Zoë Barnes was born and brought up on Merseyside, where legend has it her skirt once fell off during a school performance of 'Dido and Aeneas'. According to her family, she has been making an exhibition of herself ever since.

Her varied career has included stints as a hearing-aid technician, switchboard operator, shorthand teacher, French translator, and the worst accounts clerk in the entire world. When not writing her own novels, she translates other people's and also works as a semi-professional singer.

Although not in the least bit posh, Zoë now lives in Cheltenham where most of her novels are set. She shares a home with her husband Simon, and would rather like to be a writer when she grows up.

Zoë Barnes is the author of seven best-selling novels including BUMPS and HITCHED. The others are HOT PROPERTY, BOUNCING BACK, EX-APPEAL, LOVE BUG, JUST MARRIED and SPLIT ENDS, also published by Piatkus. Zoë loves to hear from her readers. Write to her c/o Piatkus Books, 5 Windmill Street, London, W1T 2JA or via email at zoebarnes@yahoo.co.uk

Be My Baby

Zoë Barnes

PIATKUS

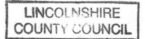
Copyright © Zoë Barnes 2005

First published in Great Britain in 2005 by
Piatkus Books Ltd of
5 Windmill Street, London W1T 2JA
email: info@piatkus.co.uk

The moral right of the author has been asserted

A catalogue record for this book is available from the British Library

Hardback ISBN 0 7499 0747 9
Trade paperback ISBN 0 7499 3617 7

Set in Times by Phoenix Photosetting, Chatham, Kent
Printed and bound in Great Britain by
William Clowes Ltd, Beccles, Suffolk

ACKNOWLEDGEMENTS

With heartfelt thanks to Vicky Ewins, midwife extraordinaire, for her professional knowledge, sense of fun and inspiration

Prologue

'It's only a sofa, love; it's not the end of the world!'

There was so much to do in their new home but at the moment Lorna Price's attention was focussed on the green Dralon monstrosity, solidly wedged at the bend halfway up the stairs. Right now there was no way it was going either upstairs to her husband's new study, or downstairs to the council tip. If only for a chainsaw. 'But Ed, I can't get to the bathroom, and I can't believe you just went to work and left it . . .'

'Don't worry, you've always got the downstairs loo. Look, I'll get Chris to come round after work and I bet we'll shift it in five minutes.'

'Bet you a fiver you don't!' she retorted.

'Right, you're on. Of course,' Ed teased, 'if you didn't keep agreeing to have your beloved sister's cast-offs . . .'

'All right, I know. But it seemed like a good idea at the time.' More fool me, thought Lorna. I should know by now that anything involving Sarah is only ever a good idea for her.

'Got to go now, darling,' said Ed regretfully. 'I'm off to inspect the new flood defences on the Chelt. Big kiss for Leo when he wakes up.'

'What about me?' she pouted.

He chuckled. 'Two big kisses for you. 'Bye, see you later.'

Lorna smiled to herself as she put down the telephone receiver and stuck her head round the living room door to check if Leo was still flat out on the sofa after a hard morning's play at nursery school. Ed might only be down the road running the council works depot, but even after all these years together, she still missed him whenever he wasn't around. And at the age of not quite four, Leo's conversation – though advanced for his years – tended to revolve around monster trucks or dinosaurs.

Most people who'd met at fourteen would probably hate the sight of each other by now, but not Lorna and Ed. They were a legend; the sort of couple people made jokes about. If one of them walked into a room, the other would inevitably follow a couple of seconds later, and it

1

wasn't because they were too bored with life to think of doing their own things.

Besides, how could any woman get bored with a man as gorgeous as Ed? Not film star gorgeous, perhaps, but rugged and dark and muscular, with the sort of twinkling grey eyes that captured your heart and never let it go. Add to that the fact that he was funny, intelligent and downright sexy, and it was little wonder that they were still inseparable after all these years. They just loved being together.

Leo was just waking up. 'Can I have a 'nana sandwich, Mummy?'

'You've already had your lunch. You'll be sick!'

'Won't.' He prodded his little round belly. 'I'm hungry. Please Mummy.'

'Oh all right then. Just a little one.' She went into the kitchen and Leo followed her, toy T Rex dangling from one hand. 'Daddy was on the phone just then. He sends you a big kiss.'

She offered puckered lips, but big boy Leo was developing masculine doubts about being smooched by his mum. 'I'd rather play dinosaurs with him when he comes home.'

Lorna laughed, and ruffled his blond curls. 'I know,' she said. Because she quite understood.

When it came to Ed, there was nothing like the real thing.

Lorna was leafing through a copy of *Midwifery Today*, glancing at the advertisements for refresher courses. She'd been more or less out of the profession ever since Leo was born, and she was beginning to wonder if she'd ever go back to it full-time. After all, despite a number of disappointments, they still hoped that Leo wasn't going to be an only child, was he? And neither she nor Ed liked the idea of leaving their kids with childminders.

It wasn't that she didn't like being a full-time mum; it was just that sometimes she felt a need to use the skills she'd been taught – a need that the odd shift at the local old people's home couldn't fulfil.

The doorbell rang, and she put the magazine back on the coffee table. Funny; she wasn't expecting anyone. Maybe it was the lady from across the road again, with her catalogue order, or her best mate Carmen, stealing half an hour from her job for a crafty coffee.

It wasn't.

On the doorstep stood two uniformed police officers, a middle-aged sergeant with a lumpy red nose, and a young female constable who looked barely old enough to be doing her mock GCSEs.

'Mrs Price?' enquired the sergeant, displaying his warrant card.

She nodded. 'Oh no, this isn't about Ed's van again, is it? I thought he explained about losing the new tax disc.'

'Er no, it's not about that,' said the sergeant awkwardly. There was a brief silence that felt like hours, and for the first time Lorna felt a slight shiver run through her. 'Is it all right if we come in and have a quiet word?'

'What's happened?' she demanded.

The female constable eased in through the door, took her gently by the elbow and guided her down the hallway. 'Best if you sit down, eh? Sarge'll make us a nice cup of tea, won't you, Sarge? Kitchen through there is it?'

'D-down the stairs, in the basement. B-but—'

Without further ado, the older officer vanished, clearly grateful to be off the hook.

'I don't want to sit down,' protested Lorna, but did so anyway. 'What's going on?'

The impossibly young girl sat down on the chair opposite and took Lorna's hands in hers. 'It's about your husband, Mrs Price,' she said softly. 'He was taken ill at work.'

Lorna leapt to her feet. 'Where is he? Is he in hospital? I have to go to him.'

The hands tightened around hers. 'They took him to hospital straight away, as soon as they realised he'd had a heart attack, but . . . I'm so very sorry . . .'

Lorna blinked at the policewoman, the words finding no meaningful echo in her brain. 'A heart attack? What are you talking about? My Ed's only thirty – he's the fittest person I've ever met. There must be some mistake.'

There was real sadness on the policewoman's face. 'They did all they could, Mrs Price, truly they did. But I'm afraid they weren't able to save your husband.'

Chapter 1

About eighteen months later . . .

'Look Mummy – three for the price of two!' crowed Leo, barging his way like a miniature tank through the shuffling mass of November shoppers and pouncing on a display of tins. At the advanced age of five and a bit – 'Almost six, Mummy!' – and bright with it, Leo seized every conceivable opportunity to try out his new reading skills.

'Leo love, that's asparagus. You don't like asparagus – especially tinned.'

'Yes I do!'

Lorna put all her weight behind the overloaded supermarket trolley. It was like trying to push a two-bedroom bungalow up a steep hill. 'No you don't, you only had it once and you were sick. Go and find Mummy a big tin of baked beans, will you?'

Leo scampered to the end of the tinned foods aisle, closely watched by his mother with a mixture of exhaustion and overwhelming love. He's the man of the house now, she thought regretfully, and at his age he shouldn't have to be. But she couldn't help smiling whenever he proudly declared that he was going to protect her from 'bad people and spiders'.

Baby Hope gurgled in her trolley seat. At only eleven months old, she couldn't miss her daddy because she'd never known him. I do wish he'd known about you though, thought Lorna for the umpteenth time. But she'd had good reasons for not telling Ed she was pregnant until she was absolutely sure. Too many false alarms and two miscarriages had left her wary and almost superstitious about telling anybody.

It was ironic really. She'd been planning to tell Ed the following weekend. She'd even been planning what to cook for a romantic dinner. And then all of a sudden, impossibly, he wasn't there any more. 'I'm so sorry, Mrs Price,' the doctor had said, 'but there wasn't anything anybody could have done. Your husband wouldn't have had the faintest idea that there was anything wrong with his heart. There are no symptoms, you see.' And then he'd sighed. 'I'm afraid it's something that occasionally happens to young, fit people.'

To young, fit people maybe, she'd thought as the numbness wore off. To *other* young, fit people. But not to him. Not to my Ed.

She had been so overwhelmed that for one crazy, grief-stricken moment she'd even thought about terminating the pregnancy she and Ed had wanted for so long. She was so very alone in the world now. Leo was enough of a responsibility: how on earth would she cope with a baby as well?

But as the months progressed, Lorna's pregnancy turned into a source of comfort, just like everyone said it would. The day her little girl was born, a ray of sunshine had parted the clouds outside the windows of the delivery room, and it felt like the first sunshine after a long, bleak night. In an instant, the baby had a name: Hope.

'I think you should hold on tight to the trolley now, Leo,' she instructed him as they headed for the corner that led to Pet Foods and Accessories. 'It's very busy here today.'

'Aw, Mu-um,' he protested, with a screwed-up face. 'I'm not a baby. And I'm helping.'

'Yes, you are. But right now you can help by not getting yourself lost. Now, let's go and buy some cat food for Clawdius. Do you think he'd like some of those nice chunks in gravy as a special treat?'

Lorna was so busy keeping one eye on her shopping list and the other on Leo that she just didn't see the trolley coming round the corner in the opposite direction. The head-on collision made such a racket that – for a moment at least – it drowned out 'Mexican Moods' on the supermarket's sound system.

'Oh dear, I am sorry,' gasped the nice forty-something man she some-times chatted to over the cheese counter.

'Don't worry, it was my fault,' she assured him, looking around for the melon, which seemed to have suddenly disappeared. 'I wasn't looking where I was going.'

'Are you all right?'

'Fine, really.' She glanced round. 'You haven't seen a melon, have you?'

'Pardon?'

'A honeydew melon – you know, one of the yellow ones. It was here a minute ago.'

Leo tugged at her sleeve. 'Look Mummy, there it is.' He pointed in the direction of the bread racks. 'It looks a bit squishy.'

Squishy was an understatement. It was completely flat on one side.

'Oh dear, never mind.' She rubbed her aching temples and smiled rue-fully at the nice man, who was still fussing as if he'd just run her over at ninety miles an hour on a pedestrian crossing. 'It's just turning into one of those days.'

He shifted awkwardly from one brown-brogued foot to the other, hands thrust deep in the pockets of his slightly baggy cords; the very picture of discomfort. 'I . . . um . . . could I, you know?'

'Could you what?'

'I think he needs the toilet, Mummy,' confided Leo in a stage whisper.

The nice man laughed. 'Actually, I was just going to say that it's one of those days for me too,' he said. 'And I was going to ask if you would . . . er . . . like to have dinner with me tonight.'

Lorna blinked. 'Pardon?'

'Dinner?' He made it sound like an apology. 'I know this really nice lit-tle place, not far from—'

The strangest feeling had invaded the whole of Lorna's body, as though it had been suddenly injected with ice water. Go out to dinner? To dinner? With a *man*? Since Ed's death she'd led such a reclusive life, seeing practi-cally nobody beyond the kids and her closest friends, that she'd managed to avoid even thinking about such things. And being suddenly confronted with her own desirability made her feel distinctly uncomfortable.

'I'm so sorry,' she cut in with a frozen smile, 'but I'm afraid I really couldn't. Come on Leo, better hurry up or we'll be late for Auntie Carmen's.'

As his mum towed him off towards the checkouts, Leo craned his head back to look at the funny man, staring after them with his mouth hanging open. All in all, figuring out grown-ups was proving a lot harder than he'd ever imagined it would be.

Lorna might think she had it bad, but her best friend Carmen Jones was having the day from hell.

'Look, Mrs—'

'Crosby,' bristled the woman with the two kids in private school uni-form and the brand-new 4x4. 'Nathalie Crosby. And it's Ms.'

'Look, Ms Crosby.' Carmen pointed to the large yellow sign screwed to the wall above the parking space. 'It says "Private Parking Only, Offenders Will Be Clamped".'

'I can read, thank you.'

'Good. Then you'll understand why you have to pay me the fixed penalty before I can take off the wheel clamp.'

'This is ridiculous.' The woman swept a Kookai-clad arm impatiently in the direction of the car. 'I have children!'

Don't you just, thought Carmen, raising an eyebrow at the sight of Crosby Junior Mark II shoving a finger up his nose and excavating the contents. She sighed. 'I realise you want to get them home as soon as you can, so if you could just sign here to say you accept liability for the penalty ...'

'I'll do nothing of the sort!'

'But you deliberately parked in a private parking space, Ms—'

'The ... the sign was obscured. Behind that tree.'

This was so patently untrue that Carmen almost laughed out loud. Though to be honest she didn't know whether to laugh or to cry. People thought being a traffic warden was the worst job in the world; obviously they'd never tried a day in the life of an immobilisation operative.

It was on days like these that she thought of her best friend, Lorna. Life had been cruel to her, taking away her husband like that; but Lorna was still young, pretty and smart. If I had half her abilities, thought Carmen with an inner sigh, I'd be doing something useful with my life – not clamping cars and having abuse hurled at me every flipping day.

'You know what you are?' demanded Nathalie Crosby. 'You're a bloody disgrace. In fact you're worse than that, you're a f—'

Carmen let the stream of expletives wash over her. There weren't many swear words Carmen hadn't heard numerous times before, but on occasions it still surprised her how inventive the chattering classes could be.

'Yes, madam, I'm sure. Have you quite finished?'

Ms Crosby's eyes narrowed. 'Look at my poor darlings! How am I going to get them home now? It's patently obvious you haven't got children.'

'Actually madam, I have four,' replied Carmen, taking out her mobile and dialling up Chappie, her supervisor. 'And they've all got better manners than you.'

Lorna felt shocked, flustered and slightly upset – without really knowing why.

OK, maybe she did know why. But being asked out to dinner by a perfectly nice, ordinary man was hardly reasonable cause for the way she felt right now. Get some perspective; it's the sort of thing that happens to people every day, she reminded herself.

Only not to me, her emotions replied. Not since ...

Just as she was gathering up the children and their assorted gear, ready to drop them off at Carmen's for the night, the telephone rang. She almost ignored it, but since the last time she'd done that she'd missed out on the Chelt FM Prize of the Week, she turned round and snatched up the receiver.

'Yes?'

'Hello Piglet. It's me, David.'

'I do wish you wouldn't call me that,' she complained, the way she did every single time her elder brother phoned her. 'It makes me feel small and fat and pink. And about five years old.'

'Well, if the cap fits,' he joked, knowing how neurotic she was about her diminutive stature and curvy figure.

'At least I'm not the one who got mistaken for a girl at the Year Ten Christmas Party!'

'That was fifteen years ago!' he protested.

'And you haven't changed a bit, Curly.'

The two of them had been like this for as long as they'd coexisted, or at least for as long as Lorna could remember. It wasn't that they didn't like each other – or at least, not *just* because they didn't like each other. Each brought out the competitive spirit in the other, and since he'd qualified as a chartered accountant, David had acquired such a penchant for pomposity that somebody had to puncture his balloon once in a while.

'You OK?' David asked.

'Oh, you know. Fine.'

'You sound a bit breathless. Have you been running or something?'

She didn't want to tell him about the man in the supermarket. He'd only have called her an idiot for turning down a bloke who probably had a four-bedroom detached in Prestbury and a major paperclip franchise. Either that, or a shameless hussy for not dressing all in black and withdrawing into a nunnery. You never could tell what opinionated daftness David would come out with next. 'Just getting the kids ready to stay the night at Carmen's. I'm on duty at The Pines tonight.'

'Oh Lorna!' The distaste in David's voice was palpable. 'Ed left you with enough to get by on. What do you want to go out wiping old people's bottoms for?'

This riled Lorna. 'Maybe I enjoy it,' she retorted. 'And maybe spending twenty-four hours a day with the under-sixes sends you a bit stir-crazy after a while.'

'Then do something ... respectable. Get a job in a charity shop or deliver soup to the poor of the parish or something.'

'David,' she cut in.

'What?'

'Shut up.'

'Charming.'

'And tell me why you're phoning me.'

'Would you believe, because I just wanted to talk to my little sister?'

'No.'

9

'All right, it's because Mum and Dad are up to something and Sarah and I thought you might know what it was.'

Lorna's brow wrinkled. 'Mum and Dad? It's the first I've heard of it. What do you mean, up to something?'

'It's kind of difficult to work out, but every time I phone them it's like they're trying to hide something, or there's something they're avoiding saying ... I don't know what. I guess it's just a feeling,' he admitted lamely.

'Did Sarah put you up to this?' enquired Lorna. Her darling younger sister liked nothing better than to stir things up, stand back and observe the results from a distance. The more collateral damage, the better.

'I don't take orders from Sarah!'

'She made you eat a live goldfish once,' Lorna reminded him.

'Why do you always have to drag everything back to things that happened when we were kids? Anyway, it's not just Sarah. I noticed it too. And when I said Maria and I were going to come up and see them in a couple of weeks' time, they went all evasive on me. Dad started babbling something about holiday arrangements – but who goes on holiday in November?'

'They're retired now; they can do whatever they want,' she pointed out. All the same, she had to admit it all sounded a bit odd. Normally her dad was compulsively straightforward. He had no concept of subterfuge whatsoever. 'And what do you want me to do about it?'

'Give them a call,' David urged. 'See if they do the same thing with you. Admit it, Piglet, there's something funny going on and you want to know what it is, just as much as I do.'

Carmen lived in an extended terraced house in St Paul's, near to the university. In the old days, the area had been populated mainly by the people who worked hard to give the posh types in Prestbury and Montpellier a nice life. Nowadays, as soon as a property came on the market it was snapped up either by an aspirational young couple, or a landlord who wanted to see how many students he could cram into it.

Carmen's house had started off quite small, but little by little extra bits had appeared on the back of it as the number of inhabitants grew. It had a basement too, and a cramped attic room that overlooked the long, straggly ribbon of back garden. Frankly it was just as well, since it had to house one adult and four growing kids but even if she could afford to, Carmen had no desire to move anywhere else. She'd lived here a long time, and nowhere else would really feel like home.

When Maurice had left her, just after Robbie – her eldest – started school, she'd never imagined she'd one day own her own house; but it

10

was amazing what you could achieve when there was no one else to do it for you. Even if you did have no qualifications and not much in the way of brains. At least, that was the way Carmen saw herself.

In the years since Maurice, Carmen had never quite given up the search for Mr Right. The trouble was that Mr Wrong came in so many alluring varieties, and Carmen invariably fell in love with all of them. Consequently she found herself, at thirty-seven, without a man but with four children – all by different fathers. Robbie, Charmain, Rosie and Becca were her life. But that didn't stop her firmly hoping and believing that the next man would be The One.

This was more than Lorna could say. For Lorna had had her One; but he was gone now and there was no way he was ever coming back.

Lorna wiggled her car back and forth until it just squeezed into the tiny space between the student wrecks. She craned her head back. 'Come on kids, let's go in and see Auntie Carmen.'

Carmen and Lorna had been firm friends for several years, ever since newly qualified Lorna had been called out to the A&E car park to deliver a baby in a Ford Fiesta. That baby had been Carmen's second eldest, Charmain; Lorna hadn't told Carmen until much later that Charmain was only her third delivery as a qualified midwife.

She unstrapped Hope from her car seat and took Leo by the hand, despite his protests that he was quite grown-up enough to cross the road on his own. Cars sometimes shot round the corner, and she wasn't taking any chances.

The front door was ajar, and Carmen was on her knees on the laminated hall floor, sweeping up the remains of a vase. 'Genghis,' she said.

'Sorry?'

'Robbie's rat,' Carmen explained, adding hastily, 'don't worry, he caught it and it's back in its cage now.' She heaved herself to her feet, her tall, muscular presence towering over Lorna's small blonde frame. Her caffe latte skin was complemented by a riot of shoulder-length black curls, held back off her strong-featured face by a knotted pink silk scarf. She ruffled Leo's hair, as soft and corn-blond as his mother's. 'Hello Leo, how's my favourite fella today?'

'I've grown,' he said proudly. 'Nearly half of a half of a half of an inch, Mummy says.'

Lorna and Carmen exchanged smiles. 'Ooh, that's a lot,' agreed Carmen, clearly impressed. 'Why don't you go upstairs and tell Becca all about it?'

Leo didn't need to be told twice. He and Becca, Carmen's youngest, were about as close to being Romeo and Juliet as it was possible to be at five and six respectively. Or maybe it was more Bonnie and Clyde, mused Lorna, recollecting the time the pair had depilated next door's dog with

Carmen's hair-removing cream. There was only a couple of months between them in age, but Becca was half a head taller than Leo and solid with it. When Carmen made children, she made big ones.

Lorna and Carmen sat down with a cup of coffee while Hope sat on the rug and played happily with a few of Becca's battered old baby toys that Carmen had kept especially for her.

'Can't stay long,' Lorna apologised. 'Only I promised I'd come on duty a bit early tonight, and sort out the residents' medication.'

Carmen raised an eyebrow. 'I bet you're not getting paid extra though, are you?'

'Well . . .'

'Typical!' Carmen shook her head. 'That's you all over, always doing stuff for people when what you really need is somebody doing stuff for you!'

'Ah well, that's life I guess. I mean, when's the last time anybody did you a favour for free?'

'Hmm.' Carmen looked at her over the rim of her coffee mug. 'What's up?'

'Nothing.'

'And now the truth?'

Lorna squirmed. 'I told you – nothing! Nothing important, anyway.' She saw that Carmen wasn't going to be satisfied until she'd spilled the beans. 'This bloke just asked me out for dinner, that's all,' she muttered.

Carmen's face registered extreme interest. 'A nice bloke? A horrible bloke?'

Lorna felt her cheeks burning. 'Just some bloke. In the supermarket. And in case you're wondering, I turned him down.'

At that moment, Hope started crying, and everything stopped until harmony was re-established and smiles returned. But if Lorna was hoping for an opportunity to change the subject, she was in for a disappointment.

'It's really shaken you up, hasn't it?' Carmen ventured. 'Being asked out.'

Lorna's attempt at a nonchalant shrug ended in abject failure. 'A bit,' she admitted. 'I wasn't expecting it.'

'But you're young and you're pretty,' Carmen pointed out. 'Why wouldn't men be attracted to you?'

Lorna stared at her knees. 'It just doesn't feel right.'

'Because of Ed?'

'I . . . guess.' She looked up at Carmen. 'Look, I know he's gone; I'm not living in dreamland. I know I have to make a life for myself now. But that doesn't mean I'm ready to forget how much I loved Ed.'

'That's OK, you don't have to.' Carmen sat down next to her on the

12

sofa and put an arm round her shoulders. 'You don't have to do anything you don't want.'

Lorna snorted. 'Tell that to the world! Everybody seems to want to forget him – that, or they want me to pretend I'm completely OK now, so they can stop feeling uncomfortable around me. You know, there are old friends I can't bear to be with any more, because every time I mention Ed they change the subject.'

'Then they're not really friends, are they?' said Carmen quietly. She picked up the tin of chocolate biscuits and plonked it on Lorna's lap. 'Come on kid, tell me all about it. The Pines can spare you for another half an hour.'

Chapter 2

'It's a good job they provide smocks,' commented Carmen a few days later when they took the three youngest children for an after-school treat. She laughed as she wiped a blob of paint off Becca's nose.

Lorna looked at Leo and wondered how one small boy could get so messy in such a short space of time. Still, that was the whole point about Smashing Times, the paint-it-yourself pottery shop: making a mess and knowing that somebody else was going to clear it up. 'Smocks?' she retorted. 'I reckon Leo needs one of those bio-hazard suits!'

Leo looked up, his brow furrowed in intense concentration. 'What's a bio-wizard suit?' he demanded. 'Is it magic?'

'Yes,' replied Carmen wryly. 'It turns clean little boys into paint monsters.'

This idea seemed to go down rather well with Becca, who started chanting 'Paint Monster, Paint Monster, Leo's a Paint Monster.' Leo of course retaliated by sticking his multicoloured fingers into the corners of his mouth and pulling it into a grotesque leer.

'Maaaa!' Hope clung to Lorna and hid her face.

'Becca, behave,' said Carmen. 'Sorry Lorna, I didn't mean to set them off.'

Lorna soothed Hope, stroking down her soft, pale curls. 'Everything's OK sweetie, Leo's just being a silly boy – aren't you, Leo? Now, let's wipe that paint off your mouth before you poison yourself.'

'Don't worry, madam,' a cheerful assistant assured her. 'It's completely non-toxic. You wouldn't believe how much of this stuff gets eaten.'

'I think we would,' replied Carmen. 'Now calm down, the pair of you. And get a move on with those works of art!'

While Becca painted some rather sturdy-looking pink fairies and Leo worked on his inevitable dinosaur, Lorna and Carmen giggled childishly over their joint attempt at a birthday present for Lorna's mum, Meg.

'I hope your mum likes pork pies,' commented Carmen as she stepped back to survey the decorated plate, 'because that's what it looks like.'

15

'It's not a pork pie, it's a birthday cake!' protested Lorna, loath to admit that the dancing pigs on either side of it gave it more than a passing resemblance to an advertisement for a pork butcher's.

'Ah yes – I know that and you know that, but it wouldn't do any harm to paint some candles on it or something. Just to make sure.'

'All right, we'll write "Happy Birthday Mum" underneath. You can do that bit though,' Lorna added. 'You're the one with the steady hand.' She blobbed half a dozen yellow and blue candles on top of the cake. 'There – how's that?'

'She'll love it,' Carmen promised.

'You really think so?'

'She has to, she's your mum. And besides, it'll probably get broken in the post, so she'll never know how awful it really was.'

'Oh, I'm not posting it,' said Lorna. She kissed Hope on the top of the head. 'We're going to travel up and see Granny and Grandad, aren't we darling? And give Granny her present on her birthday.'

Hope babbled happily.

'I like Grandad,' piped up Leo. 'He makes bottom noises with his armpit, doesn't he, Mummy?'

'Only when Granny's not there to tell him not to,' replied Lorna, making a mental note to have a quiet word with Grandad. 'And don't you dare go copying him, Leo – it's rude.'

'Why?'

'Because it just is!'

Reluctantly, Leo went back to his dinosaur.

'So when is your mum's birthday then?' enquired Carmen.

'Not for a few weeks yet. It'll be good to see them again though; we haven't heard much from them lately. They're always so busy since Dad retired. If they're not redesigning the garden or building a conservatory, they're off up the Amazon on some Saga cruise.'

'You're lucky, being so close to your mum and dad,' sighed Carmen. She and her older sister Grace had spent their childhoods in and out of foster homes. 'Really lucky.'

'I know I am, even if they do drive me mad sometimes. Mind you, I don't see half as much of them as I should. I tend to think that I don't need to see them all the time, because I know they're always there if I need them.'

'I suppose when you've always had something you take it for granted,' commented Carmen reflectively. 'Like if you've got this really reliable bloke you're happy with and then all of a sudden—' She brought herself up short. 'I mean . . . I didn't mean Ed, you know. Just blokes in general. Me and my big mouth.'

16

Lorna's brush hovered over the yellow paint. 'It's OK, honest. But you know, I reckon I did take Ed for granted. In a way. Or at least, I definitely never thought for a minute that one day he wouldn't be there any more. We had all these plans and stuff. Silly things really ... and now we'll never do any of them.'

'All the same, while you had him ...' Carmen was fighting for the right words. 'I mean, what you had with Ed was really good, wasn't it?'

'The best,' murmured Lorna.

'So at least you have good memories of a great bloke. That must count for one hell of a lot. Not everybody has that, you know.'

Lorna nodded, though sometimes the memories were the hardest part of all. But at least they were golden, and bright, and filled with joyful things. Mostly, the best memories Carmen had of her ex-partners were of the day they'd walked, stormed, flounced or been kicked out. All the same ...

Lorna nudged Carmen's arm and directed her gaze at Becca, smiling radiantly through tendrils of paint-smeared hair as she put the finishing touches to her masterpiece. 'Hey, you have some good memories too,' she reminded her. 'This one, for a start off.'

'That's very true,' agreed Carmen with a laugh. 'Though I still wonder how something so good could come out of getting myself involved with ... well, that's nature for you!' She stifled an enormous yawn. 'I don't know why kids always complain about going to bed early. I'm so tired I could sleep all day.'

'What's up – work? Kids? Late nights out clubbing?'

Carmen chuckled. 'I wish. Actually it's work. Kids I can cope with – it's the general public who wear me out.' She rubbed her eyes. 'And I missed out on a load of commission yesterday. Let some guy with nice eyes spin me a line about needing to get to hospital with his bad leg ...'

'Let me guess: there was nothing wrong with him?'

'Five minutes after I'd let him off, I spotted him sprinting across to the bookies' in Winchcombe Street. Soft touch, that's what I am.'

'Better than being a hard-faced bitch,' ventured Lorna.

'Sometimes I wonder. Maybe I'm just not cut out for the job, or for any job. Sometimes I wish I could just stay at home all day and look after my kids properly. I do worry about Robbie ... the kind of friends he's making, and what he's getting up to when I'm not there.'

'He's a good lad, you know he is.'

'Yeah, maybe, but he's just turned fourteen and it's a funny age.'

'If you ask me, they're all funny ages.' Lorna felt a growing heaviness and, looking down, saw that Hope had fallen asleep in her arms. She felt a sudden pang of guilt and wondered how she could even have considered going back to work full-time. Carmen's weren't the only kids who needed their mother. 'Do you reckon that's what I should do? Stay at home?'

Carmen looked taken aback. 'What? You? No, I was talking about me! You've got proper qualifications and skills. What am I? A glorified parking attendant, someone everybody hates. I'd hardly be giving up the career of a lifetime, would I?'

'Look, Mummy!' Leo proudly held up his plate. His design consisted of a blue dinosaur with triangular red scales all down its back. Its mouth was wide open and something orange was coming out.

'It's lovely, sweetheart.' Lorna pointed to the orange thing, hoping it wasn't meant to be vomit. 'What's that?'

Leo looked at her as though she were very old and very stupid. 'Fire, Mummy. It's breathing fire.'

'I thought it was a dinosaur, not a dragon.'

'This is a special magic dinosaur. Magic dinosaurs can do anything.'

'Oh, I see. That's all right then.'

Magic's such a wonderful thing, thought Lorna; it lets you fashion things however you want them to be. If only adults believed in it too. But no; when you were a grown-up you just had to change things the hard way – or put up with them the way they were. The question was, which did she want?

'I still haven't decided,' she said.

'About the refresher course? But I thought you really wanted to get back into midwifery.'

Lorna nodded. 'I did. I do. But ... It's not just that it feels selfish. I mean, maybe it wouldn't be entirely selfish if I knew it was going to give the children a better life.' It wasn't as if she was destitute. When Ed died the mortgage had been paid off, and she had a small widow's pension, plus what she earned from part-time work at the residential home. But it would be nice to be able to afford a few more of the luxuries that a lot of families took for granted.

'Of course it wouldn't,' agreed Carmen. 'And it's only a five-day course. So what's the but?'

'But ... even if I managed to get through the course by calling in favours and begging people to help with childcare, how on earth would I manage once I went back to work? There's no crèche, and you know how much nurseries cost: I'd probably end up worse off than I am now.'

'Tell me about it,' said Carmen. 'But maybe you could work part-time, that might work out better. And after all, Leo's started school now.'

Lorna mulled it all over, for the thousandth time. 'I'm sure you're right,' she said finally, 'and I have filled in the form. I just can't make up my mind whether or not to send it off. Maybe I should just forget the whole thing until they're older.'

Just then, Hope awoke, stretched up her arms for a big cuddle, and planted a big kiss on her mummy's cheek.

She needs me, thought Lorna, in agonies of indecision. She really does. How could I leave her with a stranger for hours on end?

Once she'd given Becca a good wash and dropped her off at her gym club, Carmen parked her old van in the supermarket car park and walked across to the Neighbourhood Centre. She'd been there so many times that she could probably have made the trip blindfold.

She pushed through the swing doors, gave her name at the reception desk and went into the waiting room. There was nobody else there, but she could hear the low murmur of voices coming from the room behind the door marked 'Counsellor'.

After a while, the door opened and a middle-aged woman came out, dabbing at her eyes. 'Thank you, you're very kind.'

The counsellor's voice followed her out. 'Just remember, it's about your future. In the end, the decision has to be down to you, not him.'

Relationships, thought Carmen with a shudder. It's always about relationships. She wondered vaguely which caused more problems: having one or not having one. In Carmen's experience, it was more or less a toss-up between being treated like a doormat and having cold feet in bed.

Janice Green, the resident counsellor, greeted Carmen at the doorway of her consulting room – if you could call it that. For most of the week it doubled as a cloakroom for the mother and toddler group, and there was no disguising the line of brightly coloured potties along the back wall.

'Didn't expect to see you again so soon, Carmen,' commented Janice. 'More problems with ... er ... Gary, wasn't it?'

Carmen came into the room and closed the door behind her. 'Oh no, Gary's no problem at all – not since I gave him his marching orders.'

'So you're on your own again with the children now?' Janice motioned to Carmen to take a seat.

'Yes.' She didn't mention the fact that she'd also experimented with Jason and Trey in the last couple of months since she'd been to counselling. It was a bit embarrassing. But how was she going to find Mr Right without eliminating all the Mr Wrongs? 'The thing is ... I'm really glad Gary's gone and all that, I really am. I mean, the way he treated me wasn't good and I should've wised up to that a lot earlier. So I ought to be happy now, oughtn't I?'

'And you're not?'

Carmen sighed. 'I'm lonely, Janice.'

'So you're having trouble adjusting to being single?'

Carmen thought about Lorna. 'I've got this friend . . . She lost her husband eighteen months ago, and she's been on her own ever since. It's not that she couldn't have a man if she wanted. She says she can't imagine ever being with anybody else.'

'A lot of people do feel that way after a bereavement,' pointed out Janice.

Carmen nodded. 'They were very close, and I can understand why she wants to be on her own. But the thing is, she thinks I'm strong like her, but I'm not – I'm a bit pathetic really.'

'What makes you say that?'

'I've never been without a bloke since I was fifteen, and I just don't know where to start.'

The kids were in bed at last, and Lorna was flopping out on the settee with half a litre of Ben & Jerry's, watching the latest reality trash TV. If she'd been expecting visitors, she'd have worn something other than shapeless joggers and zebra-print mules, but she relaxed when she heard Chris's familiar tuneless whistling.

She was at the front door before he knocked.

'Hello stranger,' he grinned, giving her hair a quick ruffle. 'Is it a bad time? Only I thought I'd fix that dodgy hinge on the kitchen cupboard.'

'What dodgy hinge?' Lorna laughed. 'How come you always end up fixing things before I even know they've gone wrong?'

'Ah well, that's the penalty of having a mate who's a carpenter. Besides, you know me: any excuse to come round and have some of your amazing chocolate brownies.'

'Oh yes, and who told you I'd just made brownies?'

'You always make brownies on a Tuesday!'

'Am I really that predictable?'

'It's OK, I like you that way.'

She followed Chris downstairs into the basement of the three-storey Victorian house, where the kitchen and utility room were situated. There was something about him that always cheered her up when things were getting her down. Maybe it was the carefree scruffiness of him; or the tanned face, bright blue eyes and sandy, windblown hair of a man who loved working outdoors. Maybe it was just the fact that he had been Ed's best friend ever since they were at primary school together. When Chris was around, it felt like Ed was never far away.

'So how's it going?' he asked through a mouthful of chocolate cake as he started attacking the cupboard door.

She shrugged. 'Oh, you know. How about you?'

'Pretty much the usual really. Fitted a load of new door frames on the Blackberry Estate, went to the dentist, got dumped by Sonia . . .'

'Oh Chris, you didn't!' Lorna looked at him with a mixture of sympathy and exasperation. 'But you were getting on so well – what happened?'

Chris concentrated unnaturally hard on dislodging a cross-threaded screw. 'She said I wasn't committed enough. That my mind always seemed to be somewhere else. Perhaps she was right.'

'Oh,' said Lorna. She didn't contradict him, suspecting there was more than a grain of truth in it.

He looked up. 'I'm not very good at the relationship thing, am I? I'm thinking of giving up and getting a goldfish.'

'Don't you dare.' Lorna assumed a stern expression and wagged a reproving finger. 'Auntie Lorna won't let you.'

Chris pulled a face. 'If you ask me, Auntie Lorna's a big bully.' He extracted the offending screw with a grunt of satisfaction. 'There. At least I'm good for something.'

'I sometimes wonder if I am,' sighed Lorna, kicking a heel into the skirting board. 'All I am these days is a mother, and I'm not even sure I'm much good at that.'

'What's brought this on?' wondered Chris, clearly surprised. 'Last time I saw you, you were full of that back-to-work course, and how you were going to make a better future for you and the kids.'

Lorna cringed at the memory of her own unfettered optimism. 'That was before I thought about the practicalities,' she confessed. 'It's really not feasible at the moment, not with the kids so young. Unsocial hours, childcare – it's a nightmare.'

'You mean you're not going to do it? You're giving up?'

'Not giving up, just facing facts.'

'Sounds like giving up to me.' Chris sat back on his haunches. 'You know, I used to know somebody called Lorna who'd never let anything get in the way of what she wanted to do. What do you suppose happened to her?'

Maybe she died along with Ed, thought Lorna in a wave of self-pity. 'Don't give me all this crap, Chris; you know how difficult things are.' She realised dimly that a part of her wanted Chris to say that yes, he understood perfectly, and give her permission to stop trying.

'Difficult, yes; impossible, no. Look at my cousin Jane – after her divorce she was left on her own with three under-sevens, and she's running her own department now.'

'Well bully for her.'

Chris gave a sigh. 'I'm sorry, Lorna. I didn't mean to sound hard. It's just that we're good mates and it hurts me to see you like this.'

21

'Like what?'

'Negative. Defeatist. Ed wouldn't have wanted you to turn your back on life,' he added quietly.

She rounded on him. 'Oh really? And what makes you think you're the world authority on what Ed would have wanted? Besides,' she added with an edge of bitterness, 'what does it matter? He's not here any more.'

'All the more reason for you to start thinking about the future,' Chris replied, methodically putting away his tools and standing up. Why is he always so calm, wondered Lorna? Sometimes she wanted to kick him, just to make him lose his cool.

'There, that should hold for a bit.'

At the door, he laid a hand briefly on Lorna's shoulder. 'Shout at me as much as you like, I don't mind. Just don't ask me to stand by and watch while you give up on life.'

Chapter 3

It's only a five-day course, Lorna repeated to herself a few weeks later as she crashed round the kitchen making Leo's sandwiches for school. A few lectures and a test on stuff you already know. Just how bad can it be?

But she really wasn't fooling herself. Maybe she hadn't been out of midwifery that long, but everybody knew the world of medicine changed at the speed of light. Everything she'd been taught was most likely prehistory by now, so she was probably destined to make a complete fool of herself, and it was all her own fault for listening to people like Chris and Carmen. Why hadn't she let herself be guided by her own gut feeling?

As she fumbled with ham and butter, Leo watched glumly from his seat at the breakfast table. 'You'd better hurry up and clean your teeth,' Lorna prompted him. 'Auntie Lennie's coming to pick you up in a minute, and you don't want to be late for school.'

Auntie Lennie wasn't really an auntie, or called Lennie for that matter. Her real name was Eleanor Spinks and she was a friend Lorna sometimes shared the school run with. They weren't especially close, but Lennie was pretty reliable, and the kids had always got on well with her. Thank goodness she'd been free to have Hope this week, and take care of Leo until Lorna got home.

Leo's lower lip quivered ominously. 'Don't want to go to school.'

Lorna slapped one round of bread haphazardly on top of the other. 'Of course you do, you love school.'

'No I don't, I hate it.'

This was a new and unwelcome development at twenty-five past eight on a Monday morning when Lorna had to be at the Glevum University campus by nine and still hadn't brushed her hair. She took a deep breath. 'What's the matter, sweetheart? You like Auntie Lennie, don't you?'

'She's all right,' Leo admitted, but grudgingly.

'So what's wrong with school then?'

23

Leo shrugged and stared at his cereal bowl, stirring a mess of Coco Pops and milk into a muddy vortex. 'School's stupid.'

Coming from the kid who thought sums were fun, this was pretty earth-shattering stuff.

'Hey, nobody at school's being nasty to you, are they?' asked Lorna anxiously. 'Because if they are—'

'If anybody was nasty to me,' Leo replied with disarming candour, 'I'd hit them. And then they'd stop.'

This might not be the politically correct response, but in a way it was reassuring. At least he wasn't letting the bigger children intimidate him. Anyhow, kids had their moods just like anybody else, Lorna reminded herself, and this was obviously Leo's day for a funny one. It would have blown over by morning break-time.

At least Hope was her usual uncomplicated self, beaming cherubically from her high chair as Lorna swabbed the scrambled egg from her face.

'Weggy,' she burbled brightly.

'Yes, lovely eggy-weggy,' agreed Lorna. 'I just wish we could've avoided getting most of it down your front.' She thought of Lennie's two, Caspian and Jacintha, who were always decked out in the latest designer gear, and wondered if there was time for an entire change of clothes. Oh sod it; what was an egg stain or two between friends?

She finally bundled Leo and Hope, rather guiltily, into Lennie's car about five minutes before she was supposed to be registering for the course. Even if she ran every red light between home and the campus she'd still be late: so much for the new Lorna Price, super-efficient work-ing mum.

The unwashed dishes in the sink beckoned evilly to her as she grabbed her handbag and made for the door. For a moment she felt quite nostalgic about potty-training and daytime TV. But it was too late to back out now. For the next five days at least, she was a career woman again.

'Excuse me, is this where to register for Midwifery Return to Practice?'

Red-faced and panting, Lorna practically skidded into the lecture room, clutching the forms they'd given her at reception. Twenty faces turned to eye her with interest – and a touch of amusement.

'Nope, this is Literary Theory, Year III,' replied a pasty youth with skateboarder trousers and dreadlock extensions. 'Try next door.'

'That's Fundamentals of Psychology,' protested the girl sitting next to him. 'She wants that new block across the park – that's where the nurses hang out, isn't it?'

'Only the student ones. The postgrads are somewhere else, aren't they?'

'I heard they were moving them all to Gloucester.'

Oh great, thought Lorna: I'm not just in the wrong room, I'm in the wrong town. She was on the point of giving up and opting for Literary Theory when the door opened and a thirty-something woman with the soft-eyed look of a golden retriever stuck her head round it.

'You haven't got any of my midwives in there have you? Only I'm one short.'

'That'd be me,' confessed Lorna. 'I got lost.'

'Hardly surprising dear, they never signpost anything properly round here. But that's academics for you.' She stuck out a hand. 'Sadie Witherspoon, course tutor. Welcome to the madhouse.'

Leo was not happy. In fact he was really, really, really not happy. If there was one thing he hated it was change, and he'd already had way too much of it in his young life.

Unlike his sister, he was old enough to remember his dad, though sometimes that made him upset because he couldn't recall exactly what his face looked like without looking at photos. And sometimes Mummy got upset when he did that too often. Leo knew it was OK to feel sad when somebody died, but on the other hand he was pretty sure feeling angry was bad, so he hadn't told his mum about the times he got mad at Dad for dying and leaving them and making Mummy cry.

Some of the other kids in his class didn't have dads who were home all the time, but at least they had them at weekends or in the holidays or once in a while or knew they were around somewhere. Even if you had a dad you never saw, that must be better than not having a dad at all.

And as if that wasn't bad enough, his mum had got out her smart clothes and started talking about going out to work. Leo knew all about mums who went out to work. His friend Harry's mum was a doctor, and she was always out taking care of ill people, and he had to be put to bed by this horrible nanny with really smelly breath and fat knees. Leo knew his mum was going to work in a hospital too, like Harry's mum, so he'd probably hardly ever see her and she'd never be there when he got home from school and wanted to tell her all the new things he'd learned.

It was story time in Leo's class, and they were all sitting on the floor round Miss Rubery's chair. It was quite a good story, and he liked Miss Rubery, but he'd decided some things were more important than stories. He had to do something, so he did the only thing he could think of.

'Yes, Leo?' asked Miss Rubery as he waved his arm in the air.

'Please miss, I feel sick and my tummy hurts.'

'Oh dear. Perhaps we'd better get you down to the nurse's room.'

25

Success. It was only a matter of time before his mum came racing down to the school to take him home.

Lorna was starting to feel a little less like a fish out of water. At least she wasn't in her fifties and desperately out of touch, like many of the other women on the course. In fact she was the youngest by a long way, except for a gazelle-like girl called Camilla whose husband was a director of Seuss & Goldman, 'Cheltenham's premier department store'. Bet she doesn't have to worry about the cost of childcare, thought Lorna ruefully. And what's the betting she gets staff discount in the babywear department too.

Sadie Witherspoon was explaining what they would be doing over the next five days, and Lorna was gradually beginning to relax. Some of the terminology and procedures might be new, but the fundamentals didn't change even if fads and fashions did. It was still all about trying to give nature a helping hand.

'Of course, midwives have to spend a lot more of their time on post-op nursing care these days,' Sadie went on. 'That's the result of a rising number of Caesareans, I'm afraid.'

'But we're not nurses,' protested one of the other women. 'We're midwives. I mean, you don't mind doing some wound care of course, but when it's every other woman . . .'

'I blame it on the doctors,' said the older woman sitting on Lorna's left. 'That and these so-called celebrities on TV. Everybody wants the quick option. In my day, you did things the natural way whether you liked it or not.'

By now, Lorna felt sufficiently confident to venture an opinion. 'Natural birth is the ideal way, I agree. But surely the important thing is to find the right solution for each individual woman?'

The older woman sniffed. 'Well, maybe . . . within reason. But all some of these young ones think about is getting their figures back.'

'Some are just scared,' objected Lorna. 'And it's our job to educate them and take away some of the fear.'

'No, it's our job to deliver healthy babies.'

The debate had barely got underway when the 'William Tell Overture' started bleeping from the depths of Lorna's handbag. Crimson-faced, she rummaged for her mobile, cursing herself for not switching it off during the lecture.

'I'm really sorry,' she stammered when she saw the caller's number. 'It's my son's school. If you could just excuse me a minute.'

She dived outside into the corridor. 'A tummy upset? You're sending him home? But I'm on a course . . . yes, yes, I appreciate that, but . . . Could you give me a moment? I need to make some arrangements.'

Oh Lennie, she said to herself as she dialled the mobile number, you are really going to hate me for this.

After an interminable delay, a voice answered. 'Hi – that you, Lorna? You'll have to speak up; it's a bit noisy in here, I can't hear very well.'

Lorna puzzled at the muffled din on the other end of the line. It sounded more like Paddington Station than Lennie's front room. 'Where on earth are you – the soft play centre?'

'The coffee shop at the hospital. Caspian swallowed a plastic sheep from his toy farm, and it's stuck halfway down.'

'Oh no! Is he all right?'

'Fine. He's just gone off to be X-rayed. Can't understand what all the fuss is about, the little sod.'

'Where's Hope?'

'She's here with me, smearing chocolate all over her face. Don't do that Jacintha, it's not nice. It's OK Lorna, don't worry, we should all be out of here by teatime. When the X-rays come back, the doctor's going to fetch a big grabby thing to pull the sheep out.' She giggled. 'He's quite sexy actually.'

Lorna apologised for bothering her, and rang off. So much for asking Lennie to go and fetch Leo from school. It sounded like she had quite enough on her plate already. So Lorna would have to bite the parental bullet, take him home herself and ditch the course after all. Maybe some things just weren't meant to be.

Then she had a thought. It was Monday – and somebody she knew could usually juggle his hours around, if a real emergency cropped up. It was a bit of a long shot, but worth a phone call. Crossing everything she could think of, she found the number and dialled.

This wasn't the way Chris had planned on spending his afternoon, but he wasn't that busy at the moment which meant he could reorganise his routine work and it was obvious Lorna was in a fix. And after all, he was the one who'd been pestering her to go on the course.

As for Leo, he wasn't as pale as Chris had expected, but he was certainly looking glum. His expression as he peered through the window of the nurse's room and saw Chris's van draw up at the school gates was pure, unadulterated disappointment.

'Oh, it's you.'

'Yes, it's me all right.'

'Where's Mum?' Leo demanded as they drove home.

'On her course, you know that.'

'But I'm ill. I've got a tummy ache. Mum always takes me home when I'm ill.'

27

'Not today, big man. Today you'll have to make do with me.'

Once back home, not even the prospect of a game of Mousetrap could lure Leo out of his gloom. Rather concerned, Chris laid a hand on his forehead, but it was quite cool. 'Are you feeling really bad?' he asked. 'Should we get the doc to come and see you?'

At this suggestion, Leo looked positively alarmed. 'I'm all right,' he declared suddenly.

'I thought you said you were feeling sick.'

'I was. But I'm not now. Can I have some crisps?'

Chris rubbed his chin thoughtfully. 'I'm not sure crisps are quite the thing if you're feeling sick. Unless of course . . . you weren't feeling sick to begin with.'

Leo avoided looking at him. 'I was ill,' he protested.

'Sure?' Chris squatted down to his level. 'I won't be angry, I promise.'

Leo swung his legs listlessly back and forth, drumming his heels against the front of the armchair. 'I was only a bit ill,' he admitted. 'A very little bit.' He looked up at Chris through his long blond eyelashes. 'Are you going to tell my mum?'

Chris shook his head. 'Not if you tell me why,' he replied. He paused. 'When I was at school, just a few years older than you are now,' he confided, 'there was a teacher I didn't like, and I used to pretend I was ill whenever he was teaching the lesson – until they figured out I was making it up, and then I got into trouble.'

Leo looked at him with round eyes. 'I like Miss Rubery,' he said. 'She's nice.'

'I know. But maybe you don't like your mum going out all day? Maybe you thought, "I know how I can get her to come back home"?'

There was a long pause. 'Am I in trouble now?' asked Leo.

Chris smiled. 'No, you're not in trouble. But you have to let your mum get on with her course, you know. It's important and she really wants to do it.'

Leo's lip trembled. 'But she'll go out to work like Harry's mum,' he blurted out, 'and then she'll never come home and I'll never have bedtime stories ever again and she'll forget all about me.'

'My mum went out to work,' said Chris. 'And she didn't forget about me. Sometimes she wasn't there, but she always made up for it and we had lots of fun when she came home.'

'Oh,' said Leo, clearly only half convinced.

'And what about your friend Becca – her mum goes out to work, doesn't she?'

Leo shrugged.

'Does that make her sad?'

28

Leo considered the question for some time. 'She says one day when her mum saves up enough money from her job, they're going on holiday to Disneyworld.'

Chris considered this at least a minor victory. 'So it's not all bad having a mum who goes out to work, is it?'

'When I had a daddy, he went out to work,' replied Leo sadly. 'And Mummy stayed at home.'

'I know, Big Man, I know. And I miss him too.' Chris stood up so that Leo wouldn't see how much. 'Hey, what do you say we have those crisps now? And then we can work out what we're going to say to your mum when she comes home.'

When Lorna did come home, she was somewhat amazed to find Leo sitting with Chris in front of the TV, accompanied by two empty crisp packets and a tube of Smarties.

'Chris, you're a life-saver . . . Oh Leo sweetheart, I thought you were really poorly!' She scooped him up and gave him a mother-hen hug. Although it was only a few hours since she'd left the house, it felt as though she hadn't seen him in weeks; as if she'd been away time-travelling in another world. 'I've been worried about you all day.' She clocked the crisps and chocolate. 'What on earth have you been feeding him, Chris? It's no wonder he's feeling sick!'

'He was quite poorly when I fetched him,' explained Chris, 'but he's feeling much better now, aren't you, Big Man?'

Leo nodded emphatically.

'All the same, you can't be too careful with tummy upsets,' mused Lorna. 'So no more chocolate for you, young man! Perhaps I'd better phone the university and tell them I won't be in tomorrow.'

Out of the corner of her eye, she thought she saw Chris give Leo a nudge, but she was probably imagining it.

'I think I'll be able to go to school tomorrow, Mummy,' said Leo, right on cue. 'We're making cornflake crispy cakes and doing adding up.'

'Well . . . if you're sure.'

'I'm all better now, Mummy,' Leo assured her. 'So you can go out tomorrow, can't you?'

By the end of Wednesday's clinical visit, Lorna's mind was buzzing but her body was giving up the ghost. Housework was one thing, but it was a long time since she'd spent a whole shift on a maternity unit. And that was only the ante-natal unit: goodness knows how she'd cope on a busy labour ward!

That evening, Carmen left the kids with her sister, and came round to

29

scoff pizza and perv over the new George Clooney film. When there was no answer to the doorbell she let herself in with the key Lorna had given her, and found Lorna on the phone.

'But we always come up and see you on your birthday!' protested Lorna.

'Yes dear,' replied Meg Scholes, Lorna's mother, 'but it's . . . well, it's just not the best time at the moment, that's all.'

'Why?' demanded Lorna. 'I mean, if you're only decorating or something—'

'No, it's not really that . . . to tell you the truth, there's a problem with the conservatory.'

'What sort of problem? Maybe I can help.'

'Oh, I don't think so, dear. And it's much too complicated to go into. Besides, your father's terribly busy right now, reorganising his fossil collection. You know what he's like when he gets engrossed in his bits of rock. We might come over and see you, though.'

Lorna scratched her head, thoroughly bemused. 'But Mum, if Dad's busy and there's something wrong with the conservatory, won't you want to stay at home?'

'Oh, I'm sure we can find time to visit our favourite daughter.'

Lorna laughed. 'You'd better not let Sarah hear you say that.'

'You're both our favourite daughters dear, you know that. Now, shall we say we'll pop up and see you on the Wednesday, all being well?'

'The day before your birthday? So you'll be staying over then?'

Meg coughed. 'Yes. I should definitely think we'll be staying over.'

Lorna put down the receiver, turned round and spotted Carmen. 'Oh hi, didn't hear you come in.'

'Parent problems?' enquired Carmen, divesting herself of her coat and launching herself at the sofa.

'I'm really not sure,' admitted Lorna. 'They say they're fine, but I've never heard such feeble excuses for not having visitors. You know, I'd swear there's something they're not saying.'

'Still, from what I heard you'll be seeing them soon, so you'll be able to give them the third-degree then.' Carmen sniffed the air. 'Is that pepperoni and ham I can smell?'

'And jalapeño peppers. Should be just about ready now.'

They sat down side by side and Carmen hungrily dismembered the pizza. 'Come on Lorna, wrap your gnashers round this before it gets cold.'

Lorna slapped her hand over a jaw-cracking yawn. 'Sorry, I think I'm too knackered to be hungry. You know, I can't believe I ever worked twelve-hour night shifts.'

'Ah well,' said Carmen, 'you'll soon get back into the swing of things.' She flexed an impressive bicep. 'Cop a look at that: the result of five years writing clamping notices, that is.' She ripped off a mouthful of pizza. 'How's the course coming along, anyway?'

'Great.' Lorna nibbled the edge of her pizza wedge. 'I'm really enjoying it. Just not entirely sure I'm up to the job any more, that's all.'

Carmen exploded into gales of laughter. 'Oh come on! You're not exactly antiquated – even if you are dangerously near thirty.'

Lorna stuck out her tongue. 'At least I'm not as old as you!'

'True,' agreed Carmen. 'When you're my age you know you're past it.'

They sat in companionable silence for a while, George Clooney's incomparable buttocks holding them so mesmerised that it was quite some time before Carmen realised the gently rhythmic sound wasn't the central heating but Lorna snoring.

Ah well, thought Carmen; waste not want not. And reaching over Lorna she helped herself to the last slice of cold pizza, then settled back into impossible dreams of her perfect Mr Right.

The week had sped by so quickly that Lorna could hardly believe it was Friday – or that she'd just sat an hour-long exam on everything she'd learned.

Sadie Witherspoon called them into her office individually after lunch, to discuss the results. When it came to Lorna's turn she felt exactly as she had years ago, when she'd gone up to the school to get her GCSE results. Hope they're better this time round, she mused; she still had unpleasant memories of that E in Geography.

'Lorna,' smiled Sadie, 'do sit down.'

'Did I pass?' asked Lorna, cutting to the chase.

'Extremely well. No problems at all with your professional knowledge.' Sadie leaned forward. 'I am a little concerned about your aims and objectives though. They seem a little . . . undefined. Are you planning to go back into full-time practice?'

That hit the nail right on the head. 'I just don't know,' sighed Lorna. 'At least I do – want to, I mean – only it's the children.'

'If you're worried about the cost of childcare, there are provisions to help with the fees,' pointed out Sadie, opening a desk drawer. 'I have a leaflet here somewhere . . .'

'It's not just that,' confessed Lorna. 'It's the thought of them being looked after by strangers. I mean, my friends have been really good, helping out this week, but they couldn't do it long term.'

The course tutor nodded sympathetically. 'Well, nobody can make the decision for you; but there are tremendous opportunities in midwifery

31

right now. The profession is crying out for keen young professionals like you. Just say the word, and I can find you a mentored placement straight away.'

As she walked back to the car park, Lorna realised she was at a watershed in her life. If she turned down the chance to rebuild her career, she knew she'd end up regretting it; but if she chose work and then the kids lost out as a result of that choice, wouldn't she feel ten times worse? Look at what had happened to Caspian when he was with Lennie – that could have been Hope . . . and it might not have ended so happily.

No matter how she looked at it, all the solutions seemed like the wrong ones.

Chapter 4

Clawdius the cat was in his element. Not only had he been allowed into the spare room, where he was practically never allowed to go, but there was loads of entertaining stuff to play with, too. And although he might be getting on a bit, Clawdius had never quite lost his sense of adventure.

In fact he'd had a pretty adventurous start to his life, being discovered at the tender age of five weeks in a sealed bin liner, floating down the River Chelt. If Ed hadn't heard his plaintive cries, he wouldn't have lasted long, but he was a survivor – unlike the other three kittens in the bag.

Ed and Lorna had already been going out for ages by then, and when Ed presented Lorna with the pitiful scrap of black fur, the two of them both knew they'd do anything to keep him alive, however discouraging the vet might be. So they took it in turns to feed him every two hours, round the clock; and against all the odds, the mewling scrap had grown into a magnificent black cat with long, lustrous fur and a tail you could sweep chimneys with.

Of course, that had been a good few years back. These days, Clawdius's coat was not so much black as rusty-coloured, faded by his fondness for spending hours snoozing in any patch of sun he could find. But apart from a slight paunch, Clawdius was still the picture of feline health.

He prowled around interestedly while Lorna rummaged in a cupboard. He had no idea what she was doing, of course, but the things she was looking at had a familiar smell: the smell of someone nice who had suddenly gone away.

Sometimes, when she was feeling especially strong or especially alone, Lorna would come up to the small bedroom that had been Ed's study, and sort through some of his things. Officially, she was going through them with a view to getting rid of some; unofficially, she was surrounding herself in memories that were irresistible yet almost too intense to bear.

At the back of the built-in cupboard, she found Ed's old climbing gear: the boots, the bag of powdered chalk, the shirt that still smelt so strongly of him. If she nuzzled her face into it, closed her eyes and breathed in, she could still almost believe he was here beside her, talking animatedly about the next mountain he was going to climb, the next daft stunt he wanted to try.

But only almost.

Inevitably as the months passed, she had felt the raw intensity of her grief begin to lose a little of its vicious edge, so that now she had to come up here and immerse herself in Ed in order to feel the same gut-wrenching loss she had felt at the beginning. This made her feel guilty – and angry. Guilty because the lessening of grief, however slight, implied a fault in her, a denial of the strength of the love they had shared. And angry because it felt as if another much-loved thing was being taken away from her, drop by precious drop.

'I've really got to do something with all of this you know,' she said out loud to the cat, who purred and rubbed himself amiably against her. 'It's getting like a cross between a shrine and a time-capsule in here.'

Lorna knew her mum and dad would have something to say about her lack of progress with the room. It wasn't that they wanted her to forget about Ed – far from it. They just worried about how healthy it was to lock grief away instead of facing up to it. Perhaps they were right. But anyway, they weren't arriving until next week, so there was no need for Lorna to do anything about it today. Maybe tomorrow, she told herself as she sat cross-legged on the threadbare old carpet Ed had resolutely refused to throw away, even when they could afford to replace it. He'd said it would be a reminder to them of times when things weren't so easy.

Now she'd have traded everything she owned to go back to those times.

Lorna took a deep breath and let it out very slowly. Yes, maybe tomorrow she'd think about sorting through some of the old computer games and sending them to the charity shop. It wasn't as if she was ever going to play them, and anyhow they were out of date already.

Out of date. Like her grief?

The thought was so sacrilegious that it revolted her. How could she even begin to think that way? Ed had been the one love of her life, and he always would be, no question about that.

She might have gone on berating herself, but the telephone rang in the main bedroom, so she hauled herself to her feet and went off to answer it. Alone in a forbidden paradise, Clawdius couldn't believe his luck. He hopped lightly into the cupboard, curled up on Ed's old shirt and went to sleep.

*

34

'Hello Mum,' said Lorna. 'Everything all right?'

'Er . . . yes, dear, of course.'

Lorna frowned. 'Are you sure?'

'Yes dear. Why ever wouldn't I be? Now, how are you and the children? Has Leo got over his tummy upset?'

'Leo's fine. It was only one of those one-day things. Chris brought him home and he was scoffing crisps again in no time.'

'You shouldn't let him eat too many of those salty snacks, you know,' her mother reminded her. 'And all that hydrogenated vegetable fat can't be good for a growing child.'

'Yes, yes, I know. Don't worry Mum, he gets plenty of good wholesome food.'

'Don't think I'm nagging, dear. I just worry, you know, with you being on your own and having so much to cope with.'

'We're doing just fine,' Lorna assured her with a confidence she didn't necessarily feel. 'Anyhow, you'll be able to see that for yourself when you come over next week.'

'Ah, yes. Next week.'

'Mum!' groaned Lorna. 'Don't tell me you're not coming!'

Meg laughed rather strangely. 'Oh, don't worry about that, we're definitely coming. It's just . . . well, we wondered if it would be all right with you if we came a little earlier than planned.'

'Oh. Yes, fine. How much earlier – you mean next Tuesday, instead of Wednesday?'

'Actually dear, we were wondering if we could come tomorrow.'

'Tomorrow!' Carmen still couldn't quite believe it. 'Your mum's going on about how much you've got to cope with, then she goes and tells you they're coming to stay tomorrow? I'll never understand parents. Sometimes I'm almost glad I haven't got any.'

'That's OK, I don't understand them either. Not mine, anyway.'

Lorna and Carmen went on making up the bed in the guest room. 'They don't usually spring this sort of thing on you, do they?' asked Carmen.

'Never. That's why I can't help thinking they're up to something.'

Carmen laughed. 'You make them sound like naughty kids.'

Lorna shook her head. 'No, with kids you *know* they're up to something. With Mum and Dad, I've just got this really weird feeling.'

'Wind,' diagnosed Carmen.

Lorna threw a pillow at her head. 'I'm serious. Parents are supposed to be boring and predictable. I mean, mine are always telling me in minute detail about everything they've done in the last fortnight, even if I don't really want to know about my dad's bunions or the woman from number thirty-seven's husband who wears ladies' knickers.'

Carmen's interest increased. 'Does he?'

'Apparently so.'

'Frilly lace ones, or big saggy white ones?'

'I thought we were talking about my parents!' exclaimed Lorna in exasperation.

'Sorry, but if you will distract me. What do the rest of the family think?'

'David doesn't know what to think, and Sarah . . . well Sarah just doesn't think.' Unless it's to do with money or expensive holidays, she added silently. 'But I don't need them to tell me there's something up.'

'Well, you don't have to wait long to find out,' pointed out Carmen, patting the last pillow into shape. 'There – all you need to do now is polish the kettle and whitewash the cat, and you're done.'

Lorna blew a straggle of blonde hair out of her eyes. 'Thanks for helping out at the last minute, Carmen. I don't know what to say.'

Carmen winked. 'Don't worry, I've got you down to baby-sit my tribe for the next ten years. That should just about cover it.'

George and Meg Scholes were not the sort of people to be late, or early, or in fact anything other than precisely on time. Indeed, even though he had taken early retirement a couple of years previously, George was still getting up at six thirty every morning, simply because he was accustomed to the routine. He was the sort of person likely to book an appointment to die, just so as not to inconvenience anybody.

Consequently, Lorna was ever so slightly concerned when three pm came round and her parents still hadn't arrived. And when she tried phoning, only to be greeted by the 'number unobtainable' tone, her mind started creating all sorts of unfeasible scenarios.

'Where's Grandad?' asked Leo for the fourteenth time since lunch.

'Gan-da,' echoed Hope, pulling herself up onto her fat little legs and toddling a few steps before falling on her bottom.

'He'll be here soon.'

'You said that before and it was ages ago and he's not here,' protested Leo.

'I know, but he'll definitely be here soon.' He'd better, thought Lorna, or I'll have a mini-riot on my hands.

There was a short hiatus. Then: 'Where's Grandma?'

Lorna sighed. 'With Grandad.'

Pause. 'Where's Grandad?'

At ten past three, when Lorna was on the point of being seriously worried, a grey Peugeot turned the corner past the church into St Jude's Square. For a split second, she didn't recognise her parents' car, so laden was the roof-rack with suitcases and – of all things – a chair. But then she saw her dad's ubiquitous tweed cap, and her mum waving at her through the passenger window. She scooped Hope up in her arms. 'Look kids, it's Granny and Grandad!'

Leo was first to the car as it laboured into the sole free parking space in the square. With the church in the middle and Cheltenham town centre only five minutes' walk away, parking was often not so much an inconvenience as a near-impossibility. Not like it was in Mum and Dad's rural Herefordshire retreat, where the only commuters were the sheep that ambled across the road from one field to the other.

'Grandma Long-Legs!' carolled Leo as Meg emerged from the driver's seat, easing out the knots in her spine. She was a statuesque woman, absolutely the physical opposite of her daughter, and it was always a challenge to cram her long limbs into any car.

'Well, well,' said Meg, beaming, stepping back to take a better look at her grandson. 'Whoever is this tall young man?'

'It's me, Grandma! Leo!'

She shook her head in mock disbelief. 'No, no, you can't be Leo. My Leo's much smaller than you.'

Leo hopped up and down in giggling frustration. 'I grew, didn't I, Mummy, tell Grandma I grew!'

'He certainly did,' confirmed Lorna ruefully. 'I've lost count of the pairs of shoes he's been through since you last saw him.'

Grandad dragged a couple of suitcases onto the pavement and opened his arms wide. 'Come here boy, and give me a hug.'

Leo obeyed with a whoop of joy, leaping into one of Grandad Scholes's special bear-hugs.

'That's Leo all right.' George liberated him, red-faced and tousle-haired, and set him back on his feet. 'Nobody hugs like our Leo. And who's this pretty little lady then?' He chucked Hope under the chin and gave her a big kiss on her curly blonde head. 'Aren't you the gorgeous one?'

'Ahem,' cut in Lorna. 'Her mum's not that bad either. Do I get a kiss too?'

'Of course you do, darling.' Her mum somehow managed to enfold Lorna, Leo and Hope in one all-encompassing embrace. Clawdius wound his tail round Lorna's leg, determinedly getting in on the act. 'How are you?' Meg asked. 'I must say, you're looking well.'

'I'm fine,' replied Lorna as they walked towards the terraced house, with its cream rendering and lopsided chimneys. 'Knackered as usual, but

37

fine.' She gave her mother a long, hard look. 'I'm more bothered about you, actually. You've never been so late before – I was really getting worried!'

'Oh,' said Meg, looking at George. 'There was no need, really there wasn't.'

George fidgeted. 'You know how it is. Delays and all that.'

'What kind of delays – traffic jams?' Lorna led the way into the hall. 'I didn't hear anything on the radio.'

'We were waiting for a telephone call actually,' advanced Meg, darting desperate glances about her. 'Oh look, George, Lorna's bought a new lampshade – isn't it lovely?'

Lorna wasn't to be put off quite so easily, particularly since the lampshade in question was at least five years old. 'What telephone call? And what's with all this luggage?' Open-mouthed, she watched suitcase after suitcase appear in the front hall, followed by an assortment of peculiar domestic items. 'I mean, who on earth takes a chair on holiday with them? And an antique brass coal-scuttle?'

George had the look of a cornered Victorian schoolboy, caught bang to rights with his pockets full of apples. Meg looked at him, and sighed. 'Tell her, George. She's got to know sooner or later.'

A surge of panic assailed Lorna. Oh my God, she thought; he's ill. Or Mum is. Dangerously ill. It's probably cancer. They were waiting for the test results, and it's really bad, and they can't bring themselves to tell me. 'Know what?' she demanded, dry-mouthed.

'The phone call was from the solicitor,' her father explained wearily. 'Until she called to say the money was through, we didn't want to risk moving out and putting the rest of our stuff in storage.'

Lorna stared blankly, not understanding any of this. 'What are you talking about?'

Meg took her hand and squeezed it gently. When Lorna looked her in the face, she saw tears forming in her eyes. 'We've sold the house, dear,' Meg said softly.

'Rainbow Cottage? But—'

'I know how much you loved it,' said her father. 'And so did we. But believe me, love, we had no choice.'

Chapter 5

Once Hope was asleep and Leo was happily playing with his toys in his bedroom, Lorna allowed herself the time to be stunned. 'Tell me this is some kind of weird joke, Dad,' she pleaded as they sat in the lounge, watching a perfectly good pot of tea go cold.

'I wish I could, love, but I'm afraid it's true. It's all to do with money, you see.'

Money? That just didn't make sense in Lorna's head. Dad had always been the sensible sort – so much so that some people might accuse him of being downright stingy, though he'd be mortally offended if they suggested it. While other families were going on foreign holidays and buying big TVs, the Scholeses were having a week's self-catering in the Lake District, playing Monopoly and reading a lot of books. Meanwhile, George was squirrelling every spare penny he could find into his company pension, or unit trusts, or anything else that would build up his 'rainy day fund', as he liked to call it. The future had been as meticulously planned as his production schedules at Incorporated Ball Bearings. How could he and Mum possibly have money problems?

'I know what you're going to say, dear,' said her mum as she opened her mouth to protest, 'and you're quite right. Dad's always looked after us all very well. But the thing is, your dad and I have had a few . . . mishaps.'

George sighed and patted his wife's hand. 'You're being too kind, Meg. Let's be honest about this, it's all down to me.'

Meg wasn't having any of it. 'Don't be ridiculous George, how could you have known the chairman was going to embezzle all that money from the pension fund?'

'What!' Lorna was knocked sideways. 'How come this hasn't been all over the papers?'

'Incorporated's only a small firm, love. The big tabloids aren't interested in us.'

'But you can get some of the money back, right?'

'Let's just say I wouldn't hold your breath. And then there's the invest-ments,' he added soberly.

Lorna shook her dazed head back into focus. 'They're OK, surely? You've always been so careful, Dad. Hasn't he, Mum?'

Meg nodded. 'Always.'

But George just sagged in his chair. 'Not careful enough, I'm afraid. Some of my investments have taken, well, let's say a bit of a dive. And did I see it coming? Did I hell. So now we're down to what's left in the savings account, and that's not going to get us far.'

'Oh Dad.' He looked so sad that Lorna wished she could hug it all bet-ter, the way she did with the children when they fell over and hurt them-selves. Unfortunately, as she knew only too bitterly, adult life wasn't quite so straightforward.

Meg filled the uncomfortable hiatus in the conversation. 'If anybody's blaming anybody,' she said firmly, 'then I'm taking my share too. If it wasn't for me going on about that blessed conservatory, we might have been able to hold on to the house.'

Her husband gripped her hand tight in his. 'You've always wanted a conservatory, right since before we even got married. Somewhere to sit on a nice evening, grow those plants you're so good with ... It was your dream, and I wanted it to come true.'

Lorna looked from her mother to her father and back again. 'What's the conservatory got to do with all this? It didn't fall down or something, did it?'

'No,' replied Meg, 'but when your dad started having his money prob-lems, we couldn't keep up the repayments on the loan, you see.' She sat back on the sofa, staring hard at the ceiling as if concentration was the only thing holding the tears at bay. 'Oh damn and blast Lorna, I feel like some feckless teenager who's run up a fortune on stupid credit cards.'

Lorna slid along the sofa so as to be closer to her. 'It's nothing like that at all, Mum. It wasn't your fault, or Dad's. Horrible, unfair things just happen to nice people sometimes.'

'You know more about that than anyone,' said her mother. 'Listen to the pair of us, George, moaning and whining over money when our daughter's lost far more than we ever have.' She wiped the back of her hand across her eyes. 'I think it's time we pulled ourselves together and acted like grown-ups, don't you?'

For the next couple of days, Lorna tiptoed around George and Meg's bombshell as if it had left an invisible crater in the middle of the floor. Nobody mentioned money, or homelessness, or the future. Nobody picked up the phone and called Sarah or David. Leo and Hope were

40

indulged, fussed over and entertained just as much as they would have been on any normal visit from their grandparents. It was as if the moment of dreadful revelation had never happened.

As for Lorna, she was too busy to spend much time speculating on what was going to happen. And she was more than a little grateful when her parents offered to take on the kids for the day and give her some time for herself.

It was a long time since she'd spent a whole day indulging herself, and she was rather afraid that she might get to like it. She had her hair done and her legs waxed – something she hadn't even contemplated since Ed died. What was the point in having stubble-free legs if there was never going to be anyone else to admire them? The luxury of a little time out made Lorna think that perhaps there was some point in doing it simply for herself. It felt undeniably nice; luxurious and not in the least bit sensible. And she'd been doing an awful lot of sensible over the last eighteen months.

Lunch in a town-centre café, accompanied by an entire, uninterrupted glass of wine, was a scarcely remembered indulgence. And to top the whole day off, she blew half the weekly food budget on a pair of impractical shoes she'd probably never wear. And she didn't even feel guilty.

Thanks Mum; thanks Dad, she thought as she walked back home. Thanks for letting me remember what it was like to be me.

It was teatime: usually a moment of total domestic chaos, but George and Meg had everything organised. Leo was happily stuffing his face with Grandma's home-made tuna-fish bake, while Grandad was pretending his spoon was an aeroplane – and getting most of the mashed potato on it into Hope's mouth, much to Lorna's surprise.

The dishes were done, there was a casserole in the oven, and the washing had been tumble-dried and folded in a basket on top of the machine. Even the small patch of front garden looked suspiciously as if it had been weeded. It isn't until somebody else cleans your house, mused Lorna, that you realise just how grubby it was to begin with. Or how untidy.

'Lorna dear, your hair looks nice.' A beaming Meg placed a cup of tea in her hand almost before she'd stepped in through the door. 'Now let's see. Your friend Carmen rang and I told her you'd call back after eight, somebody called Lennie wanted to know the date you're taking the children to the zoo, so I found it on the calendar and told her, and that nice boy Christopher says he's got a replacement bracket for that wonky shelf in the bathroom. Did you have a good day?'

Breathless just from listening, Lorna flopped onto the empty chair next to Leo. 'Not as busy as yours, that's for sure!'

41

'Grandma made cakes with blue icing,' Leo announced proudly. 'Hope had one, and I had three.'

'That was kind of Grandma,' said Lorna. 'I hope you said thank you. And I hope all your teeth don't fall out!'

'You don't mind, do you?' asked Meg, somewhat crestfallen. 'Only I do so love giving them little treats.'

'Oh, I think that's what grandmas are for,' replied Lorna with a smile. 'We'll just make sure he brushes his teeth properly. Here Dad, shall I take over doing that?' she asked, reaching for the spoonful of mashed potato.

'Don't you worry, love. Hope and I are having a lovely little game, aren't we sweetie?'

Hope gurgled in agreement, and was so entranced by Grandad's funny faces that she hardly seemed to have noticed that her mum had come home at all.

'You really didn't need to do all this, you know,' Lorna scolded, surveying the gleaming palace that had been her kitchen. 'But thanks all the same. I've had a wonderful day.'

Meg and George exchanged broad smiles. 'That's what we were hoping, dear,' admitted Lorna's mum. 'You see, while you were out your dad and I had an idea.'

'Your dad and I had an idea': that phrase flashed a big red warning light inside Lorna's head, just as it had ever since she was a little kid. Meg and George had 'had an idea' when Lorna was small that maybe the Brownies were a tad too militaristic. Consequently she'd been packed off to the Woodcraft Folk to hug trees and sing songs about peace when she'd much rather have been a Sixer like her friend Bryony and have badges all down her arm. Their other 'ideas' had ranged from Family Meetings (which always ended with Mum and Dad taking all the decisions anyway) to Nobody Spending More Than Five Pounds on a Family Present (which crashed in flames as soon as Christmas hove into view and the kids saw the price of their favourite toys).

'What sort of idea?' asked Lorna warily.

Meg sat down at the table, opposite her daughter. 'We've really enjoyed being with the children today, haven't we, George?'

George nodded. 'Oh yes, definitely.'

'And it has been useful to you, hasn't it? Having us to take care of them and the house and things?'

'Of course it has – it's been lovely. I'm very grateful, you know I am.' It's the kids, thought Lorna suddenly. They've done something unspeakable, and Mum's embarrassed to tell me about it. 'Is there some kind of problem?'

George and Meg both laughed. 'Not at all! We've had a wonderful day. So wonderful, in fact, that we were wondering how you'd feel about it always being like this.'

Now Lorna was completely lost. 'Sorry? I don't get it.'

George stepped into the breach and took over. 'What your mother means, love, is that if you wanted, she and I could be here all the time. We could look after the children and the house whenever you wanted us to.'

'We know how much you've been wanting to get back to work,' added Meg. 'With us around, you could.'

'You mean . . . buy a flat round here or something? But I thought you couldn't afford it.'

'We can't.' George cleared his throat gruffly. 'But if we were to find somewhere where we could pay for our keep another way, say by working, er . . . well . . . you've got a lot of empty space in this house, love, and we wouldn't take up much room.'

'What your Dad is trying to say so ineptly,' cut in Lorna's mum, 'is that we thought maybe we could move in here with you and the children.'

For just a split second, Lorna thought her mum was being serious. Then she realised it was a joke and let out a relieved laugh. 'Mum! Don't say things like that, you really had me going there for a minute.'

Meg looked rather nonplussed. 'You think it's some kind of joke?'

'It is, isn't it?'

'No, dear. As a matter of fact, your dad and I are deadly serious.'

Lorna was feeling tense already, and she'd only been on the phone to her sister for two minutes.

'Don't be ridiculous,' snorted Sarah. 'Of course they're not serious. Why on earth would Mum and Dad want to live with you?'

Typical Sarah, thought Lorna; wilfully refuse to understand the situation. It was easier getting through to a roomful of toddlers. 'I don't think it's a question of wanting to,' she repeated. 'They've got nowhere to live and hardly any money.'

'But that's silly,' insisted Sarah. 'Dad's got loads of shares, I know he has. If he's short of money, why doesn't he sell them or something?'

Lorna visualised flushing her sister's thick head down the toilet, and felt slightly better. 'I told you, because they're not worth anything any more. Don't you ever listen to anything I say?'

Sarah sniffed. 'There's no need to be rude. I'm having difficulty coming to terms with all of this, you know,' she added with a martyred air. 'I'm very traumatised.'

'Not half as much difficulty as Mum and Dad are having,' retorted Lorna.

'But if what you say is true, and they want somewhere to stay, surely they'd come and stay with me. My house is so much bigger.'

'Yes,' agreed Lorna. 'And you've got a husband, a gardener, a cleaner and no kids. Don't you get it? Mum and Dad aren't looking for the most comfortable place to stay; they want to move in here because they think they can help.'

'Hmm,' replied Sarah, clearly not satisfied. 'You're not the only one who could use a little help, you know. When I get one of my headaches—'

Lorna let her rabbit on for a while about how hard it was, being the idle rich wife of a man who went to work in a helicopter. It was easier than trying to chisel away at her self-centred little world. Am I being horrible, Lorna wondered to herself, or is my sister really a pain in the bum? God knows why I bothered to phone and ask her what she thought. Sarah doesn't do thinking.

At last Sarah appeared to grind to a halt. Lorna was about to get a word in edgeways, when her sister came out with, 'Does this mean Mum and Dad won't have any money again, ever?'

'I don't know, it might. Why?'

Sarah stumbled over her reply. 'Oh you know, no special reason. I'm just worried about them, that's all. Their future and stuff.'

Yeah right, thought Lorna. And you're even more worried about your inheritance.

It was early evening, and Carmen and Lorna were wandering through the annual German Market on the Promenade, in search of Christmas presents. The frosty air was full of the scent of fried onions, bratwurst and mulled wine; and for the first time Lorna began to feel some of the seasonal excitement Leo had caught weeks ago. For her at least, Christmas hadn't been the same since Ed died; but there was still a hint of something special about it as long as you had children.

'So what did your brother say?' asked Carmen.

'David? He said having Mum and Dad living with me was a stupid idea, and we'd do nothing but row all the time.'

'Maybe he's right,' ventured Carmen, leafing through a display of hand-painted Christmas cards. 'Sometimes people end up hating each other's guts when they're squashed into a confined space together.'

'The house is hardly a confined space,' argued Lorna. 'I mean, it's got three floors and with a bit of arranging Mum and Dad can have a couple of rooms to themselves. Like a sort of granny bedsit.'

'Hmm,' said Carmen with a sidelong look. 'Sounds like you've been giving this some serious thought.'

'Oh I have,' sighed Lorna, 'believe me I have. And in some ways it makes perfect sense – almost too perfect. Trouble is, I just can't get my head round it.'

Carmen picked up a fuchsia-pink woolly hat with tassels and plonked it on Lorna's blonde head. 'Maybe you need something to warm your brains up.'

'Or some brains to warm up.' Lorna found a stall selling wooden toys, and pounced on a medieval castle, complete with drawbridge and portcullis. 'Oh Carmen, look at this – wouldn't Leo love it? And these animal building blocks would be perfect for Hope. They're not expensive either.'

'Trust you've got a good place to hide them until Christmas!' commented Carmen. 'You know what kids are like. Robbie and Charmain are terrors for finding all my hiding places. It's like they've got a sixth sense or something.' She played idly with a toy train as Lorna paid for the toys. 'So, how long is it since you lived with your mum and dad then?'

'Oooh, years,' replied Lorna. 'Not since I was eighteen and went off to do my training. By the time I'd finished the course Ed and I were married.' She reeled as the memories piled in on her. 'God, it seems like a long time ago.'

'And you're worried you might end up feeling like a kid again, living with your parents?'

'Wouldn't you worry?'

Carmen laughed ruefully. 'I never did the family thing, remember. Apart from my kids, the only people I've ever lived with since I left care are my sister and the blokes I've shacked up with. And I wouldn't exactly call that an unqualified success, would you?' She gave the train a gentle push, and it trundled obediently along its wooden track into its little wooden shed. 'But that's not the same. And anyway, you're grown-up now; having your parents around might be totally different this time round. I mean, you're the one with the power, aren't you? You're the one helping them.'

'The kids would like it,' admitted Lorna.

'And you'd have somebody to take care of them, so you could go and get that midwifery job you've been hankering after.'

'And I'd have two people living in my house and making me feel like it's not really mine any more,' retorted Lorna.

Carmen cocked her head on one side, making her earrings jangle. 'You don't know you'd feel like that.'

'No,' agreed Lorna, 'I don't. The trouble is, I don't know anything really. And how can I risk saying yes when next week it might turn out to be a disaster?'

*

Talk about mixed feelings, thought Lorna. She'd retreated to the garden shed in the hope that nobody would venture out in the cold to find her. It was becoming awfully difficult to share the same space as her mum and dad without inevitably coming back to the Big Question. And she just did-n't want to address it until she had an answer to give them: an answer that she knew was right.

Even the kids had noticed that something was afoot. Leo particularly had picked up on the grown-ups' hushed conversations, and had started asking if Grandma and Grandad were coming to live here forever and ever.

Forever's a very long time, she thought as she had a desultory sort through the garden tools and assorted rubbish. And I really do want to help Mum and Dad, but . . .

The shed door creaked open and George's face appeared. 'Oh, there you are, love. I'd almost given up looking for you. There's somebody on the phone for you.'

Lorna almost told him to take a number and tell them she'd call back later, but now she'd been run to ground she thought she might as well sur-render gracefully. Taking off her muddy wellies, she padded across the kitchen floor in her socks and went to the telephone in the hall.

'Lorna Price.'

'Oh Lorna, hi! It's Sadie Witherspoon. How are you?'

'Fine, thanks. You?'

'Yes, fine, fine. The reason I'm calling is . . . you remember I told you a local midwifery placement might come up at any time?'

'Yes, but I—'

'I know you weren't sure about going back full-time, but I really thought you'd want to know about this one. A placement is coming up at the Cotswold General, just down the road from you. You'd be fully men-tored until you got your confidence back, and subject to everything going OK there's a job on offer at the end of it, hours to suit. I'd like to recom-mend you for the post. What do you think?'

Lorna sat down heavily on the chair by the phone table, not knowing what to think. 'You're right, it does sound good,' she conceded, 'and I'm flattered of course, but my family circumstances—'

'Yes, yes, of course. The children. Well, think about it and get back to me. But don't leave it too long, will you? I'll need an answer by Friday.'

Chapter 6

'We're very grateful and I promise you won't regret it, love,' Lorna's dad assured her as he put the finishing touches to the Christmas decorations in the hall. He was a bit of a Christmas addict. Ever since her childhood, Lorna remembered the Scholes household being the first in the street with its decorations up. 'Besides, if we get too annoying you can always chuck us out.'

That was more or less what Ed's parents had said when Lorna drove over to Monmouth to see them. 'It's not as if it's irreversible,' Ed's dad Myrddin had pointed out in his soft Welsh lilt, 'and besides, it's company for you and the children.' And then he'd given her a big, all-encompassing hug, and Lorna had cried a little because it felt so much like one of Ed's.

'Half the time you won't even know we're here,' added Meg. 'I've almost got your dad house-trained by now, you know. Apart from the snoring.'

'I don't snore!'

'Don't be silly, George. You sound like a rutting elephant seal. Doesn't he, Lorna?'

Lorna took a deep breath and avoided the question. 'We'll be fine,' she said firmly. No more mixed feelings or second thoughts, she'd decided. Everything was going to work out, and that was that. 'To be honest, I'm more worried about starting work than anything else.'

Her mum adjusted the skirt on the Christmas tree angel so that she wasn't flashing quite so much leg. 'The people at the hospital wouldn't have taken you on if they didn't think you were up to it, you know that.'

'What about whether I think I'm up to it?'

Meg gave one of her special wise smiles. 'It's all right dear, I do understand. I had the collywobbles for days before I went back to work, worrying about whether you'd all manage without me.' She spotted the expression on her daughter's face. 'Yes, I know it was only three mornings a week in the local chemist's and you were all at secondary school by

47

then; but that's beside the point. When you're a mum, you worry. In fact, you never stop worrying.'

'Ain't that the truth,' agreed Lorna. She looked out of the kitchen window into the small, enclosed back garden, where a frosty plastic slide sparkled in the wintry sunshine. What if Leo falls off it when Mum and Dad aren't looking, she thought, and I'm not here to pick him up? What if Hope tries to copy her big brother and hurts herself? She's already so desperate to be like him . . .

'Stop it,' her mother commanded suddenly, making Lorna jump.

'Stop what?'

'Imagining all the bad things that are going to happen because you're not here to prevent them. We have brought up three children ourselves, you know! And as far as I've noticed, none of you has grown up with any significant bits missing.'

If you don't count Sarah's brain and David's heart, thought Lorna maliciously. She followed up the thought with a mental slap on the wrist. Her brother and sister weren't really that bad. They *weren't*! 'Yes Mum, I know,' she replied, 'and it's not that I don't trust you or anything like that.'

'It's just that you feel guilty,' said her father, returning from putting the stepladder away.

'Well, yes. A bit,' admitted Lorna.

'That's OK, it just means you're normal,' said George cheerfully. 'Parents spend most of their lives feeling guilty.'

'Oh great! So I'm doomed then?'

'Pretty much. Now, stop fretting and pass me that gaffer tape. I want to see those children's faces when I switch the Christmas lights on tonight.'

The big day came around so quickly that Lorna's brain was unable to keep pace. When the alarm went off that morning and she realised she was actually going to have to get up and go to work in a proper job, the thought was so overwhelming that all she wanted to do was roll onto Ed's side of the bed, pull the duvet up over her head and tell the big nasty world to go away.

That moment didn't last long however, as Leo came thundering into the bedroom and started bouncing on the bed. 'Hope's got a stinky nappy and I'm hungry and Clawdius has sicked up all over the carpet,' he announced jubilantly. 'And I can't find my pants.'

So the day began.

Things have changed a lot since I last worked here, thought Lorna as she turned through the double gates into the staff car park at the Cotswold General's McNulty Wing.

Admittedly the fearsome statue of Mildred McNulty, Cheltenham's nineteenth-century midwifery pioneer, still loomed judgementally above the ornamental fountain that never had any water in it in case somebody drowned; but the grim old Palladian-style buildings were all but invisible behind the sparkling glass and honey-coloured brickwork of the splendid new wing.

The building had been open only six months, and – despite living less than a mile away – Lorna had never been inside. Oddly, she'd have felt less uncomfortable with the gloomy Victorian warren they'd demolished to make way for the new wing: that was, after all, where she'd worked after she qualified, and where Leo had been born, one suffocating summer afternoon. This felt a little too TV-perfect, the sort of place where nobody made allowances for newbies and their inevitable mistakes . . .

'You – yes, you! Blondie! Are you deaf?'

The sudden shout made Lorna step on her brake so hard that her seat belt nearly throttled her. A dark-haired young man in a bright red, top-of-the-range Mazda was leaning out of the driver's window. He might have been quite good-looking if he hadn't been crimson with annoyance.

Grumpy sod, thought Lorna, nevertheless manoeuvring out of the car's way so that it could glide racily towards a space on the other side of the car park. So I was a bit distracted; so would you be, mate, if it was your first day back on the ward and you had to dash out and find some triceratops underpants in your lunch break.

Leo's favourite pants had turned up in the end. What Lorna hadn't told him was that they had turned up in three separate pieces. Clawdius could be a bit overenthusiastic when he found something in the laundry basket that he really wanted to shred. And Lorna could only hope that the Kidswear department at Seuss & Goldman still stocked the same range, or there would be trouble. After all, Grandma and Grandpa Price had bought him those pants, so it was practically as if they'd come straight from his dad.

By a miracle she managed to find somewhere to park, made sure her staff permit was firmly stuck to the inside of the windscreen, took a deep breath and headed towards the electric double doors.

'I know sitting down is uncomfortable, Kelly, but you can't stay standing up for ever,' pointed out the tall midwife with the formidable bust.

All the other midwives on Honeysuckle ward were wearing white tunics with burgundy piping and burgundy trousers, but Rose Finnegan had scant regard for such modern fads. She still preferred flat black shoes, thick black stockings and the striped uniform dress that all her younger colleagues had given up wearing five years earlier; and she didn't give a damn if trousers were more practical.

'My bum's on fire,' protested the stubborn-faced girl in the fluffy white dressing gown and tiger's-feet slippers. She couldn't have been more than sixteen, but wasn't going to be daunted by the likes of Miss Finnegan. 'That doctor's a butcher, he is. Cuts me and then sews me up like he's darning a bloody sock.'

Rose Finnegan gave a sigh of impatience. There was so little respect for the medical profession these days. 'The doctor had to make an incision to get the baby out, or you'd have torn, and that would've been much worse I assure you.'

Kelly grunted. 'How'd he like it if somebody sewed up his whatnots? Put the brakes on his jollies for a bit, wouldn't it?'

The other three women in the bay fell about laughing, and one of the babies started to cry. Naturally all the others followed suit. As it happened, that was the moment Lorna chose to arrive on the scene.

'Hi, I'm Lorna Price. Is this a bad moment to say I'm new?'

Rose Finnegan promptly dumped a bawling infant in her arms. 'If you're the new student, you're late,' she said. 'Here, see what you can do with this.'

'Actually I'm not a student, I'm a qualified midwife.' Lorna cuddled and shushed the child until its crimson face faded to pink and its yelling subsided.

'Hmph. I knew the recruitment crisis was bad, but I didn't know they'd started taking children.'

Not for the first time, Lorna cursed her youthful appearance. Being small, naturally blonde and frail-looking was a definite handicap unless you were trying to travel half-price on the bus. Ed used to joke that they didn't need to buy two plane tickets when they went on holiday: he could just stick her in his suitcase.

'She is a bit young, isn't she?' commented one of the older mothers.

'My eldest looks older than her, and she's only fourteen,' agreed another. 'When you're in this place what you want is somebody with a bit of experience.'

'Hiya, I'm Kelly,' the teenager piped up defiantly. 'Take no notice of them, they're just jealous 'cause they're past it. I like your hair, do you bleach it yourself?'

'No, I'm lucky; I don't have to. I was born that way.' Lorna was relieved that somebody at least was interested in having a conversation about something other than her age. She looked Kelly up and down. 'Having trouble sitting?' she enquired. 'You look like you're in a bit of pain.'

Kelly darted Rose Finnegan a black look. '*She* says it's normal.'

'Which it is,' the older midwife retorted. 'Lots of women have stitches down there, but they don't all make an almighty fuss about them the way you do.'

Lorna made a mental note never to have another baby if Rose Finnegan was likely to be delivering the after-care. 'I know it's horrible,' she said. 'I had a lot of stitches when I had my first. But it does ease off, and we can get you a rubber ring to make you more comfy.'

'You've got kids of your own then?' one of the older mothers asked, clearly surprised.

'Two, a boy and a girl.'

'So what's your bloke do?'

It wasn't the first time Lorna had been asked the question, but somehow she was never quite ready for it. 'I'm . . . er . . . on my own now,' she said.

'Me too,' sympathised Kelly. 'It wouldn't have worked though. He supported Arsenal.'

'My God,' lamented Rose Finnegan, 'talk about the youth of today. Not a wedding ring between the lot of you. Never occurs to you to get married first and then get pregnant, does it?'

Something about the tone of her voice pressed all the wrong buttons in Lorna's usually cool head. 'As a matter of fact I'm a widow,' she said tartly. 'Now Kelly, shall we see if we can get you that rubber ring?'

As it turned out, the sister on the post-natal ward wasn't a sister at all. For one thing she was a he; and the nameplate on the ward office door read 'Senior Midwife' and not 'Sister'. More changes, thought Lorna. Mind you, he'd have looked pretty silly in a knee-length dress and black tights.

'This is Debs, she's going to be your mentor,' yawned Senior Midwife Colin Jenkins, one eye on his electronic diary. Young, brash, flash and only four years out of university, he didn't look as if he was planning on sticking around too long. Crocus ward was most probably just one small step in a carefully worked-out plan for global domination. Still, he was friendly enough in his own way. 'Debs, Lorna. Lorna, Debs. Any problems, she'll sort you out. Now if you'll excuse me, got to dash, I'm late for a meeting.'

'Don't worry, he's OK really,' said Debs as Colin's brogues marched off down the corridor to Admin. 'He's just . . . you know.'

'A man?' enquired Lorna.

Debs giggled, making dimples appear in her plump cheeks. She was thirty-five, and pregnant enough to be starting to show, but had a girlish air that appealed to Lorna. She'd already decided she was glad that Debs

51

was going to be her mentor. 'A man who happens to be a midwife,' Debs reminded her. 'And you know what that means.'

'What?' asked Lorna, though she had a pretty good idea.

'Headed straight for management, and he'd be there already if all these pregnant women didn't keep showing up.'

They laughed. 'I feel really out of place,' confessed Lorna. 'I haven't been on a maternity unit since I had my kids. It feels like . . . like I don't know anything!'

Debs shrugged. 'I've only been qualified a year, so that makes two of us.' She flashed Lorna a smile. 'Seems daft really, me mentoring you when you're the one with all the experience.'

'Hmm,' said Lorna. 'Well there might be people with more experience on the ward, but from what I've seen I'm pretty sure I'd rather have you.'

'Ah.' Debs grinned. 'You've been talking to our Rose, haven't you?'

'Well—'

'Strictly old-school, is our Rose. Won't hear a word against doctors, thinks mothers should do what they're told, and babies should be fed every two hours on the dot. I wouldn't worry too much about her though; she's all talk. Scares the pants off some of the young mums though.'

'I noticed.' Lorna nodded towards Bay C, where Kelly was singing 'Postman Pat' off-key to her baby daughter. 'At her age, I reckon I'd have run off screaming, but she seems to give as good as she gets.'

Debs nodded. 'On the surface, yes. I'm not sure she's all that hard underneath though. It can't be easy, having a baby when you're fourteen.'

Lorna's jaw dropped open. 'Fourteen! I thought she was sixteen at least.'

Debs lowered her voice to a whisper. 'That's what the lad said too, apparently. Police decided not to prosecute, and the parents couldn't give a damn. I think the social worker's due to see her before we let her and the baby go home – assuming she has a home by then. Last time I heard her mum was threatening to throw her out and get a lodger instead.'

Poor kid, thought Lorna, suddenly feeling lucky. Even with the bad things that had happened to her over the last eighteen months, she'd never felt alone: at least, not that alone.

She was brought back to the present by a nudge in her ribs. 'Talking of doctors,' whispered Debs, 'what do think of our local luurve machine? Wouldn't mind him leafing through your case-notes, eh?'

Lorna glanced behind her and came face to face with the young man who had insulted her in the car park; only this time, he was wearing a white coat and had a stethoscope hanging round his neck. Oh great, she thought. You're a doctor. I should have guessed from your social skills.

'Hello, Dr Sullivan,' beamed Debs, changing instantly from a married mother-to-be into a simpering pool of goo. 'I've got all the notes laid out in order for you, just the way you like them.'

Dr Sullivan looked right through her. 'Well, well, if it isn't Blondie,' he said in a voice that, when it wasn't bawling abuse, was a rather melodic southern Irish brogue.

'My name's Lorna Price,' she replied with, she thought, just the right degree of coolness.

'Oh really? Well, Lorna, I'm sure you're perfectly aware that students aren't allowed to put their cars in the staff car park.'

Lorna felt as if the top of her head was about to blow off. 'I am not—'

Debs stepped in before Lorna reached critical mass. 'Lorna's a qualified midwife,' she explained. 'She's come back into midwifery after having her family.'

Dr Sullivan regarded Lorna coldly for a few seconds, and Lorna stared right back, unblinkingly.

'Next time you decide to stop right in the middle of the entrance and put your lippy on, make sure you do it when I'm not around.' He snapped his fingers. 'Notes, Deborah. I haven't got all day.'

Lorna watched Debs scuttle off in his wake like a devoted dachshund, and despaired. How come some women were perfectly normal and sensible all the time, until some vaguely good-looking bloke hove into view, and then they went to pieces?

Well, not me, Dr I-think-I'm-God Sullivan, she mused defiantly. I don't like you very much at all.

Chapter 7

'It's early days of course, but so far things seem to be working out really well.' It was lunchtime, and Lorna was sitting in the staff canteen with Debs and Honey Lewis, one of the nursing assistants from Crocus ward. In the short time she'd been working with them, Lorna had become quite friendly with her two colleagues – though she'd have run a mile rather than share her lunch with Rose Finnegan. 'I must admit though, I was a bit worried in case Mum and Dad couldn't cope.'

'I wish I could come home to a nice cooked meal once in a while,' commented Honey wistfully. 'My Rick just doesn't seem to realise he's not the only one who's knackered after a long shift. I'm lucky if he bothers to put his underpants in the laundry basket. God knows what it'll be like if we ever have kids.'

'Start as you mean to go on,' advised Debs. 'Underpants on floor equals dinner in bin. That's the rule in our house. And of course there's always, you know, the Ultimate Sanction.'

'The what?' Honey looked puzzled.

Debs gave a broad wink. 'You know. Withhold the one thing he'd miss more than beer and footie.'

'Oh that! I shouldn't think he'd notice. Most of the time he just climbs into bed and falls asleep.

Lorna listened to the tales of lazy husbands and DIY that never got done, and felt a pang of nostalgia for the days when she'd ended up putting up shelves herself because Ed was away climbing something, or jumping off it with a bungee rope attached to his ankles. She might have muttered the occasional curse when he wasn't there to mend a fuse, but he was her soulmate and she longed to have him back with every fibre of her being.

Perhaps she even knew, deep in her heart, that she would have welcomed him back even if he had been the worst husband in the world, just for the comfort of having him there; of having someone in the big green armchair who wasn't her dad.

Face it Lorna, a little voice whispered to her, you're just plain lonesome.

It took a few seconds for her to realise that Honey was asking her a question.

'Sorry? What was that – did you say something?'

'I was just asking, what do make of life on Crocus ward then?'

'It's good; I'm enjoying it a lot more than I thought I would. That young Irish doctor's a bit of a pain though.'

'What – Eoin?' Debs laughed incredulously. 'But he's gorgeous!'

'Totally buff,' agreed Honey. 'Hey, when did you get on first-name terms with him?'

Debs grinned. 'Wouldn't you like to know.'

'Hands off, he's mine!'

Lorna wondered if she'd wandered into a class of thirteen-year-olds. 'Hang on, I can't believe I'm hearing this!' she protested. 'He's arrogant, he's rude to the patients, he thinks he's God's gift—'

'Only because he is,' Debs replied dreamily.

'And he's not even that good-looking.' OK, maybe just a bit good-looking, she admitted to herself reluctantly, but definitely not enough to make anyone with half a brain overlook his glaring shortcomings.

Debs and Honey shook their heads in mock pity. 'I dunno, no taste at all,' lamented Honey. 'Still, all the more for me. I've always wanted my own life-size Action Man.'

'Action Man?' Lorna pulled a face. 'Don't tell me – he's in the SAS as well.'

'I bet he could be if he wanted!' retorted Honey, staunch in his defence. 'He must be really brave – he does all that dangerous sports stuff – white water rafting, paragliding, caving, the lot.'

'Oh,' said Lorna, with a mixture of surprise and grudging interest. 'He does, does he?'

'You can tell he's got lovely muscles under that white coat,' added Debs. 'And he saved somebody from drowning when we had that flash flood last year, so he's a hero as well.'

'That was him?' Lorna recalled the story in the *Cheltenham Courant* – a woman had been swept away in her car when the Chelt flooded, and some young doctor had waded in and pulled her out seconds before the car went under the water. OK, so that was a bit brave – well reckless, anyway. Trust someone like Eoin Sullivan to get himself into the headlines.

As soon as she had the thought, she wondered if she was being a little uncharitable. Maybe she'd caught the guy on a bad day . . . no, make that a bad week. Maybe he wasn't really that bad after all.

56

Or maybe, thought Lorna, I'm just going soft in the head.

When she arrived home that evening after her late shift, she found George and Meg on their hands and knees in the front room, peering at the DVD player.

'Kids OK?' asked Lorna, throwing off her jacket and rubbing her hands to warm them up. It felt so strange, coming home this late and missing all the familiar evening rituals – bath-time, story-time and all the goodnight kisses.

George looked up. 'The children are fine, love. Both in bed, though it took a while getting Leo up the stairs. I'm not sure about this thing though.'

'What on earth are you doing?' asked Lorna.

Meg sighed. 'It was my fault really. I should have been keeping a closer eye on Hope. I mean, you give a child a banana sandwich and you expect a mess, don't you? I just didn't expect her to gum up the insides of your DVD player with it.'

Lorna tried to suppress a groan. 'Actually if it's anybody's fault it's mine. I should've told you Hope's got this new fascination with anything shiny. Looks like I'll be ringing up the insurance company then.'

'Oh dear, I am sorry. Can we pay something towards it?'

'No, no, Mum. No need.'

She was leafing through her tatty notebook of numbers when the phone rang. 'Hello? Oh Carmen, hi. How's things?'

'Oh you know . . . I just rang up to see how work's going.'

'Not too bad so far. I'd rather be on the labour ward though; the post-natal ward gets a bit boring after a while – all breastfeeding counselling and rubber rings. How's the clamping business?'

'Well nobody's actually tried to punch me yet this week, so I guess it's going pretty well. And I've . . . er . . . got myself a new boyfriend.'

Lorna held her breath for the inevitable. 'Go on then.'

'What do you mean, "go on"?'

'Tell me what's wrong with him.'

'Who said anything about that?'

'It's your tone of voice. The one you always use just before you tell me you've done something silly. Like the time you took in that lad from the night shelter and he nicked all your jewellery.'

'There's nothing wrong with this one, Lorna! And I haven't done anything silly! Not exactly.' There was a short silence, during which Lorna could imagine Carmen twisting the telephone flex round her fingers. 'I mean, everybody these days has debts, don't they? And we all need a helping hand sometimes.'

57

There was an awful sinking feeling in the pit of Lorna's stomach. 'How much?' she asked. 'How much money have you given him?'

'Nothing!' protested Carmen. 'Not yet. I just told him I'd think about it, that's all.'

Lorna groaned in despair. 'Listen to me, Carmen. Please, please, please tell him that you've thought about it and the answer's no. You can't go giving money to complete strangers, especially when you've hardly got enough to manage on yourself!'

Carmen let out a small sigh that sounded like relief. 'I was hoping you'd say that,' she confessed.

'Why me?' asked Lorna.

'Because . . . because you're always sensible and I'm not, and sometimes it's like being on a runaway rollercoaster and I just . . . I just need somebody else to say "stop", I guess.'

There was something flattering yet disturbingly dull about being thought eternally sensible. 'Yeah, well, maybe one day I'll need you to say stop for me,' suggested Lorna.

Carmen laughed. 'Don't be silly. You'd never ever get stupid over some bloke.'

It was the following day, and Lorna was perched on the edge of Kelly's bed, talking to her about going home.

'My mum says she's going to have me and the baby,' said Kelly flatly.

'That's good, isn't it?'

'No.'

'Why?'

'Because she doesn't want us. And if she chucked us out they'd have to find somewhere decent for us, wouldn't they?'

'I don't know if that's quite the way to look at it,' said Lorna. 'You're very young, after all. I don't think anybody'd want you and the baby trying to cope somewhere on your own.'

Kelly's large, doll-blue eyes narrowed a fraction. 'Are you saying I can't take care of my baby?'

'Of course not, I think you're doing really well. But maybe the social workers might worry if you didn't have anybody around in case something went wrong. If the baby got ill, say, or you had an accident.'

She could tiptoe all round the edges of what she was trying to say, but Kelly went straight to the heart of it. 'You mean they'd take her off me 'cause I'm fourteen and I must be thick as pigshit 'cause I got myself pregnant?' Kelly flopped back on the pillows. 'You're just as bad as them.'

'All people are trying to say is that maybe you'll be best off with your

58

mum for a while, just till you're a bit older and you've got things sorted out.'

'Then people are stupid, aren't they?' retorted Kelly. And she turned her face to the wall and refused to say any more.

On her way down to the vending machine for a quick sandwich, Lorna was so preoccupied wondering what was going to become of Kelly that she didn't even notice there was somebody else in the lift.

'Well, well, alone at last eh?'

She swung round and was greeted by the mile-wide smile of Geoff the porter, forty-five if he was a day but still sporting tufty blond highlights and white ankle socks. In Geoff's world time had got to 1982, decided it liked it, and stayed there.

'Oh, hi Geoff. How are you?'

'All the better for seeing you.' He leaned nonchalantly against the large bin of medical waste as though it were a plane tree on some Parisian boulevard. 'Get out much, do you?'

She looked at him, puzzled. 'Sorry?'

'In the evenings. Do you go out a lot? I mean, being on your own and that.'

'Er ... sometimes. It's a bit easier now I've got Mum and Dad to babysit. Why?'

The word was hardly out of her mouth before she realised exactly why. Oh God, she thought, with a sudden hot feeling on the back of her neck. He's going to ask me out! Geoff with the Wham highlights! Noooo!

'My sister's youngest's in the chorus of *Sweet Charity*, see,' Geoff was explaining. 'It's supposed to be very good. Thought you might like to come with me, seeing as she's given me a couple of free tickets.'

'I ... um ...'

He threw her a winning smile, clearly convinced that he was doing her some enormous favour by taking her out on the town; and Lorna felt really guilty. He might be the Eighties incarnate, but he was a nice guy and definitely not the kind you'd want to upset.

She took a deep breath. 'It's really nice of you, but ... it's on next week isn't it?'

'That's right.'

Her floor came up and the door opened with a ping of released tension. 'I'm really sorry, but I've got to do a lot of late shifts next week. Some other time, maybe.'

And she was free; scuttling off down the corridor, still wondering why she hadn't told him it was because she wasn't over Ed yet.

'He asked you out?' Meg's eyebrows shot skywards. 'Doesn't he know?'

'Know what?' enquired Lorna, emptying carrier bags into the fridge.

'About your . . . situation. You know, your bereavement.'

'Oh I'm sure he knows, everybody does by now,' replied Lorna. 'Why?'

Meg looked at George, who looked surprised. 'Well, you'd think he'd have a bit more sensitivity, love,' he replied. 'With you being not long widowed.'

Lorna sat down on the edge of the kitchen table, an aubergine in one hand. She was silent for a few moments. 'Actually it has been quite a while now, Dad,' she said quietly.

'Only a year!' replied her mum.

'Eighteen months – more, twenty months now. Soon it'll be two years.'

'That's not long at all, dear. Your Great-Aunt Beryl who was widowed in the war reckoned it took her the best part of fifteen years just to—'

'I'm not Auntie Beryl,' said Lorna, slowly but firmly. 'And I've started thinking recently that . . . that I ought to be trying to make some sort of life for myself.'

'You've got a life – you've got us, the children, and now work.'

'A life for me. And maybe sometime in the future, not just me.'

George and Meg looked at each other, dumbfounded.

'You don't mean . . . a man? You're not actually thinking of going out with this Geoff fellow? It's much too soon!'

Lorna smiled. 'No, not with Geoff. Maybe not with anybody, not yet. But as for whether it's too soon or not, I think I should be the judge of that – don't you?'

Chapter 8

The Safari Bar was not a particularly restful place to be, filled as it was with the piped sounds of African drumming and assorted animal noises. Nevertheless, Lorna yawned repeatedly and wondered if she'd get through her Pink Flamingo cocktail before she fell asleep.

'Sorry,' she said. 'I'm a bit bushed.'

'Well don't drop off,' advised Carmen cheerily, 'or you'll poke your eye out on your cocktail umbrella. And you're not allowed to fall asleep anyway. It took ages to persuade Grace to babysit for me tonight.' She plucked a maraschino cherry off its stick with her teeth. 'See?' she teased, 'this is what happens when you go out clubbing every night.'

Lorna laughed so loud that she almost drowned out the baboons. 'Carmen love, the last time I went clubbing was at my leaving do from work, and then I was seven months pregnant with Leo! And right now, I couldn't boogie the night away if you . . . if you put itching powder down my knickers.'

Carmen raised her glass in a toast. 'Welcome to the wonderful world of the working mum. You're not regretting it, are you?'

'Going back to work? No, not really. It's just that I'm so knackered all the time and I hardly ever seem to see the kids except when they're asleep.'

'Best time, if you ask me,' commented Carmen. 'At least when they're asleep they're not shoplifting or shaving the cat.'

'Mind you,' Lorna went on, 'they don't exactly seem to be missing me much. Between you and me, what with Grandma's blue fairy cakes and Grandad's magic tricks, I think I may be heading for redundancy.'

'Don't knock it,' said Carmen with the air of one who had seen it all before. 'Enjoy a bit of peace and quiet while you can – 'cause sooner or later the kids'll go down with something horrible like projectile vomiting or worms, and believe me, cleaning that up will be your job and nobody else's.'

'You make motherhood sound so ... romantic,' said Lorna, knocking back a mouthful of pink fizz.

Carmen shrugged. 'Well, there's no point pretending it's all fluffy bunnies and flowers on Mother's Day, is there? Not when your youngest wants to eat slugs and your eldest has got chewing gum stuck in his pubic hair.'

Lorna did a double-take. 'In his . . .? How?'

'Believe me, you don't want to know.'

'I always knew your Robbie would turn out creative.'

'Hmph.' Carmen made whirlpools in her drink with a giraffe swizzle-stick. 'As long as he doesn't turn out creative with other people's property, like his good-for-nothing father, that's all I'm bothered about.' She dropped the swizzle-stick into the glass with a tinkling sound. 'Men,' she sighed. 'What's the point of them?'

'I think it's something to do with cleaning behind the washing machine and putting up shelves,' replied Lorna wryly. She looked at her friend. 'I gather Brian didn't take it too kindly when you told him you weren't going to lend him the money?'

'Let's just say when I got back from the off-licence he'd gone, and taken half my CD collection with him.' She looked up. 'Where do I find them, Lorna? Are they all like that, or am I just . . . lucky?'

Lorna leaned towards her until their foreheads were touching. 'I don't know what the rest of them are like,' she replied, 'but I know at least one of them was nice. So maybe there are some more like him out there.' She wasn't sure she believed herself, but surely Ed couldn't have been the only decent man in the world?

'The trouble is, every time I meet someone, I'm convinced he's The One. And he never is. If you really do meet the right guy for you, how on earth can you tell?'

'I'm not sure. I guess you just follow your instincts and see what happens.'

'No blinding flashes of light? No violins and angel choirs?'

Lorna chuckled. 'Not as I recall. The first time I saw Ed I was only fourteen. But I just felt deep down that he was the one for me, and he never did anything to change my mind.' She toyed with the pink cocktail umbrella. 'The awful thing is, I have this terrible feeling that you can only experience that kind of certainty once in your life. Still,' she flopped back on the itchy bench seat, 'I've decided I can't live my life like a nun, whatever Mum and Dad may think.'

'Ah,' said Carmen. 'So you've been talking to them about dating then?'

'Not so much talking as being lectured,' replied Lorna. 'According to my mum it's "not seemly" for me to be seen going out with men so soon after Ed died.'

Carmen grimaced. 'Not seemly? What century is she living in? Did your dad tell her to get a life?'

'Hardly; he agrees with her. If it was good enough for Great-Aunt Beryl to be widowed at thirty and never look at another man for the next fifty years, that's plenty good enough for me. Apparently.'

'Bullshit,' Carmen declared emphatically. 'I hope you told them where to get off.'

'Not quite, but I told them I didn't agree.' Lorna scratched her ear. 'The thing I can't quite get is why they're so uptight about it when Ed wasn't even their son. I'm their daughter, but it feels almost like they care more about his memory than they do about my future.'

'I don't suppose they see it that way,' said Carmen. 'They're probably thinking: nice home, nice kids, nice job, nice memories, and us into the bargain – what does she need a replacement man for?'

'Apart from putting up shelves?'

'Yes, apart from that, obviously.' Carmen took a long pull at her drink. 'They'll come round. It's like when you turned into a teenager – they just need time to get used to the idea.' She sighed. 'And if you end up with so many men you've got some left over, you can always send them round to me.'

It occurred to Lorna that the last thing Carmen needed was more men. Men seemed to be at the root of everything that ever went wrong in her life. She didn't say so, though. Carmen would probably have socked her one with a plastic palm tree.

'Well, you're welcome to Geoff the porter,' Lorna said, chewing reflectively on a cube of fresh papaya.

'Does he have all his own teeth?'

'I doubt it. And he wears white socks.'

'Hmm, I'm not that desperate,' retorted Carmen, then paused. 'Yet.'

Lorna looked at her quizzically. 'You're not pining after another relationship already, surely? You've only just got Brian out of your hair.'

Carmen looked a little awkward, and didn't quite meet Lorna's gaze. 'Oh you know, nil desperandum, never give up, all that stuff. I mean, you never know, the next bloke might be Mr Right. What if I'm so busy feeling sorry for myself, and not going out and all that, that I miss him? That'd be it – my one big chance, gone forever. And I wouldn't even realise.'

It's one way of looking at it, thought Lorna. But she couldn't help noticing how tired Carmen looked. 'I think you should take some time for yourself,' she said. 'I really do. Chill out a bit.'

Carmen raised an eyebrow. 'Time for myself? With four kids? I'm lucky if I get to go to the toilet without an audience.'

Lorna thought about the solution to Carmen's problem; freaked out at the prospect; and then bravely bit the bullet. 'Maybe I could, er—' she ventured.

An upraised hand stopped her like one of Carmen's Denver Boots. 'God no, Lorna. Thanks for offering, but I couldn't ask you to babysit for my lot. I wouldn't wish them on anybody – especially not a real mate like you. I wouldn't ask unless I was really desperate.'

Lorna concealed her relief. 'I'm not entirely helpless you know,' she protested rather feebly.

'And my kids aren't entirely little monsters from the planet Brat . . . but even rounding them all up at bedtime takes a Land Rover and a tranquilliser gun. Believe me, it's a job for a specialist. Me.' Carmen signalled to the barman. 'Now, shut up and let me get you another drink, and we can toast your new life as a femme fatale.'

It's one of the first rules of the profession, Lorna told herself; don't get emotionally involved. They teach you that when you're a student, in your first clinical placement. The trouble is, they don't teach you how.

It was mid-afternoon on Crocus ward, and Kelly was finally going home. If you can call it that, thought Lorna, watching a big, orange-haired woman in a pink tracksuit stuffing Kelly's few possessions into plastic carrier bags as if they were so much rubbish to be put out for the bin men.

'For Christ's sake shift your arse, girl,' she snapped. 'And show a bit of gratitude. If it weren't for me and Liam, you'd be out on the street like the little tart you are. And serve you bloody well right.'

Lorna met Kelly's gaze across the ward. It was pure, naked despair. She didn't look like a cocky teenaged mother any more, but a miserable, bullied kid who knew there was no escape. I've got to do something, thought Lorna; but what?

She walked across to Kelly's bed. 'Hello, you must be Kelly's mum.' She held out a hand but the woman just glanced at it suspiciously and went on emptying the bedside locker.

'What about it?'

'I just wanted to say how much we've enjoyed having Kelly and her baby on the ward,' Lorna said, doing her best to sound bright and breezy. 'She's been a real breath of fresh air.'

Kelly rewarded her with a faint, rather crooked smile of gratitude. But her mother wasn't that easily impressed. 'She's a little cow with a big mouth. And she's nothing but trouble. I don't know why I'm bothering.'

Lorna winced but persevered. 'Lee-Anne's such a beautiful baby,' she enthused. 'You must be a really proud grandma.'

Kelly's mother looked at her as if she were some kind of imbecile.

'Proud? God help us, why would I be proud?' She paused for a moment and looked at the baby slumbering in her daughter's arms. 'It's not the baby's fault though, and she's quite pretty as babies go.' She signalled to Kelly with a jerk of her head. 'Come on then, get a move on. The car's waiting.'

'I . . . don't want to come,' Kelly blurted out.

The babble of conversation around the adjacent beds ceased, and all eyes fixed on the fourteen-year-old.

'I'm not coming, Lee-Anne and me'll find somewhere else.'

Her mother's lips formed into a hard, thin line. 'Either you get down them stairs in the next thirty seconds, or I don't want nothing more to do with you, got that? And you know what's going to happen if you've got nowhere to live.' There was an almost malicious enjoyment of the words on the older woman's face.

'Mrs—' cut in Lorna; but Kelly got there first.

'Nobody's taking my baby! She's mine, you keep your hands off her!'

'It's OK love.' Lorna put an arm round Kelly's shoulders, and felt her entire body shaking. 'Everybody wants to keep you and Lee-Anne together – don't we, Mrs Picton?'

Tracey Picton gave a grunt that might have been affirmative.

'You see? Everything's going to be OK.' Lorna hated herself for selling Kelly reassurance she didn't feel. 'But maybe it's best if you go home with your mum today. See how things work out.'

Kelly turned red-rimmed eyes on her. 'You're all the same,' she said in a tiny, weary voice. 'All of you. All the fucking same.'

Then she turned and followed her mother like an automaton, carrying herself and her baby off the ward and out of Lorna's life.

There wasn't time to brood. It was a busy day on Crocus ward. To begin with, a woman had been sent down from the delivery suite with twins; then there had been three more deliveries in rapid succession, with threats of another three to come. The ward was bursting at the seams. Suddenly it seemed as if everyone in Cheltenham wanted to have a baby for Christmas, whether it was scheduled or not.

There were decorations all over the hospital, and a big tree in the lobby of the maternity unit. The blessed Mildred McNulty would probably have loathed such seasonal depravity, but as luck would have it she couldn't see it because somebody had pulled a fleecy Santa hat down over her eyes.

The only person who didn't seem imbued with the festive spirit was Dr Sullivan. Lorna despaired of him as he stood at the bedside of a thirty-something new mum with crippling back pain, setting things out exactly the way he saw them.

'But the pain,' protested the woman, hand clasped to her lower spine. 'It's only been bad since you—'

Eoin Sullivan fixed her with a steely gaze only a fraction removed from contempt. 'Mrs Barrymore—'

'Ms.'

He let out a sort of 'tch' of annoyance. 'All right, Ms Barrymore. I can tell you exactly why your back hurts. It hurts because you are so fat.'

Ms Barrymore's jaw dropped. 'What did you say?'

'Fat, dear. F-A-T. Would you like me to write it down for you?'

Lorna flinched on the poor woman's behalf. OK so she was no super-model, but she was hardly obese either. Foolishly, she entered the fray.

'I think what Dr Sullivan is trying to say—' she began.

Dr Sullivan fixed her with a haughty scowl. 'I don't require any assistance in saying what I mean, thank you, Nurse.'

'I'm sure you don't, doctor. And I'm a midwife, not a nurse.' She lunged on recklessly. 'What I think he's saying, Ms Barrymore, is that a little excess weight can increase the chances of back problems. But back pain is very common just after delivery. You rest, and I'm sure it'll settle down.'

Dr Sullivan seemed so surprised at being interrupted by a mere slip of a midwife – and a blonde one at that – that he just stared at Lorna as she patted the bedclothes straight and headed for the sluice, to hide behind the door and ask herself, 'Did I really just do that? I must be off my head.'

She did such a good job of avoiding him that afternoon that she very nearly managed not to cross paths with him at all before the end of the shift. But only nearly. Half an hour before ward report, just after the drug round, she was crouching down draining a patient's catheter bag when she spotted Dr Sullivan out of the corner of her eye.

Damn and blast. She could hardly run away with her plastic jug of wee, and he was heading straight for her.

'Excuse me.' His voice was smoothly expressionless. 'Could I just have a private word when you've finished that?'

Jug still in hand, Lorna reluctantly joined him by the ward window. Here it comes, she thought: well, I asked for it.

'Hold out your hand.'

'Is this some kind of joke?'

'Go on, do it.'

Tentatively she did, and he dropped something into it. 'What's this? Oh my God.'

He smiled, but not quite as superciliously as she might have expected. 'Yes, it's the keys to the drug trolley. You left them sticking out of it and I thought you just might not want your boss to see.'

Lorna gawped at him. This simply did not make sense. She was still new, under supervision, and she'd got right up his nose only an hour or two earlier. He could have dropped her right in it with Colin Jenkins, and instead he'd actually helped her.

'Er ... thanks,' was all she could manage as she blinked dazedly into his blue eyes. And they were very, very blue.

'No problem,' he replied, setting off to answer his bleep. 'Oh by the way,' he added, turning back with a half-smile, 'I should get that jug emptied if I were you. You've got urine all down the front of your tunic.'

Sunday lunch had never been a particularly big deal chez Price ... until Meg and George arrived. Meg was a card-carrying member of the meat and two veg brigade, and proud of it; and if you could stand up unaided after one of her sponge puddings you obviously needed another helping.

In principle, Lorna was all in favour of a nice Sunday lunch with the family together round the old dining table Lorna had inherited from Grandma Scholes; but in practice it was sometimes more trouble than it was worth. Leo was going through a phase of not eating anything green; Hope couldn't wait until lunchtime; and more often than not Lorna either had to rush back from an early shift or rush off to do a late one. It was a recipe for indigestion all round.

Nevertheless, it was nice to have somebody else doing the cooking, and on this particular Sunday – the last one before Christmas – Granny and Grandad Price had come for lunch.

It was always something of an occasion whenever Ed's mum and dad came round. They'd only moved out as far as a village near Monmouth (Myrddin Price's native city), but it always felt like a special event when they returned to Cheltenham. Lorna found it upsetting and comforting, at the same time. Upsetting because Ed had looked so much like his dad, and comforting for the very same reason.

For once, lunch went by without a hitch, and a timely hard stare across the tablecloth interrupted Leo just as he was about to tell Grandma Scholes that there was a boiled caterpillar in the cabbage. All was harmony, until the children went off to play and Jo Price started talking about Christmas.

'At least you've got your mum and dad with you this year,' she said with a smile, patting her daughter-in-law on the hand. 'And of course we'll be here on the big day too.' She sighed. 'But it must be so hard for you without Ed.'

'It's hard for you too,' cut in Meg. 'After all, he was your only son.'

'And we'll never forget him or stop loving him,' nodded Myrddin. His big bear's arm pulled his wife towards him. 'But life has to go on, doesn't it, Jo?'

She nodded. 'Of course it does. And it has to go on for Lorna too, doesn't it Meg?'

'Well . . . up to a point,' conceded Meg.

'But everything in good time,' nodded George.

'It's been over a year and a half now,' pointed out Myrddin, 'and I'm sure Lorna's thinking about getting out and about in the world again, now she's got her new job and everything. Aren't you, love?'

Lorna was slightly taken aback. If her own mum and dad had been difficult about her future plans, surely Ed's would be even more difficult? At least, that was what she'd envisaged. 'I think I maybe . . . need to get out and meet a few more people.' She cleared her throat. 'Perhaps even . . . er . . . men.'

'Lorna!' protested Meg. 'And with your poor dead husband's mother and father sitting right in the same room!'

'That's all right.' Jo smiled. 'Ed knew how much Lorna loved him. He'd want her to make a new life for herself. Don't you worry, sweetheart. We're right behind you. And I'm sure your mum and dad will be too, once they've come round to the idea.'

Lorna took one look at George and Meg's faces. I wouldn't bet on it, she thought to herself. But then, at the end of the day that's their problem, not mine.

Chapter 9

Christmas had a habit of sneaking up on Lorna.

It wasn't as if she didn't know it was there, lurking just around the corner; and it wasn't as if Leo didn't make sure she remembered, with his daily word-perfect renditions of every toy advert on TV. But it still managed to get the drop on her every year. One minute the announcers were hailing another 'hundred and twenty-seven shopping days till Christmas', the next, it was Christmas Eve and she'd still got six people to buy presents for.

And so Christmas Eve it was once again, and Lorna was having her annual wrestling match with a turkey that thought it was an ostrich. As she heaved it into the boot of her car with a parting curse, she wondered why she persisted in buying far too much of everything every Christmas, when it was Ed who had always been the one for seasonal excess. One way of pretending he's still here I suppose, she mused as she contemplated the sprouts that nobody would dream of eating at any other time of the year. Well, that and a way of making things up to the kids. It wasn't fun and it wasn't fair, not having a daddy at this time of year, even if you did have Grandad Scholes with his rude noises and 'Uncle' Chris with his inept juggling routines.

Hmm, actually I haven't seen Chris in a while, she thought to herself as she threw in the rest of the shopping. I do hope he hasn't got himself another totally unsuitable girlfriend. Poor Chris. She smiled. Perennially hopeless in love. He really does need somebody to sort him out.

She was so lost in thought as she crossed the supermarket car park that she almost wheeled her empty trolley right into the side of Carmen's van.

Carmen braked to a squeaky halt and Lorna nearly jumped out of her skin. Carmen wound the window down and stuck her head out. 'Hey Lorna, if you want to be run over, couldn't you just lie down in front of the van and make it easier for me?'

'Oh God, sorry.' Lorna skipped to one side to let a silver Mercedes through. 'I was totally miles away.'

'Don't tell me, you were totally miles away 'cause it's Christmas and you can't wait for Geoff the porter to snog you senseless under the mistletoe.'

Lorna pulled a face. 'Actually, I'm thinking of having mistletoe banned, just in case he does. Last-minute shopping?' she enquired.

'Last-minute clamping, actually. The supermarket wants us to clamp anyone who's parking here and not using the store.'

'How seasonal,' commented Lorna. 'Bet you'll be popular.'

Carmen seized a red and white fleecy hat from the dashboard and put it on. 'Just call me Santa Claus. Now, about your present . . .'

'I haven't wrapped yours yet!'

'Ah well, yours doesn't need wrapping up at all.' Carmen waved a long white envelope at her through the window. 'Want to guess?'

'Er . . . holiday in the Bahamas? Summons for non-payment of council tax?'

'Sorry, you'll have to wait till we meet up on Boxing Day. Happy guessing!'

And with that, Carmen accelerated off into the distance, leaving Lorna feeling quite bemused.

Christmas Day itself came and went like a camera flash: a brief moment of extreme brightness that left Lorna dazed and disorientated.

To say it was exhausting was an understatement. A double shift on the delivery ward would have been restful by comparison; and in a way Lorna was glad of the distraction. There was far too much to do preventing Leo from breaking his toys and Hope from eating hers to sit down and ask herself whether she was actually enjoying herself. Far too much energy had to be expended filling in the gap left by Ed for Lorna to admit to herself that maybe she missed him more than the kids did.

On the whole it helped having Mum around in the kitchen, but it was amazing how tense people could get over something as daft as the proper way to cook a Christmas pudding. Next year a hotel, Lorna promised herself; and sod the expense.

By the time Boxing Day came, and with it advanced mince pie fatigue, Lorna was starting to fantasise about detox diets and sleeping for a month, not necessarily in that order. She almost flung her arms round her dad's neck and kissed him when he whipped out four tickets for the pantomime.

'I'm really sorry love, but they only had the four left. It's a complete sell-out.'

'Don't worry dear,' added her mother. 'Your father can stay here while you and I take the children.'

'No, no,' replied Lorna hastily, 'I wouldn't want to deprive you of all that fun. Besides, Carmen's popping round later this afternoon. We can have a nice chat while you and Dad enjoy the show with the kids.'

'Hmm,' said her mother with a sidelong look at George. 'Well, I wish you'd change your mind, dear. Your father's such an embarrassment at pantos – he always shouts, "it's behind you!" when it isn't.'

Lorna hummed to herself as she vacuumed up Smarties and broken crisps from down the back of the sofa. It was amazing how much rubbish one modestly sized family could produce in one day. At least when Leo came home she'd be able to tell him where his missing pterodactyl was – if she'd managed to extract it from the Hoover bag by then.

She paused for a moment and checked her watch. If she got a move on, she could do some of the children's washing before they got back, too. I wonder why I'm doing all this work, she thought as she plucked a sweaty strand of hair off her forehead and tucked it behind her ear. All I have to do is ask Mum and she'll be on to it in five seconds – cleaning the house from top to bottom while preparing a nutritious dinner for five with the other hand. Let's face it, I've hardly had to touch the vacuum cleaner or the cooker since I went back to work.

And maybe that was the reason why she was doing it now. Living in a clean, tidy house with clean, tidy children was nice; but sometimes it just felt good to do some of the cleaning and tidying herself, if only to remind herself that it was her house they were all living in, and not her mum and dad's.

She was ramming the last of the washing into the machine when the doorbell rang. Carmen was hopping about breathlessly on the doorstep.

'Hiya kid, sorry I'm a bit early.'

'Yeah: two hours early!' commented Lorna, letting her in. 'What's up – do you love me so much you couldn't keep away?'

Carmen targeted an armchair and launched herself at it as though she hadn't seen one in weeks. 'Actually, it's our Robbie. He only goes and gets himself into some kind of fight down the park, and the first I know of it, he's stood on the doorstep with a broken nose and a copper on either side of him.'

'No!' gasped Lorna. 'What happened – I mean, why?'

Carmen shrugged. 'Don't ask me. The police don't know and the little bugger won't say.'

'But he's OK, is he?'

'Oh yeah,' replied Carmen with a hint of bitterness. 'Couple of black eyes, big plaster on his nose, and soft in the head as ever. Thing is, my sister Grace is keeping an eye on him for me while I'm here, so I thought I'd

71

better slip out and give you your prezzie now, so as I can get back before she has to go home.'

'Oh Carmen, you could've phoned and said you couldn't make it. I would've understood, you know that.'

'I know you would.' Carmen smiled. 'That's why I wanted to come.' She picked up her bucket-sized canvas shoulder bag and rooted around in it, eventually producing the same long white envelope Lorna had seen on Christmas Eve. 'Happy Christmas, Lorna,' she said, holding it out. 'Enjoy.'

Lorna looked down at the envelope. 'What is it?' she asked, rather stupidly.

'Open it and find out.'

'OK then.' She could feel Carmen's eyes boring into the side of her head as she picked at the stuck-down flap.

Carmen let out a gasp of exasperation and grabbed the envelope. 'Don't just fiddle with it – tear it!' Ripping it open along the top, she slapped it back into Lorna's hand. 'Go on then! What do you say?'

Lorna peered into the envelope. There didn't seem to be anything inside it except a card. She slid it out, and read: '"Congratulations! You've just made the best decision of your life." What is this?'

'Read on!'

She opened the card. It contained a lot of glossy pictures of people looking very bright-eyed and happy, mostly in pairs. '"Welcome to LOVE BITES, Gloucestershire's exclusive lunch club for executive singles ..."' What!' She turned horrified eyes on Carmen. 'Carmen, this is a ... a membership to a dating agency!'

'No it isn't, it's an exclusive lunch club for executive singles, it says so on the card, see?'

Lorna felt suddenly hot and cold all over. 'I'm not an executive single!'

Carmen shrugged. 'You're single and you've got your own teeth. Believe me, that counts as executive. Anyway, it's not like a dating agency, I told you.' She flipped the card over to show the blurb on the back. 'You just meet up with people for lunch if they sound interesting, and if you don't like them all you've lost is the cost of a cheese salad.' She folded her arms and sat back, sisterly pride written all over her face. 'So what do you reckon then – unusual Christmas present or what?'

'Um ...' Lorna sat down in slow motion. 'Yes, it's definitely unusual.' She looked at Carmen over the top of the card. 'Three months' trial membership? This must've cost you a fortune.'

'Oh, it wasn't that much. And I had one of those introductory money-off coupons. Besides, you're worth it.'

Oh God, thought Lorna, feeling ever so slightly giddy. This isn't right. I'm not some desperate man-hunting spinster. I haven't even decided if I want to go out with anybody anyway! Well, not completely. 'Carmen, I—'

'Look,' Carmen enthused, ignoring her feeble attempts to protest, 'here are your six specially selected first contacts. Isn't it exciting?'

She shoved a bit of computer printout under Lorna's nose. It consisted of a list of six names, each complete with age, height, occupation ... and telephone number. Lorna swallowed hard. 'I can't—'

'Yes you can.'

A sudden thought hit Lorna. 'Hang on a minute, how did they select these six blokes anyway? How did they know who to choose?'

'From the application form.'

'What application form?'

'The one I filled out for you! It's OK, I knew all the right answers to put. Eyes blue—'

I don't believe this, thought Lorna. 'They're green, Carmen.'

'Whatever. Likes: kids, animals, singing—'

'Carmen, I'm tone deaf!'

'But you like singing in the bath. Oh, and I upped your annual salary a bit, so they wouldn't match you up with any losers ...'

Lorna sank back into the armchair with a groan, still not quite believing what her best mate had gone and done. Much as she adored Carmen, being signed up for a dating agency by her was a bit like being enrolled for marriage counselling by Zsa-Zsa Gabor. 'Carmen,' she said faintly when there was a tiny break in the conversational flow. 'Don't take this the wrong way, but—'

'What?'

'Do they give refunds?'

Love Bites did not give refunds. And even if they had done, Carmen wouldn't have had any of it. As far as she was concerned, she was on a crusade and it was pointless Lorna assuring her that she was perfectly all right without a man; even Lorna knew the words sounded a little hollow.

But this ... This was not the way Lorna had planned on getting back 'into circulation'. To be honest though, she hadn't really planned it at all. So the following day, when Carmen shoved the phone into her hand and made her make the first call, it was easier just to do it than to find a good reason not to.

Selection One sounded quite promising, she had to admit. Six foot two, athletic type, fond of kids. She cleared her throat and put on her best telephone voice.

'Hello, could I speak to ... er ...' she checked the list, 'Gerry Rawlings please?'

73

'I'm sorry, he's not in at the moment,' replied a woman's voice. 'But I'm his wife, can I take a message?'

Flushed to the roots of her hair, Lorna slammed down the phone. 'That's it, no more. I knew this was a bad idea.'

'What's the matter?' asked Carmen. 'Did he sound weird?'

'No, he sounded married.'

'Ah. Well, you do get the odd one.' Carmen brightened. 'But at least you found out now and not later, eh?' She shoved the paper under Lorna's nose again. 'Go on, try Selection Two. He likes Barry White and piña coladas.'

Lorna gave Carmen a funny look. 'I can't stand Barry White and I'm allergic to coconut!' Her suspicions grew. 'Tell me something, when you were filling in that form, did you answer the questions as me or as you?'

'As you!' protested Carmen, adding as an afterthought, 'Mostly. Look,' she went on, determined not to be defeated, 'Selection Three's a nurse – and he's not gay! Tell you what, I'll give him a call for you.'

'No you won't!'

But Carmen was already dialling. 'Hi, is that Adrian? My name's Lorna, Lorna Price. I got your details from Love Bites, and I—'

Lorna seized the telephone from her friend's – or was it her ex-friend's – hand. 'Hi, actually I'm Lorna,' she said breathlessly, before she had time to wimp out.

'Well . . . whatever,' said the voice on the other end of the line, clearly somewhat bemused. 'I mean, there's no need to fight over me, I'm not that great.'

He sounded, thought Lorna, almost normal. But what could you tell from a voice? 'I see you're a nurse,' she said. 'I'm a midwife.'

'That's nice. I'm single, how about you?'

The question smacked Lorna brutally in the face, like a cold, wet flannel. 'I suppose I am now,' she mused, half for her own benefit. The admission made her feel somehow hollow, not quite complete. 'That is, I'm, I was . . . widowed. Couple of years ago. Two kids, how about you?'

'Not yet. Never met the right person. Tell you what,' his voice sounded warm and reassuring, 'do you fancy meeting up for lunch? That pizza bar on the corner of North Street's pretty good.'

'I . . . er . . .'

Carmen snatched the phone from Lorna's hand. 'Where? When? Don't worry, she'll be there.' She slammed the phone down with a big, beaming smile. 'Guess what, Lorna? You've got a date.'

Tuesday was Lorna's day off, so she had plenty of time to work herself up into a frenzy of apprehension before the dreaded lunch date.

It's not a date, she kept telling herself. It's just . . . meeting someone. For a chat. She couldn't quite convince herself though, and what with Carmen's 'motivational' telephone call halfway through the morning, asking her if she needed any condoms for her handbag, she felt positively sick by the time twelve o'clock came round. Lunch? She'd be lucky to manage a glass of water.

When it was almost time to leave, she finished feeding Hope and then scuttled off to get dressed. It was too much to hope that nobody would comment on her sudden change from baby-food-spattered sweatshirt to a smart shirt and well-fitting denim skirt.

'You're looking nice, dear,' observed Meg, with just a hint of maternal suspicion. She doesn't miss a trick, thought Lorna. 'Off somewhere?'

'Oh, just out for lunch.'

'With Carmen, is it? Or that nice girl Miranda you used to go to Pilates with?'

'Just. Someone.' She was determined not to start an argument by confessing that this particular someone happened to be male. 'You know.' She rattled the rest off like a Grand National commentator with a caffeine habit. 'I've put Hope down and she's fast asleep, and I'll pick Leo up from school today, so you should be able to have a nice rest. 'Byee!'

Before the last word had left her lips, she was halfway down the drive to the car. The maternal interrogation could wait till later. For now, it was all Lorna could cope with just to drive herself into town.

She arrived at the car park stupidly early, and spent a nail-gnawing ten minutes tugging critically at her hair and touching up her lipstick in the rear-view mirror. Then she realised she was going to be late if she didn't get a move on, and in her haste to get out she managed to rip a hole in her tights on the car door. Damn!

By the time she'd retreated into the public loos and put on her emergency pair, she was in danger of being seriously late. So she put on a spurt and legged it across to North Street as fast as her tight skirt would allow.

The Pizzeria Bel Canto was a relatively new addition to the area. Lorna had never been there, but she'd heard it was good. Authentic food, good service, nice atmosphere. So at least this . . . Adrian . . . had good taste. And he had sounded very nice and warm on the telephone. Plus with their similar jobs they were bound to have something in common. Time to be brave and go for it.

As luck would have it, there was quite a lot of lunchtime traffic, and Lorna had to pause on the kerb opposite the restaurant, waiting for a chance to cross. She checked her watch: shit, seven minutes late, and he promised he'd be right on time: he must have been waiting for ages. Come on traffic, let me cross.

From where she was standing, she had a really good view through the Bel Canto's big picture window. As she waited, her eyes drifted instinctively to the inside of the restaurant and focused on the one and only person sitting inside. Blond hair, blue sweater, just as he'd described on the telephone.

'Oh my God,' gasped Lorna. 'You're Adrian?'

'I can't tell you how bad I feel about it,' sighed Lorna as she watched Chris sorting out the bathroom sink that Leo had blocked with the ornamental pebbles out of her best glass vase. After weeks of silence, he'd turned up out of the blue at exactly the right moment, as though he had some kind of telepathic bond with Lorna's plumbing.

'Yeah. I'm sure.'

'I mean, the poor guy – I'm sure he must have been able to tell that I couldn't get out of the restaurant fast enough. To be honest I'd have avoided going in at all but I just couldn't stand him up.'

'So what did you do then?'

'Told him there was a family emergency and I only had time for a quick drink. Then I legged it.'

'Hm,' said Chris, lying on his back under the sink. He took the plumber's wrench from between his teeth. 'So he was really big then?'

'Not big, Chris – mountainous. We're talking thirty, thirty-five stone. I know, he's probably the nicest, kindest bloke in Gloucestershire, and I feel absolutely terrible about lying to him, but I just ... couldn't.' She wilted. 'When it comes down to it I'm just a coward.'

Water drained into the basin Chris was holding, along with half a pound of multicoloured gravel. 'Lots of us are cowards,' he replied quietly.

Lorna laughed. 'Not you! You're not afraid of anything.'

He sat up and his eyes met hers, and there was an odd kind of softness in them. 'You'd be surprised, Lor. You really would.' He cleared his throat. 'Blimey, that boy of yours certainly knows how to block a drain.'

She smiled. 'He gets it from his mother. Do you remember that time I dropped the key to the Citroën down the grid in the back garden? If it hadn't been for you, there'd have been manholes up all over Gloucestershire.'

He touched his forelock. 'Happy to be of service, ma'am.'

Lorna smacked his hand playfully. 'Don't be like that – you're not a workman, you're my friend! And a very good one, too,' she added, getting up to make a cup of tea.

'A good friend,' murmured Chris, disappearing under the sink again to replace the U-bend. 'Yeah, Lorna. That's what I'll always be.'

76

Chapter 10

It was Friday afternoon, and Lorna was enjoying the start of a rare long weekend off. Or rather, she would have been enjoying it if her conscience would only let her.

Is it possible to be a mother and not feel guilty? she wondered as she sat cross-legged on the living room carpet, watching Leo teach his little sister how to make a wall with her wooden building bricks. Before, I felt guilty for being a boring, stay-at-home mum with no spare money for treats; now I feel guilty because half the time I'm not here when they want me. Can there ever be such a thing as a happy medium?

As if tuning in to her thoughts, Leo looked up and declared: 'Miss Rubery said my picture was best in the class and I could take it and show my mummy, but only Grandad was here so I didn't.'

There was a world of reproach in the look he gave her from under that sweep of golden eyelashes.

'I'm so sorry, sweetheart,' she said, stroking his curls, still baby-soft despite his self-appointed role as man of the house. 'Mummy had to go to work. But I'm really proud that your picture was the best.'

Leo's lower lip jutted. 'You always have to go to work.'

'Not always,' she protested, then added rashly, 'Tell you what, this weekend we can do anything you want.'

He looked up, his eyes brightening. 'Anything?'

Oh dear, thought Lorna; I think I'm going to regret this. 'Anything . . . sensible,' she said weakly, in case it involved intergalactic space travel.

It didn't take him more than two seconds to decide. 'Dinosaur Park!' he crowed. 'We're going to Dinosaur Park!'

'Er . . .' began Lorna, wondering how Hope would react to a park filled with fifteen-foot-high concrete dinosaurs. 'Don't you think—'

The lower lip quivered. 'Dinosaur Park, you promised Mummy, you promised!'

'Di-bo-dore,' echoed Hope, delightedly bashing two plastic bricks together. Clearly Leo's programme of indoctrination was beginning to take effect.

'OK then,' said Lorna. 'Dinosaur Park it is.'

'Just you and me and Hope, Mummy? Nobody else?'

'Just us.'

Leo beamed all over his face. 'Come on Hope, let's build a stegosaurus!'

Dinosaur Park turned out to be not nearly as bad as Lorna had expected. For a start off the whole thing was indoors, housed under a huge glass dome, and real butterflies and birds were fluttering away among the giant tree ferns and tropical orchids. So no traipsing around in the January mud, and there were lots of bright, pretty things to entrance Hope while Leo tried to sneak off and scale the brontosaurus's neck when no one was looking. There were even life-size pterodactyls, perching high in the branches – so lifelike, you'd swear they were about to swoop down and make off with your ice-cream cornet.

Barely able to keep pace with Leo's fathomless energy after a long week on the ward, Lorna was somewhat relieved when the Education Centre hove into view, and Leo begged to be allowed to go on one of the supervised 'Bug Safaris'.

'Can I go and look for bugs Mummy, can I, can I?'

'It's very well supervised,' the park ranger assured her. 'One trained member of staff for every four children, and all the bugs are perfectly harmless. He'll be back in half an hour, with a certificate and a souvenir bug.'

'A souvenir?'

The ranger lowered his voice. 'Don't worry, madam, it's not a real one.'

'Oh – go on then. But behave yourself and don't wander off!' Lorna set Hope down on her feet, took tight hold of her hand, and let her totter the last few steps to the terrace where some chairs and tables were laid out, with free tea and coffee for the grown-ups and apple juice for the children.

'It's all right here, isn't it?' remarked a man's voice just behind her. 'You could almost think you were in the Caribbean if it wasn't for the dinosaurs.'

Lorna turned her head and saw that the voice was coming from a neighbouring table, where a blond, broad-shouldered guy in his mid-thirties was sitting, surrounded by the evidence of several small children.

'Very nice, yes,' she agreed. 'It's a lot warmer in here than I'd expected.'

'I suppose they have to keep it heated for the plants,' he volunteered.
'Yes.'

'Is this your little girl?' He smiled at Hope, who gazed back at him with round eyes as if she'd never seen anything quite so fascinating in her life.

'Her name's Hope.'

'She's beautiful, just like her mum.'

There followed one of those awkward silences that scream to be filled with something – anything – and then the guy actually got to his feet and dragged his chair over to Lorna's table. 'Mind if I join you? It's a bit boring sitting on your own while the kids are off having fun.'

'Er . . . yes. I suppose it is a bit.'

He sat down rather closer than she was expecting, and she could smell his expensive aftershave. Not so much of it that it was ostentatious, just enough to whisper 'good taste'.

'Here on your own with the kids?'

'Yes.'

'Me too. Well, there is only me, actually. Now the wife's gone.'

A lump of empathy came to Lorna's throat. 'Oh dear, I'm so sorry.'

'I'm not.' He saw her startled look and laughed. 'It's OK, I didn't mean that sort of gone. She ran off with my best mate and said she didn't want any more to do with the kids.'

'Oh,' said Lorna, not sure whether to be sorry or relieved. 'That's tough.'

'You cope, don't you? Handed in my notice at the office the next day, taught myself how to change a nappy, and I've been a full-time dad ever since. Haven't regretted it for a moment, either.' His eyes met hers and she found she liked the way they crinkled at the corners when he smiled. 'How about you – is there anybody waiting for you at home?'

To her surprise, Lorna found that the directness of the question didn't hurt nearly as much as she would have thought. In fact she was almost eager to tell him. 'No, not any more. I mean, there used to be.'

'Ah,' he said sympathetically. 'Divorced?'

'Widowed. A couple of years ago. His name was Ed,' she added, as if that mattered to this man, whoever he was. She realised with a shock that she was telling her life story to a total stranger, and not feeling bad about it. That was a first, and no mistake.

'Now it's my turn to be sorry,' he said. He stuck his hand out. 'Pete Bedingfield, pleased to meet you.'

His clasp was firm and warm. Lorna smiled, a little uncertainly. 'Lorna Price.'

'You must be wondering what sort of creep chats up beautiful young widows in a kids' dinosaur park,' he went on cheerfully.

79

Lorna could feel her ears burning scarlet. 'No, really,' she protested.

'But if you'll let me take you out to dinner tomorrow night, you'll have a chance to find out.'

She was still speechless with surprise when Leo and Pete's kids came bounding up, gabbling nineteen to the dozen about bugs and dangling plastic tarantulas on the ends of bits of elastic. And she was in such a state of shock that she didn't even bat an eyelid when Leo proudly stuck his hand in his pocket and produced the special fat, wriggly earwig he'd been saving just for her.

'Carmen,' she hissed down the phone, 'you've got to help me.'

'Why – what's happened? You've not split your trousers again, have you? I told you not to wear them so tight.'

'No! Listen.' She glanced around to make sure that her mum and dad were upstairs and well out of earshot. 'I met this bloke today, at the Dinosaur Park. And he asked me out!'

'And?' demanded Carmen.

'And what?'

'What's the problem? Is he an axe-murderer or something? Has he got more than the usual number of heads?'

'Carmen, I'm being serious! I don't know what to do.'

There was a sigh on the other end of the line, followed by a short silence. 'OK. What's his name? It's not Cedric or Percival or something is it?'

'Pete.'

'That's normal enough, anyway. Do you like him?'

'Well . . . he seems quite nice, but I only spoke to him for a few—'

'Shush. Do you fancy him?'

Lorna squirmed. She could almost hear Carmen's shoe tapping impatiently on the laminated floor of her front hall. 'I . . . um . . .'

'I'm waiting.'

'I think so,' admitted Lorna in a sort of strangled gasp.

'How can you only think you fancy somebody?' demanded Carmen in exasperation.

'I don't know. It's been a long time, I'm out of practice.'

'Then get back in practice! When's he taking you out?'

'It's supposed to be tomorrow night, but to be honest—'

'You've got cold feet and you thought I could think up a way to get you out of it?' suggested Carmen.

'Something like that,' Lorna admitted.

'Sorry, kiddo. No can do. You've got to get out there and start dating sometime, so why not now?' Her voice softened. 'Admit it Lorna, you're just scared. And you're going to go on being scared until you've conquered it and realised it was nothing after all.'

But it's not nothing, thought Lorna as she put down the receiver. That's the trouble. Compared to this, going back to work was a stroll in the park. Right now this seems like the biggest, scariest thing I've ever done.

The next day, Meg Scholes was eyeing her daughter critically over the supper dishes. 'You're not going out again?'

Suddenly Lorna felt like fifteen again, with a curfew of ten pm and absolutely no snogging in the front porch. She couldn't decide whether it was irritating, exhilarating, or both. 'Why?' she enquired.

This only threw her mother for a microsecond. 'Because ... you went out for a drink with Carmen only the other night.'

'And?'

'And you've got work tomorrow.'

'Yes, I know.'

There was a short, tense silence.

'So, are you going out or not?'

'I might.'

'With a man?'

That was the final straw. Very calmly folding up the tea towel and laying it on the kitchen table, Lorna looked her mother straight in the eye. 'That's none of your business, Mum,' she replied.

It felt like the ultimate blasphemy.

It was a longer evening than Lorna had planned, and she'd drunk a lot more than she was used to. But she felt happy, relaxed, as though Ed's ghost was giving her special dispensation not to feel sad, at least for one night.

He's a nice man, she thought, looking at Pete as they strolled out of the restaurant into the surprising calm of the winter night. And yes, Carmen, in case you're still interested I do fancy him, OK?

Pete slid an arm about her shoulders. 'Taxi and then home?' he enquired.

'It's very late ... I don't usually ...' She realised that she was trembling at his touch, and that her half-drunk thoughts were racing far ahead into the realms of erotic fantasy.

'That's OK, neither do I,' he replied with a smile, and he placed a very gentle kiss upon the back of her hand. 'So – your place or mine?'

Her throat was very dry, and she was woozy and a little bit giggly from too much alcohol. 'I don't know if I should ... I mean, my kids are—'

He completed the sentence for her: 'Asleep. And being looked after by their grandparents. So?'

She swallowed hard and took a huge step into the unknown. 'Mine,' she said.

Lorna awoke with a pounding headache and the sound of the alarm clock shrieking in her ear. As she rolled across to bash it into silence, her arm collided with something in the bed.

No, not something. Somebody.

At that electric-shock, lurid Technicolor moment, Pete rolled over onto his back, grunted and opened his eyes.

'Oh God,' he said. 'Never again.'

Lorna had practically hurtled across to the far edge of the king size bed before something rather odd dawned on her: she was fully clothed. And as far as she could tell from the top half of Pete, just visible above the duvet, so was he.

He hauled himself into a sitting position, confirming Lorna's theory. 'What the hell time do you call this?' he groaned. 'It's pitch black out there.'

'Six o'clock, I'm on early shift.' She shuffled across the room and snapped on the main light.

'Jeez, that's brutal.'

'Early mornings and late nights – comes with the job.'

They looked at each other as warily if they'd both just spontaneously generated from the primeval swamp. Lorna swallowed hard. 'Did I . . . I mean, did we . . .?'

Pete laughed humourlessly, got out of bed and started rummaging around for a missing sock. 'Are you kidding? After you'd told me how much you missed your precious Ed, and I'd realised I was still in love with my ex-wife, and we'd finished off that half-bottle of brandy you found in the kitchen, it was about as erotically charged as a nunnery in here.'

'Oh,' said Lorna. An enormous wave of relief washed over her. I didn't do it, she thought; I didn't betray Ed after all. 'So it was a bit of a failure then?'

'You could say.'

Feeling stones lighter, Lorna practically bounced across the room. 'Fancy some breakfast? I could do us a fry-up.'

He scratched his stubbly chin. In the harsh light of a hangover, mused Lorna, he wasn't even remotely fanciable. 'Yeah, why not?' he said, trying to pull some of the creases out of his shirt. 'If it's a toss-up between sex and a fry-up, give me the bacon every time.'

Half an hour later, when Meg came downstairs to make George his morning cup of tea, she was horrified to find Lorna sitting at the kitchen table with a man, the pair of them reeking of alcohol and fried bread.

It didn't take her more than a cursory glance to put two and two together. 'I see,' she sniffed. 'Just got back after a night on the tiles, have you?' She spoke the words with all the warmth of liquid nitrogen. There was no need for her to add: 'You ought to be ashamed of yourself, young lady' – it was written in flaming capitals across her forehead.

Pete opened his mouth, no doubt to say something pleasant and inoffensive, but Lorna kicked him under the table and he just went 'Ow' instead.

Something overstretched inside Lorna just couldn't cope with a hangover and her mother's arbitrary moral absolutes, not at half past six in the morning.

'Actually Mum,' she replied, 'Pete stayed here last night, didn't you?'

She gave him The Look, and he mumbled, 'Yeah.'

Meg's intake of breath was clearly audible. 'On the sofa in the lounge?' she enquired, almost daring Lorna to say otherwise.

Lorna didn't reply; just pushed away her plate and got to her feet. 'Sorry Mum, can't chat now. Got to go and get ready for work.'

'I'd . . . er . . . better go too,' said Pete. 'See you, Lorna.'

'See you, Pete.' And she added, for the sheer wickedness of it, 'Thanks for a great night.'

Chapter 11

'Phone, Lorna,' her dad bellowed up the stairs. 'David. He wants a word.'

Frankly, the last person Lorna felt like having a word with was her brother David. Well, the penultimate person maybe; her sister Sarah tended to be permanently top of Lorna's 'tell them I'm not in' list.

It wasn't that she didn't like him. Not entirely. They'd been pretty close when they were kids, and Lorna had lost count of the number of times she'd weighed in to rescue him from playground bullies. Other kids threatened bullies with their big brother; David threatened his with his little sister. Lorna suspected he'd never quite got over the humiliation.

She came downstairs, picked up the cordless phone from the hall table and carried it into the front room, closing the door behind her. There might be swearing, and she was in no mood for a lecture on ladylike behaviour from her dad. 'David. Hi.'

He didn't beat about the bush. 'Dad says you've got a boyfriend.'

'Thanks David, I'm very well thank you and so are the kids. How are you?'

'Yeah, yeah, whatever. Well, have you?'

Lorna feigned stupidity. 'Have I what?'

'Got a boyfriend!'

She nearly told him to mind his own business, but she'd only just got back on reasonable terms with her mother after the Pete episode, and she really wasn't in the mood to reprise all the arguments they'd had over the last couple of weeks. 'Does it matter?' she asked wearily.

'What kind of thing is that to say?' he demanded.

Oh for God's sake, thought Lorna. 'It's the sort of thing people say when they're knackered and their brother's being pompous and asking them a load of personal questions,' she snapped.

'So Dad was right. You have got a boyfriend.'

In her mind, Lorna pictured herself flushing her brother's head down his genuine reproduction Victorian pedestal toilet with the solid brass fittings. 'David, first of all I don't see why you're so interested, and second, no, I haven't got a boyfriend.'

She should have known it was no good trying to wear her brother down with argument; he did tedious perseverance like nobody else. 'First of all,' he retorted, 'I'm interested because I care about this family, and second, if you haven't got a boyfriend, who's this Pete character Dad was talking about?'

Lorna subsided with a groan into the nearest armchair. 'Look David,' she said, 'I met a guy called Pete. We went out for dinner. Once. The end.'

'So Dad was wrong and he didn't stay the night then?'

'David! I am not even going to think about answering that. And what's all this about "caring about the family"?'

'Of course I do!'

'Not enough to bother spending Christmas with Mum and Dad though,' remarked Lorna coolly.

'The firm's always busy around Christmas,' David protested, but she knew he was squirming. David and his wife hadn't been to a family gathering since the last time a will was read out. 'I couldn't get time off.'

'What – not once in the last eight years?'

Nobody said anything for what felt like about half an hour.

'I just don't want you getting hurt,' said David sullenly. 'Or . . .'

'Or what?'

'Doing something . . . silly.'

She couldn't understand it. Her brother hadn't worried about her since she was ten and had been late back from the chip shop with his portion of battered haddock. He hadn't worried about her when Ed died, so why was he playing the concerned brother now?

Then it dawned on her.

'Oh I get it – you mean, silly as in something that might embarrass my terribly important big brother?'

'Will you stop second-guessing me for a minute?' exploded David. 'I didn't mean that at all. I meant silly as in getting mixed up with complete strangers and ending up hurt or . . . or worse.'

'Oh,' said Lorna, as all the wind went out of her sails. 'Really?'

'Really. Look sis, do you really think that's all I care about – what people make me look like, and money, and stuff like that?'

'No, of course not,' she replied, more chastened than convinced. 'But you can't just—'

'Yeah, OK, I know. I'm sorry. I was just worried.'

'There's no need, I'm fine. Besides, I'm not seeing anybody anyway.'

'Well, if you're sure.'

'I am. And Dad ought to know better than to stir things up.'

'He was worried too.'

'So now you know I'm fine you can tell him to stop.'

David's rehabilitation in Lorna's eyes lasted precisely as long as it took her mother to tell her about the Art Deco coffee table.

'Well,' she explained, 'as David said, Julia's always liked it, and it'll look so nice in their new Thirties-style drawing room.'

Lorna could hardly believe her ears. 'Grandma's table? You're letting him have Grandma's table?'

Meg smiled in a vague, faintly uneasy kind of way. 'Yes, I know you were fond of it when you were little, and Grandma may have sort of hinted that you should have it when we pass on ... But it's not as if it's really worth anything, is it? And I never could say no to David, could I, George?' George nodded benignly. She turned back to Lorna. 'You don't mind, do you dear?'

There didn't seem much point in Lorna saying yes, or explaining that it felt as if she was losing the last bit of her beloved grandma. It's only a thing, she told herself. And besides, you know David can do no wrong. He always gets everything he wants.

She cleared up the coffee cups to cover the way she was feeling, and dumped them in the sink. 'So you'll be needing a new coffee table then.'

'Oh I shouldn't think so, love,' replied George. 'I was always tripping over the damn thing.'

'Besides,' cut in Meg, 'we don't have money to burn, and your father needs a new suit for his job interviews.'

Surprised, Lorna turned round, up to her elbows in washing up. 'Have you got an interview then, Dad?'

'Er ... no,' he admitted.

'Not yet,' admitted Meg, 'but when he does, he's going to need something a bit better than his usual "hatchings, matchings and dispatchings" suit. Besides, he's put on so much weight that it's bursting at the seams.'

'I've been through a lot with that suit,' said George wistfully.

Nobody mentioned the last time he'd worn it: at Ed's funeral. But Lorna knew they were all thinking the same thing.

Meg broke the silence with a brisk: 'Yes dear, and it shows. Anyhow Lorna, we were thinking of going to that big new out-of-town shopping centre next Wednesday, the one just outside Swindon. What's it called – April Glade?'

'Wednesday ...' Lorna wiped her hands on the seat of her jeans. 'But I'm at work on Wednesday, and don't forget it's Leo's half-term next week.'

George and Meg exchanged puzzled looks. 'Is that a problem?' asked George. 'Only we thought we'd take the children with us.'

'Oh,' said Lorna, taken aback. 'Well . . . if you're sure. But it's quite a long drive, and you'll need to take Hope's changing bag, and you know what Leo's like if he sees a toyshop. You'll never get him out.'

George and Meg laughed. 'Don't you worry, love,' said Lorna's dad. 'If we managed to bring up you and your brother and sister, I think we can handle a day out with Leo and Hope.'

The next time Lorna saw Carmen, she was buying a funky new top at the Thursday market in the Henrietta Street car park.

'Don't tell my boss you've seen me shopping,' she urged, handing over a couple of fivers to a man with a money-belt and fingerless gloves. 'Officially I'm on patrol. But I just had to get something nice to wear for tomorrow.'

'So what's happening tomorrow?' enquired Lorna, parking the pushchair next to the clothing stall. She took in Carmen's flushed cheeks and sparkling eyes. 'Not another lunch date?'

Carmen grinned as she pocketed her penny change. 'I've got one lined up every day until next Tuesday. You know, you're going to wish you hadn't transferred that Love Bites membership into my name!'

'Oh, I doubt it,' said Lorna with feeling. 'I think I'm a bit too chicken for blind dates. Nice top though,' she commented, squatting down to point it out to Hope. 'Look sweetie, Auntie Carmen's got a pretty new pink top with sparkly bits on it. And oooh, isn't it low-cut!'

Hope – normally such a sucker for anything sparkly – was unusually unimpressed, and just went on smearing her face with banana.

'Is she all right?' enquired Carmen, peering into the tot's face. 'Is it me, or is she looking a bit flushed?'

'Yes, I thought that too,' nodded Lorna, laying a hand on Hope's forehead. It did feel a little bit warm. 'If you ask me, she's sickening for that sniffle Leo had. You know what she's like – whatever her big brother's got she wants it too, even if it's germs!'

Carmen's effervescence fizzed out a little. 'I wish germs were all I had to worry about,' she sighed.

'More problems? Your central heating isn't playing up again, is it? I could always ask Chris to—'

'No, it's not that. It's Robbie, always getting into fights, and I can't get a word out of him about why he does it. And then there's this boy in his class that he hangs around with: Ryan. I found out last week his dad's in prison for murder.' She looked at Lorna ruefully. 'Like father like son, eh?'

Lorna really felt for Carmen. She could only imagine how she'd respond if it was Leo in ten years' time. 'Don't jump to conclusions,' she encouraged her. 'You know what young lads are like. Chances are, he'll get it out of his system in a few months and settle down again.' She wasn't sure if she believed herself, but in all honesty Robbie had never seemed like a bad lad to her. 'Give him time, eh?'

'Yeah, I guess.' Carmen made an effort to inject the zip back into her smile. 'Ah well, better go and clamp something before Chappie notices I've been slacking. Tell Leo Becca sends her love.'

'I will. And you make sure you keep me posted on all these dates, yeah?'

Carmen turned and winked. 'Don't you worry, kiddo. You're getting the full, unedited version – whether you want it or not.'

The rest of that week passed uneventfully enough, though Hope's tetchy sniffle duly developed into a streaming cold that left her poor little nose looking like a ripe strawberry. By contrast, Leo was fit as a fiddle, and beside himself with excitement at the prospect of a trip to the far-off, exotic land that was Swindon.

'Are we going in Grandad's car?' he asked, about ten times a day. And Lorna would assure him that yes, they were going in Grandad's big car and not Mummy's little one with the girlie pink seat-covers and the smell of cat in the back; but that Granny and Grandad might not go at all if Hope wasn't feeling better by then.

'But Mummy, she's only got a snotty nose like I had,' he protested. 'And I could wipe it for her.'

And then Lorna smiled and said that yes, possibly he could, but that he'd just have to be patient and wait and see. This of course was a bit like telling a brass band to keep the noise down, and all weekend Leo watched his small sister like a hawk, to see if she was any less snotty than the last time he'd checked.

Fortunately, by Tuesday Hope was looking much better, if a bit peaky, which was just as well as one of Leo's school friends had told him that they had 'zillions' of different flavours of ice cream at the food court in the April Glade shopping centre, and a shop selling robot dinosaurs. It was more than Lorna's life was worth to tell him he wasn't going after all.

On Wednesday morning, she helped her mum and dad get everything ready for the big trek before heading off to work. Not that they seemed to need her help, which perhaps wasn't so surprising. After all, thought Lorna, they've got more experience of child-rearing than I have. And that thought made her feel just a teensy bit inadequate.

'You won't feed them too many sweets, will you?' she pleaded as her parents loaded the kids into the car.

Her mother's eyes rolled heavenwards. 'No, dear! And I'll make sure Leo uses his asthma inhaler if he needs it, and we'll make lots of stops along the way, and no, I haven't forgotten that Hope only eats broccoli if you put tomato sauce on it, not that I expect them to have any in a place like that. Now stop worrying and get yourself off to work, or they'll start having babies without you.'

It was mid-morning by the time George's big old Rover manoeuvred to a halt in the April Glade car park.

'I need a wee-wee,' piped Leo from the back seat.

'What – again?' George held his breath and counted to ten. He'd lost count of the number of stops they'd made along the road, turning a straightforward one-hour drive into a tortuous maze that took in every public loo, Little Chef and secluded hedge between Cheltenham and Swindon. 'All right, wait a minute. Just let Grandad get a ticket from the parking machine.'

'Now, Grandad!' replied Leo, reinforcing his urgency with a tortured grimace.

'Oh, well . . . look Meg, can't he do it behind the car or something?'

'No dear, of course he can't,' replied Meg with a look of horror. 'Somebody might see.'

'Want a proper toilet!' protested Leo.

'It never bothered you when our lot were little, and David got caught short behind the Co-op.'

'That was then, dear. You can't do that sort of thing these days.'

At that moment Hope woke up in her baby seat, and started to cry.

'Don't worry dear,' soothed Meg, mollifying her husband with a Murray mint. 'They'll be fine once we get them inside. This is going to be a lovely day out, just you wait and see.'

Meg stood in the atrium of the April Glade Shopping Experience, utterly aghast. Hope gazed out from her pushchair with eyes that were as round as gobstoppers, while Leo tried to pull his grandfather in three different directions at once.

'Oh dear,' said Meg faintly. 'It's a bit busy. Perhaps half-term wasn't the best time to come after all.'

To say that April Glade was a bit busy was the understatement of the year. Oxford Street on Christmas Eve was busy. April Glade was the Tokyo rush-hour times ten, with the addition of droves of schoolkids, let loose upon Greater Swindon with all the force of a locust swarm.

Leo's face lit up with a huge, beaming smile. 'Ice cream! Look, Grandad – ice cream!'

George and Meg exchanged looks. 'How about a bit later, eh?' suggested George bravely.

'Ice cream! You promised! Grandma, he promised, didn't he?'

And so ice cream it was: large, multicoloured, covered in hundreds and thousands and with a Flake stuck in the top. Not that Leo was selfish with it – he made sure his little sister had her share, albeit mostly down the front of her clean white top.

'Oh Hope,' sighed Meg, ineffectively tackling her face with a wet wipe. 'What are we going to do with you? You're all sticky.'

'Bung her in the washing machine, clothes and all,' replied George jovially; at which Leo's jaw dropped.

'Won't it make her dizzy when it spins round, Grandad?'

George blinked in incomprehension; realised what Leo was on about; and laughed. 'I didn't actually mean it, Leo.'

'But you said—'

'Come on Leo,' said Meg, deciding it was time somebody displayed a bit of authority. 'Let's go and buy Grandad a new suit.'

'I can't be a forty-four short!' protested George. 'Last time I bought a suit, I was only a thirty-eight.'

The young assistant in Supasuits draped his tape-measure back round his neck. 'And . . . er . . . when was that, sir?'

'Nineteen seventy-four,' replied Meg. 'But that was before he got so fat, wasn't it, George?' George looked daggers. 'This last year, he's done nothing but comfort-eat.' She nudged him. 'Go on George, take the forty-four short and let's see what you look like in it.'

Muttering something inaudible, George reluctantly took the hanger with the dark grey suit on it, and vanished through the Portal of Doom into the men's changing cubicles.

Hovering outside, Meg fervently hoped he wouldn't be too long. To be perfectly honest, she was beginning to feel her age just a little, though she'd have died rather than admit it. And keeping a close eye on two children at once seemed somehow more difficult than it had done thirty years ago. Was it that children had become more of a handful; or was she just getting old? No, no, it couldn't be the latter; she and George could give any of the younger generation a run for their money. Well, maybe not a run; but a brisk walk anyway.

'Don't wander away, Leo,' she told him as he messed around in the racks of jackets, alternately disappearing and re-emerging like an intrepid explorer from a tweed jungle.

'Not wandering, Grandma,' he said. 'Just 'sploring.'

'Well do it where I can see you, there's a good boy.'

Hope chose that moment to start grizzling. As Meg bent down to comfort her, she stretched out her pudgy little arms and demanded to be picked up. Her sciatica complaining at the weight, Meg hoisted the sturdy tot onto her hip.

'Now, now, what's the matter? Are you going to be a good girl for Grandma?'

Hope's response was to vomit prodigiously, all down the front of Meg's anorak.

'Oh no,' lamented Meg. 'I knew all that ice cream was a bad idea, after you'd just been poorly . . . Now, where did I put those wipes? Gosh, we'll have to get you to a washroom, young lady.'

It took her a good few minutes to clean up Hope and herself as best she could; and then another couple of moments to realise that something wasn't quite right. She looked around. 'Leo?'

Nothing.

'Leo, where are you?' She slid the jackets along the rail. 'Are you in there? Come out of there right now.'

Still nothing.

Panic rising in her throat, she tapped the assistant on the shoulder. 'Excuse me, have you seen my grandson – the little boy in the blue jacket with the green woolly hat?'

'I'm sorry, madam, I thought he was with you.'

'Leo!' A thousand terrible images flashed through Meg's mind as she gathered Hope up in her arms and rushed into the men's changing rooms, paying absolutely no heed to the outraged exclamations of semi-clad customers. 'George!' she shouted. 'George, come out this minute.'

He emerged from behind a curtain, clad only in trousers, vest and socks. 'Whatever's the matter, Meg? Can't it wait?'

'No!' she snapped. And she dragged him out. 'Don't you understand? I've lost Leo!'

Chapter 12

The mall's security staff couldn't have been more helpful; but at that moment, the only thing that would have calmed Meg down was the sight of her little grandson, holding on firmly to his grandad's hand. And the centre manager's soothing words only served to irritate her: she'd seen the news stories, read the papers. She knew what happened to innocent little children whose careless grandparents let them wander off.

'You have to find him!' she begged, through floods of tears.

'We will,' promised the chief of security, a motherly woman in her forties who was plying Meg with tissues. 'We've radioed all our staff and put out announcements throughout the centre, and if—'

'Not if, now! Before something terrible happens to him.'

The centre manager was still desperately trying to find the right words. 'This does happen a lot, you know, Mrs Scholes. You mustn't blame yourselves. It's very hard keeping watch on kids all the time, especially when you're . . . well . . . not quite as young as you used to be.'

Normally, George would have been outraged at the implication that he was past it. Now, he was beyond protesting. 'Look, I don't care how often it happens.' He put a protective arm round his wife's shoulders. 'Please – never mind looking after us. Just get out there and find our grandson.'

Meg's hand hovered over the mobile phone in her handbag. 'Do you think we ought to ring Lorna?' she asked George anxiously.

He thought for a moment, then shook his head. 'Not until we know something,' he said grimly. 'We caused this mess, and it's up to us to sort it out.'

Breaks were a standing joke on Crocus ward, mainly because nobody ever got any, except Colin Jenkins, and he was the boss so he could have pretty much anything he liked. Including the domestic services supervisor over his desk, if the scurrilous rumours were to be believed.

Today was a bit different from usual, though. Half the beds on the ward were empty, and for once the staff were actually hunting around for things to do. Colin had got so bored that he'd gone off 'coordinating', with a sheet of A4 paper in his hand for effect.

Debs was by the window, resting her increasingly ample belly on the sill. It was amazing how much fatter a person could get in the space of a few weeks. 'Am I the only person in Cheltenham who wants to have a baby any more?' she wondered. 'I'm beginning to think we're permanently running out of customers.'

'Don't you believe it,' flashed back Lorna, busying herself making up one of the empty beds. 'They're just all keeping their legs crossed until that new Orlando Bloom serial finishes on Channel Six. Wouldn't want to miss the end of that, would they?'

Honey the nursing assistant grinned lasciviously. 'I wouldn't keep my legs crossed if Orlando Bloom was around.'

Rose Finnegan gave her a look that said: 'No surprise there, then.' She glanced at the clock on the wall and gave a sniff. 'It's only ten to, but I suppose somebody could go off on their break, if they wanted to.'

Lorna looked up. 'You go if you like, Rose.'

Rose drew herself up to a starched five foot five, and patted the front of her dress. 'Not me, no. Whenever I get near that canteen my willpower fails me.' She compared her flat stomach with Debs's ample swell. 'You go, Lorna, and for goodness' sake take Deborah with you before she goes into premature labour on the ward floor.'

'Silly old bat,' Debs muttered as she and Lorna headed down to the staff canteen. 'She's living in the Stone Age if she thinks pregnant women should be sitting around doing nothing.'

'It'd be good practice for me though,' said Lorna with a grin.

'What would?'

'You giving birth on the ward. I haven't done a single delivery since I came back to work.'

'I'd rather you didn't practise your emergency interventions on me, thanks! I'm having the full water-birth treatment: soft music, warm water, Jeremy rubbing my back with baby oil . . .'

Lorna raised an eyebrow. 'No analgesia then?'

Debs exploded into laughter. 'Are you kidding? I'm a fully paid-up coward. First contraction I get, bet you I'll be begging them to knock me out and tell me when it's all over.'

'Tell me about it,' sympathised Lorna as they walked down the corridor that led to the canteen. 'Natural birth's a great thing – until it starts to hurt.' She stopped as she spotted the staff payphone by the door and unzipped her purse to find some change. 'Tell you what, you go in – I just want to call Mum and Dad and check everything's OK.'

Debs wagged a chiding finger at her. 'Now, now, Mrs Neurotic. They won't thank you for checking up on them every five minutes, will they?'

Lorna hesitated, her hand hovering over the receiver. 'I suppose not,' she admitted.

'And they'd ring the ward if there was anything wrong, wouldn't they?'

'Well ... yes. And to be honest I sometimes wonder why they bother having a mobile.'

'Why's that then?'

'Because Dad's too deaf to hear it, and Mum can't get it out of her handbag before it's stopped ringing.' She put the change back in her purse and zipped it up. 'Perhaps you're right. Come on then, I'll buy you a chocolate muffin.'

The staff canteen at Cotswold General gleefully thumbed its nose at every government edict on healthy eating. Apart from a token range of sad salads that nobody ever bought, the place was a cross between a greasy spoon and a school tuck shop. And that was exactly how the staff liked it. Many exhausted junior doctors had been heard to say that it was only the cholesterol stiffening the walls of their arteries that was keeping them standing upright.

Dr Eoin Sullivan was certainly standing upright, but it didn't look as if the drinks vending machine would be for much longer. Not if he kept kicking it like that.

Lorna suppressed a giggle. Debs gave her a look. But the devil was in Lorna that day. 'Having trouble?' she enquired in her most innocent voice; arms folded, leaning casually against a pillar. 'And I thought you got on so well with machines.'

It was true, after all. Other doctors believed in natural birth; Eoin Sullivan had the mothers wired up like Frankenstein's monster the minute they came through the hospital doors.

He swung round and glared. 'Oh ha ha, most amusing.' He grunted. 'Might've guessed it'd be you, Blondie. I wouldn't put it past you to have sabotaged the bloody thing.'

'But I'm far too busy touching up my lippy,' she reminded him. 'Tell you one thing though,' she went on. 'If you stick your penknife in the slot like that, you'll probably end up electrocuting yourself.'

Debs's eyes widened in alarm. 'Oh dear, yes, Dr Sullivan, she's right.' She fumbled in her purse. 'If you've lost your money in the machine, I'm sure I've got some change and—'

He reached out and snapped her purse shut. 'Good God woman, don't fuss! I'll just do without my shot of caffeine for once.' He eyed Lorna.

'Who knows, maybe without it I'll be a bit less beastly to all and sundry. What do you think, Nurse Price?'

She refused to rise to the obvious 'nurse' jibe. 'Oh, I doubt it,' she replied with the sweetest of smiles.

The corners of Dr Sullivan's mouth twitched, as though threatening sarcastic retribution. Then he laughed. 'You don't like me much, do you Lorna?'

'Whatever gives you that idea?' she enquired.

'Oh, you know – just the way you stick pins in wax effigies every time I go past – nothing specific. You're probably right about me though; I am a complete monster and an unreconstructed misogynist, after all.'

Debs cut in with a hasty, 'Don't be silly, Dr Sullivan,' but nobody was listening. Lorna and the doctor were gazing at each other as though nobody else existed; like two deadly rivals, each willing the other to blink first, or two people who'd only just become aware of each other.

Lorna heard herself say, 'Oh, I don't expect you're all bad.'

'You should let me prove it sometime,' he replied, refusing to let her gaze escape from his.

'Maybe I will.'

She tried to sound defiant, but as she went off with Debs to buy coffee and muffins, her heart was pounding and her ears were fiery red. She didn't dare look back over her shoulder. If she did, she was convinced Eoin Sullivan would perceive the shameful truth: that she fancied him like crazy.

April Glade might be a kids' paradise, but Leo was not having the time of his life.

He really did wish now that he hadn't wandered off. But it was so boring, waiting in the suit shop with Grandma and Hope while Grandad tried stuff on. Maybe it wouldn't have been quite so boring if they'd given him something to try on too, or if they'd brought some of his toys to play with.

Leo hadn't meant to wander off so far, but first he'd caught sight of the man in the rabbit outfit, with the big bunch of balloons, and then he'd found the shop with all the robot dinosaurs in. When he'd turned round to show Grandad what he'd found, he'd suddenly realised that he didn't know where Grandad was. Worse, he didn't know where he himself was, either.

The question was, what to do. Mummy had always told him not to talk to strangers, so he didn't dare go up to anybody, not even people who looked quite nice, just in case they weren't. So he'd wandered around for a bit, hoping that perhaps round the next corner he would wander back into the shop where he'd left Grandma and Grandad.

His lower lip began to quiver. He was tired, he was hungry, and he wanted his mum.

Sadly, he dragged his feet across to the big fountain in the middle of the central court, knelt up on it and gazed down into the water. There were big golden fish in there, and he could see some coins in there too. Grandad had told him people threw coins in sometimes to make their wishes come true. He felt in his pocket but he didn't have any coins.

If he could get one of the pennies from the bottom of the fountain, one of the ones that contained somebody else's wish, could he throw it back in and make his wish come true too? He didn't want much after all; just to go home.

It was a bit of a stretch, but if he got up on tiptoe, bent right over and plunged his arm into the water, right up to the shoulder, he might just manage it.

Tongue in cheek, concentrating like mad, he bent over the marble edge of the fountain. Just a little bit further and he'd have that twenty-pence piece, which must surely be worth more wishes than a penny or two-pence piece.

He stretched so hard, and the marble was so slippery, that all of a sudden he felt himself losing his grip and sliding forwards, towards the cold, blue water and the big-eyed fish.

Then somebody shouted, and just as Leo's nose touched the water, a huge hand grabbed him by the waist of his trousers and yanked him backwards as if he weighed no more than a ball of wool.

'Well, well,' said the security guard, pushing his peaked cap back on his head. 'Is your name Leo? Leo Price?'

Leo nodded, which wasn't quite as bad as actually talking to a stranger. Besides, this one knew his name.

'I think you'd better come with me, young man. Your gran and grandad have been searching high and low for you.'

Meg held Leo's hand so tightly that he winced. 'Grandma, you're hurting me!'

'I'm sorry, darling.' She relaxed her iron grip, but only fractionally. 'I'm just scared of letting go in case you run off again.'

'I won't, Grandma,' he said.

George eased his aching joints into a crouch, so that he was on eye level with his grandson. How did you explain to a five year old boy that he'd nearly given his grandparents multiple heart attacks and had them imagining everything from kidnapping to grisly accidents? How did you explain to him that he'd made them seriously question their own competence to care for him?

97

'Do you promise you won't do anything like that ever again?' he asked his grandson, holding him by the shoulders and looking him straight in the eye.

Leo nodded solemnly. 'I promise, Grandad.' He was quiet for a long moment, then asked, 'Are you going to tell Mummy I was naughty?'

George and Meg looked at each other. That was the sixty-four thousand dollar question.

Meg swallowed. 'She's got a lot on her plate, George.'

'Yes. Maybe we don't need to worry her with this.'

'It's probably for the best, dear.'

It was an excuse and they knew full well they were chickening out, but maybe it was true. Maybe there really was no point in frightening Lorna when, after all, in the end Leo had come back to them safe and sound.

'As long as you keep that promise,' said George sternly.

'I will,' said Leo. And – at least for now – he truly meant it.

That evening, when Meg and George arrived home with the children, Lorna was there to greet them with home-made chocolate chip cookies, still warm from the oven.

'Did you have a lovely day?' she asked, hugging Leo and taking Hope in her arms. 'Gosh, you must've done. This one's got ice cream all over her!'

Meg gave Leo a surreptitious nudge. 'Yes, Mummy. We had a very nice time, thank you.'

Lorna looked at him quizzically. This wasn't like Leo; normally he flew in, frantically gabbling out all the things he'd been up to before he'd even got through the door. 'You're a bit quiet,' she said. 'Are you feeling all right? Only I made chocolate chip cookies, and—'

At the magic words 'chocolate chip cookies', Leo was off into the kitchen with a whoop of delight.

'He's fine, love,' Lorna's father assured her. 'Just a bit tired – it's been a long day.'

Lorna glanced down and saw that Hope had dozed off in her arms. 'So I see! I must send them out with you more often, if they come back this well-behaved! Come on, sweetie, let's wipe off some of this gunk and put you down for a sleep.' She turned round as she reached the door. 'Oh, by the way, did you get Dad a suit?'

Meg and George looked at each other. 'Er, no,' confessed Meg. 'You know the funny thing is, there was such a lot to do there that we just didn't get round to it in the end.'

A little while later, Lorna finished drying the dinner dishes and tiptoed upstairs to say goodnight to Leo – she hoped without waking Hope as she passed the open door of her bedroom. Normally, Hope slept right through, but once she woke up, she tended to stay that way; and that could mean driving round the streets of Cheltenham at two o'clock in the morning, trying to lull her back off to sleep again in her child seat.

As she reached the door of Leo's bedroom, Lorna heard her father's voice: the same deep, gentle, humorous voice that had held her spellbound when she was Leo's age. Not wanting to disturb him, she stood just outside the doorway and listened as he told Leo the same stories he'd told her and David and Sarah: The Adventures of Fat Penguin.

'. . . and Fat Penguin lived in the great Penguin City at the South Pole,' George went on. 'A beautiful city entirely carved out of the ice. Nobody knew it was there, because it was underground, but it wasn't dark because it was made of ice and the sunlight shone right through it, all shades of sparkly green and blue and white.'

'Grandad,' cut in Leo, 'why was Fat Penguin so fat? Did he eat a lot?'

'Oh yes, he ate all the time. Eating was his favourite hobby.'

'What did he eat?'

'Fresh herrings and strawberry jam.'

'Ewwww!' Leo pulled a face.

'And he lived in a lovely ice apartment at the very top of the city, with his pet lemming, Eric, who'd come there from the Arctic because it wasn't nice there any more . . .'

Lorna smiled to herself. Fat Penguin's nightly adventures had been a precious part of her childhood, and now they were a part of Leo's too. It wasn't all plain sailing of course, but she was glad now that her parents had moved in. Glad not just for the freedom it had given her, but for what it was giving the children.

Only one tiny niggle clouded the way she felt; and it was a silly thing. If she was honest with herself, she had to admit that something juvenile and petty inside her had secretly hoped her mum and dad wouldn't find caring for their grandchildren quite so effortless. After all, she thought: I'm their mum, I want to matter as much to them as they do to me.

I want to be irreplaceable. And I'm not sure I am any more.

Chapter 13

'Hold the bucket still, Lorna! Another load coming down.'

Chris was perched at the top of a very tall ladder, which Lorna was far too cowardly to climb herself, and was cleaning out her guttering. She braced herself as another disgusting ball of mud, twigs and leaves hit the bottom of the bucket.

'It's very good of you to do this,' she called up to him.

He turned his head round and looked down at her. 'You do realise I'm expecting payment in cake?'

'Cake on standby,' she promised. 'Home-made, with butter icing.'

She gazed up at him working away, selfless as ever, and wondered what she'd done to deserve such a good friend. Since Ed's death, Chris had been her confidant and her handyman, and she'd soaked the shoulders of most of his jumpers with tears. When other friends had got bored with her grief, Chris had never once implied that it was time to pull herself together and stop moping. If it hadn't been for him and Carmen, she'd have long since fallen apart.

Of course, he and Ed had been closer than a lot of brothers, so maybe Chris was just looking out for her because of that. But it was an awfully long road he'd travelled with her, never asking for anything in return. She couldn't help but see the irony when she thought about her own brother, David, whose sole contribution to her recovery had been to turn up at Ed's funeral. Even then, he hadn't stopped looking at his watch.

I guess some people are just naturally nicer than others, she told herself; and it doesn't matter a damn whether they're related to you or not.

The mobile in her back pocket started to warble, and she prised it out with some difficulty, making a mental note to lose a bit of weight before she wore these jeans again. She flipped open the phone and saw Carmen's number on the screen.

'Hiya Carmen, sorry I didn't phone you last night, only one of the gutters overflowed and we had a bit of a flood in the utility room.'

'I was wondering what had happened to you. Thought maybe you'd been whisked away by your Prince Charming or something. To tell you the truth, I almost didn't call you in case I caught you in a compromising position.'

Lorna laughed. 'Not unless clearing out the gutters is compromising.'

'You're up a ladder? Wow, I'm impressed – do you want to do mine too?'

'Nice try, but Chris is up the ladder; I'm just holding the bucket.' She held the phone vaguely in Chris's direction. 'Say hello to Carmen.'

'Hello to Carmen,' he repeated dutifully.

'Lucky cow. Wish I had a man on tap whenever I needed one. Anyhow, I won't keep you,' Carmen went on. 'Just thought you might like to know that I've finally found him: the man of my dreams.'

'That's what you always say,' Lorna reminded her.

'Well . . . possibly. But this time I really mean it. He's tall, young, single, has a steady job – I can tell from the profile he's going to be perfect.'

'Hang on, Carmen. You mean you haven't even met him yet?'

'No, but I've got a date with him tonight. I'm so excited about it I thought we should go for dinner rather than lunch – more romantic. Don't you worry anyway, it's just a formality. I'm telling you Lorna, we were made for each other. Even my next-door-neighbour's tarot cards said so.'

Carmen rang off and Lorna squeezed the phone back into her pocket. 'Carmen's got a hot date,' she explained.

'So I gathered.'

He didn't seem over-interested, but Lorna felt it was her duty to encourage him. 'You know, a good-looking young man like you really ought to be—'

'Hold the bucket still,' Chris cut in. 'I don't want to drop all this gunge on your head.'

It was visiting time on the ward, and naturally all the babies were crying. And crying babies did nothing to improve Rose Finnegan's temper.

'Honest to God,' she seethed as she stood outside Colin's office, surveying the ward, 'is it any wonder the little devils are screaming their heads off, with all these gormless relatives making faces at them? It should be one visitor per bed, and no exceptions.'

'Why don't we give them all an IQ test before we let them in?' suggested Lorna innocently.

'Good idea, I'm all for it.' Rose flashed a lightning-bolt of a look at a young man perched on the end of his girlfriend's bed. 'Off the bed please, if you don't mind, it's unhygienic.'

'Rose,' said Lorna gently, 'I was joking about the IQ test.'

Rose glanced at her in a disappointed sort of way. 'Were you? Pity.'

'Excuse me,' said a diminutive middle-aged lady, barely visible behind an enormous pink and white bouquet. 'Do you have anything I could put these in?'

'Try the bin,' snapped Rose, turning on her heel.

The bouquet quivered. 'I beg your pardon?'

Lorna stepped in. 'Gosh, aren't those roses lovely? And such a gorgeous scent. Tell you what, let's go to the ward kitchen and see if we can find a nice vase to put them in.'

A few minutes later, when the flowers had been neatly arranged and a sheaf of pink and silver balloons tied to the end of another patient's bed, Lorna went off in search of Rose.

She found her in the staff changing room, dabbing cold water on her face.

'What was all that about?' she asked, pushing the door to behind her.

'All what?'

'That lady – you were really rude to her. You're not ill or something?'

Rose looked at her as though she were mad. 'Ill? I'm never ill. When was the last time I took a day off sick? Not like some people round here. I mean, employing pregnant midwives – whose stupid idea was that? Stands to reason they won't be able to cope with the pace.'

'Debs is very good at her job,' said Lorna quietly.

Rose just sniffed.

'You don't like people very much, do you?' Lorna remarked.

'What is there to like?' Rose snapped back. 'Now, you may not have any work to do, but I have to get back to the ward and sort out all those screaming infants.' She reached the door and turned back. 'Oh, by the way – remember that girl you were so fond of . . . Kelly something?'

'Picton. Kelly Picton. What about her?'

'I saw her down the Lower High Street the other night. Must have been at least half-past ten. I said to myself, "There you go, I knew it – out all hours and not a sign of the baby. She's gone and dumped it on her mother."'

'You don't know that,' protested Lorna.

'She looked miserable anyhow. Well, serves her right, the irresponsible little cow.'

Rose Finnegan left, leaving the changing-room door to close in painfully slow motion.

I'm sure Kelly's not like that, Lorna said to herself; I'm sure she's not like that at all. But she couldn't for the life of her think of any reasons why.

*

'Now just you listen to me, Robbie,' Carmen warned him as she came downstairs in all her finery. 'Sharon from down the road is being really kind, taking care of you lot while I go out. And yes, I know you think you're too old for a babysitter, but last time I left you in charge, Becca was up till eleven o'clock watching videos. You give Sharon one word of cheek and you're grounded for a month. Got that?'

Hands in his pockets, Robbie gazed sullenly at his trainers and mumbled something inaudible.

'What did you say?'

He looked up. 'I said, "Yes, Mum." OK?'

Carmen looked at him and couldn't decide if she wanted to shake him or hug him. In the end she confined herself to patting imaginary creases out of his oversized basketball shirt.

He flinched. 'Mum!'

'All right, all right. I'll see you later, and you'd better be asleep or there'll be trouble.' She called down the passageway to the living room. ''Bye Sharon, I shouldn't be late ... well, not too late anyway. Don't let them give you any lip. With a bit of luck, Becca and Rosie will sleep right through.'

And then she was walking down the front path to the taxi because, after all, you couldn't really turn up for the hottest date of your life in a white van with NORTH GLOS CLAMPING CO on the side, could you?

She checked her watch as she quickened her pace across the Royal Well bus station. One or two lads were cruising around in souped-up Fiestas, trying to impress each other, but apart from them the place seemed eerily deserted. It was as though there were only two people in the world that really mattered right now: Carmen Jones and her dream date.

She glanced at the piece of paper in her hand for the hundredth time. Alex. That was all she knew about him: a name and a few statistics. But she could tell that he was going to be special. That's why she'd agreed to an evening date rather than the usual lunch.

They'd arranged to meet in the Indian restaurant behind the auction rooms. Nothing too posh and a bit heavy on the sitar music, but at least there were plenty of nice quiet booths where you could have a discreet conversation without the rest of the world hearing.

Carmen reached the door of the Simla Brasserie, pushed it open and walked into a pleasant, spicy fug, warm with the aromas of coriander and tandoori paste. It was still early, and it seemed the restaurant was empty, but you never could tell. A waiter glided forward to greet her, and she was about to ask if him someone called Alex had arrived yet when she spotted a familiar face looking at her furtively round the side of one of the booths.

'Chris? Is that you?'

Reluctantly he emerged from the booth. 'Carmen . . . er . . . hi.'

'Waiting for someone?' she enquired. A smile of delighted realisation lit up her face. 'You're on a date, aren't you? Me too. Go on, tell me all about her.'

Chris looked profoundly uncomfortable. 'I can't. I've . . . not actually met her yet. All I know is, she's called Alyssa.'

Carmen very nearly took a tumble onto the mock-Afghan carpet 'Alyssa? Oh shit. Don't tell me, she thinks you're called Alex.'

The date might be dead in the water, but a babysitter was a babysitter. And the Simla Brasserie did do a lovely chicken dhansak.

'Why on earth did you call yourself Alex?' demanded Carmen as she mainlined lime pickle until her sinuses hurt.

'I *am* called Alex,' replied Chris, looking deeply uncomfortable. 'Alexander's my real first name. I thought it sounded . . . well, posher. More impressive. So why did you call yourself Alyssa?'

'Have you any idea how many jokes people make when you have a name like Carmen?' she replied. 'Besides, being called Carmen, men always expect you to be some kind of voluptuous femme fatale. I thought I'd try using my middle name for a change and see if the men I attracted were any less sleazy.'

'Ah. And you got me.'

'Well, you're not sleazy, are you?'

Chris had to admit that this was true. 'Boring yes, sleazy no. Everybody wants to be something better than they are, don't they?' he went on with a sigh, jabbing a shard of poppadom into the mango chutney.

Carmen looked at him sharply. 'Oh dear, that sounds heartfelt.'

'Well it's true,' he insisted. 'You want to be Alyssa who goes out with non-sleazy men, and I want to be posh Alex who goes to work in a suit and doesn't construct built-in wardrobes for a living.'

Carmen wrinkled her nose. 'Why? What's wrong with who you are? From where I'm sitting you look pretty good to me.'

'Don't fancy me though, do you?'

'Well . . . no,' she admitted. 'But that's only because you're not my type, just like I'm not yours. Any woman with any sense would snap you up.'

'No she wouldn't,' said Chris dully.

Now, Carmen Jones might not be much good at managing her own love

105

life, but she was all ears when it came to anybody else's. And she'd been around long enough to know a case of unrequited love when she saw it.

'Who is she?' asked Carmen.

Chris looked at her with a mixture of guilt and surprise. 'What are you on about?'

'Don't give me that. I want to know who she is, this woman you're lusting after.'

'I'm not!' he protested. 'Or at least . . . Look, it's not like that. She's just not interested in me. Doesn't see me that way at all. End of story, OK?'

Carmen shook her head. 'Not OK. Tell me who she is, Chris, or I'll shove this lime pickle up your nose.'

She stared at him so intensely that he caved in. 'Look Carmen, if you ever breathe a word of this to her—'

'Yes, yes, OK. Cross my heart. Now, who is she?'

He swallowed hard. 'Lorna.'

'Oh,' said Carmen.

'See – even you think it's ridiculous.'

'No I don't, I just . . .' Carmen swallowed three forkfuls of rice in quick succession, while she thought of something to say. 'I think it's great, I just don't know why you haven't said anything to her, that's all. Or anybody else come to that.'

Chris looked at her in despair. 'Tell Lorna? Are you kidding? Do you know what she once told me? That she sees me as the favourite brother that David never was. Does that sound like a recipe for romance to you?'

Carmen had to admit that it wasn't the most promising start. 'But feelings can change,' she pointed out.

'With some people, maybe that's true. But I was Ed's best friend since school. Lorna's known me that way ever since she was a kid herself. And besides, out of respect for Ed's memory—'

'Ed would want you to be happy. Both of you.'

Chris pushed his food to the side of his plate. 'Carmen, I appreciate what you're trying to say, truly I do; but honestly, it's hopeless. I realised that ages ago. That's why I keep on with this stupid dating lark, in the hope that one day I'll meet someone who'll make me forget about Lorna. So far, it's been a complete failure,' he added.

Failure, thought Carmen. I know a song about that. 'Look,' she said, 'when it comes to romance there's nobody in the world who's had more failures than I have. Believe me, I'm not exaggerating. But I still go on hoping, don't I? Otherwise, would I have come here tonight to meet the gorgeous Alex?'

Chris didn't answer.

106

'All right, maybe that just means I'm a complete saddo who's living in a fantasy world. But I prefer to think of myself as an optimist.' She speared the choicest piece of chicken from the dish and offered it to Chris. 'Call me stupid, Chris, but I truly don't believe that anything is ever hopeless. Not even you.'

Chapter 14

It was the day before Valentine's Day, and most of the world was out buying red satin underwear, or writing bad love poems inside heart-shaped cards.

Carmen was sitting on the toilet, gazing forlornly at the plastic stick in her hand. She'd hoped her instinct was wrong this time round, but after four kids and a host of false alarms, you pretty much knew when you were pregnant. And like the little blue stick said, this was no false alarm.

Downstairs, her two youngest were coming to blows over the ownership of a teddy bear, the front door was still reverberating with the aftershock of Robbie slamming it on his way out to school, and if it hadn't been for his younger sister, sweet, calm, helpful Charmain, Carmen would have long since yielded to despair.

With a sigh, she wrapped the remains of the pregnancy test in a plastic bag, away from juvenile curiosity, and stood up. There was work to go to and children to be sorted out, and really and truly there was no point in moping up here. The only decision that mattered had already been taken, and now it was just a question of when, where and how.

Because no matter which angle she viewed the problem from, Carmen knew in her heart that she couldn't have another baby.

Lorna was just getting off shift when Carmen turned up at the hospital. She found Carmen hovering like an unhappy ghost outside the ward entrance, hands thrust deep in her pockets and wearing what her mother was apt to call an Eleanor Rigby face.

'Good God Carmen, what's happened?' gasped Lorna at the sight of her friend's expression. 'It's not one of the children, is it?'

Carmen smiled faintly. 'Not exactly,' she said. 'Is there somewhere we could go? Only I'm desperate and I really need to talk.'

'Well, I did tell Mum and Dad I'd be back . . .'

'Lorna, please.'

Lorna weighed up the situation, and decided that whatever it was had to be a lot more important than her mum's over-fifties' yoga class. 'OK, just let me phone Mum and tell her I'm going to be a bit late. Then we'll go and have a coffee and sort things out.'

'I wouldn't bank on it,' said Carmen flatly; then she fell silent. In fact she didn't say another word all the way between Crocus ward and the coffee shop, which Lorna found distinctly worrying. Normally the only way to shut Carmen up was to give her mouth something else to do, as many of her boyfriends had discovered over the years.

Situated on the ground floor of the maternity wing, the coffee shop was open twenty-four hours a day, seven days a week, providing black coffee by the gallon to anxious expectant fathers whose unreasonable partners went into labour at inconvenient times, kept it up for seventy-two hours straight, and then finally gave birth at three in the morning. There was always a small huddle of them outside the door too, chain-smoking in the rain and hoping that nobody noticed them doing it on hospital premises.

Carmen chose the remotest table, in the darkest corner. 'I'm in a mess, Lorna,' she confessed. 'And it's all my stupid fault. As usual.'

'Come on, chin up,' urged Lorna. 'Is it a bill you need help with, or anything like that?'

'No, it's a lot worse than that. I'm pregnant.'

Lorna blinked. 'But you're on the Pill. Aren't you?'

'Yes ... well, no ... I mean, I was, only it gave me these terrible headaches and made my backside so fat that I just couldn't cope with it. And you know what condoms are like.'

'Oh Carmen,' groaned Lorna.

'I do always use them though, really I do! But well, accidents can happen. They're not always a hundred per cent reliable, are they?'

Lorna looked up. 'Oh God, what a nightmare.'

'Tell me about it.' Carmen gazed glumly into the murky depths of her coffee.

Poor Carmen, thought Lorna. You work so hard, you love your kids, you care about other people more than you care about yourself. Why do these things always happen to you?

'So what are you going to do?' asked Lorna gently.

'What can I do?' Carmen's dark eyes sought out hers, as though pleading for some obvious answer she hadn't spotted herself even though she knew it didn't exist. 'Having Becca was tough enough. But now she's at school it's just begun to get easier. How would I manage with five? Another little one's out of the question, you know that.'

Lorna nodded slowly, uncritically. She imagined how things might have been if Ed hadn't left her with a house and a pension, and if Hope

110

had turned out to be twins, and it was all too easy to see herself in Carmen's situation, making the same unpalatable choices. On the other hand, there was one avenue they hadn't yet explored.

'What about the father?' she asked. 'Couldn't you get help from him? Child support or whatever?'

Carmen's cappuccino skin reddened slightly. 'Possibly,' she said. 'If I knew who he was.'

Even coming from Carmen, this was a bit of a revelation. 'Oh,' said Lorna, not concealing her surprise very well. 'I didn't realise.'

'You must think I'm terrible,' sighed Carmen. 'Go on, it's OK, you can admit it. I mean, how can a woman my age, with my experience, manage to get herself up the duff and not even know who by? It's a bit pathetic really.'

'Haven't you any idea who it might be?' asked Lorna. 'I mean . . . were you that drunk?'

'No, I wasn't drunk,' replied Carmen with a hint of indignation. 'It's just that I had a couple of one-night stands recently, and there was this one time when I got a bit . . . um . . . carried away and we didn't actually use a condom at all.'

'So you do know who he is then?'

Carmen looked like she wanted the tiled floor to open up and swallow her whole. 'Assuming it actually was him – and I can't be sure, can I? Assuming it was him, I don't know anything about him, except that he was called Dean and he drove a blue Renault.'

'You don't know his surname then?'

'Not a clue. I met him in a bar. And if by some miracle I did manage to track him down, do you really think he'd want anything to do with me or the baby?'

'He might,' ventured Lorna doubtfully.

Carmen gave her a cynical look. 'He didn't care enough to see me twice, did he? Face it Lorna, when it comes to choosing men I'm the worst. Anyway,' she closed her eyes, gave a long sniff and for the first time Lorna saw that she was holding back tears, 'this is about me, not him.'

She returned an expectant father's inquisitive gaze with a venomous glare as she took Carmen's hand. 'It's going to be OK,' she said quietly.

'No it's not,' said Carmen, slowly shaking her head. 'But it's going to be the best I can manage.' She reached into her pocket, extracted a crumpled tissue and blew her nose. 'The counsellor managed to get me an appointment at the clinic for three o'clock and seeing as I'm not very brave . . . I was sort of hoping you'd be able to come with me.'

'Of course I will,' said Lorna. 'Hope you've got your van with you though, 'cause my car's in for a service today.'

Carmen ran the back of her hand across her snotty nose. 'I don't think I could drive like this,' she said. 'It's OK, it's only in Gloucester city centre; we can get the bus.'

Being pregnant is a damned nuisance. That was the number one lesson Mel Janucek had learned over the last eight and a half months. It makes you fat, constipated, waddle like a duck and develop peculiar cravings for All Bran with mustard. It gives you backache, stops you wearing your favourite clothes, and – worst of all – it never ends.

It was a long time since Mel had taken a bus to go anywhere, but since her waistline had expanded beyond the gap between steering wheel and driving seat, she didn't have much option. Her husband had taken to calling her Fatso. She was thoroughly fed up. And now she had indigestion as well. There really was no justice in the world.

'Cheltenham town centre please,' she panted as she hauled herself and her shopping on board the single-decker.

'That'll be one-twenty. You all right love?' enquired the bus driver. 'Only it's ice-cold in here and you look a bit hot.'

'I'm fine,' Mel replied tetchily, a fraction of a second before the most tremendous pain surged through her, and she finally realised that she wasn't all right at all.

'I thought the doctor was very understanding,' said Lorna as she and Carmen headed back to the bus stop by the thermal underwear store.

'Yes,' said Carmen flatly.

'And the nurse talked a lot of sense.'

'Of course she did.'

Lorna slipped an arm through Carmen's. 'Hey, is there anybody in there?'

Carmen gave her a woebegone look. 'No,' she replied, with just a ghost of a smile.

Worried, Lorna wondered whether it was better to keep talking, or keep her mouth shut and let Carmen brood over the last couple of hours. Surely brooding couldn't be a good idea. 'Are you sure this is what you want?' she asked.

Carmen stopped in her tracks, turned to look at Lorna and replied, 'Of course it isn't.'

'In that case why do it?'

'Because I don't have any choice, do I.' She took a deep breath and tried to throw her shoulders back, the way she did when she had to be brave and go and clamp a Mercedes full of snotty-looking business types. It wasn't all that convincing. 'Anyhow, it'll all be over and done with this

112

time next week, and believe me, I'm making sure this never ever happens to me again. Because if it did . . .'

'I know.' The number ninety-four to Cheltenham rumbled to a halt and disgorged its cargo of noisy schoolkids. 'Come on kid, let's go home. I think we've both had enough for one day.'

The bus was about halfway between Gloucester and Cheltenham when the young woman let out a howl of agony, and the driver stamped on his brakes so hard that he left rubber burns on the road.

'You OK love?' he asked for the third time.

'Of course I'm not bloody all right!' spat the woman, who was kneeling in the gangway with her hands cradling her very obviously pregnant stomach.

''Ere,' cut in an old crone in the front seats, 'State she's in, I reckon she's 'avin' 'er baby.'

The young woman looked up in desperation and fury. 'I can't be! I've still got a month to go! And I've left a casserole in the aaaagh . . .!'

'Anybody know what to do?' enquired the bus driver, whose face had turned completely white.

'I'll phone for an ambulance on my mobile,' volunteered a middle-aged man. 'Shouldn't we have hot towels and water, or is it the other way round? I'm sure it's something of the sort.'

Carmen looked at Lorna. 'I think this is your cue.'

Mel was squatting at the back of the bus, behind a screen of overcoats that had been generously donated to lend a bit of privacy. Her knuckles were white from clenching around the chrome rails on the backs of the seats, and the sweat was pouring down her face.

Dear God, thought Lorna. All this time working on Crocus ward, and my first solo delivery for six years has to be on a bus.

'Don't worry,' she said, mopping her patient's brow, 'the ambulance will be here any minute now.' Not that your baby's going to wait that long, she added silently.

'Shouldn't you . . . be telling me . . . to push or something?' gasped Mel.

'No need. Your body will tell you when you need to.'

'Shouldn't I be lying down then? It's always lying down on the telly.'

'Most women find it much easier to deliver squatting,' Lorna assured her with a smile. 'Now, take deep breaths and hold onto Carmen's hand.'

'That's right,' said Carmen. 'Grab hold and squeeze, tight as you like.' She suppressed a wince of pain as Mel crushed her fingers to a pulp. 'That's the way,' she said, smiling through clenched teeth.

113

The bus driver's head appeared above the overcoats. 'How's it going in there?'

Carmen met his enquiry with a furious snarl. 'Oi you, bog off! This isn't a free show, you know. How'd you like having all your bits exposed to all and sundry? Hmm?'

The head disappeared as quickly as it had appeared.

'Oh!' said Mel suddenly. 'Oh dear, I think it's happening again, I think I . . . aaaagh!'

Lorna did a quick check. 'You're crowning, I can see your baby's head. A couple more like that, and we'll be there.'

'Promise?'

'Promise. It'll all be over soon.'

And it was. A couple of minutes later, when Carmen had given her hand up for lost, Mel Janucek let out a scream that drove the rooks off a potato field half a mile away, and a very red-faced Janucek junior slid out into Lorna's hands, adding his own lusty protests to his mother's cries.

Another head appeared above the coats: this time young, male and very anxious. 'Mel – Mel are you all right? Oh God, is that . . . is that our baby?'

Mel looked up at her husband through a tangle of sweaty hair. 'Trust you to miss the main event,' she said.

And then everybody started cheering.

'What a day,' groaned Lorna as she kicked off her shoes and slumped on the sofa with a child on either side. 'Thanks for the steak and kidney pie, Mum, it was just the job. And I'm sorry I was so late – something really important came up.'

'Snake and pigmy, snake and pigmy!' giggled Leo, who'd obviously been listening to his grandfather's jokes again. 'I like snake, but pigmy tastes funny.'

'Shush Leo, settle down and don't be silly,' said Meg. 'Well dear, I'm sure it was important if it kept you so long.' Lorna could see she was expecting to be told exactly what had kept her, but she wasn't about to reveal Carmen's plight to her mother, who already had Carmen marked down as being the wrong side of unconventional. 'Well, if you really want to know I delivered a baby on a bus,' she replied. 'The ninety-four from Gloucester.'

'Is that a joke, dear? Only I'm not very good with "modern" humour.'

'No, I really did! Who'd have thought it: there I was, panicking about whether I was going to cope in a fully equipped delivery suite, and when it came down to it, I didn't have any of that and it still went OK. Of course, Carmen was a big help.'

Meg's ears pricked up. 'Carmen? What were you and Carmen doing on the Gloucester bus?'

Oops, thought Lorna. 'Oh, she just fancied popping over there for an hour and I thought I'd go with her . . .' She grabbed at the first opportunity to change the subject. 'Gosh, is that a cup of tea you've got there? Don't suppose any left in the pot? I'm parched.'

Lorna and the children were settling down to watch *Bambi* when the doorbell rang.

'I'll get it,' said George, who'd never much cared for *Bambi* on the grounds that it always made him cry and crying wasn't manly.

A moment later he returned. 'It's somebody for you, Lorna. Karen Green, I think she said her name was.'

The name meant nothing to Lorna. 'Perhaps it's somebody from Leo's PTA,' she mused aloud. 'I did say I'd get some stuff together for the next jumble sale.'

But the woman standing at the door didn't look like a parent from Leo's school. For a start she didn't look nearly harassed enough. And what kind of busy parent had time to look after waist-length blonde hair?

'If you're selling anything, I'm not interested,' said Lorna with a yawn.

Karen Green laughed. 'If anything, I'm buying,' she replied. 'Or at least I'm in the market for information.' She reached into her pocket and handed Lorna a business card. It read: Karen Green, News Desk, *Cheltenham Courant*. 'The thing is, a little bird tells me you did something rather heroic on a bus today.'

Lorna paled. 'I wouldn't say that,' she parried.

'But I'm sure our readers would. Do you mind if I come in for a minute?'

Even if Lorna had minded, it was a bit late in the day; the reporter was already three feet down the hallway. 'Only I'd really like to get all the details, right from the horse's mouth. You're front-page news you know, Mrs Price.'

115

Chapter 15

The following day at work, Lorna didn't know where to look. It might be Valentine's Day, but the focus of attention had little to do with Cupid and his cutesy little arrows, and a lot more to do with the big colour picture of Lorna on page one of the *Cheltenham Courant*.

Honey was in her element, reading out chunks of the article for the benefit of patients or indeed anyone who happened to be within a fifty-yard radius. 'Listen, this bit's really good. "Lorna, twenty-nine" – gosh, are you? You don't look it – "raced into action as Mrs Janucek writhed in agony on the floor of the number ninety-four bus."'

'No more, Honey,' pleaded Lorna, 'please.'

'Don't you take any notice of her,' the sturdy-looking mother of eight in Bay C advised Honey. 'She's just shy.'

'Yes, go on, read us the rest,' urged the frail girl in the next bed, who looked quite incapable of having given birth to her ten-pound sumo of a baby son. 'It's just like the telly.'

Lorna cringed as the stirring tale of her exploits was broadcast to the entire ward. 'Look, I was only doing my job!' she protested to Debs. 'What was I supposed to do – leave the woman to get on with it?'

'Oh, let them have their fun,' advised Debs. 'It's the most exciting thing that's happened to Crocus ward since we nearly had a visit from Judith Chalmers.'

'I'm ... er ... flattered,' said Lorna, frankly not sure whether she should be or not.

Eoin Sullivan swung by with an even more sarcastic expression than usual. Great, thought Lorna; just when I was beginning to think he wasn't that bad after all. 'Well, well, if it isn't Wonderwoman,' he remarked. 'Perhaps you should start wearing your knickers over your trousers.'

'Perhaps you should wear yours stuffed down your throat,' muttered Lorna, then added out loud, 'Don't take any notice of the *Courant*. You know what local papers are like, any excuse to put a baby on the cover.'

'A babe, more like,' he replied, managing to make it sound like a capital offence.

'Sorry?' demanded Lorna.

'Oh come on, it stands to reason. Pretty, blonde, petite – you're a local reporter's dream. No doubt it'd have been different if you were a forty-five-year-old matron with a moustache and blotchy legs. Or a bloke.'

Debs giggled teasingly. 'You're not jealous are you, Dr Sullivan?'

You know something, Debs, thought Lorna, for once I reckon you might be right about Eoin Sullivan. He's having an attack of the green-eyed monster. And any guy who's that jealous of some ordinary girl getting her picture in the local rag must be hellishly insecure and vulnerable underneath all that brashness and over-confidence.

In a funny way, that made him seem less arrogant, more appealing. She still wanted to dislike him on principle, but in practice it was getting harder. Come on Lorna, she scolded herself, you're making excuses for him just because he's hot; but it was no use. She didn't care. She even tried to make him feel better.

'Oh, I'm sure there was a much bigger photo of you when you rescued that woman from the river,' she said encouragingly.

He frowned. 'I really can't remember. You see, I don't travel with a media crew just in case I happen to find somebody to save from drowning. And anyway, that's not why I did it.'

'Exactly. These things just happen to people when they're least expecting it.'

'Hm,' he replied, and Lorna decided to take that as a sign of agreement.

'In any case, by tomorrow people will be lining litter trays with my precious photo, and my mum will be the only one who bothers to keep a copy.'

When she headed off to the midwives' station he followed her, in search of a set of case-notes. 'Have you got Violet Hanson here? Skinny woman, no front teeth?'

'On the desk. The pharmacist's just been round checking the drug charts.'

'Thanks. I guess I'd better go and examine her.'

Eager to maintain harmony, Lorna proffered a hand. 'Truce?'

After a moment's hesitation, his fingers curled around hers. The clasp felt warm, strong and surprisingly companionable, and she probably let her hand linger in his just a fraction longer than absolutely necessary.

'All right then,' he said, with a flash of a smile that reminded her of the sun breaking out from behind leaden grey clouds. 'But only if you'll do something for me.'

She folded her arms and waited for the impossible demand. 'Go on, what is it – you want me to start walking to work, so my offensive little car never blocks your parking space ever again?'

'Actually no,' he replied. 'I just want you to be my Valentine. Will you come out for dinner with me tonight?'

'Mummy!' squealed Leo, racing down the front path to meet Lorna and encircling her legs with his plump little arms. 'Mummy's home!'

She gave him a big kiss and cuddle, hoisted him up and swung him round until he was giggling helplessly. 'Hello sweetie, did you do anything exciting today?'

'Yes Mummy,' he replied with breathless enthusiasm. 'Grandad set fire to the kitchen.'

'What!' In white-faced panic, Lorna scanned the outside of the house for signs of charring.

'And there were two fire engines and firemen with yellow trousers just like Fireman Sam, and one of them was a lady!' gabbled Leo, as if nearly burning the house down was the best thing imaginable. For a five-year-old boy, it probably was.

Before Lorna had a chance to quiz Leo further, Meg appeared in the front doorway, with a happily babbling Hope in her arms. One look at Lorna's face revealed that her grandson had been telling tales.

'Mum, Leo says—'

'It's all right dear, don't worry,' Meg said, hastily drawing Lorna inside the house. 'Your dad did have a slight mishap with the kitchen grill, but everything's absolutely fine now.'

'What sort of "mishap"?' demanded Lorna, making a beeline for the kitchen with visions of water cascading down the blackened walls like a deleted scene from *Titanic*.

Her mother put on a spurt and managed to overtake her at the last minute, neatly blocking the kitchen door. 'Now, don't get overwrought dear, you know it gives you headaches. Dad just forgot about some bacon he'd left grilling . . . you know he gets a little absent-minded sometimes.'

'He forgot? Oh Mum, I'm always reminding him not to leave things unattended!'

'So of course the smoke alarm went off, and you know how safety-conscious Sheila next door is with her Neighbourhood Watch. The next thing we knew, we had the fire brigade on the doorstep and nothing at all for them to do. That mini fire extinguisher you bought was a real godsend, by the way.'

'Mum, let me through,' ordered Lorna sternly, and at last Meg stepped meekly aside.

By this point, Lorna had convinced herself that nothing short of a

119

brand-new kitchen would put things right; so she was extremely relieved to find nothing more than a patch of singed tiling above the cooker, and a black mark on the ceiling. But the children must both have been in the house when it happened, and her stomach turned over as her imagination went into overdrive. A thousand ghastly what-ifs crowded into her mind, sending cold shivers down her spine, and she swung round to have the whole thing out with her mother.

Her father was standing next to Meg and Hope, his eyes downcast and his hands thrust in the pockets of his saggy cords, looking for all the world like a sad, grey version of Charlie Chaplin.

'You don't have to say it, love,' he cut in before Lorna had a chance to give him a piece of her mind. 'I know I was stupid and something terrible could have happened to the children.'

Lorna felt a prickle of tears behind her eyelids. 'Dad ... Dad, what if—'

'I know love, I know.' He wrapped his arms around her and, perhaps for the first time, she felt the diminished strength of his embrace. He wasn't young, dynamic Dad any more; slowly and silently, when she wasn't looking, he had taken several long strides towards old age. 'But it won't ever happen again, I promise. And your mother will make sure it doesn't, won't you Meg?'

'I certainly will,' said Meg firmly. 'And Lorna, you're not to worry about the mess in here either. Your father and I will clean it up tomorrow and you'd never know anything had happened.'

'I could always ask Chris,' began Lorna.

Meg shook her head firmly. 'No you won't, dear, there's no need. Besides, you expect far too much from that boy. Anybody'd think he had no life of his own; no wonder he's not married yet. Now George, put on the kettle and we'll have a nice calming cup of tea.'

George had moved only fractionally in the direction of the plug socket when Meg laid a hand on his arm.

'Second thoughts dear, I'll do it myself.'

Carmen arrived just as Lorna was clearing away after the children's tea, and simultaneously plucking up the courage to tell her mother exactly why she wouldn't be in for supper – even if it was a particularly succulent home-made chicken and asparagus pie.

'Hello Carmen dear,' said Meg, opening the front door to her with some trepidation. 'It's not another crisis is it? Only I think Lorna's been having one her difficult days.'

'I promise I won't keep her long, Mrs S,' said Carmen. 'And I really think this is something she'd want to know.'

120

Leo was on his hands and knees under the kitchen table when Carmen entered the room, helping his mum pick up the myriad stray bits of fish finger and carrot that always ended up strewn across the floor whenever Hope ate anything. Or at least, whenever Lorna fed her. There never seemed to be half as much mess when her mother did one of her family Sunday lunches. Then again, Mum didn't hold with all that modern nonsense about letting babies explore food with their fingers. If she'd had her way, no baby would emerge from the womb before it had mastered the use of a knife and fork.

'Hello, anybody in here?' enquired Carmen. Two heads appeared from under the table.

'Hello, Auntie Carmen,' chirped Leo. 'I've found a pea.' He exhibited it for inspection as though it were a missing fragment of the Crown Jewels.

'Good for you,' said Carmen.

'It's Carmen, dear,' announced Lorna's mother, rather superfluously.

Lorna backed out from under the table with extreme care, anxious not to bang her head again on the underside. She had so many bumps on her head these days that it was starting to resemble the cobbled street in an old Hovis ad.

'Hi Carmen – everything OK?'

'That's what I asked,' said Meg. 'Only she hasn't actually said yet.' She hung around for a minute, waiting for somebody to say something, then succumbed to the weight of Lorna's meaningful stares. 'Oh well, I suppose I'll make myself scarce then.' She held out a hand and clicked her fingers, and Leo trotted to her side like a pet spaniel. 'Come along Leo, let's see what Grandad and Hope are up to.'

Lorna allowed sufficient time for her mother to get out of earshot before asking, 'Well?'

'Well what?'

'Have you already . . . you know?'

Carmen pulled out a chair, sat down, sprang up again and deftly removed the remains of something sticky. 'No,' she said, 'I haven't. Have you got a damp J-Cloth? I think I just sat in some banana custard.'

Lorna hastily dampened a sponge. 'Sorry, I thought I'd found the last of it. I'm afraid Hope's reached that stage where meals are all about how many times Mummy will pick the spoon up if she throws it on the floor.' She rubbed away at the seat of her friend's jeans. 'So you're sticking with the original appointment at the clinic then? I'm still happy to come along if you want me to.'

Carmen shook her head, then eased the damp denim away from her knickers, and went to lean her bum against the kitchen radiator to dry it off. She took a deep breath. 'Actually, I've decided not to go through with it, and I wanted you to know.'

Lorna blinked. 'But I thought you couldn't afford to have another little one.'

'I can't.'

'So how are you going to manage?'

'God knows. I certainly don't. But when I saw you delivering that woman's baby on the bus ... hell Lorna, you know what it feels like, watching something coming into the world. Kittens, puppies, little fluffy chicks ... I guess I'm just a sucker for all that stuff. I thought about it over and over again, and the bottom line is, I just can't go through with the termination.'

They stood close together by the wall, bottoms comfortably resting on the hot radiator. 'You know, we used to do this when I was at school,' reflected Lorna.

'What?'

'Warm our backsides on the radiator. Those prefab classrooms were bloody freezing.' She chuckled. 'Our History teacher used to tell us we'd get piles.'

'And did you?'

'Yes.'

'Oh great.' Carmen moved her bottom half an inch away, thought about it and then sat down again. 'Sod it. Piles are the least of my worries.'

'You've really made up your mind then?'

'Yup. Fool that I am.' Carmen patted her stomach. 'Number five here I come.'

'You know I'll help you any way I can, don't you?'

Carmen laughed. 'Too right you bloody will. I'm counting on you delivering it, just for starters.' She mused for a moment. 'I hope whatever it is, it turns out to be less trouble than its elder brother,' she sighed.

Lorna's heart sank. 'Robbie? He's not been fighting again?'

'Nope. Truanting this time. I just don't know what to do with him, Lor. I mean, he won't even talk to me about it. He hardly says a word to me any more.'

'He will,' Lorna promised her. 'When he's ready.'

'Well I just hope it's before he gets himself arrested,' said Carmen soberly. She glanced at Lorna and changed the subject. 'Any good news to cheer me up? Any more hot dates?'

Lorna turned red. 'Well ... um ...'

Carmen clapped her hands. 'You have! That's great! I want to know all the details. Who is it?'

'It's Eoin Sullivan, actually.'

Carmen's face froze in an expression of utter disbelief. 'Him? The snooty doctor who gives you all that grief? You're having me on!'

'No, I'm not.'

'Then you've gone mad.'

'Probably,' admitted Lorna. 'But it's a bit late to back out now. He's taking me out for dinner tonight.'

Meg closed the door behind Carmen's retreating back.

'Honestly dear, all that hush-hush nonsense. I don't know why she didn't just come straight out and tell me she was expecting again.'

Lorna wagged a finger in her mother's face. 'Mum! You've been listening at keyholes!'

Meg looked indignant. 'I most certainly have not!' she sniffed. 'I didn't need to. It's patently obvious she's pregnant; you can tell that just from the size of her bottom.'

'You can? It looks exactly the same to me.'

'Darling, a mother knows these things. When you were first pregnant with Leo and you wore those grey trousers, from the back you looked exactly like an elephant.'

You can always rely on your mum to give it to you straight, thought Lorna. And it was high time she reciprocated.

'I'm going out tonight,' she announced before she lost her nerve.

'I rather figured that out, dear,' replied Meg with the faintest touch of sarcasm, 'seeing as you said you wouldn't be in. Going anywhere nice?'

'The Black Tulip, I think.'

This scored a direct hit. Meg's eyebrows rose in twin arcs of surprise. 'The Black Tulip – on Valentine's Day? How on earth did you get a table?'

'I didn't. I'm going with somebody. A man. A doctor actually,' she added in the hope that it might take the edge off her mother's determined opposition to dates in any shape and form. Seeing her mouth open to say something, Lorna kept rabbiting on. 'He happened to have a couple of tickets for their Valentine's dinner ... you know. I expect somebody let him down at the last minute.' She ran out of steam. 'Or something.'

Meg's mouth twitched ever so slightly in amusement. It's no good, thought Lorna. I can't lie to her; she's a walking polygraph. 'And you just sort of happened to be free?'

'Yes. Something like that. Anyway, who's going to say no to a five-course dinner at the Black Tulip, with live cabaret?'

She had hopes that the matter might end there, but before she'd managed to skip out of the room, Meg had launched into the usual list of questions. 'So who is this doctor, exactly?'

'Oh you know, just someone from work.'

'Not that awful spotty man you got to examine your father's ears?'

Lorna counted silently to ten. 'No! That was just somebody Debs happened to know in ENT. This is somebody from Obstetrics and Gynae.'

'He is single, isn't he?'

'Mum!'

'You can't be too careful. Goodness knows, it's a lesson your friend Carmen would do well to learn.'

Lorna didn't admit that she'd never got as far as enquiring about Eoin Sullivan's marital status. 'Well he is, OK?'

'And does this paragon of manhood have a name?'

'Yes thank you,' replied Lorna with a grin. 'Now if you don't mind Mum, I really must go and give Hope her bath and read the kids a story before I get ready.'

The Black Tulip might not have the most Michelin stars, but it was certainly one of Cheltenham's most exclusive – and most unusual – restaurants.

Originally a cinema, its Art Deco architecture had been so perfectly preserved that as you walked in through the swing doors at the front, you'd swear you were being transported into a première of Greta Garbo's latest romantic epic. Lorna didn't feel remotely glamorous enough, in her simple black wrap dress and the pink pashmina a friend had bought her in Goa for the equivalent of fifty pence.

I'm still not quite sure why I'm doing this, she thought to herself. It's not as if I can be that bothered about the man, is it? I mean, I'm not even wearing my best knickers.

'Do you have a booking, madam?' asked the maître d' at the front desk.

'Yes . . . I mean no, not personally. I'm meeting somebody here. A Mr Sullivan. Has he arrived yet?'

'Ah yes, that would be the gentleman at table six. If you'd just follow me.'

Lorna was half expecting the whole Valentine's date thing would turn out to be some kind of bad-taste joke, expressly devised to bring her down a peg or two. So it was quite a shock to see Eoin actually sitting there at a table, with a menu and a glass of wine in front of him. Red and pink heart-shaped balloons were tethered to an aspidistra behind him. From where Lorna was standing, it looked as if they were growing out of his head. The image was so silly that all at once she wasn't nervous any more.

'Hi Eoin.'

'Wow. You came.' Was that a flicker of apprehension in those steady blue eyes? Surely not. Jitters were a foreign concept to the Cotswold General's king of cool.

Lorna handed her wrap to the waiter and he glided discreetly away. 'Did you think I wouldn't?'

'Do you want the honest answer? Yes, I did. We've been putting the boot into each other for so long, I had a feeling you were going to stand me up just to teach me a lesson.'

She decided not to admit that she'd been thinking precisely the same thing about him. '*You've* been putting the boot in,' she corrected him. 'I've just been defending myself.'

'Would you like to punch me now, or would you prefer to wait until after dessert?'

'Good question.'

They sat and eyed each other for what seemed like ages, then Lorna decided that an evening of black looks and sarcastic comments wasn't likely to be much fun, even if the food was free. 'Tell you what, I'll say sorry if you do.'

'Ah, but are you sorry?'

'No,' admitted Lorna, 'but hey, it's the thought that counts.'

He looked at her as though he was going to say something really cutting; and then, without warning, burst out laughing. 'That's what I love about you, Lorna. You're the only person on that ward who's not afraid to say what she really thinks. As a matter of fact,' he confided, 'I was quite surprised when you agreed to come out with me. I was half expecting you'd tell me to shove it.'

Lorna leaned forward with a smile. 'As a matter of fact, so was I.'

'You're slipping then.'

'Yeah, must be.' She picked up the menu and flipped it open.

He raised an eyebrow. 'Planning on staying a while?'

'Well, if I'm going to punch you later, I might as well do it on a full stomach.'

Oh my God, thought Lorna as she started on the heart-shaped crème brulée. I'm flirting and I'm laughing at his terrible jokes, and I'm not even drunk!

The evening so far had been a revelation. Not in terms of the food or the schmaltzy entertainment, but because of the company. Lorna had been dreading a puffed-up monologue on the theme of Dr Eoin Sullivan, so it came as a complete shock when he started asking questions about her, and actually seemed interested in the answers. It was as if Eoin's place had been usurped by some bloke who looked just like him, but who was different in every other way.

'It must be hard, being alone again,' he remarked. 'Especially with young kids.'

125

'I'm not strictly alone,' she reminded him. 'I have my mum and dad living with me now. They help a lot with the children.'

Eoin couldn't conceal a grimace. 'Still, that can't exactly be easy,' he reasoned. 'God, it must be just like being fourteen again. Don't they cramp your style?'

'No, not really,' she said. Then she saw the cynical look on his face and admitted, 'Well, maybe just a bit. They . . . er . . . don't really approve of my being here tonight.'

'Really?' He chuckled. 'I'd no idea my reputation had stretched that far.'

Lorna burst his bubble. 'It's nothing personal,' she assured him. 'They just don't think I should be dating again so soon after Ed.'

'But it must be getting on for two years now. That's a long time to go without companionship.'

'That's what I told them. But sometimes I think to myself, maybe they've got a point. Sometimes I do feel guilty.'

Eoin took a large swig from his wine glass. 'That's perfectly understandable. But if you let yourself be ruled by the guilt, you'll get to the end of your life never having done anything.'

You intrigue me, Eoin Sullivan, thought Lorna as they finished their desserts. After all this time, and all your showing off, you're still a mystery to me.

'What about you?' she said, pushing away her empty plate. 'You haven't told me anything about yourself.'

He sat back in his chair, peeled off his napkin and tossed it onto the tablecloth. 'Thirty-four, divorced, a kid I never see because my ex won't let me, and a whole lot of unresolved issues. Next question please.'

'I didn't mean to pry,' said Lorna, taken aback by the cool, almost cold way he'd reeled off the facts.

'Course you did. Same way I wanted to pry into your life. What's the point of knowing anybody if you don't really *know* them? Let's just say I can be a bit of a complicated bugger, but I do find jumping off mountains helps me straighten out my head.'

Lorna fiddled with the stem of her wine glass. 'Ed was into extreme sports,' she said quietly.

'Oh. I'll keep quiet about it if you'd prefer—'

'No. I'd rather you told me about it. It's not like I was ever into that stuff myself, but I miss hearing about it. If anybody I know goes skydiving or bungee-jumping or something, they seem to think it's taboo to tell me about it now. As if remembering Ed was inevitably a bad thing.'

'Remembering isn't bad,' said Eoin, his eyes meeting hers. 'But it does hurt sometimes.'

126

The waiter chose that moment to appear from nowhere. 'Would sir and madam like coffee now?'

'Coffee?' Eoin asked Lorna. 'Or are you in a tearing hurry to get away from me and tell everybody how weird I am?'

She laughed. 'Coffee would be nice. But I do need to be home soon because Mum and Dad don't like staying up too late, and sometimes Hope wakes up in the night and wants her mummy.'

He chuckled. 'Like I said, just like being fourteen again. Except for the kids. OK then,' he capitulated. 'Make it a large coffee, and then I'll make sure you get home safely before your mum turns you into a pumpkin.'

Lorna felt torn. She wanted to get back home and check that everything was OK, but she also wanted to stay here and laugh at some more of Eoin's jokes. You couldn't be fourteen all the time.

'I meant to ask you,' she said, 'about these Valentine's Day tickets of yours. I take it somebody let you down at the last minute? Go on, tell me how many other women turned you down before you asked me.'

'Four hundred and seventy-three.'

'I'm serious!'

'All right then, if you're serious: none. Because nobody let me down. The other ticket was always meant for you.'

'Oh come on!'

He then did something Lorna had never seen him do before. In fact she would never have believed he was capable of it. He blushed. 'It's true. I bought the damn things two months ago, but it took me until this morning to get the balls to ask you out. Pathetic, or what?'

Lorna wasn't quite sure what to think at that moment. But if she'd been asked to describe Eoin Sullivan in one word, the word would definitely not have been 'pathetic'.

Chapter 16

Time had passed swiftly in the couple of months since Lorna had started work on Crocus ward. Because the next day was Debs's last day on the ward before her maternity leave, she didn't have a lot of leisure time to think about Eoin, or the very gentlemanly way he had seen her home and said a chaste goodnight, without so much as a hint of coming up for coffee.

Perhaps that was just as well. If he had propositioned her she wouldn't have known how to respond. She certainly wasn't looking for a repetition of the Pete episode. And perhaps if she thought about last night too much, that awful uneasy feeling of betrayal would come back; either that, or the new improved Eoin Sullivan would simply vanish in a puff of ether-scented smoke.

Then there was the announcement from Colin that she was being transferred to the labour ward the following week. It was what she'd been waiting for – the whole point of being a midwife – but that didn't make it any less scary. New ward, new demands, a new mentor ... part of her wanted to say 'no thank you' and vegetate forever on Crocus ward, even if she did have to put up with Rose Finnegan day in, day out.

'It's going to feel so strange,' said Debs, tears welling up in her eyes as she clutched the little pair of fluffy pink bootees Honey had bought for her.

'The poor child certainly will if it's not a girl,' commented Rose Finnegan, who for once was in quite a mellow mood, perhaps because of the large bottle of Bailey's Irish Cream that had been doing the rounds in the staff changing room. 'Pink bootees on a boy? Dear God, it'll be scarred for life.'

'Or gay,' ventured one of the new mothers cheerfully.

'Hey, there's nothing gay about my Jeff!' protested the woman in the next bed. 'He wears pink shirts, and this is our fourth baby.'

'It won't be a boy anyway,' Honey assured Debs. 'I've had a good feel of your bump, and according to what my granny says about the shape and how low it's hanging, it's definitely going to be a girl.'

'Don't tell me that!' giggled Debs, 'I don't want to know. It's supposed to be a surprise.'

Honey gave the bump a sympathetic pat. 'Sorry mate, but Granny's never wrong. Better start stocking up on Lil' Bratz and My Little Pony.'

'You all right Lorna?' enquired Debs as she unwrapped the rest of her presents. 'You're very quiet today.'

Lorna was startled out of her daydream. 'What? Why?'

'I said, you're awfully quiet.'

'Oh, sorry. Had a bit of a late night last night, you know how it is.'

Everybody went 'Ooooh!' in a knowing way except Rose, who was too busy lecturing a patient about her 'sacred maternal duty' to breastfeed.

'Was he tall, dark and handsome, love?' asked the woman whose husband wore pink shirts.

The woman in the next bed gave a dirty laugh. 'Give me short and bald as long as he's rich. I'll put a bag over his head.'

'Don't be silly,' laughed Honey. 'I bet you a fiver Lorna wasn't out with a man at all last night. She was most probably up all night with the kids again, mopping up sick. Go on Lorna, I'm right aren't I?'

Agreement struck Lorna as the easiest way of avoiding a lot of embarrassing questions. 'Oh dear, is it really that obvious?' she asked with a smile.

''Fraid so love, those dark circles are a dead giveaway. That's a fiver you owe me, Mrs Denton,' Honey added smugly.

'Ah well, years of self-sacrifice and chronic insomnia . . . that's motherhood for you,' said Debs, patting her bump affectionately as though this was her sixth baby instead of her first. 'One minute you're swearing nothing's going to change; the next, it's taken over your life and things can never be the same again.'

'Oh God now she tells us!' quipped a woman with twin boys. 'I could've done with knowing that last May, before I let Jason convince me that pregnant women were sexy.'

Debs looked impressed. 'Your bloke fancies pregnant women?'

The mother of twins snorted. 'He thought he did – until he saw me nude in a G-string. Killed his libido stone dead, it did. Poor lad's taken to spending most of his time in the loft, making Airfix planes.'

Lorna's mind drifted back to her first pregnancy; to the way she and Ed had discovered the experience together, like two clueless kids who'd stumbled on an enchanted forest. With hindsight, it was true that their sex life had dwindled when she was whale-sized and knackered; but she still remembered the loving cuddles and the nights curled up with Ed, his ear

130

to her belly, listening for the heartbeat. She'd never felt so close to any-body in her whole life; and probably she never would again.

'Well, well, what have we here?' boomed a familiar voice. 'The Mothers' Union Knitting Circle in full session?' Eoin Sullivan strode onto the ward, white coat flaring out behind him and making him look like a bleached vampire. He picked up a shapeless crocheted woolly hat between thumb and forefinger. 'I sincerely hope this wasn't made to fit your baby's head,' he remarked. 'Unless of course it's the offspring of the Elephant Man.'

Debs and Honey giggled, and Honey told Dr Sullivan he was a caution. Rose – the creator of the offending hat – merely glared. Lorna felt her cheeks burn as Eoin looked in her direction, and tried to avoid his gaze.

'Right, I've got work to do,' he announced. 'Is there anybody here who isn't either drunk or skiving?' Lorna felt his eyes fix on her. 'Oh well Lorna, you'll have to do. Rose is half-cut and Deborah looks like she's about to drop her litter any minute. Come along, don't dawdle; we've got a ward round to do.'

It wasn't until they were out of earshot of the others that he threw her a wink and said: 'Everything OK when you got back last night?'

'Yes, fine.'

'Fancy doing it again?' She opened her mouth. 'And please bear in mind that you're not allowed to say no, because I've just gone out and bought the tickets.'

'Isn't it wonderful?' enthused Meg that evening, as the family stood round gaping at the enormous pallet of tins in the front hall. 'A whole year's supply, and I won it!'

'Mum,' said Lorna gently, 'it's a whole year's supply of dog food.'

Leo, never one to let an opportunity pass him by, immediately piped up: 'Can we get a dog, Mummy, can we?'

Lorna placed a restraining hand on his wildly bobbing head. 'One day maybe, but not now.'

'But Mummy, we've got all the food for it and it can sleep in bed with me and I'll take it for walks and everything!'

She smiled to herself, remembering the identical conversations she'd had with her own parents twenty years earlier. She'd been through every-thing in the zoological dictionary, from aardvarks to zebu, and in time had managed to wear her mother down into accepting two gerbils and a stick insect. But she knew no invertebrate or tiny mammal could match up to something big and furry that listened to all your woes, loved you no mat-ter what you said or did, and ensured that you were never lonely, even when your best friend wasn't talking to you.

131

'Perhaps,' she said. 'But not now. Whatever would Clawdius think?'

Leo considered this. 'Mummy.'

'Yes?'

'Can we get a kitten?'

Lorna swiftly steered the conversation away from animals before her nerve went and they ended up acquiring a menagerie. 'Mum, what did you think you were doing, entering a competition to win dog food?'

'Mm?' Her mother left off counting the tins and turned to look at her daughter. 'Oh, I didn't, dear. The dog food was only the third prize. I was trying to win the holiday home in Corfu or the VIP trip for four to the Monaco Grand Prix.'

Lorna scratched her head. 'But Mum, Dad comes out in prickly heat whenever you go abroad and you both hate motor racing. Why would you want either of those?'

Her mother sighed at this display of utter obtuseness. 'We might not but somebody else would, wouldn't they? Just think how much those prizes would sell for on the Internet.'

'Ah,' said Lorna, finally getting the point. 'So this is another of your money-making schemes?'

'Of course it is, dear. We're being very scientific about it, aren't we George? Your father is applying for every job that doesn't stipulate "young and dynamic", and I'm entering every competition I can get my hands on. That's why we've been eating so many baked beans lately, you see. If I can collect another thirty labels, I'll automatically qualify for at least a runners-up prize.'

'And what's that?'

'Vouchers for money off more baked beans.'

Lorna was about to suggest, tactfully, that man could not live by baked beans alone when Clawdius ambled into the room, mewed piteously at Lorna and threw up all over her shoes.

'Oh,' said Meg, her voice filled with disappointment.

'Looks like the dog food experiment wasn't a complete success, love,' commiserated George.

Lorna was more horrified on Clawdius's behalf than she was about her ruined trainers. 'You've been feeding him dog food? Oh Mum, how could you? You could have poisoned him.'

'Ah well, never mind,' said Meg. 'Thank goodness for eBay. It just seems such a waste . . .'

The following day, a Saturday, Lorna was on an early shift; but Hope was already wide awake long before her mother was washed and dressed.

'What's wrong, precious?' Lorna whispered, lifting her little daughter out of her cot and cuddling her. It was so unlike Hope not to sleep right through. She was quite different from Leo, who'd spent his first two years lustily waking the neighbourhood at two-hourly intervals, and still had a tendency to be a restless sleeper.

Hope just grizzled and buried her face in her mother's dressing gown.

'Aren't you well, sweetheart?' She felt her forehead. It was a little warm, but nothing out of the ordinary. 'Come on now, Mummy kiss it better.'

Hope whined piteously and then she gave a great big, humungous sneeze that sprayed dreadful goo all over Lorna's front. It wasn't the best start to a working day.

If she hadn't been able to rely on her mum and dad to take care of Hope, she'd have been tempted to call work and say she wasn't coming in. But they were terribly short-staffed on Crocus ward now that Debs had gone off on maternity leave.

Hope might be coming down with the snuffles, but Leo was full of the joys of imminent spring. 'Saturday, Saturday!' he yelled, bouncing up and down on his bed so hard that the floorboards protested.

'Hey, steady on, or you'll break the mattress.'

'But Mummy, it's Saturday! I can stay at home all day and watch the telly with Grandad!'

Not all day I hope, thought Lorna. 'Grandma and Grandad will take you out for a nice walk, I expect,' she prompted him. 'You can go and see if there are any newts in that pond I showed you.'

Leo had to concede that this might be interesting. 'But it's *Captain Crucial* today, Mummy. It's always *Captain Crucial* on Saturday if Mummy's at work.'

A small alarm bell rang in Lorna's head. *Captain Crucial*? Surely not the same *Captain Crucial* whose intergalactic exploits were so graphically violent that she'd explicitly banned Leo from watching them?

She sat down on the edge of Leo's bed. 'Grandad lets you watch *Captain Crucial*?'

'Only when you're at work, Mummy. He says it's all right and you won't mind.'

'Oh, he does, does he?'

As usual, George and Meg were up before dawn. Lorna found them in the kitchen, amid a tantalising aroma of sizzling bacon and mushrooms.

'Sit down, love,' said George, beaming. 'Your mother's making you a proper breakfast.'

Instead of sitting down, she rounded on him. 'Dad, have you been letting Leo watch those cartoons I told you and Mum he wasn't to watch?'

He rubbed his chin. 'What? Oh, you mean Captain thingy? Yes, good

133

harmless rubbish. Cowboys and Indians in space. Don't know why you were fussing about it.'

Meg interjected. 'Yes dear. It's not very well made, I grant you, and the plots are rather rudimentary, but it does keep him quiet for hours while I'm cleaning the bathroom.'

'Mum!' Lorna exploded in exasperation. 'What's the priority here, cleaning the bathroom or not bringing up Leo to be a psychopath who thinks killing is fun?'

Meg and George exchanged pitying looks. 'Don't be silly dear,' said Meg. 'You used to watch all sorts when you were a little girl. When you were five, your auntie Jean let you stay up and watch *Dracula Has Risen from the Grave*, and you haven't grown up to be a serial killer, have you?'

'That's not the point, Mum! I specifically asked you not to let Leo watch that programme, and now he tells me he's been watching it every Saturday when I'm not here. How do you think that makes me feel?'

'Love,' said George gently, 'you don't think this full-time job of yours is getting a bit much, do you? Only it seems to be making you awfully tense.'

Clawdius sat huddled under the radiator in the bathroom as Lorna got dressed. She looked at him and wondered ... was it just her, or was he a bit thinner than the last time she'd taken a good look at him? Maybe it was just the fact that Meg had groomed him the other day and he was still mourning the loss of half his fur, or just that she'd been feeding him dog food, but Clawdius certainly didn't look very happy.

'You and me both mate,' she said aloud, reaching down and scratching the back of his neck. He gave a soft 'Mrrrrrowrrr', closed his eyes and started purring. Oh well, can't be much wrong with you then, thought Lorna. 'Now listen, you.'

The cat cocked an ear.

'I want you to keep a close eye on Grandma and Grandad today, because between you and me, I'm not sure they're taking this childcare thing as seriously as they ought to be. What do you reckon?'

Clawdius opened one eye and said, 'Eeeow.'

'Well exactly. I mean, I know they managed to bring up Sarah, David and me without any of us ending up in jail, but things have changed a bit since their day. So if you don't mind, I'd like a full report when I get home, and you have my permission to sit right in front of the TV screen if there's the slightest hint of *Captain Crucial*.'

Despite Leo's protests, *Captain Crucial* was duly consigned to the interstellar wastes, and replaced by regular doses of *The Animals of Farthing*

Wood ... though Lorna wasn't quite so enthusiastic about it when she found out that half the animals got eaten or shot on their cartoon pilgrimage to White Deer Park. Leo, on the other hand, was delighted. Apart from dinosaurs and bottom jokes, there was nothing he liked better than gore.

Meanwhile, Lorna was learning to cope with two new ingredients in her life: Eoin Sullivan and the labour ward. She wasn't sure which took more getting used to: delivering babies or being somebody's girlfriend for the first time in fifteen years. It certainly wasn't easy going out on dates, when she'd only had one boyfriend in her whole life before, and that boyfriend had been Ed. And now she had to adapt to being with Eoin.

But she couldn't say she was unhappy about what was happening to her. On the contrary, the adrenalin surging through her veins made her feel more alive than she had felt since Ed ... well, for a very long time.

One evening, the inevitable happened: Eoin showed up at the house to take Lorna out, and Meg got to the door first.

She took him in with one calculating sweep of her brown eyes. 'Good evening young man, you must be Eoin. A strange way to spell a name, but I'm sure your parents had their reasons.'

He laughed. 'They're Irish.'

'Well there you are then. Now you must come in and say hello to Lorna's father. You're a very bad girl Lorna, not bringing him to meet us before now.'

Lorna bit her lip and refrained from reminding her parents that they had practically threatened to disinherit her if she so much as thought about dating another man. Meekly she trailed her mother into the kitchen, trying not to laugh as Eoin turned and pulled a face at her.

'George, this is Eoin. He's a doctor.' Meg spoke the word as though it had some quasi-religious significance. Oh I get it, thought Lorna. I can't date any nobodies like Pete or that porter from the hospital, but bring a doctor home and they might just be willing to stretch a point.

'I'm quite a junior one really,' Eoin assured her, turning on the charm that came so readily when he wanted it to. 'Just a cog in the wheel, you know.'

'He's a senior house officer, in line for promotion to registrar,' said Lorna, 'and don't let him tell you he's not very clever. He can do *The Times* crossword in four and a half minutes. Disgusting, isn't it?'

Meg gaped in utter admiration. Her limit was the short one in the *Daily Mail*, and then only if George helped. George himself seemed to be hedging his bets about the new arrival.

'So, you're on Lorna's ward are you?'

'I cover all the maternity wards in rotation, yes.'

135

'And what do you do with yourself when you're not . . . doctoring?'

'I'm a big fan of the great outdoors, aren't I, Lorna?'

She took her cue. 'Yes, and he's into all the dangerous stuff too: white-water rafting, caving, cliff-diving'

'Oh really?' said George, looking at Lorna. She knew what he was thinking: that Ed had been into all those things too. And that whatever else he might be, Eoin Sullivan certainly wasn't Ed.

Irritated, she determined not to let her father's wariness put her off. Couldn't he appreciate how difficult this was for her? Couldn't he just loosen up, and be pleased that she'd begun to find her feet again? Did he have to play the heavy-handed father, just when she so wanted things to be all right?

'Eoin's promised to take me to Selsley Common next weekend,' she enthused, 'to watch him hang-glide.'

Eoin nudged her with his elbow in a matey sort of way. 'Who knows, we might even get you up there too, eh? Riding the thermals, looking down at the world – there's nothing like it.'

George's face emptied of colour. He cut in abruptly: 'I'm afraid Lorna really doesn't care for that sort of thing, do you Lorna?'

'Well . . . maybe I didn't used to be that keen, but—'

'You can't stand heights, Lorna, you know you don't.' His voice was positively stern.

'That's very true,' chimed in her mother. 'When you were little, you screamed and screamed if we tried to make you go down the big slide. Once, you got so het up, we had to take you home and change your knickers.'

'Mum!'

Lorna groaned inwardly. Please, no, not the embarrassing baby stories. She stole a sidelong look at Eoin. He looked as if he was about to burst out laughing or – worse – say something really sarcastic. But to his eternal credit, he managed to confine himself to a rather strangled, 'You don't say? That's really . . . fascinating.'

'I'm just going up to get my coat,' said Lorna, desperate to bring this torment to an end before the conversation turned to infant bowel movements or worse. 'Eoin can tell you all about his vintage motorbikes.'

'Gee, thanks,' Eoin mouthed behind her mother's back as she headed for the stairs.

Lorna's escape was all too brief. Hard on her heels was her perspiring father. 'Lorna!'

Teeth clenched, she stopped halfway up the stairs and turned round. 'Yes, Dad?'

'You are absolutely not going up in a hang-glider. Do I make myself clear?'

136

All this did was stir up Lorna's blood. 'What's it got to do with you? I'll go hang-gliding if I want!'

'You can't!'

'Why not?'

'Because it's dangerous, and . . . and because you're a mother!'

Lorna looked at her father's face and wanted to laugh, but couldn't. He looked so deadly serious, as if she'd just hinted that she was thinking of taking up wing-walking for a living. 'Dad – Dad, what is this all about?' She came down a few steps so that they were eye to eye. 'All I said was, I might just possibly think about it! And I most probably won't anyway, and what's being a mother got to do with it?'

George took his daughter's hand in his. 'You've got two little ones upstairs,' he said, with a tremble in his voice. 'They've lost their daddy and I don't want to have to tell them they've lost their mummy too.'

'Oh Dad – you big soppy, sentimental . . .' Lorna felt a prickle beneath her eyelids. 'I wouldn't do anything that would risk hurting the children, you know that!'

'Good. Because I don't want to lose you either.' He gave her a hug. 'You may think you're all grown up, but you're still my little girl. And I'm going to be watching that flash young doctor of yours very closely, I hope you realise that. 'Cause if he does anything to hurt you—'

She nestled into her dad's arms, the way she'd done when she was six. 'He won't, Daddy,' she promised. 'I won't let him.'

Chapter 17

The next time Lorna saw Carmen was in the coffee bar by the entrance to the maternity wing.

Carmen was in stoic mood. 'First hospital check-up already! I dunno, I couldn't believe it when they told me I was already three months gone. I just thought I'd had one too many takeaways.'

'You'll have to get one of those T-shirts that says "I'm not fat, I'm pregnant",' suggested Lorna.

Carmen considered the idea as she bit into a tuna sandwich. 'I'd have to modify it a bit, so it said, "I am fat, but I'm pregnant too."' She glanced down at her magnificently blossoming boobs and readjusted them so that they weren't escaping quite so flamboyantly from her bra. 'Mm, yes, I should think I could fit all the words on.'

'Well, I think you look great, being pregnant suits you,' declared Lorna. She lowered her voice to a confidential whisper. 'And believe me, it doesn't suit every woman. You should see some of the poor souls we get in the Delivery Suite. Jabba the Hut isn't in it.'

'Lorna!' Carmen clapped a hand to her mouth to stop herself spraying crumbs all over the table. 'Can you say things like that?'

'Not around the patients I can't,' admitted Lorna. 'But in any case, it's nothing compared to some of the names the women call their partners when they're in labour. It's an education, I can tell you.'

'That's a point,' said Carmen. 'Who am I going to swear at when I have Number Five?'

'Me, probably. If last time's anything to go by.'

Carmen chuckled. 'I must say, I thought it was amazingly restrained of you, not punching me.'

'Ah well, you did calm down in the end,' Lorna reminded her, nibbling off the chocolate round the edges of a Kit-Kat finger. 'Most people do when they realise who's in charge of the gas and air machine.'

139

'You sadist! I've a good mind to drop this sprog at home, with nothing but calm thoughts and an Enya CD.'

Lorna's jaw dropped. 'You're kidding!'

'Actually yes,' Carmen admitted. 'After that forceps delivery I had last time, I want all the pethidine you've got in the hospital, and you can hit me on the head with a brick as well, just in case I'm not sufficiently out of it.'

Lorna licked the crumbs of chocolate wafer from round her mouth. 'You'd better not let the doctors hear you saying that! Some of them would just love it if every woman was unconscious and incapable of arguing. Midwives included.'

Carmen shook her head uncomprehendingly. 'I don't get you sometimes, Lor. Doctors give you all this shit about how rubbish midwives are, and what do you do? You go out with one!'

'But Eoin's not like that!' protested Lorna. 'He respects me as a fellow professional.'

This met with a look of pure cynicism. 'Are you sure he doesn't just respect you as a pretty blonde with nice boobs?'

A titter ran round the adjacent tables. Lorna's voice dropped to a mortified stage whisper. 'Shut up Carmen, everyone's listening! And yes thank you, I'm quite sure.'

'Well I'm not,' replied Carmen. 'Not about the respect bit, anyway. I mean, I was watching just now when he went back up to the ward, and he patted you on the head like you were some kind of spaniel!'

'He did not!'

'Did.'

'Didn't.'

'Did to the power of infinity plus one.'

An overwhelming sense of the ridiculousness of it all descended upon Lorna. This wasn't just embarrassing, it was irritating. 'Oh, who bloody cares anyway? If it doesn't bother me, why should it bother you?'

'Because it gets up my nose seeing you being treated like that. I'm the one who's supposed to let herself get walked over by blokes all the time, remember? I'm the one with two GCSEs and no common sense. Not you. You're supposed to be common sense incarnate.'

This pressed all the wrong buttons as far as Lorna was concerned. 'You make it sound like I'm a half-wit and he's some kind of Nazi!'

'Hope you don't mind me butting in,' chimed in the twenty-something girl who was busy clearing the tables, 'only I couldn't help overhearing. You want to watch them doctors if you ask me.'

'Oh I do, do I?' snapped Lorna. 'And I suppose you're going to tell me why.'

140

Apparently taking this as an invitation, the girl promptly left off wiping the table down with a damp J-cloth, folded her arms and launched into her manifesto.

'My sister-in-law's cousin's best friend went out with a doctor,' she said earnestly, 'and it wasn't till he'd emptied her bank account and shagged her sister that they found out he was wanted by the South African vice squad. Very nicely spoken, he was. Big feet.' She squeezed out the cloth, tossed it onto her stack of trays and picked them up. 'Yes love, you want to watch out for them doctors, I'm telling you. Half of 'em's up to no good, and the other half don't know what they're doing. You want to steer clear of hospitals, like what I do.'

Carmen looked at her in puzzlement. 'But . . . you're working in one.'

'Yeah, but only in the café, where it's safe. You won't catch me in any of the bits that smell of sick people.'

With that parting shot, the girl in the blue and yellow overall headed back to the kitchen.

'Great,' said Lorna acidly. 'So according to Little Miss Cheerful, I'm either seeing a con-merchant or a man who can't tell his arse from his elbow.'

'There's always the odd exception,' Carmen pointed out. Then she added reflectively: 'Of course, Eoin Sullivan might not be it.'

The rest of that week was pretty uneventful, apart from one insane evening when all the rooms in the delivery suite were already occupied, and then three more mums in advanced labour turned up at reception. Even Lorna's new mentor, a seasoned campaigner called June Godwin, was hard-pressed to keep up. By the time Lorna finally got home, almost twelve hours later, she felt she had finally perfected the art of being in three places at once.

I've had my baptism of fire at last, she realised with a surge of blessed relief; and I didn't make a complete fool of myself. For the first time since her return to work, Lorna really felt like a proper midwife again.

The luxury of a weekend off didn't generally crop up more than once a month, so when she got home at teatime on Friday, Lorna was full of the same excitement she'd always felt after the last lesson of the week at school. Double Maths with Miss Fereira, and then: freedom! Lorna felt a great big smile spread across her face. All day Saturday to be with the kids and take them out somewhere fun; and then Sunday . . . with Eoin.

Saturday's trip to a Thomas the Tank Engine fun day passed by in the blink of an eye, leaving precious memories of Leo's soot-speckled face, and Hope gazing up in fascination at the Fat Controller's enormous padded stomach. Only one thing was missing, and that was the chance to

141

share those memories with Ed when they got home. Since his death, Lorna had always imagined him as an invisible presence at every family event, but this time she couldn't sense him by her side ... almost as if she'd driven him away with her thoughts of building a new life. It was a silly thought, but it wouldn't disappear.

'It's hard sometimes,' she told Eoin the following day, as they drove to Selsley Common, 'trying to be as good as two parents and knowing you can't possibly succeed.'

He shifted down a gear, and the 4x4 he used at weekends bounced left onto a country road that meandered between hawthorn hedges, just beginning to display their first juicy green buds in the pale March sunshine.

'Being a good parent is never easy,' he replied. 'But at least you have the chance to try.'

Well done Lorna, she told herself; you put your foot in it good and proper there. 'I'm sorry,' she said, 'I was forgetting you don't see much of your little boy. Have you heard anything from your ex lately?'

He shook his head. 'Solicitors' letters, that's all it ever amounts to. I don't even know where they're living, she's that determined to keep me away from Dominic.' His fingers were so tight on the steering wheel that his knuckles shone white through the skin. 'She's a smart one, I'll give her that. God only knows what she's punishing me for, but she couldn't have found a better way of doing it.'

It was hard to think of anything to say that wouldn't sound like palliative nonsense. As the road began to rise and the spectacular view spread out beneath her, Lorna turned her head to look out of the window. 'I can't imagine what it's like to have your child taken away,' she remarked. 'I can only hope I never find out.'

'You won't,' he assured her. 'You'd kill anybody that tried. And who could blame you if you did?'

'Kill somebody? Well, I don't know if I'd go that far.'

'Oh you would. Believe me.'

Lorna realised with a start that he wasn't joking. He'd said it with such grim sincerity that for just a moment, a chill ran right through her and she had to pull her jacket more tightly around her.

'Cold?' Eoin enquired.

'Oh you know, just a shiver.'

As the car slowed to enter the car park, he turned and looked at her. 'You don't want to take too much notice of what I say,' he said. 'It just gets to me sometimes.'

His mood changed abruptly as they got out of the car. 'Look.' He pointed up at the sky. 'See that rig up there? That used to be mine – sold it

142

my mate Roger Tate. Nice bit of kit, but not really fast enough for a serious flyer.'

Lorna squinted up, shielding her eyes against the low-slanting sun. A huge, orange and pink silk bird was moving across the bright sky, as smoothly and soundlessly as an eagle on the hunt for prey. Only this particular bird had a man dangling underneath it, and as it soared overhead she saw him wave to the watchers on the ground.

'Very impressive,' she said, her heart slightly in her mouth.

Eoin must have guessed what she was thinking, because he laughed and took her by the hand. 'Don't worry, they won't let you go up until you've had the proper training. I can have a word with somebody now and arrange it for you, if you like.'

She stared at him in horror. 'Me? Up there?'

'Why not?'

'Because I'm bloody terrified, that's why. And I've only come to watch you.'

Eoin shrugged. 'Where's the fun in anything if there's no adrenalin rush?'

Lorna heard her father's stern words in her head, positively forbidding her to get involved in anything more hazardous than competitive Tiddlywinks. There was a momentary tingle of temptation ... and then she visualised herself coming down, head-first, in a patch of thistles.

'Thanks, but no thanks. I'd rather be boring and stay alive.'

'Well ... whatever.'

She could sense that he was disappointed, yet unsurprised; and she almost ran after him and said yes, she would do it, just to prove that women could be daring and adventurous too: even midwives. Then common sense kicked in and she remembered not only that she hated heights and had no sense of direction, but that Ed had never once criticised her because she preferred to keep her feet on the ground while he got his kicks jumping off things; any more than she'd criticised him for not wanting to deliver babies or take up embroidery.

One by one, the hang-glider pilots and the paragliders had their gear checked out. Eoin of course looked superbly nonchalant as he took his run up, stepped off the edge of the hill and let the air currents lift him up above the Gloucestershire countryside.

For a moment, as the hang-glider was silhouetted against the sky, Lorna's mind flashed back to other times, other hills, and to someone who had taken her heart with her whenever he flew.

Yes, just for that brief moment, as the bright triangle passed overhead and the pilot waved to her, his face a dark oval against the bright blue of the sky, Lorna could have sworn that it was Ed.

*

143

'The children are watching *Sleeping Beauty* dear, and somebody phoned for you,' announced Meg as Lorna came through the front door. 'Sasha something. She left a number for you to call tomorrow.' She handed Lorna a scrap of paper with a Gloucester number on it. 'Any time after ten, she said.'

'Sasha? Sasha who?'

'I can't remember dear, and she did talk awfully quickly. Now hurry up and get those muddy shoes off, your lamb cobbler's going cold and Leo wants to show you his new stegosaurus. Its eyes light up, apparently.'

That night in bed, Lorna racked her brains to think who Sasha might be. The only one she could think of was Sasha Perkins, whose dad owned a string of filling stations, and who'd pulled a handful of her hair out in Year Seven because the boy she fancied said he preferred Lorna. Surely it couldn't be that Sasha? They hadn't seen each other since just after GCSEs, when Sasha had reputedly run off with a PE teacher from the boys' school next door. It's not like they'd ever liked each other much anyway.

No, that Sasha would hardly wait the best part of fourteen years to come back and ask for the thirty-seven pence Lorna still owed her. Would she? Maybe she knew some other Sashas, if she could only remember.

She drifted off to sleep and dreamed that everybody she knew was called Sasha, and that she owed all of them so much money that she had to buy a disguise and move to Kidderminster.

Lorna wasn't due on duty until lunchtime on Monday, so when she got up that morning she shoved a load of washing into the machine, made Leo some extra-special sandwiches for school, put on a CD of 'Baby Mozart', and then sat down to play with Hope and her pretend kitchen. It was much more fun than Lorna's real kitchen. The toast always popped up when it was ready, the fridge was always full of yummy things, and you never needed to clean the oven, because everything was made of wood.

Hope pulled the wooden bread out of the toaster and thrust it at her mother. 'Mmm, yum, yum, this toast is lovely,' said Lorna, pretending to eat it. 'Can I have some jam too?'

Hope answered with a giggle and her favourite word of the moment: 'No!'

'Some butter then?'

'No! No, no, no!'

Lorna was trying to extort some pretend Marmite from her giggling daughter when the phone rang in the hall. A few moments later, her mother appeared holding the cordless set. 'It's for you, dear,' she said. 'That Sasha woman. Here, let me take the little one while you're on the phone.'

144

Meg went off with Hope. 'Hi,' said Lorna. 'Lorna Price here. I was about to ring you, actually.'

'Ah, Lorna ... hi! So good to talk to you at last. My name's Sasha Temple-Marsh, from Avocado Productions. We're planning a new reality TV series for Channel Six, and we were wondering if you'd be interested in taking part in the pilot programme.'

Lorna eyed the phone with suspicion. 'Is this some kind of wind-up?'

Sasha let out a little tinkly laugh, like broken glass going down the sink only more genteel. 'Heavens no! It's just that one of our producers spotted the bit in the *Cheltenham Courant* about you delivering a baby on the bus, and thought you'd be perfect for *Rather Your Job*. I haven't seen the article myself, but I hear it's wonderful stuff.'

'What on earth is *Rather Your Job*?'

'It's a series of programmes in which people swap jobs for a day. For future programmes we've lined up a judge who changes place with a lavatory cleaner, and an absolute scream of an undertaker who's going to swap with a supermarket checkout girl.'

'Oh,' said Lorna, who liked the idea less with each second that passed. 'Well, it all sounds very interesting.'

'I knew you'd love it!'

'But I don't really think it's for me. I'm quite shy really; I'm sure I'd go to pieces on the telly.'

The tinkly laugh made Lorna wince again. 'Darling, don't be so modest. I'm sure you'll be a natural. Now why don't I just come over and see you one day this week, and tell you a bit more about the project?

'I ... er—'

'Say Thursday, around two pm? Excellent. Oh, and just one other thing. Do you have a best friend?'

'Um ... yes.'

'What does she do for a living?'

'She clamps cars. Why?'

'Oh how super! A midwife and a car clamper. What a marvellous swap that will make! You must invite her round on Thursday too. Must be going now, but if you have any questions—'

'Actually I do have one,' said Lorna. 'What school did you go to?'

There was a short silence. 'Roedean actually. Why do you ask?'

Lorna heaved a sigh of relief. 'No reason. I'll see you on Thursday then.'

Sasha Temple-Marsh was nothing like Sasha Perkins. For one thing she didn't look much in need of thirty-seven pence; in fact, she didn't look as if she'd know the meaning of any sum of money less than about five

145

thousand pounds. Which, by Carmen's calculations, was about what she'd paid for her rather gorgeous Vivienne Westwood ensemble. Obviously Avocado Productions paid better than the NHS.

Sasha was also infuriatingly wafer-thin, ice-blonde without a hint of vulgar regrowth, and utterly relentless.

'What interesting china,' she commented, smiling from behind one of Meg's best teacups. 'Very nouveau-rustic in an ironic kind of way.'

Lorna winced. She just knew that her mother would be listening behind the sitting-room door, and could well imagine the look on her face. 'Actually it's—' she began, but Sasha's juggernaut was rolling on regardless.

'Anyhow, as you'll see from the background material I've given you, all we require of you is to be yourselves. No acting necessary! And having chatted to you both, I can see you're going to be naturals! Now, if you'd just like to sign here . . . and here.'

'Hang on a minute,' cut in Carmen. 'We would get paid for this, I take it? I'm not humiliating myself on TV for fifty p and a jam sandwich, and I shouldn't think Lorna is either.'

'Yes, of course you'll be paid!' laughed Sasha, flipping through the contract to the appropriate page. 'Quite a generous fee considering it's only the pilot, I think you'll agree.'

Carmen's eyes widened. Generous it was indeed. Not huge or life-altering, but certainly enough to make you think if you were a single mother with four children and another on the way. 'Hmm. Well, it looks OK . . . but what about you, Lorna? What do you think?'

Lorna wasn't at all sure about the whole thing. At school she'd avoided anything that smacked of acting, even going so far as to save up her dinner money and bribe somebody to take her place when she was supposed to be a dancing tiger in 'Captain Noah and his Floating Zoo'. The thought of appearing on television was frankly even worse than the thought of hang-gliding, or at my rate almost as bad. On the other hand, she knew what the extra bit of money could mean for Carmen.

'What if – what if our employers won't cooperate?' asked Lorna. 'And a lot of patients might not be happy about having the TV cameras around when they're giving birth.'

Sasha laughed again in that irritatingly tinkly way. 'Oh, we've already spoken to your employers, didn't I say? They're both happy to take part, as long as we indemnify them against any complaints from members of the public.' She beamed triumphantly. 'So you see, we really have thought of everything.'

'Yes,' said Lorna with an awful sinking feeling. 'You have, haven't you?'

*

146

That night after work, when the children were in bed and Meg and George were engrossed in front of *Celebrity Knitting School*, Lorna slipped away to the Goose and Gannet with Carmen and Chris for a final summit meeting.

'Do you really think this TV thing's a good idea?' Lorna was practically pleading with Carmen to say no.

'Of course it is!' replied Carmen, downing an orange juice and casting longing looks at Lorna's pint of Guinness. 'It's money for nothing.'

'Yes but ... I don't know the first thing about clamping cars!'

'And I don't know much about delivering babies, but that's the whole point! They want us to look like bumbling rookies. It's not entertaining otherwise, is it?'

'I suppose not,' agreed Lorna gloomily. 'But what if one of us really messes up and something dreadful happens?'

Carmen wore her most patient expression. 'You heard the woman. We'll have people with us all the time – proper qualified people – so if anything gets a bit hairy they'll step in and sort it all out. And they certainly won't let me do anything dangerous, like delivering babies!' She opened the prawn cocktail crisps and shoved the bag in Lorna's face. 'Look Lor, if you really don't want to do this I'll understand. I won't hold it against you, honest I won't.'

Lorna chewed slowly on a crisp. The mixture of prawn cocktail and stout was a piquant one to say the least. 'But it means a lot to you, doesn't it?'

Carmen chuckled. 'If you mean does it mean a lot to me to be pratting about on TV, then no, it bloody doesn't! But if you mean would the money come in handy for the new baby ... well yes, I'm not going to deny that.'

Like it or not, there really was no answer to that. 'In that case, I guess we're doing it,' said Lorna.

'Sure?'

'No. But we're doing it anyway.'

Chris re-emerged, shouldering his way through the late evening crowd with a bag of pork scratchings and a half of lager. He looks tired, thought Lorna. And that shirt of his could do with a good iron. It was pretty plain that nothing much had changed in his social life – or lack of it.

'Blimey,' said Chris, 'the time it takes to get served in here, you could brew the beer yourself.' He sat down in the remaining chair, on the opposite side of the table to Carmen and Lorna. 'So, girls, have you made your minds up?'

Carmen pointed to Lorna. 'She has. She says we're doing it.'

Chris looked genuinely surprised. 'Really, Lorna? You're a lot braver

147

than I am then. You know they once made a safety training video at our workshop, and I threw a sickie just so I wouldn't have to be in it.'

'Shame on you,' said Lorna. 'You could have been in the Hollywood A-list by now.'

He chuckled. 'Yeah I know, but Brad Pitt couldn't handle the competition.' He sat back and looked at the two women. 'Well! Who'd have thought this time last week that I'd be down the pub tonight with two TV starlets?' He raised his glass. 'Here's to your new career.'

Carmen drank the toast in orange juice, then got up. 'Have to love you and leave you for a bit, I'm afraid,' she announced. 'Number Five's making me widdle for Britain.' She turned and directed a wink at Chris. 'Mind you two behave yourselves while I'm gone.'

For a little while after Carmen had left for the Ladies', they didn't say anything at all.

It was Chris who broke the silence. 'I ... er ... heard you're seeing someone.'

'Yes.'

'Serious?'

Lorna swallowed. It felt really, really uncomfortable being asked about Eoin by Chris, though she couldn't figure out why. She found she couldn't look him in the face. 'No ... yes. I mean, I don't know. Early days.'

'Right.' Chris stared down into his glass.

'How about you?'

He looked up. 'What?'

'Are you seeing anybody?'

'Oh. Not at the moment, no. I'm too busy really. You know how it is.'

'Right.'

'Actually Lorna,' Chris went on after a short pause, 'I did come here meaning to ask you something. And it's a bit personal, so seeing as it's just you and me now ...'

Their eyes met, and a funny sort of frisson made all the tiny blonde hairs on the backs of Lorna's hands stand up.

'Oh,' said Lorna. 'What sort of thing?'

'About the band. The Long Stands.'

'The band?' said Lorna. She didn't know quite what she'd expected, but it wasn't this. 'But it doesn't exist any more. Not since Ed died.'

'No, it doesn't,' said Chris. 'Not at the moment. It was always Ed's band. He was the lead singer and the real frontman, and after he died it didn't feel right to go on without him. Only lately, a couple of the lads have been talking about how much they miss playing together.'

'You mean you want to start up the band again? Without Ed?' She saw

148

the pain cross his face; sensed that he assumed he had hurt her. 'I'm not saying you shouldn't, it's just . . . a surprise.'

Chris reached across and took her hand, very gently, as if it were made of thistledown that might blow away in a single breath. 'We wouldn't do anything without your complete agreement,' he promised her.

'I know you wouldn't.'

'And if I did revive the band, we wouldn't be nearly as good as we were when we had Ed, I do realise that. I mean, for a start-off you'd have to put up with me as lead singer, and—'

'Yes,' said Lorna, out of the blue.

'Pardon?'

'Yes, Chris. It's a good idea. I'd really like it if you got the band back together.'

Startled, he looked into her face, searching for signs that she was just saying it to please him. 'Are you sure? It wouldn't hurt you to see us on stage again? Wouldn't bring back painful memories?'

'Not at all.' It was true, and that fact surprised Lorna as much as it evidently surprised him. 'I'd be really touched, Chris.' She squeezed his hand and was glad of its warmth. 'Go on – do it for me. And for Ed.'

Chapter 18

Lorna had never been a fan of big charity dinner-dances, but Eoin would-n't hear of her saying no, and perhaps he was right: after all, the Mildred McNulty Appeal for an extension to the Special Care Baby Unit was a good cause. It's just that Lorna would really rather have donated the money and spent a relaxing evening at home with Eoin and the kids.

Whatever must he think of me? she wondered as she stood in front of the bedroom mirror, zipping herself into the slinky black number Eoin loved but which her mother said made her look like a sea lion. I may not be thirty yet, but I'm getting old and boring and if I'm not careful he'll start telling me so. Next thing you know, I'll be taking up macramé and going crown green bowling with my dad. Lorna Price, she declared silently, the rot stops here!

Padding over to the wardrobe in stockinged feet, she surveyed the shoes on offer. Hmm. It was going to be a long evening, so it would make sense to wear something comfortable on the toes, maybe with an ankle strap and not too high a heel . . .

Stuff that. She reached to the very back and took out the breathtakingly gorgeous red stilettos she called her Toe Stranglers. They'd sat there gath-ering dust for aeons because frankly, wearing them was penitentially painful, but what did pain matter when you knew they gave you the sexi-est-looking legs in town? Admittedly her feet had swollen up a bit during the long day at work, but with a little perseverance she managed to cram them in.

She stood up, wobbled to her full height and looked at herself in the mirror, awkwardly aware that she hadn't made this much effort since was a kid, going steady with Ed. It wasn't that she'd let herself go, just that she'd always imagined her days of fashion torture were behind her, along with Union Jack dresses and that Jennifer Aniston haircut.

As she slipped on her jacket ready to go downstairs, Clawdius slunk past and tried to climb into the wardrobe.

'No you don't. Come here and give me a hug for luck.' Oblivious to Clawdius's long, straggly hairs, she swung him up, cuddled him on his back like a baby, and kissed him on the nose. This was his cue to purr, chirrup and wriggle, but he just lay there looking daft; and when Lorna set him down again, he slunk off under the bed, leaving just the very tip of his tail sticking out.

Lorna bent down – with some difficulty because of the shoes – and peered at his little downcast face. 'You're really not yourself, are you? Trip to the V-E-T for you if you don't pull your furry socks up, m'lad.'

The sound of the doorbell made her tummy turn a somersault. It really was like being fifteen again. She half expected her father to take one look at her and tell her she wasn't setting foot outside the house dressed like that.

But Meg and George were sitting in the front room, listening to some play or other on the radio now that the children were asleep. They'd obviously decided that if Lorna insisted on dating, she could answer her own doorbell.

She gave her clothes and hair a final smooth down, then opened the door with a flourish and plunged face-first into a huge bouquet of spring flowers. Eoin's head appeared from behind them and he planted a kiss on her cheek. 'Happy un-birthday!'

'Oh Eoin, they're beautiful!' She returned the kiss with enthusiasm. 'They must have cost a fortune.'

He gave her a wicked look. 'They did, but you're worth it. Especially in that dress.'

Lorna sneezed the pollen out of her nose. 'Hang on a minute, I'd better pop these in water before we go out.'

She'd got halfway to the kitchen when the phone in the hallway rang.

'I'll get it,' volunteered Eoin.

When Lorna returned a few minutes later, he was just putting the phone down. 'That was your friend Eleanor,' he said.

'Lennie? Gosh, I haven't heard from her in ages. Is she OK?'

'Actually no. Her nanny's been deported.'

'No! She never has!'

'And now the police have hauled her husband down to the nick – something to do with him running a racket in forged visas apparently.'

'Gregor? Oh my God! It sounds like an episode of *The Bill*.'

The door to the living room opened and Meg came out. 'What's the matter, dear? We can hardly hear our radio play. I thought you'd be gone by now.' It sounded rather like an accusation.

'Lennie just rang,' explained Lorna. 'Her nanny's been deported and Gregor's down the police station.'

'Oh dear,' said Meg. 'Mind you, I always said that girl had very piggy eyes, didn't I George?'

George ambled up behind her. 'Didn't you what, love?'

'Say Eleanor Spinks has piggy eyes. It's an infallible sign, you know.'

Lorna couldn't look Eoin in the face. She could feel him vibrating with silent laughter through the sleeve of his dinner jacket. 'Poor Lennie. I'd better give her a call in the morning and see how she is. Shall we go then, Eoin?'

'Not yet,' he replied. 'There was one other thing. She needs to go down to the police station to see her husband and bail him out, but she can hardly take two little children with her, and because the nanny's been deported . . .'

'She's got nobody to look after them?' Lorna had a horrible premonition of what was coming next. Visions of the dreadful Spinks children entered her mind like images in a particularly nasty horror movie. She wasn't sure who was worse: Jacintha, who screamed the place down if she didn't get everything she wanted, or Caspian, whose inventive experiments with everything from beads and plastic farm animals to saucepan lids had earned him a permanent seat in A&E.

'Exactly,' said Eoin with a nod. 'So she asked if she could drop them off here, just for tonight, and of course I said sure, no problem – your mum and dad will look after them. What's a couple more kids?'

'Oh!' said Meg, a little of the colour draining from her cheeks.

'Eleanor's children?' said George, rather faintly.

'That's right.' Eoin looked from one to the other as though addressing a group of medical students. 'That's not a problem, is it?'

'No,' said Meg, swallowing hard. 'No problem at all. Is it, George dear?'

'There you are! All sorted out,' declared Eoin.

Lorna wasn't so sure. 'You're absolutely certain you don't mind, Mum? I mean, Lennie's kids can be a bit . . . you know.'

Meg mustered up a brave smile. 'Don't be silly. Just you go out and have a nice time. Everything will be absolutely fine.'

Carmen was going out too, though not to anything half as posh as Lorna's charity ball. She'd planned on staying home and helping the kids with their homework, then at the last minute some guy called Trevor had rung up from Love Bites, and before she knew it she'd arranged a date and a babysitter.

As she was putting on her coat to go out, she had second thoughts. The three youngest were downstairs with Sharon from down the road, but Robbie had shut himself away in his room as soon as he came home from school, and had only emerged for five minutes, to cram a pizza into the microwave. Not that that was unusual for Robbie. He'd taken to teenage moodiness as if it were some kind of trendy new religion.

Uneasy for no good reason, she turned the handle on his door; it was locked.

'Robbie?'

There was a short pause, then a voice from inside the room: 'You can't come in.'

'Come on Robbie, I only want to talk.'

'I'm doing my homework, Mum. Go away.'

'Do you want me to help?'

'You're going out, aren't you?'

She paused. 'Well, yes – but I don't have to. I could stay at home and we could do your homework together. I used to be quite good at English, well, not as bad as I was at everything else. What do you say?'

'Go out, Mum. Have a good time or whatever. I'm fine on my own, I always am.'

She hesitated. 'All right . . . but I'll see you later.'

Silence.

Reluctantly, Carmen went off down the stairs, wondering with each step whether she ought simply to phone up this guy Trevor and tell him she'd got a headache. To be honest she wasn't really in the mood for a night out anyway. Being pregnant was a real passion-killer. And yet . . .

And yet she was lonely, unbelievably so. And with every day and night of loneliness that passed, the desperation inside her grew until she sometimes wondered how she could face another day without someone to love.

It wasn't that she didn't love her kids; she adored them, would give her life for them. But they had her to talk to when things got rough; who did she have to cuddle up to in bed and tell her troubles to? Being strong all the time was the hardest thing in the world, and now that even Lorna didn't have to face it alone, Carmen felt like the last unwanted turkey in the shop on Christmas Eve: the one with one leg, a crooked beak and three wings. And pregnant!

'There must be someone out there for me,' she whispered to herself. 'But how am I ever going to find him if I don't keep looking?'

Sharon looked up from *Coronation Street*. 'What's that, Carmen?'

'Oh, nothing important. There's food in the fridge and Becca's apple juice is there too. And you've got my mobile number if anything goes wrong.'

Sharon yawned. 'It won't. Have a nice time.'

With that, she turned back to the screen and Carmen had nowhere left to go but out.

*

154

'I said back to bed!' repeated Meg for the seventh time, trying to ignore the slight tremor that had crept into her voice. 'Now!'

Jacintha Spinks sat down defiantly on the stairs and dumped her doll head-down beside her. 'Don't want to,' she replied. 'Mummy and Daddy let me stay up.'

'I'm sure they don't,' said George, as calm as he could manage to be under such trying circumstances. 'Now come along, it's almost half-past ten. Little girls should have been asleep hours ago.'

The word 'little' ignited a warning spark in Jacintha's dark eyes. Her mouth twisted in fury. 'I'm not a little girl! I'm six and three quarters and a week and four days! And I'm not going to bed.'

'Oh yes you are, young lady,' said Meg grimly.

'Can't make me.'

Meg advanced another step.

Jacintha played her trump card. 'I'll tell Daddy you hit me and he'll get the police on you.'

George and Meg exchanged looks that stopped perilously short of murderous. 'I don't think your father is in any position—' snapped Meg, momentarily losing it and flexing her smacking hand; but her words ended in a sharp 'Ow!' as George kicked her on the shin.

'If you're not a good girl, Jacintha,' he said, 'I shall have to tell your mummy and daddy you've been bad, and they won't like that very much, will they?'

This, alas, failed to impress. 'If you don't let me stay up, I'll scream!'

At that climactic moment, there was an almighty crash from above. Even Jacintha was thrown off her stride sufficiently to shut up and stare, round-eyed, at the ceiling.

George took the stairs two at a time. At the top, he found the door of Leo's bedroom open, the toy fort upside down on the floor and Leo and Caspian rolling around, trying to beat each other's brains out with Action Men.

He did his best to remember his authoritarian father routine, but it was such a long time ago, and it had never worked that well the first time round. 'What on earth are you doing?' he demanded. 'You're supposed to be in bed asleep.'

'Leo made me have the bottom bunk.'

'Caspian climbed up and pulled me out of the top one, and I fell on the floor. And his hamster escaped.'

'What hamster?' demanded Meg, puffing up the stairs trailing a wriggling Jacintha behind her.

'Captain Hook,' replied Caspian, as if anybody who didn't know that was a moron. 'He was in my pocket. He's only got three and a half legs.'

'I bet Clawdius has eaten him,' declared Leo with relish.

'No he hasn't!'

'Yes he has, he's chomped him into little shreds and eaten him up.'

'Oh for goodness' sake!' exclaimed Meg as Jacintha started to bawl her head off again. 'I've never known such badly behaved children.'

A moment later, an answering howl shook the walls of Hope's bedroom. 'Ma-ma-maaaaaa!'

It was going to be a long night.

It took an inordinately long time to ascertain that Caspian's hamster was not inside Clawdius's stomach or trapped down the back of a radiator, but in fact asleep inside one of his discarded socks. Still, at least after the frantic search all over the house the kids were all so exhausted that they climbed back into bed without a murmur. All except for Hope, that is. She was wide awake and managed to fill her nappy twice before tiredness finally got the better of her.

Downstairs once more, Meg and George did their best to relax while keeping one ear cocked for the sounds of mayhem upstairs.

'Do you think we're past it?' asked George.

'Don't be silly, dear. We're in the prime of life.'

'But they've been running rings round us.' He took out his handkerchief and mopped his brow. 'I'm completely done in.'

'It's just those horrible Spinks children. It's quite obvious their parents haven't taught them any discipline at all. Stupid do-gooders, all "spare the rod" and expressing themselves.' Irritably, she flicked the pages of a magazine. 'Look – a competition to win ten thousand pounds' worth of plastic surgery. And no proof of purchase necessary!'

George looked at her, aghast. 'I wouldn't have thought you'd need quite that much, love. Maybe a nip and tuck here and there, but—'

'It's not for me!' He quailed under her oxy-acetylene glare. 'If I won, we could sell it and have the money.' She scribbled away on the entry form. 'A, B, D, oh that's ludicrous, everybody knows that, C, A. There, that's the multiple-choice questions done. Now all we need is a slogan.'

'Don't look at me, love. I'm rubbish at slogans. What's it for?'

'Dr Finckel's Age-Defying Facial Scrub.'

George wrinkled his nose. 'Sounds revolting.'

'Of course it is, it's supposed to be. It's ninety-two per cent pure senna. Now, let's see. "A slogan that combines the way Dr Finckel's gives the skin a feeling of youthful health and elasticity, with the rejuvenating powers of skilled cosmetic surgery." Hmm . . .'

George scratched his thinning hair. 'Scrub up nice with Dr Finckel's?' he ventured.

Meg didn't even look up. 'Don't be silly dear.'

'I'm not! I told you I was no good at this.'

'Wait a minute, how about ... "Keep old age at bay, the Finckel's way"? No, that's no good.'

'Why not?'

'Not specific enough. You really need to mention the product. That's what it said in my competitions magazine.'

'Oh. All right then.' George chuckled. 'Get this: "Beat the wrinkles with Dr Finckel's."'

'Oh George, that's terrible!'

'Yes, I know.'

They looked at each other and burst out laughing. 'Well, I can't think of anything better, so it'll have to do,' decided Meg, writing it in the box, clipping out the entry coupon and slipping it into an envelope. 'Now, let's fill in some of those application forms you got in the post yesterday ...'

Hardly had George put his reading glasses on when the sitting room door clicked open, and two small faces appeared in the gap.

'I'm hungry,' announced Jacintha.

'I'm thirsty,' said Leo.

George hauled himself wearily to his feet. 'All right, all right, back to bed and I'll sort you out.'

'Grandad,' added Leo, turning as George was shepherding him out.

'What now?'

'Caspian's got his finger stuck in the bathroom tap.'

It wasn't that late when Carmen got home, but she felt weary and a tiny bit demoralised.

The evening hadn't been a failure, but then again it hadn't exactly been a Rudolph Valentino romantic epic either. Trevor had turned out to be yet another in the long line of guys for whom women were always laydeez, and any kind of fun mean having a larf. Normally she'd have joined in his jokes, if only politely. Tonight he just seemed tedious, and she hadn't been particularly grief-stricken when he didn't invite himself home for a nightcap. Or surprised for that matter – the moment she'd mentioned she was pregnant, he couldn't get out of the restaurant quickly enough.

All she really felt like doing was going home, checking up on the kids, and heading for bed. Alone.

As she turned the key in the front door, she heard the TV droning in the front room but apart from that, nothing. That was a relief at least: no misbehaving kids, no domestic crises to be sorted out once again. Alone.

Sharon was still sitting on the sofa as she walked through into the living room and threw her coat across a chair.

157

'Everything OK?' asked Carmen, reaching into her bag for the money to pay the babysitter.

Sharon kept on watching the TV. Some mesmerising tosh about space-aliens taking over Halifax, delivered with all the mad-eyed sincerity of a party political broadcast. 'I tried phoning you,' she said. 'On your mobile.'

Carmen stopped rummaging in her bag. 'Why? What happened?'

'It was your Robbie.'

A knot tightened in Carmen's stomach. 'What about him?'

'He went out just after you did, then he comes in again about half an hour later. Looked like he'd been in a fight or something. Anyway, he goes up to his room, then a few minutes later he goes out again with a bag and he's not been back since.'

'Where did he go?'

'I dunno.'

'Didn't you ask him?' demanded Carmen in disbelief. 'You just let him walk out without even asking him where he was going?'

Sharon shrugged. 'He didn't look much like he was going to tell me even if I did,' she reasoned. 'So I waited till he'd gone, then I phoned you. Your phone just kept ringing.'

Carmen's heart was racing. Oh shit, oh shit, oh shit. She'd been sitting in a noisy pub with some stupid guy called Trevor she didn't give a toss for, and when her own kid had needed her she hadn't even heard her phone go off.

'Oh God,' said Carmen. 'What if something's happened to him? What am I going to do?'

Sharon yawned, stood up and slipped on her coat. 'I wouldn't worry, he probably does this kind of stuff all the time, you just haven't noticed.'

'And that's supposed to make me feel better?'

Sharon held out her hand. 'Can you give me my money now? Only I need to get back, or me mum will start worrying.'

Chapter 19

Tonight could be the night; she knew it could. If she wanted it to be.

Lorna sat in the back of the cab, with Eoin's arm round her shoulders, and tried to abandon herself to the moment. They'd had a good time together at the dinner-dance, with plenty of wine and laughter, and up till now she had felt perfectly relaxed. It was only now, as the taxi sped back towards Cheltenham, that the jitters began to creep in.

His hand slipped under the pashmina and caressed her shoulder. 'You know Blondie, you're incredibly desirable in that dress,' he murmured, and nuzzled a kiss into the crook of her neck. 'A guy could lose control.'

Lorna saw the cab driver grinning to himself as he watched them in the rear view mirror, and felt her cheeks burn with embarrassment. 'Left or right here?' he asked as they approached a major junction.

Left or right. It was decision time: his place or hers?

Eoin looked at her. 'Well?'

Her mouth was horribly dry.

The driver's fingers were tapping on the steering wheel. 'Make your minds up folks, I haven't got all night.'

'Go right,' said Lorna, not sure even now, as the car took the turn and headed for St Jude's.

Eoin looked mildly surprised, impressed even. 'What about The Parents?' he asked, making them sound like cartoon monsters.

'They'll be . . . fine.' The big question is, will I? thought Lorna, immediately telling herself off for being such a big girl's blouse. None of this bothered me when I took Pete home, did it? she recollected – or at least, not until afterwards. And Eoin's far more attractive than Pete was. I'm a bit uptight, that's all. Perhaps I'm just not drunk enough.

Eoin's fingers explored the tiny blonde hairs at the back of Lorna's neck, making her shiver. 'Cold?'

She shook her head. 'Not really.'

He whispered in her ear, 'Don't worry, I'll keep you warm.'

159

By the time the cab pulled up outside Lorna's house, she could feel her heart thudding inside her ribcage like a little man with a very big hammer. She vaguely recollected it feeling a bit like this when she was fourteen, and Ed had walked her home from the school disco and got his hands under her T-shirt in her mum's front porch. She'd sensed he was going to make a move, and she'd wanted him to all night; but when he actually did, she was too over-anxious to relax and enjoy it. It hadn't helped that they'd been spotted by the old spinster at number thirty-two, who'd made a point of giving her mother an enhanced account of what she'd seen the following morning.

Yes, it felt a little bit like that, but not quite. This time she felt somehow more detached from the experience. There was a little more apprehension and a little less excitement. She wondered why. Well, everybody said there was nothing like the passion of your first love; maybe the older you got, the less you felt. Eoin was a sexy guy, no doubt about it, but she still couldn't quite see herself racing Eoin to the bedroom, leaving a trail of discarded clothes behind her.

Oh God, Lorna thought; I hope it's not the early menopause.

While Eoin paid the taxi driver, she walked up to the front door, fumbled in her bag for the key, promptly dropped it in a rose bush and cursed loudly. Eoin stooped down and picked up the key. 'Calm down,' he said, in much the same voice he would have used with one of his patients.

It wasn't the best thing he could have chosen to say. If there is one thing calculated to make the average woman lose her cool, it's telling her to calm down. She glared at him. 'I am calm.'

'If you say so.'

'What's that supposed to mean?'

He put up his hands in mock defence. 'Hey, no need to get touchy.'

'I'm not touchy! I told you, I'm fine.'

If that statement wasn't entirely true when she made it, it became a downright lie the moment she stepped into the front hallway.

'Meeee-owrr-owr-yowww!'

As Lorna opened the front door, Clawdius shot out into the night, ears flat against his head, as if all the hounds of hell were after him. And who could blame him? Jacintha Spinks was standing in her nightie halfway up the stairs, red-faced with fury and screaming her head off; George was trying to prise Caspian and Leo apart, and in the distance Lorna could hear her daughter's plaintive wail.

Eoin winced and stuck his fingers in his ears. 'What in the name of God?'

Lorna gave him one of her looks. 'What was that you said? A couple of extra kids won't make any difference?'

Her mother appeared at the top of the stairs, looking distinctly ruffled, her normally perfect coiffure slipping down over her forehead in limp tendrils. Hope was now grizzling half-heartedly in Grandma's arms and rubbing her tired eyes with her little fists.

'It's not as bad as it looks, dear,' Meg shouted above the general cacophony. 'I'll be down in a minute.'

'Come along you boys,' urged George. It was more of a heartfelt plea than an order. 'Time to stop fighting and go to bed.'

Unsurprisingly, nothing happened.

'Leo!' barked Lorna; and the fighting paused, at least momentarily. 'Stop kicking Caspian and go back to bed this minute!'

Leo pulled himself free with the sound of a rending pyjama sleeve. His lower lip jutted. 'But he kicked me first!'

'I don't care. Up those stairs. Now.'

Leo followed the pointing finger with bad grace, but at least he followed it; though he paused to turn and stick his tongue out at Caspian as he circumnavigated his petulant sister. As for Jacintha herself, thankfully her screams began to subside as it dawned on her that nobody was paying her any attention.

Eoin bore down on the smirking figure of Caspian with an expression that had reduced many a student midwife to tears. 'You – what's your name?' he snapped.

'Caspian.'

'How old are you? Come on, I'm waiting.'

'N-nearly six,' replied Caspian, somewhat taken aback by Eoin's Gestapo style of interrogation.

'Do you want to grow up to be seven?'

Caspian nodded warily, his eyes round as marbles.

'Then you'd better get your backside up those stairs before I lose my temper. Because believe me, you really wouldn't like me when I'm angry.' For added effect Eoin cracked his knuckles with a sound like machine-gun fire. And Caspian scuttled up the stairs faster than you could say 'child psychologist'.

Jacintha's vocalisations screeched to a halt, and she glowered down at the world from her perch on the stairs. 'I hate you!'

Meg appeared behind her on the landing. 'Somebody round here is asking for a smacked bottom,' she declared, with more than a hint of intent.

Lorna decided she had better intervene before Eoin, George and her mother suggested reintroducing public flogging for the under-eights. She climbed up the stairs and sat down next to Jacintha. 'What's the matter?' she asked, as gently as her frayed nerves would permit. 'What's made you so upset?'

161

'I want Danuta!'

'Danuta? Who's she? Is she your dolly?'

'She's my nanny!' wailed Jacintha, burying her face in Lorna's pashmina. 'Danuta tells me stories about bears and gives me sweets and her hair smells nice.'

Ah, so that was it. 'I know you're going to miss her,' Lorna sighed, stroking Jacintha's hair. 'But Danuta had to go away.'

'Why?'

Oh dear, thought Lorna. How do you explain illegal immigration to a small child with a big temper? She opted for the big cop-out. 'Ask your mummy. She'll explain. I tell you what though,' she went on, 'there's no need to be sad.'

Jacintha raised her head just enough to open one questioning eye. 'Why?'

'Because Grandad Scholes knows wonderful stories too, don't you Grandad Scholes?'

George, who had been gazing gloomily into space, started at the mention of his name. 'What? Oh, stories . . . yes, well . . . after a fashion.'

'Wonderful stories,' Lorna repeated with emphasis.

'What sort of stories?'

'Stories about a really big fat penguin who lives in an ice city at the South Pole, and has lots of adventures.'

Jacintha sniffed doubtfully. 'Exciting adventures?'

'Very exciting. And funny. And if you go to bed right now, like a good girl, Grandad Scholes will come up and tell you one of his stories. But only if you go right now.'

She had severe doubts that it would work but, after a moment's thought, Jacintha picked up her doll by its leg and stomped off up stairs. 'It had better be a good one,' she warned as she reached the landing and disappeared into her room.

Meg clumped wearily downstairs. Hope had at last given over snivelling, and was struggling to keep awake. 'I'm sorry dear,' said Lorna's mother. 'You came home at rather a . . . er . . . difficult moment. Honestly, they were good as gold until Caspian got his finger stuck and—'

'Stuck? Stuck in what?' demanded Lorna. 'You know what he's like, always sticking his fingers in things.'

'Oh, it was nothing, and at least it was only his finger this time, not his head. A bit of butter soon sorted it out. We didn't need the fire brigade in the end, not this time. Well, only for rescuing the hamster from the drainpipe.'

'The fire brigade! Again!'

'They were very good about it, dear. Apparently it happens all the time.

162

Anyway, it's just that the children were a little overtired by then, and you know what children are like when they don't get enough sleep. Now, why don't I make us all a nice cup of tea, and you can tell us all about your lovely evening?'

Lorna and Eoin looked at each other.

'Actually I'm quite tired,' Eoin said meaningfully. 'Aren't you tired too, Lorna?'

'What?' She twigged. 'Oh yes, I'm tired too. Actually we were just thinking of, well, you know, bed.'

Wilfully or not, Meg chose not to get the drift. 'Oh well, if Eoin needs to get home to his bed and get some sleep I quite understand. I expect he's got a busy day tomorrow. Shall we call you a taxi, Eoin? Or George could put his coat on over his pyjamas and get the car out . . .'

Lorna was trying to find the right words to explain that the particular bed Eoin was thinking of was hers, when the telephone rang on the little hall table right next to her, making her jump. She picked up the receiver. 'Hello?'

'Is that you, Lorna? It's Carmen.' Her voice was breathless. 'I really need your help.'

'Whatever's the matter? You sound terrible. Have you been crying?'

All of Carmen's distress poured out in a torrent of sobs. 'It's Robbie. He's gone!'

'Gone?' puzzled Lorna. 'Gone where?'

'I got home tonight and Sharon told me he just picked up some of his stuff and walked out without a word. Lorna, what am I going to do? What if something terrible happens to him? What if he's planning never to come back?'

If there was one thing Eoin really excelled at, it was telling people what to do. Within ten minutes of Carmen's phone call, he and Lorna were at her house and he was making her recall every tiny detail.

'Think,' he commanded Carmen. 'You have to think of all the places he might go.'

'Don't you think that's what I've been doing?' She dabbed her red and swollen eyes with a tissue. 'I've already looked everywhere.'

'There must be somewhere you haven't thought of,' replied Eoin.

'But where?' she protested. 'I've driven round town God knows how many times, just on the off-chance I might see him. I've been to the train station, the bus station – everywhere. And I've been through it all with the police as well. Not that they seemed to care.'

'Well, we do,' said Lorna firmly. 'So you can go through it again with us.'

163

Carmen shook her head sadly. 'It's so hard to know what Robbie might do. These last few months he's been getting more and more secretive, and hanging around with all sorts – boys whose dads are in jail, kids who carry knives. Getting himself into fights and God knows what else.' She looked up, guilt written all over her honest, open face. 'I should've known, Lorna. He's my son. I should've made him tell me what he was doing, who he was seeing.'

Lorna took her hands. 'It's not that easy though, is it? Come on now, you've been a teenager yourself, you know what it's like. Kids that age are naturally secretive. But Robbie's a bright boy, he'll be OK.'

'You really think so?'

Lorna couldn't bring herself to lie to her dearest friend, however much she might yearn to. 'I don't know for sure,' she admitted. 'But I really believe he will.'

Eoin was up and pacing the room. Lorna had never seen him so involved in anything before – except for the arguments she'd heard him having on the phone about custody of his son. The penny dropped. He really feels for Carmen because he has a child of his own, she realised suddenly. A child of his own, who's been taken away.

Eoin reached the end of the room, by the three-foot-tall china Dalmatian, and turned round. 'What did he say to this Sharon girl, before he went out the second time?'

'Nothing. She said he just went.'

'And what did he take with him?'

'A bag, a few clothes, a bit of money I think . . . and a couple of toys he had when he was a kid.'

Eoin rubbed his chin. 'He's a bit old for toys, isn't he? What's so special about these?'

'Nothing really.' Carmen searched her mind for an answer. 'Only that his dad gave them to him.'

Eoin stopped in mid-step. 'His biological father?'

'That's right. Maurice.' She spoke the word as thought it left an unpleasant taste in her mouth.

'Wasn't that the guy who, er . . .' began Lorna, not sure how to put it delicately.

'The smooth-talking scumbag who promised us the earth and then got himself sent straight back to jail?' Carmen's expression was more rueful than angry. 'That's the one. We've never heard another word from him since the day he was released from prison. It broke Robbie's heart.'

'Maybe that's it,' said Eoin with a snap of his fingers. 'Maybe it's got something to do with his father.'

Lorna frowned. 'Why? Why would this necessarily be about his father after all these years? You can't look at everything from the perspective of your own experience,' she added quietly. 'Not everything is about estranged dads.'

He swung round and for a moment there was hostility in his eyes. Then the anger subsided. 'I don't know,' he admitted. 'Maybe it's not . . . maybe I'm on completely the wrong track. Maybe you're right and I'm just an obsessed lone father with a persecution complex.' Eoin chewed on the end of his pen. 'I've just got this feeling.'

Carmen sighed. 'I guess even a feeling is better than nothing.'

Outside, thunder rumbled and big, fat drops of rain began to pitter-patter on the flat roof of the porch.

'Poor Robbie,' murmured Lorna, imagining how she would feel if it were one of her children out there in the darkness and the wet. 'I hope wherever he is, he's indoors.'

'Look Carmen,' said Eoin, 'I want you to think really, really hard and tell me if there are any places Robbie might associate with his dad. Anywhere that might be special to him.'

'Think, Carmen,' Lorna urged her. 'I know it's a long shot, but Eoin might just be on to something.'

They would never think of looking for him here. Assuming they bothered to look for him at all.

Everybody else had forgotten every single thing about his dad; everybody but Robbie. And Robbie thought about him every day, though it was many years since he'd seen or heard anything from him, and even the visual image his memory held of him had faded to little more than a blur.

It wasn't that Maurice had ever been a good dad. By all accounts, he was just about the worst sort you could have, but you couldn't choose your relatives, could you? Whatever else he was, he was still Dad and that wasn't going to change however much some people might want it to.

Perhaps Dad wouldn't have come to matter to him so much if it hadn't been for the way Mum was. Or rather, the way she'd become. When you're a mixed-up fourteen-year-old boy who finds it hard to express himself at the best of times, how do you tell your own mother that when she runs around with every guy in town, she's doing more than just embarrassing you? How do you explain that when you come home in trouble again, with another crop of bruises and black eyes, you were only fighting because of her?

He loved his mum. Loved her so much it hurt like a knife-cut in his heart. And when the other kids taunted him about her, made out that she was some kind of cheap slut, it filled him so full of rage that he wanted to kill the whole world. If it wasn't for Ryan, whose mum was on the game

165

and whose dad was doing a ten stretch in Parkhurst, he probably would. Ryan was the only one who really understood. And Mum thought Ryan was scum.

What Robbie was going to do next, he wasn't sure. He hugged his blanket tighter about his shoulders and contemplated the bare brick walls around him. It was no palace, but he could hear rain drumming on the corrugated iron roof and he was glad to be inside. In any case, coming here was only a first step, a chance to think without interruption for as long as he needed to. Maybe eventually he'd try and find his dad, or maybe that wasn't such a great idea. Maybe he'd just try and find some place where things didn't make him feel so angry and confused.

But anyway, for the time being he was safe enough.

It was a long night.

In his flat near the High Street, Chris lay looking up at his bedroom ceiling, watching the patterns the occasional car headlights made as they swished past in the rain. Was that a speck of grime up there, or a spider? Was it moving, or was it just his imagination?

He lay very still, hardly daring to breathe in case he woke the girl who lay snoring next to him in the bed. Actually turning to look at her filled him with a feeling that was uncomfortably like shame. It wasn't that he was ashamed of bringing a girl home for the night, only that he couldn't seem to find one who meant anything more to him than half an hour's animal warmth. When he cast his mind back over the last few weeks, and the few 'conquests' he'd made, he found it embarrassingly hard to remember any of their names.

Worst of all, he dreaded that inevitable moment in the morning when the girl turned to him for a goodbye kiss and he'd say, 'I'll call you,' all the time knowing darn well he was lying. Chris didn't like lying about anything, which was why sometimes he didn't say very much at all, for fear of blurting out the truth.

But there was more than one way of telling the truth. That thought occurred to him as he lay in the darkness, trying to force himself to sleep but instead driving himself mad with one of the tunes Ed had arranged for the band.

More than one way.

The girl muttered something in her sleep, rolled away from him and flung her arm across her pillow. Chris chose this moment to roll the other way, reach for the scrap of paper and pencil he always kept by the bed, and click on the tiny reading light.

For a moment, he froze, sure that the girl would wake up and want to know what he was doing. But she was fast asleep.

166

Reassured, he sat up in bed, closed his eyes, and waited for inspiration to strike.

'It's hopeless,' said Carmen as the van drove slowly through the streets of Cheltenham for what seemed like the hundredth time. 'I've lost him.'

'No,' insisted Lorna, 'you mustn't give up. We have to go on looking.'

'But there's nowhere else to look!' Abruptly, Carmen stamped on the brakes and the van lurched to a halt in the middle of the empty road.

Eoin peered forward between the front seats. 'You can't stop here.'

'I can stop where I fucking well want,' snapped Carmen, dissolving into tears as she bent forward over the steering wheel.

'Well if you don't get some petrol soon, stopping is all you'll be doing,' replied Eoin. 'Have you seen that fuel gauge?'

'Petrol,' said Carmen softly.

'Yes, petrol.' There was a note of irritation in Eoin's voice. 'You put it in engines, it makes them go.'

'Petrol!' Carmen hammered the steering wheel with the flats of her hands. 'Why didn't I think of that before?'

She rammed the van into gear and it juddered off along the road in the direction of Tewesbury.

'The nearest petrol station's that way,' suggested Lorna, pointing in the opposite direction.'

'Not the one I'm looking for,' replied Carmen, and put her foot down on the accelerator.

Eoin quite clearly did not understand.

'We've come to look for petrol here?' he said, climbing out of the van and staring up at the semi-derelict pile. 'Excuse me, but this place looks like it's been closed for about the last ten years.'

'Nine,' Carmen corrected him. 'But it's eleven since Robbie's dad worked here.'

Lorna clambered out of the van into the driving rain. What had once been the Sunshine Filling Station was now little more than a crumbling brick box in the middle of a vacant lot, overgrown with fireweed and festooned with signs that read: 'Under Offer'. It had been that way for almost as long as Lorna could remember. 'This is where Maurice worked?'

Carmen nodded. 'It's the only place he ever did a decent day's work. He used to bring Robbie here sometimes, when he was little, though I don't suppose he remembers that much about it. For a while, it was almost like being a normal family.'

'What happened?'

167

'They sacked Maurice for stealing from the till, and he came back two months later tooled up with some of his stupid mates and tried to rob it. He made a hopeless job of that as well,' she added bitterly.

Eoin turned up his collar against the rain. 'He can't be here, there's barbed wire all round it.'

'Except for over there,' Lorna pointed out. A small section at one corner was flapping free, neatly snipped away from the post that secured it.

'We can't go in there,' declared Eoin, reaching for his mobile. 'We'll cut ourselves to ribbons on the barbed wire. Probably better to phone the police.'

'My son might be in there,' said Carmen acerbically. 'Do you really expect me to wait outside?'

'Hang on then,' said Lorna, 'wait for me. If you're going in there, so am I.'

Eoin raised his eyes to the teeming skies, muttered something inaudible, and followed them through the hole in the wire.

The boy did not wake as the torchlight touched his face. Swathed in a blanket, knees drawn up to his chin, he looked incredibly young and innocent: more like a baby than a teenager. At his feet lay a battered Action Man and a teddy bear with one ear.

'Robbie!' Carmen rushed forward and he started into wakefulness – at first puzzled, then afraid.

'Mum?'

She flung herself at him, almost suffocating him in her embrace. 'Please God Robbie, don't you ever, ever do that again. I thought I'd lost you . . .'

Lorna looked at Eoin, laid the torch on the ground and backed away. 'We'll wait in the van, Carmen. Come on,' she said, 'I think we're in the way here, don't you?'

Outside, as they sat in the van, Eoin started to talk about Dominic; about the joy he'd felt the day he was born, the pride in being somebody's dad, and the pain when the marriage went wrong. It was a side of him that Lorna had never really been allowed to see before, and it made her feel close to him.

'You don't know how lucky you are,' he said. 'Having kids who love you. Thanks to her, my boy hardly knows I exist.'

'I wish I could help somehow,' she said.

He looked into her eyes. 'You do.'

When Carmen brought Robbie back to the van, ten minutes later, Lorna and Eoin were so engrossed in each other that she had to thump on the side window three times before they let her in.

168

Chapter 20

Lorna stole a moment's rest in the ward kitchen, kicked off her shoes and flexed her aching feet. They don't call it the labour ward for nothing, she thought. I've never worked so hard in my life. Not much prospect of sneaking off for an hour at lunchtime, to buy Leo his birthday present.

'Well, I'm racking my brains,' announced Andrew Rennie, the male midwife, as Lorna re-emerged, fortified by a couple of swigs of black coffee, 'but I can't for the life of me work out what it was.'

'You've lost me,' said Lorna. 'What is this, some kind of riddle?'

'Kind of.' Andrew gave her one of the crinkly-eyed grins that had the prettiest students falling at his feet. 'I'm trying to work out what happened nine months ago to drive the people of Cheltenham to such wanton copulation. I've never known a baby boom like it.'

'Cold weather and power cuts,' declared June Godwin, with the air of a woman who knew these things. 'You know what it's like – come to bed love, it's the best way to keep warm. Now Andrew, stop distracting my right-hand woman. Lorna, come with me. There's a breech delivery coming into room four, and it's got your name on it.'

When Lorna finally emerged, several hours later, Eoin was deep in conversation with Kathryn, one of the other midwives. Lorna was rather hoping for a roguish wink, or at least acknowledgement by way of a knowing smile. After all, they had spent the previous night in the same bed, and she'd have liked to know that he'd enjoyed it as much as she had. But as soon as he saw her, he cut to the chase. 'Why's Mrs Harris not wired up to a monitor?'

Oh. And a very good morning to you too, thought Lorna, her flush of girlish effervescence promptly evaporating. 'Because she's in perfect health and she wants a natural birth.'

'Exactly what I told Dr Sullivan,' agreed Kathryn. 'But he doesn't seem to think—'

'What I think,' Eoin cut in sharply, 'is that we shouldn't be pandering to some woman's foolish fancies when there are good medical reasons why we shouldn't.'

'With respect,' said Kathryn through a forced smile, 'you always think there are good medical reasons for technological intervention, even when there aren't.'

Lorna was torn between sexual chemistry and professional integrity, but when it came down to it there was no contest. 'I don't really see why we should intervene when the mother expressly doesn't want us to, and when there's no evidence to suggest that we need to.'

She thought that sounded quite reasonable, but Eoin clearly disagreed. 'So now we're all doctors, are we?' he said acidly. 'And we can conjure evidence out of thin air without the aid of modern technology?'

'Of course not,' retorted Lorna, 'but sometimes all these women need is time.'

'Very true,' nodded Kathryn. 'It's hardly surprising labour sometimes slows down when they come into hospital. They're stressed, they're in pain, and then somebody sticks electrodes all over them. How would you feel in their place?'

'Well it's pretty bloody obvious I'm never going to find out, isn't it?' replied Eoin, slamming the patient's notes shut with extremely bad grace. 'But never mind, I'm still the doctor round here, and I'm telling you I want Mrs Harris on a monitor. Stat,' he added, with an ironic *ER* flourish, before turning his back on them and stomping off.

Andrew stuck his head out of the sluice. 'Is it safe to come out now?'

'Coward,' sniffed Kathryn. 'You could have backed us up.'

'No thanks, I don't want to die just yet. Not while I'm so young and gorgeous.' Andrew looked Lorna up and down. 'Speaking of which, aren't you and he – you know?'

Lorna glanced at the ward door, still juddering in its frame. 'God knows,' she replied with a shrug. 'Ask him.'

Half an hour later, when her patient begged her to go down to the café for some double-strength espresso and a Kit-Kat, she almost collided with Eoin on the stairs.

'Hello, fancy meeting you here.'

'Oh, so you are still speaking to me then?'

He gave her a funny look. 'What? Oh, you mean our little professional disagreement back there? Come on, Blondie, you've got to learn not to take these things personally.'

'I wish you wouldn't call me that,' she said.

'What?'

'Blondie.'

He laughed. 'But it suits you – and it's sexy. I like it.'

170

'Well I don't, all right?'

She carried on down the stairs, and he turned round and followed after her. Catching up with her at the bottom, he took her by the shoulder and swung her round. 'You drive me crazy, Lorna, do you know that? Last night, you and me – wow.'

Lorna turned the colour of a pickled beetroot. 'This is hardly the place, Eoin. I'll see you later, OK?'

He pressed his lips to hers, and she heard him whisper, 'As long as it's not too much later.'

Then he was gone, and the girl who cleared the tables in the coffee bar was looking at Lorna and shaking her head knowingly.

In the days since Carmen had found Robbie and brought him back home, something very big and very significant had changed.

She had begun to feel as if her entire self was crumbling away; all that she was and all that she had been, disintegrating bit by bit as she took stock of the thousand ways in which she had failed. All that time, when she'd thought she was doing right by her kids, she'd really been doing no more than trying to find solutions to her own stupid problems; she realised that now. Instead of keeping her eyes open, listening, taking stock of what the kids really needed, she'd subconsciously decided what she needed and projected it onto them.

All that time she'd needed a man; but all they'd needed was a mother. Why hadn't she seen that for herself? Was she really that self-obsessed?

Lorna understood better than anyone, but Carmen knew that nobody could ever grasp how truly ashamed she felt. The only thing she'd ever tried really hard to be was a good mum, and look what a mess she'd made of it.

Under the circumstances, all she could do was listen to every word Robbie said, promise him she'd try to do better, and then make an appointment down at the Resource Centre, so that she could pour the whole sorry tale out to Janice Green.

Unfortunately there was one small bit of information that nobody bothered to impart until she bustled into the waiting room with just thirty seconds to go.

'Ms Jones. I've got a three thirty appointment with Ms Green,' Carmen told the receptionist in a breathless rush.

'I don't think so,' replied the receptionist, looking up from her appointments book. 'Janice left about a month ago.'

'Left?' That knocked Carmen sideways. 'When's she back then?'

'I've no idea, I'm afraid. She's in Ouagadougou right now, teaching beekeeping to native tribeswomen. But don't worry, we've put you down for an appointment with our new counsellor. Victor's very good.'

171

'He's . . . a man?'

The receptionist gave her a slightly pitying look. 'Well, yes. I mean, he is called Victor.'

'Oh.'

'Is there a problem?'

Carmen imagined the sheer, hellish embarrassment of revealing all her shortcomings to a man. All things considered, it would be a bit like consorting with the enemy, only worse. More like a compulsive eater baring her all to a chocolate éclair. 'I don't know if I can,' she admitted. 'Not with a bloke. I mean . . . it's very personal.'

'Oh. It's one of those, is it?' With an irritated hrrumph, the receptionist rattled away on her keyboard. 'I can put you in with Beatrice for half an hour in June. If she has a cancellation.'

'June! But that's months away! I need to talk to somebody now!'

Right on cue, the door marked 'Private' clicked open.

'Denise, has Mrs Jones arrived yet?'

He stepped out into the waiting room, and Carmen's apprehension turned to surprise. Victor was not, as she'd imagined, another twenty-something psychology graduate, bursting with ambition and busily collecting nutters for his PhD thesis. Victor was short, fat, balding, bespectacled and – to Carmen's experienced eye – definitely well on his way to fifty.

'She says she doesn't want to see a man,' said the receptionist, before Carmen had a chance to speak.

'Ah well,' said the counsellor sympathetically, 'that's quite understandable. Not everyone is comfortable with a member of the opposite sex.' He walked over to the computer and started fiddling with it, to Denise's evident irritation. 'Let's see if we can rearrange Beatrice's appointments and squeeze you in somewhere.'

'Actually,' said Carmen, getting to her feet, 'I don't mind. You'll do.' She just managed to stop herself adding, 'Because you're not really a man, are you? You look like somebody's dad.'

Victor ushered her into his office. 'OK then, but be sure to tell me if you change your mind at any time.'

They sat down facing each other, on either side of the desk. The multi-coloured row of potties had been joined by a life-size cuddly St Bernard and three plastic pedal cars.

'I'm sorry I'm not Janice,' began Victor, 'but I'll do my best.'

'I'm sorry I'm, you know, a bit funny about men.'

'Is that what you've come to talk to me about?' he asked, so kindly that Carmen felt a great big ball of emotion rise up inside her.

In fact Victor only just managed to get the box of tissues into her hand before the floodgates opened and she started sobbing, in a way she hadn't done since Maurice broke her heart.

'I'm s-sorry,' she managed to blurt out between tissues. 'I'm s-so very sorry.'

'Just take your time,' said Victor. 'Take all afternoon if you need to. But don't you dare apologise again, or I shall have to send you home in disgrace.'

It was the first time Carmen had smiled since Robbie ran away.

Outside in the waiting room, someone else was trying to get help.

'I have to speak to somebody, don't you understand?'

Denise the receptionist studied the teenage girl before her with a practised eye. Underage, common as muck, probably pregnant. 'Have you told your mother you're here?' she enquired.

The girl stared at her. 'I told you, it's me mum who's the cause of all this! She's the one who's trying to take my baby away from me!'

'What about your doctor then? Or your social worker?'

The girl's eyes were wild with distress. 'They're all on her side! Don't you listen to anything, you cloth-eared bitch?'

Denise's expression hardened from flint to granite. 'There's no call for that sort of abuse,' she said curtly, pointing to a notice on the wall that read, 'We are a Zero Tolerance Facility.' 'Any more of that and I'm afraid I shall have to ask you to leave the premises.'

Tears were welling up in the girl's eyes, but they were tears of anger as well as desperation. 'Oh don't worry, I'm not going to stick around and make your precious waiting room look untidy. I might as well just fuck off and die, and then maybe you'll all be happy.'

Swinging round, she made a grab for the first thing that came to hand, which proved to be a vase of daffodils, and hurled it at the wall. The receptionist ducked just in time, and the vase smacked into the plasterboard, leaving a trail of greenish water as it tinkled to the ground.

'How dare you!' gasped Denise in outrage.

The door to Victor's office opened, and he came out to see what all the fuss was about.

But it was too late. Kelly Picton had gone.

After tea, George and Meg drove over to Nailsworth to see some friends who had just bought a converted mill, leaving Lorna and the kids to an evening of jigsaws, Mousetrap, and Teletubbies DVDs. Leo wasn't exactly a Teletubbies fan, but repeated hints that his forthcoming birthday present might be in proportion to how well he behaved had done wonders for his tolerance levels over the past few days.

As Hope slumbered in her cot, and Leo put on his pyjamas, he launched into the nightly interrogation routine.

'Is it a dinosaur?'

Lorna laughed. 'Not saying.'

'Is it a game?'

'You'll have to wait and see!'

'But Mum!' He hiked up his pyjama bottoms and made a beeline for the bathroom. 'Look Mum, I'm brushing my teeth.'

'Good boy.'

'I'm being good and doing it properly.'

She stuck her head round the bathroom door. 'I'm very glad to hear it.'

'Now will you tell me what my birthday present is?'

'Sorry sweetheart.' She kissed the top of his head. 'You'll still have to wait.'

Leo pondered as he scrubbed at his molars. 'Mum.'

'Yes?'

'Can I have a woolly mammoth?'

It was Lorna's turn to wonder. 'I'm not sure if you can get toy mammoths,' she confessed. 'But we can have a look if you like.'

Leo spluttered foam everywhere. 'Not a toy mammoth. A real mammoth!'

'There aren't any real mammoths, not any more.'

'Yes there are. I saw it on TV. Some scientists were digging one up and they said they were going to make lots of real live ones out of it. They did!' he protested at the half-smile on Lorna's face.

She sat down on the edge of the bath. 'Sweetheart, it's going to be years and years before they can make a real live mammoth, and they might not even manage it then. And think about how big they are. We'd never fit one in our tiny garden.'

Leo rinsed out his mouth and wiped it on the towel. 'We could keep him in the park,' he reasoned. 'It's only round the corner, and there's a pond for him to have a wash in.'

'I suppose so,' conceded Lorna, 'but if he stomped on all the flower beds the council would send us a great big bill and make us get rid of him. Besides—'

The doorbell rang downstairs. George and Meg must have decided to come home early and forgotten their keys. Or maybe it was Chris, with the new head for the downstairs shower.

'Get yourself into bed,' she told Leo, 'and Mummy will come up and tell you a story.'

'About a mammoth?'

'We'll see.'

174

She ran downstairs and opened the door. It wasn't her mum and dad standing out there, but Eoin. 'Oh, it's you.'

'Oh dear,' said Eoin, assuming a very downcast expression. 'Am I still persona non grata? Shall I go away again?'

'Don't be silly.' She pulled him inside and closed the door. 'You're the one who got all uppity and pulled rank on me.'

He grabbed her round the waist and pulled her towards him. 'Ah well, if you women would only learn your place . . .'

She wriggled free. 'What!'

'Hey, lighten up, I was only joking.'

'You'd better be, buster.' Her words were almost entirely lost as he drew her into a powerful kiss that made her bones melt and knocked all the breath from her body.

Abruptly, Eoin took a step back. 'The kids,' he said suddenly.

'In bed. What about them?'

'They have had their jabs, haven't they? The MMR I mean.'

Lorna frowned. 'Yes, of course. Why?'

'Haven't you heard? There's a mumps epidemic and it's heading straight for Gloucestershire. And you know what that means to any red-blooded male who's never had it.'

Lorna stifled a giggle. 'Oh Eoin, you're not scared are you? A big, grown-up man like you?'

'Big and grown-up my arse. Threaten any man with sterility and balls the size of party balloons, and he'll revert to a gibbering toddler. So they've definitely been done then?'

'Yes, I told you. I'd better phone Lennie though. I don't think she's had hers done – I did try to persuade her, but with all the scares she wasn't convinced.'

Eoin gulped. 'Lennie's kids? The kids who were here a few days ago? The ones who sneezed and dribbled on me? Oh great. Have you got any whisky? I hear it's good for killing germs.'

A small voice came from upstairs. 'Mummy, where's my story?'

'Coming, Leo. In a minute.'

'Now! You promised.'

Lorna threw Eoin an apologetic look and started on up the stairs.

'You spoil those kids,' he grumbled. 'A bit more discipline wouldn't go amiss. You know, I'm starting to wonder if that little boy up there deserves the super-deluxe birthday present I've just bought him.'

Lorna turned round, came back down the stairs and led him into the living room, away from Leo's radar ears. 'What birthday present?'

Eoin took out his wallet and extracted a sheaf of tickets. 'A VIP trip to the Natural History Museum, that's what.' He saw the look on Lorna's face and followed up with, 'What's the matter, don't you think he'll like it?'

'I think he'll love it,' replied Lorna. 'But I also think this is way too generous. I'm not sure I can accept it. It's not as if we've even known each other that long.'

'Does that matter? I'd really like to give you a nice day out too, not just Leo. Come on,' he urged, 'it'll be fun.'

Fun, thought Lorna with vague unease. Not much doubt about that – for Leo at least. But she couldn't help thinking that a toy mammoth and a Dinotopia DVD were going to look awfully pathetic compared to Eoin's VIP day out in London. And somehow that didn't feel quite right.

Chapter 21

Silence had at last fallen over the Price-Scholes household. The dishes were washed, the last game of Mousetrap had been played, and the children had finally been persuaded into bed – without the aid of an electric cattle-prod.

George and Meg were slumped together on the sofa like a pair of drugged walruses, glassy-eyed with fatigue and scarcely noticing that *Gardeners' Choice* had just given way to *Busty Belgian·Housewives* on Channel Six.

'No rest for the wicked,' murmured Meg.

'I don't remember being this wicked,' replied George. 'I'd like to think I'd have enjoyed it more.'

'I suppose we really ought to tell Lorna. About it all being a bit much.'

'We can't do that!' protested George. 'She needs us. Besides, we're not completely ready for the knacker's yard just yet. We're just ... getting into our stride, that's all.'

'Don't you think we ought to have got into it by now? It's been months.'

'Well ...'

'And it's not just the tiredness, is it? Everything's so different from when we had our three. All this no-smacking nonsense, and letting them eat with their fingers and do whatever they like. And as for the potty train-ing—'

'Let's not go into the potty training, love,' pleaded George. 'I've had enough for one day.'

He might think he had had enough, but clearly Fate thought otherwise; because just then the telephone rang.

'Leave it, George,' groaned Meg. 'The answering thingy's on.'

But George lumbered to his feet regardless. 'Better answer it, it might be Lorna. She might have been in an accident.'

'That's my George. Ever the optimist.'

George made a weary grab for the phone. 'Hello? George Scholes speaking.'

'Hello Dad,' David boomed over the phone. 'Is Piglet there?'

George yawned and picked a stringy bit of ham from between his teeth. 'No, lad. I'm afraid your sister's still at work. Anything I can help with?'

David clicked his teeth, the way he always did when things weren't proceeding precisely according to his specification. 'Still at work? It's nearly ten o'clock at night! You should have a word with her, Dad.'

'Why?' enquired George, who was not always terribly quick on the uptake.

'Because it's not right!' replied David. 'Out all hours, with two young kids she hardly ever sees.'

'Oh, I wouldn't go quite that far, David,' protested George mildly.

'Well I would. And coming home late at night, when there are God knows how many crackpots and perverts prowling the streets of Cheltenham.' He managed to make it sound like downtown Los Angeles. 'She ought to stay at home and spend more time with her children, like my Maria does with our Lily. It'll be on her own head if they grow up to be juvenile delinquents or socialists or something.'

'Each unto their own,' said George, who hated to get into arguments. It seemed positively dangerous to point out that the only job Maria had ever had was two weeks in her uncle's Mayfair art gallery, and that she'd got bored and walked out on that. Or that Maria had a full-time nanny to help with the immense burden of parenting one small girl, and spent more time at coffee mornings or in posh dress shops than she did in the purpose-built nursery. 'Live and let live, that's what I say.'

'Oh Dad,' sighed David, 'you're too nice for your own good, that's what you are. You do know she's using you, don't you? Taking advantage of your good nature.'

'Now, now, lad, Lorna's had a very bad time of it these last couple of years. She needs all the help she can get.' Meg joined George by the telephone and he put his hand over the mouthpiece. 'It's David,' he said.

'Yes, I gathered that, dear. What's the matter with him?'

'He says Lorna shouldn't be out this late.'

'Why?'

'He thinks she's taking advantage.'

'But that's just silly, George!'

'There's no need to take it out on me, love! David's the one who said it . . . here, tell him yourself.' He thrust the receiver into his wife's hand.

As ever, she inspected it almost as if she half-expected it to blow up in her face before tentatively placing it to her ear. 'David, is that you? What's all this nonsense about Lorna?'

178

David's voice came back loud, clear and determined. 'It's not non-sense, Mum. Much as I love her, my little sis has got you on a string and it's not right.'

'Now don't exaggerate, David. You always were a terrible one for exaggeration, even when you were a little boy. Remember that time at Cubs when you got a splinter in your toe, and you were convinced you'd have to have your whole leg off? Not to mention the occasion when you caught your—'

'Mum,' David cut in insistently, 'we're not talking about me, we're talking about you and Lorna and her kids. And the fact is, she's getting an awful lot from you for free, and you're getting nothing in return.'

'That's not strictly true, David,' she reminded him. 'Lorna was kind enough to take us into her home when we had to sell up and we had nowhere else to go.'

There was a significant pause.

'I'm hurt, Mum,' declared David. 'I really am. Are you honestly saying that Lorna was the only one of us who'd have offered you a home? OK, I know Sarah's not big on entertaining, but what about us?'

'Well,' said Meg, somewhat flustered by the turn of the conversation. 'I'm sure if you'd had to, and we'd been absolutely pushed.'

'Not at all,' replied David with almost Biblical sincerity. 'Maria and I would be glad to welcome you into our house, any time. And when's the last time you saw Lily?'

That hit home. George, who had been listening in with his face close to the earpiece, nudged his wife. 'Tell him we'll be up for a few days at Easter.'

'Your father says we'll be up at Easter.'

'In that case, I hope it'll be for more than a few days. Because little Lily's really missing her nanny and grampy, and she's absolutely shot up since you last saw her. Did I tell you she's starting piano lessons? Oh, and you must see the photos of her as a pixie in the carnival procession.'

Meg and George shared a guilty look. David had always had a natural talent for below-the-belt warfare, and it was true – at least in part – that they'd been so engrossed in life with Lorna and her kids that they'd neglected David, Sarah and their other grandchild. But all the same . . .

'We'll definitely be up for Easter,' said George, taking the phone from his wife. 'But it'll only be for a week at most, because Lorna starts on nights the week after, and she's going to need all our help. Don't forget that she's on her own in the world,' he added, 'not like you. You've got Maria.' Not that she'd be much good in a crisis, he thought to himself. Not unless it was a crisis involving nail extensions and heated rollers. Wisely he didn't say so.

179

David sighed. 'Yes, yes, I know. Poor little Lorna, who was managing perfectly well on what Ed left her, and had no need to go out to work. Poor little Lorna, who couldn't wait for Mum and Dad to move in, so she could get out and date half the men in Gloucestershire.'

'That's enough, David,' said Meg firmly. 'I think you're being very unfair to your sister. And so does your father. What's brought all this on?'

David grunted. 'I just miss you, Mum. Both of you. It's ages since you came to visit us for more than a day, and you've hardly seen the new house.'

'We'll be up soon.'

'You won't have to do any babysitting,' he wheedled.

'We don't mind babysitting.'

A faint note of desperation entered David's voice. 'But what about the garden? There's two and a half acres of jungle out there, and I haven't got a clue! And you did promise—'

George had sensed all along where this was leading. 'I said we'd help you sort out your garden, and we will. But you'll just have to be patient and wait a bit longer. You could always get somebody in to clear it in the meantime.'

'Have you any idea how much that costs?'

George bit his tongue. 'Now David, what was it you wanted to talk to your sister about? Do you want me to pass on a message?'

'What? Oh, I just wanted to tell her I'd put something in the post for Leo's birthday.'

'That's nice, dear,' said Meg. 'And will you be coming down for his birthday then?'

There was a brief pause. 'No,' said David curtly. 'Just tell Lorna I'm really busy.'

When you're six years old, only one day in the year can come anywhere close to Christmas for sheer excitement, and that's your birthday. Not even black clouds and the promise of persistent drizzle could dampen Leo's enthusiasm.

He was awake before the sparrows, and bounced into Lorna's bedroom wearing one sock and his sweatshirt back to front over his pyjamas. 'I'm dressed, Mummy,' he announced. 'Can I have my presents now?'

Lorna opened a pseudo-critical eye. 'Oh, let me see, I don't know about that.' She made great play of rolling over and pulling the duvet over her head. 'I might just have another sleep first.'

'You can't go to sleep, Mummy!' protested Leo, trying to pull back the duvet. 'It's my birthday!'

Fast as lightning, her arms shot out, grabbed him round the waist and

180

started tickling him till he was helpless and squealing with laughter. 'Happy birthday to you' (squeal), 'happy birthday to you' (squeak), 'happy birthday dear Leee-oooo, happy birthday to you!'

They fell over in a mass of rumpled duvet and shared giggles.

'Six years old today!' exclaimed Lorna. 'You're such a big boy now.'

'Big enough to look after you, Mummy?'

'Oh, definitely.'

'So you don't need Eoin to take care of you then?'

Lorna cocked her head on one side. 'Don't you like Eoin?'

Leo thought for a moment. 'Yes,' he said slowly. 'Mostly. But sometimes I think he's making jokes that I don't understand, and I don't like that. And I don't like him much when he makes you angry.' He looked at her with his large, thoughtful eyes. 'Why does he make you angry, Mummy?'

That was a big question. She hauled him onto her knee. Ruefully, she reminded herself that she wouldn't be able to do it for much longer. Even Hope wasn't quite a baby any more, and Leo would soon reach that age where he was too embarrassed to sit on his mother's knee or let her rumple his hair – especially if there was anybody else around to see it happening.

'People do make other people angry sometimes,' she reasoned. 'You got angry when Hope was born, do you remember?'

'She was ugly,' Leo reminisced in a matter-of-fact way. 'And all red, like she'd been boiled.'

'Babies mostly are quite ugly,' Lorna confided. 'Only their mummies think they're beautiful, so it doesn't matter.'

'Was I beautiful, Mummy?'

'Oh yes. Of course. All squidgy and pink.' She stroked his hair, which was still baby-soft and just a fraction too long because she couldn't quite bring herself to lop off the delicate blond curls. 'I think you were a bit jealous when you first saw Hope,' she said gently. 'I was holding her instead of you, and that made you angry. Is that how Eoin makes you feel?'

'No,' replied Leo firmly. 'But he doesn't make me feel like Daddy did.'

A little arrow of sadness shot through Lorna's heart. 'No,' she admitted. 'He doesn't make me feel like Daddy did, either. Because nobody else could be Daddy but Daddy, could they? But that doesn't mean that other people can't be nice people, does it?'

'Granny and Grandad are nice,' agreed Leo. 'And Uncle David is sometimes. And Miss Rubery. And Uncle Chris.'

'Yes, Uncle Chris is very nice.'

'I was sick on his best trousers and he wasn't even angry or anything,

181

so he must be really, really nice. We haven't seen Uncle Chris for ages, Mummy. Why not?'

'I don't know,' she admitted. It was a thought that hadn't occurred to her before, but Leo was right.

Another thought entered Leo's mind like a sudden bolt of lightning. 'Mummy, if Uncle Chris is really nice and you like him and everything, why don't you—'

Before Leo got any further, Meg's voice came trilling up the stairs: 'Where's my little birthday boy? I hope he's awake, because Granny's making him a special birthday breakfast.'

George's voice followed close behind. 'With green dinosaur eggs and brontosaurus bacon!'

Leo leapt off the bed with a 'Yeeeeeah!' of sheer joy, and went pounding down the stairs in his pyjamas, all other thoughts instantly dismissed from his mind.

Lorna flopped back onto the pillows. Oh to be six years old again, when everything was either good or bad, nice or nasty, and never anything in between.

She thought about Eoin. He was an in between kind of person, she supposed: neither so good that she'd jump into hellfire for him, nor so bad that she'd push him in first. Some might call it a mediocre kind of romance. But they liked each other, most of the time; and they had a lot of fun, under and out of the sheets; and when it came down to being brutally honest with herself, maybe that was exactly what she needed – or at least, all she could cope with after Ed.

Eoin arrived with the 4x4 just as Leo was polishing off the rest of the green dinosaur eggs.

'Oh my God,' he said, peering at the remains on Leo's plate. 'Botulism.'

'Green food colouring actually,' Meg assured him. 'Can I do you some?'

'No thanks, I never eat anything green on principle.'

Leo was highly impressed. 'Not even peas?'

He winked. 'Especially not peas.'

'Why?'

'Because they're not vegetables, they're space aliens.'

Lorna contemplated him with folded arms, trying not to smile. 'Stop it, Eoin – he almost believes you. You'll give him a phobia or something!'

Eoin laughed and gave Leo a matey sort of pat on the shoulder. 'Take no notice of me, birthday boy, and eat your vegetables or your mother will never let me hear the last of it. Will you?'

She stuck her tongue out at him. 'Depend on it. Now, sweetheart.' She turned back to Hope and finished wiping the bits of egg off her chin. 'Mummy and Leo and Grandad have to go out with Eoin today, but you're going to have a lovely day at home with Grandma! Aren't you a lucky girl?'

Hope banged her spoon on the tray of the high chair, and showed all her bright little teeth in a big smile. 'Gan-ma. Gan-ma dolly.'

'That's right, Grandma bought you a lovely new dolly, and you're going to do lots of playing, and go for a nice walk in the park and feed the ducks. And Mummy will be back very soon, and give you lots and lots of hugs and kisses.' Lorna kissed Hope, breathing in her uniquely comforting baby scent. 'Mum, are you sure you don't mind staying home with Hope?'

'To be honest dear,' Meg replied, vigorously scrubbing egg off the pan, 'I was rather dreading trekking all the way to London with my veins. And it's not as if there was anybody else to mind the little mite – Carmen is at work, so is Chris, and as for Eleanor, well, frankly I'm not at all sure I'd want Hope learning any new tricks from those two spoilt brats of hers.' She dunked the gleaming pan in the washing-up water. 'No, you just get George out from under my feet and I'll be happy.'

'Thirty-five years of marriage, and now she tells me,' grunted George, shrugging on his jacket.

They left Eoin's car at the station, and took the direct train to London.

For George at least, this was the best bit of the whole day. 'I think I need the toilet,' he announced just past Swindon.

'But Dad, you've already been twice,' said Lorna. 'You're not ill are you?'

'Ill? No, no, it's just that I've never been on a Pendolino before,' explained George. 'And I simply must have another go on those push-button electric doors. It's all space-age in there, you know – there's a button for everything. Mind you, train toilets aren't like they used to be.' His eyes glazed over with fond remembrance. 'When we were courting, your mother and I once had a very romantic tryst in one on the way from Penzance to Coventry . . .'

'Dad,' hissed Lorna, with a meaningful look at Leo.

'What? Oh. Right.'

'What's a tryst, Grandad?' asked Leo. 'Is it something to eat?'

'It's – er—'

'Oh look, Leo,' cut in Eoin, looking up from his *Visitors' Guide to London*. 'It says here that they've got some komodo dragons at Regent's Park Zoo. Bet you don't know what they are.'

183

Leo forgot instantly about trysts. ''Course I do! They're just like real dragons, only smaller,' he said, wriggling enthusiastically on his seat and spraying everybody with crumbs. 'If they bite you it goes all bad and smelly and then you die,' he added, biting into his piece of jam sponge-cake with obvious relish. 'I saw it on the telly. Can we go and see them? Can we?'

'Well, we might have time after we've been to the museum,' replied Eoin.

'Dragons, dragons! We're going to see dragons!'

'You've done it now,' commented Lorna, easing herself into a comfort-able snuggle with his arm around her waist. 'If he doesn't see dragons, there'll be hell to pay.'

Eoin settled back into his seat and yawned. 'Oh, he'll see dragons. With my irresistible charm, they'll probably rustle up some unicorns too if I ask them.'

Leo was unimpressed. 'Unicorns aren't real, everybody knows that!'

Lorna drew in her legs to make way for George, back from his expedi-tion to the loo. 'Take no notice of Eoin, Leo, he was just being silly,' she told him. 'He's full of silly things, aren't you, Eoin?'

'He's certainly full of something,' commented George.

The train pulled into Paddington Station just before eleven, and despite the crowds and the usual Underground hold-ups, they emerged from South Kensington Tube station around half past. The sky had brightened at last, it had stopped drizzling, and there was even a hint of spring sun-shine, making the wet pavements look like sheets of rippled glass in the light breeze.

Leo raced out of the station, so full of beans that Lorna had to pant to keep up with him. 'Are we there yet, Mummy? Where's the museum? Is that it?'

'No, sweetheart, that's not it, that's an embassy or something, where the ambassador lives. It's just a little bit further. Eoin, are you sure you've got the tickets?'

He patted the breast pocket of his jacket. 'Stop worrying, everything's under control. Come on Leo, best foot forward. I'll race you to the dinosaurs.'

As they crossed Cromwell Road, the sheer enormousness of the Natural History Museum had Leo gaping in wonderment. Lorna felt his hand tighten around hers, and she gave him an encouraging smile. The steps leading up to the vast, ornate entrance awed even her; it wasn't diffi-cult to imagine what a six-year-old dinosaur-freak was feeling. This must be Heaven, Disneyland and Jurassic Park all rolled into one.

The man at the reception desk took the details, checked the tickets and made a phone call while they waited, all gazing in wonderment at the huge Victorian entrance hall, the curving staircases and the bridge that ran across. Unlike most things, thought Lorna, this seems even bigger than it did when I came here as a little girl. A few minutes later, a youngish, dark-haired lady in a red suit arrived, and introduced herself.

'Hi there,' she beamed, 'you must be Leo. Happy birthday!'

'Thank you miss,' said Leo politely as she handed him a large birthday card with 'Six Today!' across the front in glittery blue letters.

She laughed. 'I'm sure we're going to be very good friends, so you can call me Aileen. Now, I'm going to be taking you on a special tour around the museum,' she went on, 'and we'll be meeting the new life-size inter-active T-Rex, of course. And then afterwards we'll have orange juice and cake. How does that sound?'

It was pretty obvious from Leo's face that it sounded damned good. In fact, thought Lorna, he looked as though he was so sure this couldn't be for real that he was making the most of every moment, just in case he woke up.

'How much did you pay for this?' Lorna hissed in Eoin's ear as they followed their guide through the galleries.

Eoin just shrugged self-effacingly. 'Oh, you know. You're worth it. Getting the right date was a bit awkward, but it helped having a university mate who's a curator.'

'Is there anywhere you haven't got mates?' enquired Lorna, with amusement.

He tapped the side of his nose knowingly. 'Never underestimate the value of networking, that's what I say. Why do you think I've applied to join that posh golf club over Tewkesbury way?'

At the word 'golf', George stopped gazing at the skeleton of a giant Irish Elk and transferred his attention to Eoin. 'You play golf? I didn't realise you had any interest in the game.'

'I don't,' Eoin replied candidly. 'But my consultant does. And after all, it's not what you know . . .'

George grunted and turned back to the elk.

'Look, Mummy!' squealed Leo, momentarily forgetting his good man-ners and causing a mass outbreak of shushing. He tugged at her jacket and towed her across the gallery to another glass case. 'Look, it's a mammoth! A real mammoth!'

Aileen followed them across. 'Actually that's a mastodon,' she said with a smile. 'See the information board over there?'

Leo pressed his nose against the glass, leaving a halo of breath and a greasy smudge. 'It's a mammoth!' he insisted. 'It is!

185

Eoin laid a hand on Leo's shoulder. 'Calm down,' he said. 'I'm sure the lady knows what she's saying.'

'Mummy, it *is* a mammoth,' Leo appealed to Lorna. 'Its back slopes and it's got a lumpy head and its hair is lots of different colours, and its tusks are—'

'Leo, be quiet,' said Eoin ill-temperedly, with an apologetic look at Aileen. 'I dunno. Kids, eh?'

Lorna felt a rush of annoyance. If anyone ought to be telling her son to be quiet, it was she, not Eoin. And besides, she knew that spark in Leo's eye. He was very seldom wrong about anything prehistoric. 'It's all right Leo,' she said. 'Don't worry about it. It doesn't really matter, does it?'

'But Mummy—'

'Wait a minute,' said Aileen slowly, peering hard at the stuffed creature behind the glass, 'he's right. That is a mammoth. Somebody's mislabelled the display. Well spotted, Leo.' She patted Lorna on the back. 'Mrs Price, that's a smart boy you've got there.'

'I know,' Lorna replied. 'We don't need anybody to tell us that, do we, Dad? Well done, Leo.'

George beamed with grandfatherly pride. Eoin said nothing.

They carried on through rooms filled with everything from fleas to flamingos, Leo's eyes growing rounder with every exhibit. At this rate he'd probably spontaneously combust with joy when they finally reached the dinosaur collection.

At that moment, every single person in the gallery turned round and stared. Not because Leo had got overexcited, or George had done one of his armpit noises; but because the '1812 Overture' started sounding from the depths of Eoin's jacket pocket.

Aileen did not look pleased. Neither did anybody else for that matter. A lady in a tweed suit pointed aggressively at a sign depicting a mobile phone with a red line through it.

'I'm sorry, didn't anyone tell you? We don't allow mobiles in this gallery,' said Aileen.

'Switch it off, quick,' said Lorna, reddening with embarrassment.

Eoin fished in his pocket, drew it out and checked the display. 'Oh, it's Hans van den Vries from Harley Street. Sorry, I'll have to take this.' Seeing the look on Aileen's face, he added loudly, 'I'm a doctor, OK?'

While everybody else stood around dying of embarrassment, Eoin talked uninhibitedly into his phone. 'Yeah – yeah, sure I would. Right now, you say? That's terrific, I'll be over in thirty.'

He flipped his phone shut.

'Well?' said Lorna.

'Have to go, I'm afraid. This consultant obstetrician mate of mine has a patient in his private clinic – really unusual presentation, highly abnormal. I happened to mention I was going to be in London today, and he wants me to pop over and take a look, give him a second opinion. Should be really interesting.' He grabbed Lorna and planted a kiss on her lips. 'You don't mind, do you?'

'Well . . . as a matter of fact—' she began.

Leo gazed up at Eoin, his eyes filled with recrimination. 'You said we'd see dragons. You promised!'

Eoin looked down, his expression blank for a moment before he remembered. 'What? Oh, yes, the komodo dragons. Well, never mind eh? We can always see them next time.'

'But it's his birthday today!' protested Lorna, so flabbergasted that she hadn't even had time to get angry yet.

'See you later,' said Eoin, already halfway to the Exit sign. 'Should be at the station in time for the train, but if need be go back without me. 'Bye!'

George, Lorna, Aileen and Leo stared at the empty doorway where Eoin had stood a moment earlier.

'He said we'd see dragons,' said Leo quietly, quite obviously trying not to cry.

'When I get my hands on him,' muttered George under his breath, 'I'll . . . something.'

Lorna crouched down and gave her son a huge hug. 'Don't you worry sweetheart,' she told him. 'We don't need Eoin to take us to the zoo. If you want to see dragons I'll make sure you do – and that's a promise.'

Hope was having her after-lunch nap and Meg was dozing on the sofa when the telephone rang. Still bleary-eyed, she picked up the receiver. 'Hello, Lorna. Are you having a nice day?'

'It's not Lorna,' came the voice on the other end of the line. 'It's Carmen. Isn't she there then?'

'No dear, she's gone to London for Leo's birthday.'

'Oh damn, I forgot. I was going to pop round with his present. Oh well, never mind, I suppose I can drop it round later. Thanks Mrs S, 'bye.'

Meg had not worked in a chemist's shop for fifteen years without knowing how to tell when there was something somebody wasn't telling her. 'Hang on a minute, Carmen, is there something wrong?'

Yeah, thought Carmen. Only everything. 'Oh, I'm OK really,' she said. 'It's just all this business with Robbie . . . and the new baby . . . and work. You know, nothing special – just the usual mess I get my life into.'

'Would you like to talk about it, dear? I'm a good listener.'

Carmen was rather taken aback. She'd always had the distinct impres-

187

sion that Lorna's mum didn't quite approve of her. Nevertheless, it was the best offer she'd had all day. 'I'm a really bad mother,' she lamented. 'I mean, I always knew I wasn't going to win any prizes, but I never realised I was so bad . . . not until Robbie ran away.'

'Ah yes, all that trouble with Robbie. That was very unfortunate,' agreed Meg.

'It wasn't just unfortunate, it was all my fault!'

Meg weighed this up. 'I think you're being a little hard on yourself, dear,' she concluded.

'You do?' Carmen couldn't believe what she was hearing.

'Yes. After all, Robbie's at that difficult age, isn't he? A boy's very close to his mother, especially when he doesn't have a father-figure, and when he reaches his teens, well, let's just say it doesn't take much to set them off. As I recall, my David once knocked a boy's front teeth out because he made lewd suggestions to his sister.'

'At least your David had a dad when he was growing up,' replied Carmen ruefully. 'If Robbie hasn't got a father-figure, whose fault is that?'

'Maybe it's his father's,' replied Meg. 'From what I hear he's never exactly been a pillar of social responsibility.'

'But I was the one who was stupid enough to hook up with him and believe all his stupid promises!'

Meg sighed. 'True, dear. But you were young, and which of us hasn't fallen for an unsuitable man sometime in our lives? You know, if George hadn't come along when he did, I might quite easily have married Ronald Crenshaw-Smith, and ended up having to run away with him to the Costa del Crime. Don't tell George that though; he thinks he's the first man I ever had eyes for.'

'OK, so you nearly made a bad choice in men. Once. But I make a habit of it, don't I? And I keep having kids by them. The counsellor says I'm a "serial romantic".'

'Well, perhaps so,' conceded Meg. 'But there's nothing wrong with romance as such, you know. Still, maybe next time you should try for a little less moonlight and roses and a little more contraception?'

'Maybe I should just give men up, full stop.'

'That's the alternative,' agreed Meg. 'But I can't quite see you taking the veil.'

Ain't that the truth, thought Carmen, chain-eating her way through a box of Galaxy truffles. Carmen Jones: love addict. Maybe if I'm really fat and spotty, she reasoned, nobody will fancy me, so it'll be physically impossible to get myself into any more trouble . . .

'I appreciate the chat, Mrs S, I really do,' she said, unwrapping another chocolate with a rustle of cellophane. 'You've really helped me get things clear in my mind.'

'You're very welcome, I'm sure.'

'Actually, I could do with a spot of advice now,' she admitted. 'About this silly TV programme I've got myself and Lorna mixed up in. I'm beginning to wonder if I shouldn't pull out.'

Meg stopped smoothing imaginary creases out of her skirt. 'Why's that, dear? Have you got cold feet?'

'It's not me, it's Robbie. I'm worried about showing myself up on the telly and upsetting him even more. I just want to do the right thing, you see, and I guess I'm not very good at working out what that is.'

'Has Robbie said he doesn't want you to go on TV?'

'Well . . . no. Actually he seems quite interested, but even so.'

'Not that my opinion's worth much,' said Meg, 'but if it was me, I think I'd go ahead and do it. Go out and show Robbie and everybody else what a great mum he's got.'

'But I'm not a great mum,' protested Carmen. 'I'm a failure.'

'Says who?' Meg didn't give her a chance to answer: 'says me.' 'Come on Carmen, be yourself and concentrate on being a mother to those children of yours. For what it's worth, I think you're doing a pretty good job,' she added.

'Really?' Stunned, Carmen halted in mid-chew.

'Really, but don't quote me on it. Now, I know you're eating chocolates, I can hear the rustling. Pull yourself together and put them away. Do you want the new baby to look like a sumo wrestler?'

'I need a wee-wee,' announced Leo loudly, in the middle of the interactive science display. A few giggles from other people in the gallery greeted this announcement, but Leo was unabashed. 'I really, really do,' he added, hopping from one leg to the other just to convey the urgency of the situation.

'No problem,' smiled Aileen. 'There's a Ladies' just through the next gallery. You and your mum can go in together.'

Leo looked horrified. 'Don't want to go in the Ladies'! Want to go in the Boys'!'

'It's all right, I'll take him,' volunteered George, taking Leo by the hand. 'Just point me in the direction of the Gents' and we'll see you back here in a few minutes.'

A few minutes passed, then a few more. Aileen started glancing more frequently at her watch. 'Perhaps I'd better go and see if they need anything.'

'Perhaps there's a big queue?' wondered Lorna out loud. But that didn't sound right: everybody knew there were never queues in men's loos, only women's.

She and Aileen were about to head off towards the Gents' cloakroom when George reappeared, short of breath and very red in the face.

'What's the matter – where's Leo?' demanded Lorna, heart in mouth.

'He gave me the slip! One minute I'm in the cubicle and he's standing right outside. "Don't you move from there," I tell him. "No, Grandad," he says, all sweetness and light. And two minutes later, when I come out, the little blighter's wandered off!'

A thousand horrible scenarios instantly entered Lorna's head, turning her blood to ice. 'No! Leo – my baby! You've got to find my baby! What if something horrible's happened to him? What if he's been abducted?'

'It's OK, Mrs Price, we'll find him,' promised Aileen, and she switched on her walkie-talkie. 'Reception? I want you to broadcast a missing child alert.'

George was caught between anguish and fury. 'I told him! He promised! Last time it happened, he promised he wouldn't do it again . . .'

Lorna looked at him sharply. 'Last time? What do you mean, last time? Are you telling me this has happened before?'

George cowered under her laser-beam glare. This was no time to fudge the issue; he was going to have to come clean about the April Glade Shopping Experience.

As luck would have it, it took all of five minutes to track Leo down. He was precisely where Aileen predicted he would be: back in the Dinosaur Gallery, with the animatronic T-Rex.

Only he wasn't just looking at it: he was climbing up one of its back legs.

'Leo Price, get down here this minute!' roared George.

'Don't shout at him!' pleaded Lorna. 'He might fall off! Oh Leo, what are you doing?'

Leo spotted his mother, gave a cheery wave, and slid back down the leg as though it were a banister. 'I want to see its teeth,' he declared, 'but I can't reach.'

Aileen bent down to his level. 'That was a very silly thing to do,' she said. 'You could have hurt yourself and then how would your mummy and your grandad feel? Hmm?'

Leo had the good grace to look slightly downcast. 'I only wanted to see its teeth,' he protested.

Lorna didn't know whether to hug him or strangle him. 'Leo, you promised your grandad you'd never run off again. You broke your promise.'

190

Their eyes met. And perhaps Leo could see the pain in his mother's gaze, because his lower lip started to tremble, and he blurted out, 'I'm sorry. I won't do it again, I promise.'

'Proper promise this time?' demanded Lorna sternly.

His round blue eyes shone wetly as he nodded. 'Proper promise.' He sniffed. 'Are we not going to see dragons now?' he ventured fearfully.

Lorna suppressed a smile. 'It's your birthday and I promised, remember? And mummies always keep their promises. Just be sure you keep yours too.'

The trip to Regent's Park Zoo passed off uneventfully. The komodo dragons were suitably scary, the bug house had sufficient mini-beasts to delight the most discerning six-year-old, and nobody ran off, went missing, fell in the canal, or was abducted by aliens.

The only flaw in the great master plan was Eoin. All his assurances about getting back to them 'in good time' for the return journey sounded pretty hollow when they tried to contact him with ten minutes to go before the train left, and found his mobile phone was switched off.

'I'm going to kill him,' George declared very calmly and quietly, as they climbed aboard and went off in search of their reserved seats.

'Don't be silly, Dad. I'm sure it must be something important that's held him up if his phone is off.' Lorna heard herself talking the talk, but even she wasn't sure she believed what she was saying. The feeling was more one of disappointment than of anger. He's let me down and he's let Leo down, she told herself; and a little bit more of the gilt has fallen off the gingerbread.

There was still no sign of him when the whistle blew and the Cheltenham Spa express laboured out of Paddington Station, leaving London and all its dinosaurs and dragons behind.

Lorna sat back in her seat and watched Leo kneeling up, face to the window, trying to catch farewell glimpses of the darkening city. 'Did you have a nice birthday, Leo?'

He screwed his head round. 'Yes thank you, Mummy. And I'm sorry I ran away.' He paused. 'Where did Eoin go, and why didn't he come back?'

'I'm not sure,' confessed Laura. 'I think he had to see a lady who was having a baby.'

Leo digested this piece of information. 'I liked it better when he went away,' he said, matter-of-factly, and went on staring out of the window.

It's funny, thought Lorna suddenly, but do you know what? So did I. Drop-dead sexy you may be, but you're going to need a damned good excuse if you're going to worm your way back into my good books, Dr Eoin Sullivan.

It was past Leo's bedtime by the time they arrived back home, and all three of them were exhausted.

Meg, on the other hand, was crisp, fresh and had a three-course meal on the table before they'd even got their coats off. 'Did you have a lovely time? That's wonderful. Leo, go and wash your hands and we'll all have something nice to eat. George, sit down before you fall down. You look completely worn out.'

'How's Hope?' asked Lorna.

'Oh fine, fine. You'll never guess what – I was leaning over to tuck her in, and she looked up at me and smiled, and said "Mama"! Isn't that cute? I suppose it's with me spending so much time looking after her.'

'Cute. Yeah,' said Lorna, feeling a pang of resentment deep in her guts. What sort of mother has a little girl who thinks Grandma is her mummy? she asked herself. Not a good one, that was for sure.

'Oh, some people phoned while you were out,' Meg went on. 'Carmen and I had a little chat.'

'Is she all right?'

'What dear? Oh yes, fine, fine. Just gets herself into a tizzy, that girl. Then that Sasha girl from the television rang up.'

Lorna's stomach plummeted from a great height. She'd been trying to put *Rather Your Job* to the back of her mind, in the forlorn hope that if she ignored it, it might obligingly go away and get itself cancelled. 'Oh. What did she say? Is there a problem?'

'Not as far as I could tell. Apparently they're planning to film the pilot programme the week after next. That's good news, isn't it?'

'Great,' Lorna agreed weakly.

'But I've saved the best for last.' Meg's eyes sparkled with secret excitement. 'Sarah rang too, and guess what? She's expecting a baby!'

Lorna's jaw dropped. 'Sarah? My sister, who said she'd rather die than spoil her figure having babies?'

'Yes! I knew Jeremy would get her to change her mind. Isn't that just wonderful?'

Chapter 22

Sasha's eyes narrowed to critical slits in her porcelain-perfect complexion. 'The hairstyle's fine darling, but the bleach-job's a bit, well, chav.'

Lorna bristled. It was bad enough having to invite a TV crew into your bedroom and feed them all your chocolate biscuits, without them doing a demolition job on your appearance while you paraded up and down in your smalls like a reject from the Damart catalogue. 'It's not a bleach-job, it's natural!'

'Oh,' said Sasha, looking surprised. She peered more closely. 'Are you sure?' When Lorna replied with a stony-faced glare, she shrugged her shoulders. 'Ah well, when all's said and done I suppose that's what our viewers are looking for: the common touch. Now then, let's see you in the uniform.'

Lorna struggled into the jacket and skirt Carmen's boss Les had provided. It was made from hairy bottle-green polyester, was tight and baggy in all the wrong places, and smelt strongly of wet dog.

'Oh dear,' said Sasha. 'Jolyon – I don't suppose you've time to put a few darts in that jacket?'

'Sorry love,' replied Jolyon the wardrobe man, who – despite all appearances to the contrary – was in fact rampantly heterosexual, with a wife in Stroud and a mistress on the Isle of Wight. 'I've got my work cut out re-making that tunic for that girl who's going to be a midwife. You might have warned me she was up the stick, I've had to put Velcro all over the place.'

Sasha was contemplating Lorna's legs and biting the tip of her beautifully-manicured scarlet nail. 'I don't suppose you have any higher heels than those?'

Lorna looked down at her feet. She was wearing her favourite sleek black shoes with the Louis heel – smart, but nothing she couldn't walk all day in. After all, she was going to be clamping cars, not dancing the

193

Can-Can. 'What's wrong with these?' she demanded. 'They're my interview shoes.'

'They're dull, darling – dull, dull, dull!' exclaimed Jolyon. 'What we want here is more colour and style ... think hidden passions surging within ...'

'I'm supposed to be a wheel-clamper,' protested Lorna, 'not Mata Hari. And I get blisters the size of coconuts if I wear high heels.'

'No problem, let's compromise,' said Sasha, her head and shoulders buried in Lorna's built-in wardrobe. 'Here, wear these.' She re-emerged with the three-inch designer patent wedges, half a size too small, that Lorna had bought long ago in a moment of madness from the Seuss & Goldman sale. She had never worn them. In fact she hadn't even seen them since the day she shoved them at the back of the wardrobe and tried to forget they existed.

They were truly hideous.

'I can't wear those!'

'Don't be silly. Go on, put them on.' Sasha clapped her hands triumphantly as Lorna took a breath and rammed her toes in. 'See? Style and comfort. The perfect combination. Now, let's go downstairs and record the opening chat with Melissa.'

Across town, Carmen breathed in hard and fastened the white tunic over her tight, stretchy maroon trousers. It wasn't the fashion look of the decade, but as she looked at herself in the mirror, for a fleeting moment she felt like ... well ... someone.

She went along the landing to Robbie's room, knocked and went in. He was huddled among the chaos of books, discarded clothes and bicycle spares, busily zapping something on his X-Box.

'What do I look like?'

He paused the game and spun round on his chair. 'Fat,' he replied, and then turned back to the screen.

'Oh,' said Carmen, instantly deflated. Mind you, she could see what he meant. 'That's not fat, that's baby,' she countered, prodding her stomach as she perched on the end of her son's bed. 'Well, some of it is. The rest's probably chocolate mini-rolls.'

He shrugged. 'I didn't say you looked bad, Mum,' he said. 'Just fat. You'd look all wrong if you were thin.'

'You're thin,' she pointed out. 'Mind you, you take after—' She stopped and bit her lip, cursing her clumsiness.

'My dad, I know.'

There was a short silence.

'Robbie.'

'What?'

'Do you want me to pull out of this silly TV show? I can if you want me to.'

He looked at her. Behind him, a couple of Airfix planes hung from the ceiling on lengths of cotton, swaying gently in the warm air rising from the games console. 'Why?'

'Because I don't want to embarrass you. I think I've been doing too much of that lately.'

He shook his head. 'I'm sorry Mum,' he mumbled. 'I'm sorry I ran away. And I'm sorry I told you that stuff the other lads said about you.'

Carmen looked him straight in the eye. 'Well I'm not. I'm glad you did. You can't change something if you don't know what it is, can you?'

He considered this for a moment. 'Don't change too much, Mum. I like you the way you are.' He looked up. 'And I want you to do the TV thing.' His downcast face cracked into a smile. 'It'll be a great.'

'People look even fatter on the telly, you know. I'll be the size of a house.'

'I don't care.'

Carmen got up to go. 'See you later then. Wish me luck.'

'Yeah.' Just as she got to the door, he stopped her. 'Mum.'

She turned back. 'Yes love?'

'About Dad.'

Her heart sank but she tried not to show it. 'Yes?'

'I know he wasn't a nice person and I don't suppose he is now either. But . . . but I'd like to meet him, face to face. Just to see, you know. To see the other half of where I come from. Would you be really upset if I—'

'Tried to find him?'

'Yeah. Would you?'

She wanted to shout out 'you bet I would', but instead she smiled and shook her head. 'Of course not love. If you want to find your dad we'll do it together.'

And then she put on the bravest face in her collection and stepped out into the limelight.

After thirty years in the clamping business, Les 'Chappie' Chappell was not the calmest man in the world, and his knuckles were white as they clutched at the dashboard of the elderly van.

'Bleedin' 'ell woman, you nearly had us in the 'edge!'

'Look I'm doing my best, all right?' Lorna struggled with the gear-stick as they juddered round the roundabout on Tewkesbury Road. It was like wrestling a rusty tin-opener through a can of concrete, and it didn't help that there was a camera mounted in the back of the van, and another in the Channel Six car in front, recording her every moment of humiliation. 'When's the last time you had this thing serviced?' she panted. 'Ten Sixty-six?'

Chappie picked his teeth with a credit card. They were irregular, yellow, and smelt of rancid cheese. 'Don't look at me, that's Head Office's responsibility, I'm just Area Manager, me.'

'Area Manager? There's only you and Carmen!'

'That's right. She's the area and I'm the manager. Simple, see. Now, take the next right into World of Sheds – we've got a contract to clamp anyone without a permit.' He screwed his head round and gave the camera behind him the benefit of a winning smile. 'How'd you fancy tackling your very first serious offender, Lorna my girl?'

'You make it sound like the Bronx or something,' commented Lorna, turning into the car park.

'Well it has its moments. Did I tell you about the time that woman whacked me with a frozen chicken? Three separate skull fractures I had. And then there was the other time—'

Lorna got out of the van. 'I think I'll just watch for now, if that's OK with you.'

Chappie laughed. 'You're not getting out of it that easily, my girl. You know what they say, there's only one way to learn a job and that's to do it.' He reached behind him and thrust several large yellow lumps of metal into her arms. 'Off you go, kid. Search and destroy.'

And then he settled back in his seat and got out his sandwiches.

An hour into her day as a midwife, Carmen was beginning to wonder if she'd missed her vocation in life.

OK, so this was only the Post-Natal ward, and she wasn't going to go near any of the serious giving-birth stuff until the afternoon, but hey, this was easy. After four babies of her own and another on the way, stinky nappies and cracked nipples held no fear for Carmen Jones.

On the other hand, Rose Finnegan was enough to scare any baby straight back inside its mother. And Carmen was already getting tired of hearing her tell anyone who would listen that Crocus ward was a 'serious clinical environment', which had no place for this 'media sideshow'. Especially since the awful woman seemed to worm herself into every single shot.

Not that she was the only person fascinated by the cameras. Colin Jenkins, normally the original invisible man, had suddenly found that he had no important meetings to go to, and Honey had taken to making frequent trips to the ward kitchen – a journey that just happened to take her right past the sexy lighting man with the impressive halogen spots. As for the patients, if there were a law against excessive eye make-up they'd have been facing a life-sentence. Everybody was smiling like their lives depended on it.

In fact it was all going remarkably smoothly. Which was probably why the unit director was so pissed-off. He snapped his fingers tetchily. 'Hey, you – Sister – Florence – whatever your name is.'

Colin's smile slipped a fraction and the patient whose drip he was checking let out a giggle. 'Senior Midwife Colin Jenkins,' he reminded the director for the fourth time.

'Yeah, right, whatever. Look, can you find something a bit more challenging for this Carmen girl to do? Otherwise I'm going to have to resort to a comedy bedpan-dropping incident. And I want you to know, I really don't want to have to do that in a quality show.'

Rose Finnegan's eyes rolled back. 'Quality! Is that what you call it?'

The director frowned in her direction. 'And while you're at it, Corin—'

'Colin!' he repeated through clenched teeth.

'Yeah, whatever. While you're at it, can you find something else for the old witch to do? This is going out at tea-time; we don't want her scaring the little kiddies.'

Carmen tried not to look too pleased as Rose Finnegan was dispatched, scowling, to Pathology with a crate of nasty-looking biological specimens. 'What do you want me to do then?' she asked Colin.

He pondered. 'Well, you could assist me in removing some sutures from Mrs Finch over there.'

Mrs Finch beamed. 'Ooh, fame at last.'

The director brightened. 'Sutures? That's stitches, right? Great, a bit of real medical action – the punters love that. Now, where exactly are these stitches, so we can get the lighting right?'

'In her perineum.'

'Her what?'

'You know – down below.' Colin mimed something between the stern and the water-line.

'My God,' exclaimed the director, blanching. 'We can't have that on early-evening TV! Haven't you got any elbows or ears or something she can practise on?'

Carmen burst out laughing. 'Since when do babies come out of ears?'

The director sighed and struck a line through the notes on his clipboard. 'OK, I give in. Go and fetch the bedpan.'

*

197

Lorna was loath to admit it, even to herself; but this clamping business was rather addictive. And even Chappie had a grudging admiration for her natural knack with a Denver Boot. The funny thing was that although she'd always hated conflict, laying down the law to peeved motorists didn't seem to bother her in the least. Matter of fact, it was quite liberating – and she even said so, to camera.

'Where next?' she enquired as they climbed back into the van after clamping a couple of illicit hatchbacks behind World of Sheds and sticking tickets on their screens.

Chappie checked his list. 'Car park behind that big video rental place. Loads of people think they can get away with parking there for nothing.' He rubbed his hands together. 'Not while we're around they can't.'

The camera operator in the back of the van stuck his head between the seats. 'You really love your job, don't you Chappie?'

Chappie guffawed. 'What – bein' paid to make other people's lives a misery? What's not to love? Best job in the world, this is.'

He was certainly right about there being rich pickings in the car park behind Starstruck Video. There probably wasn't a single driver in Cheltenham who hadn't left their car there at least once and then sneaked off to the High Street to do a spot of shopping. The trouble was, it was just too darned convenient. Lorna felt a pang of retrospective remorse as she recalled all the moments she'd parked there – and she'd never rented a video in her life. But it was only a small pang. Basically she was having too much fun to feel really guilty.

Good job I don't do this permanently, she thought as she wrote out another ticket and tucked it under a windscreen wiper; I'd probably end up as weird as Chappie, putting in unpaid overtime just for the buzz. Scary.

As Lorna stalked the rows of parked cars, she spotted one she recognised. Red, sporty, distinctive . . . well, well. She took a quick look round her but there was no sign of its owner and there was definitely no Starstruck parking voucher in the window, so she signalled to Chappie and he brought over a clamp.

'You're good at this,' he remarked as she fixed the big yellow lump of metal securely in place. 'I hope you're not thinking of takin' it up full-time, 'cause I'm not sure I can take the competition.'

'You're all right,' she replied over her shoulder. 'I haven't got the muscles for it.'

'Ooh, I dunno.' Chappie's cheesy teeth reappeared in a smutty grin. 'They look all right from where I'm standin'.'

Lorna looked down, blushed, readjusted her top and hoped that bit didn't make it to the final cut. As she stood up and wiped her oily hands on the seat of her uniform trousers, she happened to look in the direction of the High Street – at the very moment that Eoin Sullivan came striding round the corner into the car park.

Lorna called to the director. 'Stop filming for a minute.'

'Why?'

'I want to go and have a word with a friend, OK? And then I'm just popping inside for a wee.'

'What – again? Go on then, but make it a quick one.'

Lorna scooted across the car park in Eoin's direction. He didn't spot her until she was almost right in front of him. Mind you, he wasn't accustomed to seeing her dressed like a World War Two tank driver.

'Blondie?' He guffawed. 'Oh my God, what have they done to you?'

'Oh, so you do remember who I am then?' replied Lorna coolly. 'I mean, I couldn't help wondering. You've been avoiding me at work all week.'

Eoin assumed a look of wounded innocence. 'Oh come on, you're not still angry with me about London, are you? I sent you a really big bunch of flowers.'

'It's not me you should be apologising to,' Lorna replied. 'It's Leo.'

This provoked a look of faint exasperation. 'Lorna love, he's a little boy. And it was only a trip to the zoo. Little boys forget stuff like that all the time.'

She looked at him steadily. 'You don't know much about kids really, do you? Considering you've got one of your own.'

Eoin's brows knitted. 'Is that supposed to be some sort of veiled insult?'

'Eoin, if I wanted to insult you I wouldn't bother veiling it. No, it's just a statement of fact. There's some stuff kids remember forever, especially stuff that happens on their birthdays.'

Eoin deflated ever so slightly. 'All right, all right, I admit it was a bit selfish of me, but one minute this woman's undergoing a routine examination, the next she's in labour, and it was such an unusual case of conjoined twins I just couldn't resist tagging along.' He looked earnestly into her eyes. 'I do have to think of my career, you know.'

'Yes, you do, don't you,' replied Lorna dryly.

The barbed comment bounced off, leaving not so much as a scratch. 'Anyway Lorna, we can talk later, yeah? How about dinner tomorrow night and then back to yours?' He didn't give her a chance to answer, just brushed a swift kiss across her lips. 'But I have to rush now, the other TV crew are doing the labour ward this afternoon, and they specially asked me to be there.'

'Oh,' said Lorna.

He raised an eyebrow. 'Oh what?'

'Oh, I don't think you're going to be rushing anywhere just yet,' Lorna replied sweetly.

'Why's that then?'

'Because I've just clamped your Mazda.'

Everybody within range took an instinctive step back as Eoin stormed into the labour ward, half an hour late and in the foulest of tempers.

'Seventy-five quid!' he seethed as he stomped past Andrew Rennie. 'Seventy-five bloody quid it cost me to get my car unclamped!' He caught sight of the TV crew and mellowed slightly. 'Sorry I'm late, got held up – medical emergency, you know how it is.'

Carmen exchanged amused looks with the cameraman. 'Sorry doc,' she said, 'but you've been rumbled. Everybody knows Lorna clamped you.'

Eoin's face fell.

'Don't worry, it'll make for great TV,' the unit director assured him. He lowered his voice. 'By the way, I was meaning to ask you – have you and the lovely Lorna got a bit of a thing going on? Only viewers love that – bit of the old sexual tension.'

Before Eoin had a chance to reply one way or the other, June Godwin arrived with important news. 'You all know Deborah Grant – she's a mid-wife on Crocus ward?'

Everybody nodded except Carmen. 'Is that Debs – the one Lorna worked with when she first started?'

'That's right. Well, she's just coming up to us from Ante-Natal. First baby, two weeks overdue, they've done a sweep—'

'A what?' Carmen whispered to Andrew.

'Sort of internal rummage,' he explained. 'Brings on labour sometimes.'

'Oh, one of those. A James Herriot.'

'—and they were about to send us up to her to be induced, when she went into labour spontaneously,' June went on. 'Carmen, could you assist Andrew and Dr Sullivan in the delivery suite when she comes up?'

Carmen's eyes grew round with excitement. 'You mean I'm actually going to deliver somebody's baby?'

'Not if I've got anything to do with it,' Eoin snapped. 'You'll stand well out of the way, keep quiet, and leave all the technical stuff to the pro-fessionals.'

'Ja, mein Führer,' muttered Carmen mutinously.

Andrew winced. This was not going to be the easiest of working rela-tionships.

Lorna was getting used to the sound of Chappie's mobile phone, as alter-nately distressed and infuriated drivers rang him to pay up and get their cars released. It came as more of a surprise when her own phone burbled into life.

'Lorna Price ... who did you say? Sarah? Oh, hi.' She tried to sound enthusiastic at the sound of her sister's voice. 'No, of course it's not inconvenient. They're what? Turning brown? Well yes, actually it is normal. Completely normal. No, you don't need to see the doctor. Yes, of course I'm sure. 'Bye.'

She ended the call and turned to Chappie. 'My sister,' she explained. 'Pregnant and neurotic.'

Five minutes later, it rang again. 'Sarah? No, I told you, it's not a problem at all. Green? No, not necessarily. Have you eaten anything? Well there you are then. Just have a dry biscuit and see if that calms it down.'

'Perils of being the only midwife in the family,' she explained with a weak smile.

It went on like this for the next half-hour, until finally Lorna's patience ran out. 'Sarah?' Oh God, she groaned inwardly, not again. 'Well yes, actually it is rather inconvenient – I'm in the middle of being filmed for that TV show Mum told you about. So if you don't want your swollen nipples all over Channel Six South-West, I'd hold off phoning for a few hours if I were you.'

Unbelievably, ten minutes later – when Lorna really thought Sarah had got the message – her phone rang again.

'Sarah, I ... Oh Jeremy, it's you! Debs is in labour? Hey, that's great. Now keep calm, and remember it'll probably be ages, with it being her first. Yes, hours and hours I'm afraid. Keep me posted, and I'll be over to see her as soon as we've finished filming here.'

'Friend having a baby,' she explained to Chappie and the crew.

'Is everybody you know pregnant? Chappie demanded.

'Mostly,' she admitted.

He edged away slightly. 'Nothin' personal love, I'm just not takin' any chances, see.'

Debs had always wanted Dr Sullivan to see her naked; only perhaps not quite like this.

She filled the bath like a big pink whale, displacing almost all of the water, while Carmen rubbed her back, Jeremy said encouraging things and Debs occasionally swore as the contractions got stronger.

'I phoned all your friends, like you asked me to,' said Jeremy. 'And Lorna's promised to come as soon as she can. Is this making you feel better, darling?' he enquired hopefully.

'Is it fuck,' spat Debs.

'Bugger, we'll have to bleep that bit as well,' said the cameraman.

201

Meanwhile, Andrew and Eoin were huddled in the corner of the delivery room, having a lively discussion about the foetal heart monitor. 'But you always use one,' protested Andrew. 'You're obsessed with technology.'

'Well today I'm not using one,' hissed Eoin. 'She's a perfectly normal, healthy woman, and I can see no need for continuous monitoring in this particular case.'

Andrew twigged. 'You mean, you overheard the director wittering on to that Melissa woman about natural birth, so you figured that's what they want to see?'

Eoin gave him a withering look. 'Just go and get on with whatever male midwives do.'

'We deliver babies. Safely.'

'Well you're not delivering this one. Haven't you go some other patient to practise on?'

Melissa the presenter chose that moment to come over and join the conversation. 'So, everything is fine?'

Eoin offered the camera a dazzling smile. 'Absolutely, Melissa. And as you see, we're allowing our patient to give birth in as natural a way as possible.'

'So I see,' smiled Melissa. 'So you're a believer in making your patients feel at home?'

'Oh definitely. You see, we often find that a cold, clinical environment with lots of tubes and monitors frightens mothers-to-be and it can even halt labour. I've always felt that minimal intervention was the best course wherever possible.'

'Liar,' mouthed Andrew, clearly hoping that the camera would pick it up.

'So we won't be needing you,' Eoin went on with a sort of ferocious smile. 'You can go and do something else, can't you Andrew?'

'With *respect,* Doctor, I really think I ought to stay,' Andrew objected, with an expression that looked about as far from respectful as it was possible to get. 'There'll be no qualified staff in here, and nobody to supervise Carmen, and what if—?'

'*I* will be here,' said Eoin through clenched teeth. 'So you can go. Now.'

Andrew went with bad grace, leaving the field open for Eoin to show off.

'So, how's our midwife-for-a-day doing?' asked Melissa, with a cheery wave to Carmen.

'Oh, fine, fine,' replied Eoin, his smile never slipping even for an instant. 'She's a natural. Mind you, with four children already and another on the way that's hardly a surprise, is it, ha, ha?'

'And she's provided us with quite a few amusing incidents, hasn't she? Like when she was talking to that girl's mother, and she turned out to be her lesbian partner. And when she tripped up carrying that bedpan . . .'

Eoin fell about laughing as if that were the funniest thing in the entire world. Carmen would have liked to throw in some appropriate insult, but Debs was having another contraction.

'Aaaaaaagh!' she roared, clutching at the edges of the bath. 'That bloody hurts.'

'I know darling,' soothed Jeremy, stroking her sweat-matted hair. 'I know.'

'No you bloody don't, and it's all your bloody bastard fault! AND I WANT AN EPIDURAL!'

'Doctor,' said Carmen, 'I think Debs wants an epidural.'

Eoin spun round and took Debs's hand. 'Are we absolutely sure about that? Wouldn't we prefer to give nature's endorphins a chance to—'

'No we damn well wouldn't! Get me out of this bath and give me an epidural NOW!'

'Oh for God's sake,' Eoin hissed under his breath. 'Can't you wait a bit, till the anaesthetist comes back?'

The door opened and a nursing assistant's head popped round. 'Phone call for you, Dr Sullivan.'

'Can't you see I'm busy?' he snapped. 'We're trying to film a television programme here.'

'Sorry Doctor, but it's a Mr Hans van den Vries, from Harley Street. Something about a patient with conjoined twins . . . Apparently he'd like your opinion on something.'

Eoin's ears pricked up like radio antennae and his chest swelled like a bullfrog's. 'My opinion, you say?'

'Yes, Doctor. And there's a courier downstairs at reception with a package for Melissa.'

Eoin rubbed his hands. 'Right then. I'd better go and answer that phone call. You'll keep an eye on Deborah for me while I'm gone, won't you Carmen?'

'What about my epidural?' demanded Debs. 'Come back here, you—!' But Eoin had already gone. 'Bloody doctors.'

Melissa eyed the scene, hands on hips. Fat pregnant woman in bath making the occasional strangled hippo noise, other fat pregnant woman watching, first fat pregnant woman's husband faffing around. Not exactly the stuff of great TV. 'Hmph. Doesn't look like there's going to be much action here for a while. Keep filming; I'll be back in a couple of minutes.'

*

203

Suddenly Carmen had the sobering realisation that she was alone with a woman in labour, a cameraman and a man who would probably have been much happier pacing up and down in some distant waiting-room.

'The doctor will be back soon,' Carmen said, as much to encourage herself as the other two.

Debs looked up at her sheepishly. 'It hurts,' she said, very quietly. 'And he's a bastard.'

'You're telling me,' nodded Carmen. She squeezed Debs's hand. 'But you'll be OK. You're doing great. Isn't she, Jeremy?' she added, poking him in the ribs.

He started out of his daze. 'Y-yes, darling. You're very brave.' He looked anxiously at Carmen. 'Should I be telling her to push or something? Or breathe? I can't remember?'

That's OK, thought Carmen; neither can I. 'Just do what feels right,' she said. 'Let nature tell you what to do. Jeremy – you couldn't stick your head out of the door and see if the doctor's on his way?'

Jeremy got up and opened the door to look outside.

And then something happened. Debs went rigid with pain; not just the pain of the regular contractions, but something huge and terrible and overwhelming, that took over her whole body and drained all the colour from her face. A pain so bad that she couldn't even cry out.

And suddenly, all in a rush, the water in the bath turned a deep, opaque crimson.

'Ugh,' said the cameraman, recoiling.

'Oh my God,' gasped Carmen, 'that's not right'. And she leapt for the emergency bell on the wall, letting all Hell loose.

Lorna was just taking the clamp off a sales rep's car when her phone rang again. She almost didn't answer it, since it was probably Sarah again, wanting to know if being pregnant was going to make her eyelashes fall out, or give her rampant acne. But then she thought about Debs, and relented. This might be news about Crocus ward's latest happy event.

'Lorna Price.'

'Lorna, it's Jeremy, something's happened—'

A finger poked Lorna in the back. 'Excuse me, but while you're enjoying a nice little chat, I'm missing out on valuable commission.'

She put her hand over the mouthpiece. 'I'm sorry sir, I'll only be a minute. Jeremy, are you still there?'

'It's Debs, Lorna. I'm really worried. One minute she's fine, and then the next . . .'

Lorna felt a cold shiver. 'What's wrong?'

204

'There was blood everywhere, Lorna. I don't know anything, except that they've rushed her off to theatre. Lorna – what if she dies?'

'I'm sorry sir,' she said, getting to her feet and handing the tools to the sales rep, 'but you'll have to take the clamp off yourself. Chappie, give me the keys to the van. I have to get to the hospital. Now.'

Chapter 23

Lorna, Andrew and Honey sat in an adoring semicircle around Debs's bed, while little Erik Jeremy Kiefer Sanderson slumbered blissfully in her arms, totally unaware of the fuss that had surrounded his arrival. Jeremy senior had finally been persuaded that his wife and baby son were going to be all right, and had crawled off home to snatch a few hours' sleep. Carmen had just about recovered from her moment of unwanted glory. As for Debs, she was wearing the pink-cheeked exhilaration of hard-won triumph.

'You must be exhausted,' said Lorna. 'Perhaps we should go and let you get some rest?'

'Don't you dare!' retorted Debs. 'I already feel like a total fraud, lying here in this private room. Anybody would think I was ill or something.'

'Debs love,' pointed out Andrew, 'you've had an emergency Caesarian and a blood transfusion. And you're a member of staff. If that doesn't entitle you to a private room I don't know what does.'

'Quite right,' agreed Lorna. 'It's not as if you get any other perks in this job, is it? If I were you, I'd just lie there eating chocolates and enjoy the rest while you can.'

'After all,' Honey pointed out with a smile, 'you won't get any rest once you get home! Little Erik will make sure of that. So you'll have to hurry up and get better.'

Debs looked down dotingly at the sleeping bundle nestling in her arms. 'Oh, we're just fine,' she smiled, stroking the soft white-blond fluff on her son's tiny head. 'Aren't we, sweetie? Which is more than I can say for some people,' she added, raising her head to look at Lorna. 'How on earth did you get that black eye? Brawling in the street with Rose Finnegan?'

Everybody laughed except Lorna, who was mortified. It was bad enough having a black eye, without having to admit how she'd acquired it. 'The TV crew were filming the last sequence in the car park,' she admitted. 'And Chappie called me over, and what did I do? I tripped over one of my own wheel clamps and bashed my eye on some bloke's stupid hood ornament.'

Honey clapped a hand to her mouth. 'You mean they filmed it? Oh God, I can't wait to see it on TV.'

'Well I'm glad somebody's looking forward to it,' said Lorna dryly. 'But pardon me if I emigrate or disappear or something before then.'

'If anybody ought to be doing a runner,' opined Andrew, 'it's Eoin bloody Sullivan. And yes, Lorna,' he added, 'I know you're going out with him but that doesn't stop him being an incompetent tosser. Sending me out like that, and then buggering off to answer the bloody telephone. If it hadn't been for your mate Carmen, Debs could have died.'

'He's right you know,' said Honey.

'I know,' sighed Lorna. 'Don't worry, I'm not going to defend him. From what I've heard, he was completely unprofessional.' She had to ask the question that had been troubling her ever since she arrived at the hospital. 'Are you going to lodge a complaint about him?'

Debs looked surprised. 'Complain about Dr Sullivan? Of course not! I mean, anybody can make a mistake, and – well – Erik and me, we're here aren't we? And we're both fine.'

'Only because the people in theatre knew what they were doing,' countered Andrew.

But Debs wasn't having any of it. 'Oh, these things happen. And you know me, I'm not one to cause trouble.'

'You won't have to,' pointed out Honey. 'They filmed the whole thing, remember? If you ask me, he's stuffed.'

Lorna couldn't have put it better herself. Things were not looking at all good for Eoin; and disturbingly, she wasn't even sure how she felt about that.

'Stuffed' was not a word in Eoin Sullivan's vocabulary; or at least, not unless it was followed by 'quails' eggs in a light sauce béarnaise'. And he had no intention of being eaten for breakfast.

He had chosen the restaurant with care: nothing too pretentious – just a tasteful little French bistro he happened to know on the outskirts of Winchcombe. It was small, authentic, and exactly the right place for a quiet discussion over dinner with someone from the TV.

'I'm really not sure why you've invited me here,' confessed Melissa, accepting a second glass of red wine. 'I'm the presenter, not the producer.'

Eoin leaned forward to give her the full benefit of his intense blue eyes. 'Yes, but I know you have a great deal of influence. After all, you're a household name. A lot of people say you're the most important person at Channel Six.'

Melissa looked amused. 'Do they? They don't say it to me.'

'You're far too modest. I'm quite sure that anything you happened to say would be taken very seriously by the Channel Six Editorial Board.'

Slowly, she twirled her wine glass by its stem, watching the flickering candlelight turn the wine to dozens of different shades, from pink to deepest crimson. 'And what exactly is it that you want me to happen to say?'

Good, thought Eoin. Cut to the chase. No beating about the bush. 'I want you to tell them that when they screen the pilot for *Rather Your Job*, it would be a really bad idea to include the delivery-room footage of myself and Mrs Sanderson. There's a chance it might be ... misinterpreted.'

The television presenter looked back at him coolly. 'Misinterpreted in what way precisely? I'd have thought it was all perfectly clear.'

He felt a rush of annoyance, but fought it down. It wouldn't do for him to lose his temper in this situation. 'Not at all, Melissa – can I call you Melissa?' He didn't wait for her to reply. 'You see, we're dealing with very technical matters—'

'As I understand it, a woman very nearly bled to death and lost her child.'

'As I said, it's all very technical. And it's far better, surely, to concentrate on Lorna and Carmen and their exploits? Give the masses what they want, all that?'

Melissa dabbed the corners of her mouth with her napkin, folded it neatly and replaced it on the table. 'Thank you for the dinner, Dr Sullivan, but I'm afraid I can't help. I really don't see how doctoring the evidence is going to give us a better programme, and besides, I really don't have nearly as much influence as you imagine.'

It was a pity she'd taken that stance. He'd hoped his softly-softly approach would have the desired effect. Just as well he'd been careful to procure a get-out-of-jail card; and now was the time to play it.

'Actually,' he confessed, 'I asked a friend of mine to have a chat with your Chief Executive while they were out playing golf.' He sipped at his wine. 'Terrible game, golf,' he reflected, 'but I can't deny you do find a fascinating cross-section of influential people playing it. Perhaps I ought to take it up.'

She eyed him warily, trying to weigh up whether or not he was joking. 'You know the Chief Executive?'

'Not personally no. A friend of a friend, you might say. Anyway, this friend of a friend explained about what had happened, and the potential misunderstandings, and the damage that might be done ... and he was very sympathetic. He could quite appreciate why I might want the footage pulled.'

'But he still turned you down, right?'

Eoin smiled broadly. 'Actually that's where you're wrong.'

Melissa's normally inscrutable expression cracked. 'I don't believe you.'

'Fine, I didn't expect you to.' Eoin settled back into his chair and drank a hearty slug of wine. 'Why don't you call him yourself and check? Now, shall we order? I'm really getting rather hungry.'

Lorna gave a huge, jaw-cracking yawn. She really wasn't at all sure why she'd agreed to go to the pub with the others. It wasn't as if she really knew the girl who was getting married; Cherie worked at the other side of the hospital. But she was a friend of June and Kathryn, and everybody else who wasn't on duty was going, so it seemed churlish not to join in.

She was awfully knackered though. An early night with *Heat* magazine and a mug of cocoa would have been more her scene.

Carmen arrived with her youngest while Lorna was putting her coat on to go out. Becca burst through the door like a small and very sturdy tornado: 'Hiya Auntie Lorna, where's Leo? I want to show him my new pyjamas.'

She thundered off into the living-room, like a miniature stampede.

'Wish I had her energy,' Lorna remarked wistfully as Becca disappeared.

'Me too,' admitted Carmen. 'Is it still OK for this one to sleep over? I can take her over to Grace's with the other three if it's not.'

'It's fine,' Lorna assured her. 'Matter of fact, Dad's been looking forward to it all week. He's made up some more Fat Penguin stories to tell them at bedtime.' She chuckled. 'He's a bit of a big kid himself, bless him. Anyhow,' she dotted a kiss on Carmen's cheek, 'I'd better love you and leave you. Shouldn't be too long – I'll just stay long enough to be sociable.'

'I thought it was a hen party,' Carmen called after her as she headed for the door.

Lorna stopped and turned round. 'It is. Sort of.'

'Won't you be the only one not wearing false breasts or *Playboy* bunny-ears or whatever?'

She shrugged. 'Bet I'm the only one with a black eye as well.'

While Lorna was enduring Happy Hour at the Red Pig with a bunch of boozed-up nurses, Carmen was busy helping to round up the children, get them all bathed and persuade them into bed. This was no mean feat with Leo and Becca under the same roof. If they weren't bashing each other with pillows or bouncing up and down on the beds, they were chasing

210

each other up and down the stairs or rolling about on the floor in fits of giggles.

When they were finally all tucked in, with Hope settled down in her room and the bunk beds set up in Leo's, Carmen, George and Meg stole a few blissful moments of rest, perching in a row on the nearest thing to hand – which happened to be the edge of the bath.

'You look tired, dear,' observed Meg.

'So do you, Mrs S,' replied Carmen.

'Yes, but I'm not expecting,' pointed out Meg.

'I should hope not,' grunted George, mopping the sweat from his brow. 'Is it me, or do children have more energy these days?'

'I'm afraid it's you, George,' replied Meg. 'Well, actually it's both of us. We're neither of us getting any younger,' she said to Carmen. 'It's not that we don't love looking after our grandchildren, but – just now and then – I do wonder if we're really up to the job.'

'Of course you are,' Carmen said firmly. 'But I do understand how you must feel. It's a tough job, bringing kids up; and when you're tired you start worrying that things might go wrong.'

'Exactly,' nodded Meg.

'Well they won't,' declared Carmen. 'Because people of your generation are made of sterner stuff. It's true,' she insisted. 'We youngsters are namby-pamby compared to you. I think I'd die if they banned disposable nappies.'

A duet of small but insistent voices came from the bedroom next door. 'Story! Story! We want a story!'

George heaved himself to his feet and adjusted his spectacles. 'I think they're playing my song,' he said wearily; but there was a twinkle in his eye. Carmen could see that Lorna was right. George might be tired out, but he loved telling his children's stories.

'Mind if I listen in?' she asked. 'Nobody ever told me stories when I was little.'

Meg looked utterly shocked. 'Of course you must. Just don't expect too much – I'm afraid they are a little . . . peculiar.'

Two pairs of eyes sparkled in the glow from the Pooh Bear nightlight. As she leaned against the doorframe, just outside the bedroom door, Carmen couldn't remember the last time she'd seen two children so enraptured.

'. . . but Fat Penguin didn't know that the ice was very thin just there,' George went on. 'And what do you think happened?'

'The ice broke!' chorused the children.

'Exactly. As he ran away from the fearsome Black Penguin, his weight

211

started to make the ice quiver and shake and crack. And the little cracks turned into big cracks, and suddenly . . . SPLASH! He fell right into the cold, dark water.'

'But he's a penguin,' pointed out Leo. 'So he's all right, 'cause penguins can swim.'

'Very good Leo, yes that's true. But you're forgetting: he was wearing the disguise he'd put on to hide from the Black Penguin, and the heavy cape and boots pulled him right down under the water. No matter how hard he flapped his flippers, he just sank down and down and down. He couldn't breathe! And then—'

George left a long dramatic pause.

'What, Grandad, what?' demanded Leo.

'Something enormous came whooshing up out of the deep water. Something as big as a submarine and grey like an elephant. And as it shot up towards the surface, it caught Fat Penguin and pushed him up too.

'All of a sudden, it popped up through the broken ice, and Fat Penguin found himself bouncing up and down on top of a huge jet of water that was coming out of the top of the creature's head. Do you know what sort of creature it was?'

Leo did, and opened his mouth, but George signalled to him to give Becca a chance. She thought very hard. 'A fish?'

'Almost. Something much, much bigger.'

'A whale!' blurted out Leo, who couldn't keep silent any longer.

'Yes, it was a whale. With a great big squirt of water, it blew Fat Penguin onto a safe part of the ice. Fat Penguin was terrified. Was the whale going to eat him? Then it opened its enormous mouth and said: "Good afternoon, the name's Bill Krill, pleased to meet you. Don't suppose you'd know the whereabouts of an evil villain called the Black Penguin?"'

There was an 'Aaaw' of disappointment as George announced that that was the end of tonight's part of the story, and that it was time to go to sleep. With a start, Carmen realised that she too was disappointed that it had come to an end. And that gave her an idea.

'That was brilliant, Mr S,' she enthused as he emerged from the bedroom.

'Oh, just a silly old story, you know,' he replied modestly.

'No, really, it was great. I was wondering . . . would you mind writing some of your stories down for me?'

Meg rolled her eyes. 'Don't go encouraging him Carmen dear, he's already more than halfway to his second childhood.'

George blinked. 'Write them down? I've never really thought about writing them down. Why?'

'Well, I'd really love to read them to my kids at bedtime. I know it'd help me to get them to bed on time. And I thought, a mate of mine helps out at our local nursery – maybe she could try them out on the children there? Only if you don't mind, of course.'

George laughed. 'Mind? Of course I don't mind. Do whatever you like with them. If you ask me, there's nothing in the world more rewarding than making a child laugh.'

The Red Hen was not a sophisticated venue. Indeed its facilities were so basic, it was rumoured that on Saturday nights the landlord hired bouncers to throw people in.

But drink was cheap, and therein lay the secrets of its survival. If you were an underpaid nurse or midwife, with a powerful desire to get completely bladdered, the Red Hen could fulfil your every need and still leave you with enough money for a kebab on the way home.

Long before the second tray of tequila shots came round, Lorna was busily thinking up excuses to leave. Everything from death of the family stick insect to the outbreak of interstellar war passed through her head as she fought a losing battle to stay sober.

'Fancy another?' asked Cherie, who was sporting L-plates, a red and white lace garter and a white T-shirt with 'BRIDE' on it in red capitals.

'Just a Coke,' pleaded Lorna.

Cherie laughed. 'A Coke, right.' She winked. 'One vodka and Coke coming right up.'

Kathryn nudged her elbow. 'Might as well relax and concentrate on getting drunk,' she said cheerfully. 'The male strippers aren't on for ages yet.'

Her neighbour leaned over and chuckled dirtily. 'Mind you, they don't call the big one Chopper for nothing, know what I mean?'

Oh God, thought Lorna. I'm only twenty-nine, and I think this is Hell. I ought to be downing triple vodkas and showing my pants with the rest of them, but I just can't. That's not me any more. I'm not sure it ever was.

She was about to make an excuse to go to the Ladies' and see if she could climb out through the window, when a couple more nurses arrived from the hospital, still in uniform. One was very tall, dark and willowy, the other rather petite and blonde and highly made-up – a kind of pocket-sized Marilyn Monroe.

'That's her, Sadie,' said the dark one, pointing at Lorna. Lorna vaguely recognised her from one of the ante-natal clinics. 'She's the one who's going out with him now. Lorna Price she's called.'

'Good God,' said Sadie, taking a few steps forward. Lorna shrank back into her seat, half-expecting to get punched in the face without even knowing why. The Red Hen was the sort of place where things like that happened all the time. 'You look like shit.'

'Oh,' said Lorna. 'Do I?'

Sadie wasn't smiling, but somehow she didn't look exactly aggressive either. She reached out and touched the bruising around Lorna's eye. 'I see the bastard's already been up to his old tricks then.'

'What? Who?' Lorna looked from Sadie to her friend and back, in hope of some explanation. 'I got this hitting my head on a car,' she explained.

'Yes, of course you did,' said Sadie with a humourless laugh. 'Budge up,' she said to Kathryn, who made room for her on the seat. 'Look Lorna, is it? Believe me, I used to say all those things too when people asked me where I'd got the bruises. Anything rather than admit that piece of shit Eoin had been knocking me about.'

'Nobody's been knocking me about,' protested Lorna. 'I told you, the black eye was a stupid accident. Are you trying to say you went out with Eoin Sullivan and he used to hit you?'

Sadie clapped her hands slowly. 'Give the girl a prize.'

'B-but that's rubbish! He couldn't. He just . . . wouldn't.'

'That's what I thought too, till I found out what he used to do to his wife and kid. And even then I didn't believe it. I thought his ex was making it all up, just being malicious, the way he said she was. Then it started. I put up with it at first. In fact I put up with it far too long. Then, the week before Valentine's Day, he went a bit too far and broke two of my fingers.'

No, Lorna told herself. This is rubbish; malicious rubbish spouted by a jealous ex-girlfriend. I am not even going to listen to this.

'Why are you telling me all this?' she demanded.

'Why do you think?' Sadie exploded in exasperation. 'To try and warn you before he does something worse to you, you daft cow.'

'I know he's got his faults, and maybe he even has flashes of temper, but he would never lay a finger on me,' said Lorna.

'You think so? And what about your kids? Would you trust him not to hit them? Ever?'

Lorna wanted to reply 'Of course', but somehow the words dried in her throat.

'Look,' Sadie went on, 'I'm not just doing this for you, I'm doing it because I feel guilty. I should have done something back in February, when he hurt me. But I didn't. I'm still not sure why. Anyhow, the least I can do is tell you what I know. It's up to you whether you listen or not.'

She got up. 'Enjoy the rest of the party'. And she turned to leave with her friend.

'Wait,' said Lorna, and she stopped. 'Just one question before you go. Were you still going out with him back in February?'

'Yes, I told you so.' She grimaced at the remembrance. 'Believe it or not, he was going to take me out to some fancy restaurant do on Valentine's night. He had it all planned – the tickets, the champagne . . . And then he did what he did, and I dumped him. Why do you want to know?' she enquired.

'No reason,' replied Lorna dully. But all of a sudden those tickets for dinner at the Black Tulip didn't seem quite so romantic any more.

Chapter 24

If Lorna had been hoping that everyone would forget about *Rather Your Job*, she was destined to be sorely disappointed. She might just as well have hoped that it would rain marshmallows for all the good it did.

On the evening the pilot programme was due to be aired, her front room looked like Screen Two at the local Odeon, only more crowded. It wasn't just that everyone she knew from the hospital had turned up; Lorna had no idea who half the people were.

She caught up with her mother in the kitchen, humming 'Another opening of another show' as she made industrial quantities of popcorn. 'Who's that woman with the tea-cosy on her head?' she demanded, helping herself to a handful.

Meg administered a tap on the wrist and whisked the bowl away. 'Don't be unkind dear, that's Mrs Paterson from Over-Fifties' Fitness. She wears the hat to hide her nervous alopecia. Amazonian Indians made it, apparently.'

'The alopecia?'

'Now you're just being silly.'

'Well what about that dreadful man with the BO and the creepy smile?'

Meg looked quite shocked. 'Lower your voice, dear, that's the vicar. Now, bring that tray of home-made biscuits and those paper napkins; we don't want greasy crumbs all over your sister's nice sofa, do we?'

Lorna suppressed a wish that Sarah's cast-off green sofa would crumble to dust and take the vicar with it. She had hated that sofa ever since the day it came into the house: the same day that Ed had died, and her whole life had crashed to a cruel standstill. But somehow she'd never summed up the energy to get rid of it, and since her mother liked it so much, it had insinuated its fat Dralon body into a corner of the sitting room, where it sat looking smugly superior to all the other furniture.

I'll get you one day, she promised silently as she passed it on the way to deposit the food on a coffee table.

'Oooh, it's the star of the show!' exclaimed Mrs Paterson, nudging her neighbour. 'Come and sit next to me, Lorna. You can talk me through the programme. I'm a little hard of hearing, you know.'

Lorna's heart sank at the prospect of having to provide a fortissimo commentary. Then she felt a tug on the back of her T-shirt. It was Carmen. 'It's OK,' she said, 'Chris and I have saved you a seat at the back, so we can run away if it's too embarrassing.'

'Bless you,' said Lorna, with an apologetic wave at Mrs Paterson. 'I thought I'd had it there.'

Chris and Carmen had commandeered the old wooden chest that Lorna had used for her toys when she was little. It wasn't very big, and even with cushions on it wasn't the most comfortable of things to sit on, but it was right next to the door marked 'get me out of here'.

When he saw her, Chris pulled Carmen closer to him so that Lorna could perch on the end; but Carmen shoved him right back again. 'Come on Lorna, sit between us. That'll be nice and cosy, won't it Chris?'

Chris mumbled something, and turned very slightly pink as Lorna insinuated her bottom into the small gap between them. 'Hey, I haven't seen you for ages,' she remarked to Chris.

'Oh, you know. Busy. The band, and work . . . all that stuff.'

'Leo keeps asking when Uncle Chris is going to come out for the day with us again. He really enjoyed it, that time we all went looking for water voles, and you fell in the river.'

'Funnily enough, so did I,' replied Chris softly. 'I . . . I've been meaning to tell you—' He looked at Lorna and she felt something – she wasn't sure what – pass between them. Then it was gone.

'Meaning to tell me what?' asked Lorna.

'Oh look!' squealed Honey, who was sitting right at the front, with her nose jammed up against the TV screen. 'It's starting!'

'Nothing important,' replied Chris, and turned away.

Just as the music started and the titles rolled, an unexpected late arrival slipped into the room and tapped Chris on the shoulder. 'You don't mind do you? Only I'd like to sit next to my girlfriend.'

There wasn't much point in arguing, and Chris knew it. 'Go ahead,' he replied. 'I was just leaving anyway.'

Lorna turned just as Eoin sat down in Chris's place. 'What – where's Chris?'

Eoin smiled. 'He had to go. Aren't you pleased to see me?'

'Well I'm surprised,' she replied, not entirely warmly. 'You've hardly said two words to me since the filming ended. I thought you must have found somebody more interesting to spend your time with.'

218

He laughed. 'Who could be more interesting than my little Blondie? I've just had a few . . . things to take care of, that's all.'

'Really? That's nice. I've been out and about too, actually.'

'Hmm?' Eoin was barely listening.

'Met someone who knows you the other night – a nurse on Hyacinth Ward. What was her name? Oh yes, Sadie, that's right.'

Eoin froze momentarily, then relaxed again. 'Sadie, eh? How is she?'

'Fine at the moment,' replied Lorna, watching his face for a change of expression as she added, 'or at least, better than she was when she was with you, apparently.'

His head snapped round so that he was looking her in the eyes. 'What's she been saying about me?'

'What do you think she's been saying?'

'She's a malicious little bitch,' he replied coldly. 'She could have been saying anything. We went out for a couple of months, but it was a big mistake. I've never met a more jealous, possessive woman. And ever since I ended it with her, she's made it her business to ruin my life.' His voice softened. 'Please believe me, Lorna, that woman is poison.'

'So she didn't cry off the Valentine's dinner at the Black Tulip because you broke two of her fingers then?'

He took a sharp, indrawn breath. 'My God, she said I did that to her?' He shook his head. 'I never thought she'd go that far. Look Lorna,' he said, 'I admit I bought the tickets for her and I lied when I said I'd got them with you in mind. That was wrong, and I'm sorry. But break her fingers? She got those falling over in the kitchen at her flat when she'd had one too many. Jesus, Lorna, what do you think I am?'

He sounded so convincing that Lorna wasn't sure what to believe any more. All she knew was that all through her life with Ed, she'd never had to make the effort to disentangle truth from lies. And she didn't want to have to make that effort now.

'I don't know,' she replied dully. But Eoin wasn't listening any more. He was much more interested in watching her on the screen. Suddenly he let out a guffaw. 'My God – look at the state of you in that uniform! What is it – Soviet army surplus?'

'Eoin, what she said . . . it frightened me.'

He squeezed her hand. 'Don't you worry, Lorna. I'll have a word with her. She'll not upset you again.'

'But—'

'She's a liar, Lorna. End of story.'

And as far as Eoin was concerned, the subject was clearly closed.

A peal of laughter ran round the watching throng as Lorna was shown completely failing to clamp a van, and having to stand there helplessly as it drove off into the distance. 'I don't think you're supposed to do it like that, dear,' her mum called back to her, wiping tears of mirth from her eyes.

'God, you look a fright,' chortled Eoin.

'Thanks Eoin, but I don't need you to point out how shit I look,' replied Lorna, trying not to look at the screen but failing. There was a horrible fascination about seeing yourself made to look like a complete idiot on television.

'Never mind,' counselled Carmen, 'he'll be laughing on the other side of his face when he comes on and it's him they're making look stupid.'

'Actually no, I won't,' replied Eoin serenely, 'because I'm not in it any more.'

Carmen and Lorna both stared at him. 'What?'

'I told them I wasn't happy with the footage . . . you know, had a quiet word. And they agreed to cut me out. Their Chief Executive was very reasonable about it.'

Now Lorna knew why Eoin had decided to brave the screening of a programme that might wreck his career. He had nothing to be brave about at all. 'How the hell did you manage that?' she demanded.

'Like I've always said, it's just a question of networking. Making friends with the right people. Oh dear Carmen, I don't think you're quite cut out for a hospital career, do you?'

On the screen, Carmen's bedpan scene was being shown in all its stage-managed glory. She groaned. Everybody else practically wet themselves laughing. And the canned laughter track didn't make the experience any more pleasant. 'They're making us look like . . . like—'

'Complete dimwits,' said Lorna, finishing the sentence for her. 'Yeah, I noticed. So much for "quality TV showing what life is really like".'

'Oh, by the way,' Eoin went on, helping himself to some popcorn and clearly thoroughly enjoying himself, 'I'm off to the Massif Central in July with a couple of mates, to do some base-jumping. You know, pick a big mountain, jump off the top, hope your parachute opens . . .?'

'I know what base-jumping is,' said Lorna. 'Ed tried it a couple of times.'

'Well why don't you come with us? You don't have to jump if you don't want to – but I thoroughly recommend the buzz.'

'I sometimes wonder if that's all you care about,' she said, 'the buzz.'

'Don't talk rubbish. I care about you, don't I? So how about it then?'

He looked genuinely flabbergasted when she replied, 'I'm not sure. I'll have a think about it and let you know.'

She was still having a think about it – and everything Eoin had said about Sadie – when she awoke the following morning.

220

Maybe I've just been incredibly lucky up till now, she thought as she got dressed. Maybe all the glossy magazines are right, and every other woman in the world is having drama-packed relationships with dodgy blokes all the time. Maybe not being sure you can trust someone is just par for the course. It certainly seems to be that way in Carmen's world. But all I have to measure Eoin up against is Ed; and if Ed really was the one and only hundred-per-cent-decent man in the entire universe, how on earth am I ever going to get used to having less?

On the other hand, she reminded herself, I could have this all wrong. Eoin may not be perfect, but that doesn't necessarily mean he's not telling me the truth about Sadie. God knows, there are plenty of jealous, vengeful women in the world – probably just as many as there are untrustworthy men.

So how can anyone ever know the truth about anyone else?

Still mulling this over, she went downstairs and found her mother sitting on the third stair from the bottom in a state of total shock, clutching a letter.

'Mum!' exclaimed Lorna, hurrying down. 'What's the matter? Are you ill? Is it bad news?'

Meg swallowed hard, and handed the letter to her daughter with a shaking hand. 'Read that,' she said in a hoarse whisper, 'and then tell me I'm not dreaming.'

Lorna did as her mother asked. '"Dear Mrs Schools – Mrs Schools"?'

'Don't worry about that, they're always getting it wrong. Read on.'

'"Thank you for entering our recent Dr Finckel's competition. We are writing to inform you that you have won . . ."' Eyes widening, Lorna collapsed onto the stair next to her mother. 'It says here you've won first prize, twenty thousand quid's worth of plastic surgery! And an all-expenses-paid trip to South Africa to have it done!'

'So I'm not dreaming?'

'Not unless I am as well.' She raised her voice. 'Dad? Dad, come here, Mum's got some amazing news for you!'

George bumbled out of their downstairs bedroom, still in his pyjamas and carrying his false teeth in a glass of water. 'What amazing news?' he demanded gummily, rummaging around in the glass and shoving the dentures into his mouth.

'George darling, do you remember that competition I did, the one where we submitted that terrible slogan?'

'"Beat the wrinkles with Dr Finckel's". How could I ever forget?'

'Well, I've won it! Look!'

Extracting his reading glasses from the pocket of his pyjama jacket, George read through the letter, read it again, and then read it a third time for good measure. 'Good Lord Meg, you have won! Well, if that isn't a turn up for the book and no mistake. Mind you, I dread to think what the other slogans were like.'

Meg clapped her hands in excitement. 'I don't care! Just think – we'll be able to auction the prize on eBay, and we're bound to get thousands for it, and—'

'Wait a minute love,' cut in George. 'I'm just reading this fine print on the back. Ah, right. I thought as much.'

Lorna and Meg's smiles faltered ever so slightly. 'What's up, Dad?'

George jabbed a finger at the paper. 'Here – Rule Six, sub-section 2b: "The prize may only be taken by the winner him/herself and is in no way transferable. There is no cash alternative."'

Meg's lip trembled. 'You mean . . . you mean I can't sell it?'

'Sorry love. That's what it says. Do you want me to ring them up and tell them to give it to somebody else?'

'No!' exclaimed Meg indignantly. 'It's my prize and I won it fair and square.'

'But if you take it you'll have to have a load of plastic surgery, Mum,' Lorna pointed out.

Meg sniffed. 'Well why shouldn't I? Why shouldn't a woman of a certain age want to look younger and more glamorous? Yes,' she declared, seizing the letter from George's hands as she swept past, 'the more I think about it, the more I think I might just go ahead and do it.'

It was many years since George Scholes had tried to change his wife's mind about anything, and the last time she'd locked him in the coal-cellar; so all in all he didn't much feel like starting again now.

'But Dad, you can't just let her,' Lorna had protested. 'She might come out looking like that awful American woman who tried to turn herself into a cat. Or worse!'

'It's your mother's decision, love,' was all that George would say. And the topic was studiously avoided around the breakfast table.

But that didn't mean he wasn't thinking about it. Indeed, he'd been thinking about it so much that he couldn't sleep; which was why he came to be padding downstairs to the kitchen in the middle of the night, for a cup of tea and a helping of leftover trifle.

At first, when his bare foot collided with something furry, he thought it was one of the children's discarded cuddly toys. But then he clicked on the kitchen light and saw that it was Clawdius, stretched limply across the tiles, his eyes half-open and his flanks quivering as he panted for breath.

His throat tightened with fear. 'Clawdius?' Crouching down, he tried stroking the cat but after a brief attempt at purring, it sank back, utterly exhausted.

George was no vet, but he knew when something was seriously wrong. And, gently scooping Clawdius into his arms, he hurried back up the stairs and went to wake Lorna.

Lorna's eyes were misted with tears as Emily the out-of-hours vet ran the stethoscope over Clawdius's prone body.

'Please help him,' she heard herself beg, though she knew it was a silly thing to say. 'Please – you have to make him better. He's a very special cat.'

'We'll do our best,' promised Emily. 'We always do. But Clawdius isn't a young cat, and I'm afraid he's very poorly.'

A head popped round the door of the consulting room, and a tired-looking young vet with a coat on over his pyjamas handed Emily a piece of paper. 'Those blood results you wanted. I'm off back to that calving now. See you later.'

Emily glanced at the paper, nodding as she read.

'What is it?' whispered Lorna, her heart in her mouth, her hand gently stroking Clawdius's rusty old pelt and feeling the ribs underneath.

'Well, it seems Clawdius has developed severe diabetes. Have you noticed him drinking more than usual? Spending a penny especially frequently? Has he lost any weight?'

Guiltily, Lorna realised that she'd noticed all of these things, and had even told herself several times that she ought to take him to the vet; but had never actually got round to doing it. And now this had happened. She would have given anything to have been more observant, to have somehow prevented this happening. 'Maybe,' she said. 'A little.'

'The thing is,' the vet explained, 'not only is his blood sugar very high, but he's also developed a lung infection. I can definitely hear some fluid in there – that's why he's having so much difficulty breathing.' She paused. 'The question is, how far do you want us to go with treatment?'

The question came as a shock. 'Is there any chance you can make him better?' she asked, trying to sniff back her tears but watching them fall onto Clawdius's fur.

'A chance, yes. Not a big chance, but definitely a chance. We can put him on a drip to rehydrate him, give him insulin and antibiotics, and he may pull through. But I can't promise anything. And it will be expensive.'

Lorna felt the softness and warmth of Clawdius's paw in her hand, and bent to kiss his head and whisper nonsense in his ear. 'I don't care what it costs,' she declared. 'Just don't let him suffer.'

Outside, sitting in the car, Lorna let the pain overwhelm her and sobbed until it felt as if there could be no more moisture in her body.

'Oh Clawdius,' she whispered, and in her mind she was simultaneously whispering, 'Oh Ed. Why did you have to go away? Please don't take Clawdius away from me too, he's all I have left.'

She remembered the day Ed had given him to her; recalled the damp, terrified bundle of fluff wriggling as she tried to wrap it in a towel and calm it down. 'He's got huge claws,' Ed had said. 'I think we ought to call him Clawdius.' And Lorna had laughed, and Chris had gone out to buy some cat food and a basket while she and Ed played with the kitten.

She reached into her handbag and took out her mobile. There was only one person she could ring at this time of night and who wouldn't mind. Only one person who understood all that Clawdius meant to her.

Just as she was calling up Chris's number, the phone rang. It was her mum and dad's private line. Wiping away the tears that were dripping off the end of her nose, she answered. 'Hello?'

'Lorna dear? It's your mother. How's the cat?'

'Not very well. But they're doing all they can. I'll be back home in a few minutes.'

'That's just as well,' replied her mother, 'because there's a very strange girl in the kitchen, and she says she won't go away until she's spoken to you.'

All manner of bizarre scenarios trooped through Lorna's head during the short trip back to the house. But whatever she'd expected, it certainly wasn't the sight of Kelly Picton, soaked to the skin, swathed in a blanket, and huddled over the kitchen table with a mug of Bovril and some Twiglets. The bedraggled brown rat's tails of her hair were dripping water onto the floor with an insistent 'pit-pat'.

'Kelly?'

The girl's expression switched instantly from misery to elation at the sight of Lorna. 'Oh great, it's you! I knew you'd come.'

'Well ... yes. This is where I live,' pointed out Lorna. 'How on earth did you find me, and what are you doing here?'

'I'm sorry dear,' cut in Meg, 'but I could hardly leave her shivering on the doorstep in that condition, could I?'

Lorna pulled out a chair and sat down, the sheer vulnerability of the girl taking the edge off the shock. 'What's happened to you, Kelly? How did you get like this?'

Kelly's smile faded. 'It's me mum,' she said. 'That bitch hates me – you've see what she's like. And she'd do anything to please that creepy bloke of hers. So she takes Lee-Anne off me and throws me out on the street, and what does she tell the social worker? "Kelly's walked out and left her baby for me to bring up," that's what she says! And the daft cow believes her!'

'That's terrible,' sympathised Lorna. 'But surely somebody—?'

'Nope. Nobody. They couldn't give a flying toss, any of 'em. Thing is, the other night I saw you in that job programme on TV, taking crap from all those snotty drivers, and I thought, "She's not like the others, she'll help me."'

'Oh,' said Lorna, more startled by the moment. 'But how on earth—?'

'Oh, it wasn't that hard to find out where you live,' Kelly replied brightly. 'When I was on your ward I heard you telling that Honey you lived in St Jude's Square, so I just went and told her you'd invited me round only I couldn't remember the number.'

Lorna's jaw dropped. 'Honey told you!'

'Yeah. Nice girl, but I wouldn't tell her any secrets if I was you. Anyhow, the last few weeks, I've been sleeping on my mate's floor and trying to get somebody to listen to me and get my baby back. Only they won't. And then tonight there was no room for me to stay any longer, so I went out to find a bench or something. I was in the park and some lads stole me money and threw me in the river, and that's when I knew I had to come and see you. Where else could I go?'

She looked up at Lorna with such desperation in her eyes that Lorna did not even consider the possibility that she might not be telling the truth. It was a look of almost animal distress.

'She's took me baby off me, Lorna!' she repeated, in increasing agitation. 'Won't you help me get her back?'

Chapter 25

When Lorna went into Hope's bedroom the next morning, she was surprised to find her cuddled up with Kelly on the Z-bed. The pair of them seemed fast asleep, but as she was deciding whether or not to tiptoe out and come back later, Kelly opened one eye.

'You don't mind, do you?' she whispered. 'Only she was crying and I didn't want to wake you up.'

'That's kind of you,' said Lorna, sitting down as quietly as she could on the end of the folding bed, which let out a protesting creak after years of disuse. 'Are you OK?'

'Fine,' replied Kelly, but she didn't look it. Scared stiff and completely lost would have been closer to the mark, thought Lorna.

Lorna hesitated for a moment and then asked the question that had haunted her dreams all night. 'I've been wondering, Kelly … why did you decide to come and find me? Why me and not somebody else? Haven't you got any aunties and uncles, or family friends you could confide in?'

Kelly rolled onto her side and propped herself up on one elbow, easing herself up very slowly and gently so as not to wake Hope. 'Well, there's me Auntie Doreen,' she recollected. 'She buggered off to Australia before I was born, and nobody's heard from her since. Then there's Dad's brother Steve. Only he won't speak to us since Mum chucked Dad out. And as for Dad, he died five years ago. Oh, and there's Linda – she's my big sister.'

'Couldn't she help you?'

'Oh yeah. Social Services really love Linda,' Kelly replied with more than a dash of sarcasm. 'She lives in a squat in Birmingham and she does that many drugs she needs a map to find her own backside. Would you want her helping you to get your baby back?'

Lorna had to admit that the teenager had a point. 'And there's really nobody else?'

'If there was, don't you think I'd be pestering them instead of you?

You're my only hope, Lorna. You're the only one who hasn't treated me like shit ever since I got myself pregnant. And I mean yeah, I know it was a pretty stupid thing to do but the condom split and I really don't need people looking down their noses and reminding me how crap I am all the time. Do I?'

'It must be hard,' Lorna agreed.

'Well, when I was in the hospital, you didn't do any of that. You weren't like that cowbag midwife with the bad smell under her nose. You didn't say, "stupid little slut doesn't deserve to have a baby," you just . . . helped me.'

'Helping's all I can do,' pointed out Lorna. 'It's not like I have magic powers or something.'

'No, but you've got qualifications and that. People respect you. So Social Services'll have to listen if you speak up for me, won't they?'

Kelly's blind faith was touching, but Lorna wasn't sure how best to respond. Instinctively she liked the kid, sensed that everything she was saying was true; but when all was said and done, Kelly was practically a stranger, just a patient she'd looked after once for a few days.

'There's one thing I don't understand,' she said, thinking back to the sour-faced woman in the pink tracksuit who'd come to the ward to take Kelly home. 'Why would your mum want to take your baby off you? Are you sure this isn't just a misunderstanding or some kind of family argument that's got blown out of all proportion? You didn't just leave Lee-Anne with your mum overnight and she maybe thought the worst—?'

There was a universe of hurt in Kelly's eyes. 'Why doesn't anybody believe me? You *are* just the same as all the others!'

'No I'm not, really I'm not,' Lorna reassured her, alarmed by the vehemence of the teenager's reaction. 'I'm just trying to understand. How can I help you if I don't understand?'

Hope stirred in her sleep and snuggled closer to Kelly. 'Third time lucky for me mum, isn't it?' said Kelly quietly.

'How do you mean?'

'Well, she really fucked up with Linda, and now I haven't turned out right either. And she's got this new bloke banging on about how he loves kids and he wants to start a family, only she can't, can she? 'Cause she had her tubes cut after she had me. So she's scared she's going to lose him, isn't she?'

'You think she wants Lee-Anne because she can't have another baby of her own?'

'I don't think she gives a toss about Lee-Anne,' replied Kelly bitterly. 'She just doesn't want her precious Rick going off with some other woman.' She reached out and gently stroked Hope's pale golden curls as they spilled across the duvet. 'You're really lucky, you are.'

228

Lorna smiled. 'I know.'

'Mum told the Health Visitor and woman from Social Services and everybody who'd listen that I didn't look after Lee-Anne. She said I just bogged off and left her, like she was a doll I was bored with or something.' Kelly looked up, and as their eyes met Lorna saw how bright and moist the younger girl's were, as though she was struggling not to blink, because if she did, tears would overflow and tumble down her cheeks. 'Will you help me, Lorna? Please will you help me?'

Hope gave a little sigh and rubbed her eyes. 'Mum-mum! Juice.'

Lorna helped her out of bed and hoisted her onto her hip. 'Yes, lovely juice and toast. Shall we get you dressed first? And then we'll ring the vet and see how Clawdius is feeling today.'

'Meow-meow!' piped Hope. She wasn't the only person hoping the cat would be back home soon. Lorna couldn't get over how empty the house seemed without him, even though with Kelly in it, it was now stuffed to the rafters.

'Will you?' repeated Kelly, sitting up in her shapeless Snoopy night-shirt and catching at the hem of Lorna's dressing gown.

Lorna hesitated. This was a big commitment to make to a kid she barely knew. And yet she sensed that if she didn't, nobody else was going to. And sometimes you just had to trust to the best and act on your instincts. 'No guarantees,' she said, 'but I promise I'll do my best.'

News of Kelly's arrival got round fast, and before you could say 'eviction order', Eoin was on Lorna's doorstep, determined to give everybody the benefit of his opinion. Then Chris turned up with a replacement bulb for the back yard security light, and George found himself trapped in the front room with two men who clearly loathed the very sight of each other.

'Talk about naïve!' raged Eoin. 'What kind of person takes in some empty-headed teenage slag off the street and gives her a bed instead of calling the police?'

'A nice person who doesn't spend all her time thinking about herself?' suggested Chris, quietly but pointedly.

George scratched his balding head and took a seat in the nearest arm-chair. 'I have to admit it's a little worrying,' he conceded. 'But Lorna's no fool. If she thinks this Kelly girl is all right, perhaps we ought to go along with her.'

'Oh, right,' retorted Eoin. 'So if Jack the Ripper turns up tomorrow and you invite him in for tea, we should go along with that too?'

'Now you're just being facetious,' said Chris. He ignored the scathing look he received from Eoin in return. 'From the little I've seen of her, Kelly seems like a pretty normal fourteen-year-old kid. Well, as normal as you can be when you've had a baby and your mother's stolen it off you.'

'It must be difficult for the girl I suppose,' pondered George. 'If she hasn't anybody else to turn to.'

'Of course she has!' exploded Eoin. 'This isn't the Nineteen-bloody-Fifties. These days you can't move out there for social workers and youth workers and sexual health counsellors and God knows what else.'

'Not much use if none of them believe you,' pointed out Chris.

'Oh for God's sake, get real. You know why this girl's targeted Lorna? Do you? Well I do. She knows when she's on to a good thing, that's why. She saw Lorna in the hospital and she thought, hey, I can't lose here. Face it, Kelly reckons Lorna's the soft touch of a lifetime, and it's our job to make her see sense.'

Turning round, he saw Lorna standing in the doorway. Without a word, she looked from Eoin to Chris to George, and then back again.

And then she turned on her heel and left, banging the front door behind her.

At least Mary, the hospital social worker, wasn't surprised. 'Believe me I've heard it all,' she told Lorna. 'Abuse, neglect, babies abandoned in phone boxes . . . even infanticide. Sometimes you wonder if you can take any more, but of course you always do.'

'Kelly didn't abandon her baby,' Lorna reminded her. 'Her mother just wants the social worker to believe that, so she gets to keep it herself.'

Mary drummed her fingertips on the desktop. 'Yes. I do see what you're saying.'

Lorna could sense a 'but' from fifty yards away. 'So what's the problem?' she demanded.

'What if this child – and after all that's what she is, a child – did leave her baby? Say she got stressed, or bored; fancied a night out with her friends . . .'

'She wouldn't do that,' Lorna said firmly.

'How do you know that? You haven't exactly known her long.'

'I don't know how I know,' she replied. 'I just do. You know how it is: sometimes you meet someone and you just click. You have a kind of sixth sense that tells you whether that person's basically good or basically bad.'

'You could be wrong,' Mary pointed out.

'I could, but I'm not.' Lorna leaned over the desk, eager to get through to Mary how urgent this all was. 'Look: all I want from you is to know what has to be done in order for Kelly to get her baby back. Surely you can go that far to help the poor kid?'

Mary's expression softened, and her tone became less defensive. 'Don't get me wrong, Lorna. I'm not trying to make problems for her, and

230

I'm not saying I don't believe her story. Goodness knows, if what she says is true, then something has to be done. I just don't want you to be—'

'Taken advantage of?'

'Well . . . yes.'

'I'll take that risk,' Lorna said firmly, slightly surprised by her own certainty. 'I'm not in the habit of taking in waifs and strays, you know. This one's special. Now, tell me. What does she have to do?'

Mary sat back in her chair. 'It's not all bad news,' she said. 'Social Services and the courts always try to keep mothers and their babies together, if humanly possible. They're not in the business of breaking up family units.'

'But?'

'But . . . Kelly's fourteen years old and homeless, and she's certainly not getting any support from her family. That's hardly an ideal situation. What Kelly needs to be able to offer is a stable environment, under close adult supervision. For example, we might be able to get her a place in a children's home with a mother and baby unit.'

Lorna could just imagine how that would go down with Kelly. 'Or?' she demanded.

'A suitable foster home, perhaps. Though God knows, it's hard enough to find families willing to take in problem teenagers, let alone ones with babies. The thing is, what she needs is what we call a "suitable supervising adult" – someone mature and willing to be responsible for her and the baby.'

'Somebody with training, you mean?'

Mary shook her head. 'Not necessarily. Just somebody with experience of family life and its ups and downs. Somebody with a good, strong personality who can guide Kelly into making the right choices . . .'

Do I know anybody like that? wondered Lorna. Straight away, something went 'ping' inside her brain, like a microwave hitting zero. Do I? You bet I do.

The question is, what on earth is she going to say when I ask her?

For the first few seconds, Carmen didn't say anything at all. But her complexion turned pale beneath its caramel sheen, and half the bacon in her bacon double cheeseburger fell out of the bun and landed on her bump like some peculiar garnish. 'Me? A responsible adult? You're having me on.'

'I most certainly am not,' replied Lorna, picking at a curly fry. She wasn't a great lover of fast food, but Carmen's latest craving meant that she could never resist the offer of a free Massiveburger with extra gherkins. 'I talked it over with Mary, and then I had a chat with Social Services, and you're exactly what they're looking for.'

231

'What – a fat, pregnant underachiever with four kids and the world's worst taste in men? I doubt it.' Carmen peeled the bacon off her stomach and ate it, then rubbed at the grease stain it had left behind. 'Have you actually told them about me?'

'Well ... yes,' admitted Lorna. 'But only in general terms; I didn't mention any names. That wouldn't be ethical – or fair.'

Carmen shook her head in mild amusement. 'But it's fair to come telling me tragic tales about homeless fourteen-year-olds with babies when you know I'm a sucker for a sad story? Lorna love, it's about as fair as sticking a six-week-old kitten in front of me and telling me it's going to be drowned tomorrow if I don't adopt it.'

'I do feel a bit bad about it,' Lorna admitted. 'But you can always say no.'

'Hmm,' was Carmen's response, muffled by a mouthful of burger. She chewed and swallowed. 'Why me, anyway? Why not pick on some other complete failure?'

'Because you're not a failure. You're my best mate, and you've done an amazing job, bringing up those kids on your own. If anybody knows about the "ups and downs of family life", it's you. Besides,' she added guiltily, 'there's your basement.'

'Aha,' declared Carmen. 'I was wondering when we'd get round to that. Lorna, my basement is a hole, filled with junk. It's been that way for the last decade.'

'Yes, but you've said yourself, it could easily be turned into a bedroom and a sitting room.'

'Yeah – with the aid of four tons of plaster and the entire contents of B&Q.'

'Help is available,' Lorna replied promptly, flourishing a fistful of leaflets.

Carmen eyed her with a mixture of despair and admiration. 'You really have thought of everything, haven't you?'

'I hope so.' Lorna nibbled nervously on a battered fish ball. 'So ... what do you think?'

'I think you're a manipulative cow, Lorna Price.'

'And?'

'And ... I don't know what else. This really means a lot to you, doesn't it?'

Lorna nodded dumbly. 'I'm sorry,' she said. 'I mean ... I'm really sorry. You mustn't take any notice of my obsessions. When I said you could refuse, I meant it. If you really feel it isn't you, just tell me to bog off.'

Carmen wiped a mixture of grease and ketchup off one of her pre-baby chins. 'Don't worry, I will,' she replied. 'But first, I have to talk to Victor.'

Lorna's ears pricked up. 'Who's Victor? A new boyfriend?'

Carmen waved away the suggestion. 'Hardly, he's pushing fifty and he's practically bald. No, Victor's my counsellor. I told you, I'm a reformed character. No more boyfriends for me. Ever.'

Lorna stared down at the table top and fiddled about with a sachet of tomato ketchup, pushing the contents up into one end, and then back again to the other.

'What's the matter?' demanded Carmen.

'What do mean, what's the matter?'

Carmen stuck a finger under Lorna's chin and tilted it up, forcing her to look at her. 'You're doing that compulsive fidgeting thing, Lorna. You only ever do that when something's really bugging you. Come on, out with it.'

It was at once a gargantuan effort and an immense relief to reveal what was on her mind. And who else could she talk to about it, if not Carmen? 'It's Eoin,' she confessed, staring at the table top again. 'I think he . . . I think he may have a history of hitting women.'

She dared steal a look at Carmen's face, but there wasn't a trace of shock on it. It was almost as if she had been half expecting something of the sort. 'Says who?' asked Carmen.

And Lorna let out the whole story of the hen night, and Sadie, and Eoin's angry denials, which had frightened her almost more than his ex's allegations. 'What do I do, Carmen?' she agonised.

'Who do you believe – him or her? Or neither?'

Lorna expelled a long, defeated breath. 'I don't know. But I do know that when he lost his temper with me, for a moment I did think it might be true.'

Carmen rubbed a hand wearily over her eyes. 'You do realise I'm the wrong person to ask, don't you? My love-life's been a catalogue of disasters from start to finish. And you know I think Eoin's a complete tosser.'

'But maybe that makes you exactly the right person to ask,' countered Lorna.

Carmen squeezed Lorna's hand with fingers that were sticky with mayonnaise and barbecue sauce. 'I can't tell you what to do, love,' she said regretfully. 'All I can say is, be very, very careful. But I know you will, because you're not a sentimental idiot like me. Now,' she wiped the last of the smears from round her mouth, 'buy me a hot cherry pie and tell me some more about this girl Kelly.'

Lorna would have spent the rest of the day in a horrible state of suspense – if it wasn't for Clawdius. Around two o'clock, the surgery rang to say that he was much better, and would she like to take him home? There'd be

233

insulin injections to get the hang of, and antibiotics, and special food; but Lorna's heart soared at the news.

At least something's going right, she thought as she made a grab for the car keys. Maybe it's a sign and other things will start going right too. She tried not to add 'like Kelly', but it wasn't easy to censor her thoughts.

Clawdius greeted her with a 'rowwrrr' and a chirrup of recognition, and pressed his soft, furry face against her cheek when she lifted him gently out of the vet's hospital cage. He felt even thinner than before, but his eyes were bright and when he started nibbling at her necklace, she knew he was on the mend.

'Thank you so much,' she said, trying not to look like a big, sentimental wuss and failing. 'Thank you for making him better. I really thought—'

The vet nodded. 'So did we. But he's really turned the corner. Now, you're sure you're OK with giving the injections? I can run through it all again if you need me to.'

'I'm fine thanks,' replied Lorna. 'He probably won't like me much for a while, but I guess we're both just going to have to get used to it!'

As she carried his box out to the car, she couldn't express the happiness and relief that was coursing through her. This wasn't just a much-loved family pet coming home; it was much more than that. It was a re-forging of the link with Ed too, as he clasped her hand once again and – through Clawdius – helped her to remember things she could never bear to forget.

One day, she knew she'd have to face that possibility. But not now. For now at least, things were once again the way they ought to be.

Clawdius was welcomed home with much rejoicing and several helpings of tinned tuna. After half an hour of the children's hugs though, he padded off up the stairs to find one of his favourite sleeping-spots and enjoy a little peace. Lorna knew how he felt. There seemed to be people everywhere she looked. If it wasn't her mum and dad, still arguing the toss over cosmetic surgery, or Eoin, trying to persuade her that Kelly was going to run off with the family silver any moment now, it was Kelly herself, trying much too hard to be helpful and getting in the way instead.

She sat at the bottom of the stairs and pushed a hand through her dishevelled hair. The thought struck Lorna that, if Carmen turned her down – which she well might – she could be stuck with Kelly forever. Well, not forever maybe, but for a very long time. After all, she'd taken her on as a responsibility now; she couldn't just turn her away, could she?

God, I'm tired, she thought, stifling a yawn. And I still haven't done the dishes.

At that moment the phone rang in the hall, practically next to Lorna's ear. 'Hello?'

234

'Lorna, it's Carmen.' A very deep breath followed. 'I've talked it through with Victor, and I'm prepared to give it a go.'

'Carmen!' Lorna exclaimed in jubilation. 'Oh Carmen, do you really mean that? That's amazing.'

'Hold on a minute,' Carmen intervened. 'This thing has to be done slowly, right?'

'Right. How do you mean, slowly?'

'First, I have to meet the girl!'

'Oh. Yes. I hadn't thought of that,' confessed Lorna, feeling stupider than usual.

'And so do the kids. If they don't like her, I'm afraid it's no go. You do understand, don't you?'

'I do. And even if you end up saying no, I want to thank you for even thinking about doing this.'

Carmen laughed. 'Don't thank me, thank Victor. If it wasn't for him, I'd never dare.'

As she put the phone down, Lorna's mind reeled through the thousand and one things that would need to be done . . . assuming Carmen and her children felt they could get on with Kelly, and could cope with having not one but two babies in the house. And supposing Kelly could actually persuade Social Services to let her have Lee-Anne back . . .

Her mind was reeling. But she still climbed the stairs with a light heart, looking forward to the look on Kelly's face when she heard the news.

The door to the spare room – Ed's room – was ajar. Lorna smiled to herself. Only a cat as smart as Clawdius could have worked out how to open the door, standing on his hind legs and pawing at the handle until it dipped and the door swung inwards.

She peeped inside, half-meaning to shoo him out. But when she saw him curled up in the corner, on Ed's favourite old slippers, she knew she wouldn't have the heart.

Silently she tiptoed across the room, fully expecting one ear to shoot up and an eye to open at her approach. But Clawdius did not stir. He must be very deeply asleep.

Kneeling, she reached out to stroke his silky, rusty-black fur . . . and a horrible shiver ran through her as her fingers touched flesh that was not warm and soft but cooling, stiffening.

'No,' she whispered, scooping him up in her arms and willing him to wake up, though she knew he never would. 'Clawdius, no!'

And she prayed and begged and pleaded as the tears poured silently down her cheeks, but to no avail.

Clawdius was dead.

Chapter 26

Eoin was sitting at Lorna's dining room table, irritably jabbing at the keys of her PC. 'My God this is slow,' he muttered. 'You really ought to get something faster.'

Lorna was sitting limply on her mother's old Windsor chair by the fireplace, half watching Leo playing on the rug, half hugging the hairy old cushion that had been Clawdius's favourite. 'What?' she asked, vaguely aware that Eoin had spoken.

'This computer of yours. It's out of the Ark. Are you listening to me?' he asked, twisting round on his chair.

'Yes. Whatever. Why don't you go home and use your own computer?'

'Because it's on the blink, remember?' Eoin turned back to the screen. 'You know, I really do need to know if you're definitely coming on this base-jumping trip with me. I have to let people know, so they can make arrangements.'

'I'm still thinking about it,' replied Lorna dully; though in truth she hadn't been thinking about it at all. The only things she'd been thinking about over the last couple of days were Clawdius, and Ed . . . and the allegations that Sadie had made about Eoin. Were they, as he claimed, nothing more than a malicious lie by a jealous ex-girlfriend? Was Lorna imagining it when she saw a glint of cold fury in Eoin's eyes? 'Well hurry up and make your mind up,' grunted Eoin.

'Bang! Bash! Pow!' yelled Leo, crashing his toy cars together on the rug.

Eoin stiffened, turned round and fixed the child with a glare. 'I've told you twice already, Leo, either shut up or go to bed!'

'But—'

'I said shut up!'

Leo blinked, first at his mother and then at Eoin. 'But it's not my bedtime. And Mummy said I could stay up.'

'Well Mummy was obviously out of her tiny fucking mind,' muttered Eoin under his breath.

'What's that you said?' Lorna sat bolt upright.

'Nothing.'

'That's not what it sounded like to me.' She turned to Leo, his eyes still fixed on Eoin, trying to work out what it was that he'd done to make him so angry. 'Leo sweetheart, why don't you take your cars and show them to Grandma and Grandad? Mummy and Eoin have to talk about something.'

When Leo had left the room, Eoin gave a sigh of relief. 'Thank God for that. He must drive you nuts.'

Lorna rounded on him like a lioness with a wounded cub: not just angry, but afraid – for herself and her son. 'Actually there is one person in this room who drives me nuts, but it's not my son,' she spat. 'How dare you use that kind of language in front of him?'

Eoin flopped wearily back in his chair. 'I know what this is all about,' he said. 'You're still moping about that bloody cat.'

'Clawdius was a member of the family, and we loved him very much.'

'Too bloody much if you ask me. He was just a cat, Lorna. A flea-bitten bag of fur with four legs and no brain.'

'If you had a grain of sensitivity in you, you'd know that wasn't true.'

'And if you had a grain of sense, you'd see that what that boy of yours needs is some old-fashioned discipline.'

Lorna could hardly believe what she was hearing. 'Leo's a perfectly normal little boy. And he's only six years old! What are you suggesting – leg irons and six strokes of the birch?'

It was meant to be a sarcastic joke, but evidently Eoin didn't take it quite that way. 'It's never too soon to discipline children – give them rules they have to abide by. And in my opinion physical discipline should be an integral part of that.'

'You mean – you think hitting kids is a good idea?'

'I wouldn't put it quite that way.'

Lorna folded her arms combatively across her chest. The combination of Eoin's comments about Clawdius and his medieval ideas on childrearing had got her blood well and truly up. 'Oh really? Well I would. And I bet you think women need the odd slap to keep them in line too, don't you?'

'Now you're just being hysterical,' replied Eoin, but he didn't deny it.

She jammed her face right up against his. 'Was that why your ex threw you out? Is that why she doesn't want you having anything to do with your son? Well, is it?'

Eoin's steely blue eyes flashed with temper. 'Women! You're all the bloody same.' For a split second, Lorna caught a glimpse of something very dark and angry behind that handsome face. Sadie's words came back into her mind, unbidden: 'I had to warn you . . . before he does the same to you.'

Instinctively, she took a step back. And the spell was broken.

Eoin rubbed a hand across his forehead as though awakening from a bad dream with an even worse headache. 'Oh God Lorna, I'm so sorry. I really didn't mean to lose my temper there, I'm just tired. Will you forgive me?'

There was real sorrow in his eyes, and when he took her hands in his, his touch was gentle as a child's.

She moistened her parched lips with the tip of her tongue. 'I . . . maybe. I guess.'

He smiled. And, as if nothing at all had passed between them, he sat back down at the computer. 'So, shall I tell them you're coming on the trip with me?' he asked.

Without answering, she turned and walked out of the room, trying to conceal the fact that she was still shaking.

'They're going to hate me,' obsessed Kelly as she got out of Lorna's car and looked up at Carmen's rambling terraced house. 'I just know they are.'

'Why do you think that?' asked Lorna.

'Everybody hates me.'

'I don't,' Lorna pointed out.

'Yeah, well, you're a bit weird then aren't you? And that boyfriend of yours looks at me like I just cracked one off under his nose.' She took a deep breath. 'Come on then, let's get it over with.' And she marched up to the front door and rapped hard on the knocker.

It wasn't Carmen who answered the door, but Robbie. Damn, thought Lorna. Of all the Jones family, why did it have to be the mean and moody one? His recent acquisition of a James Dean-style sneer didn't exactly make him look any more welcoming, either. According to Carmen he thought it made him look hard, but in reality it looked more like a bad attack of indigestion.

His and Kelly's eyes met. 'Hi,' said Kelly.

'Er . . . hi.'

'I'm Kelly. Kelly Picton. The one with the baby.' She stuck out a hand. As Robbie fumblingly accepted it, Lorna saw a crimson flush rise from the neck of his T-shirt to the tips of his ears. 'And I bet you're Robbie. Lorna's told me all about you.'

At this, Robbie looked not so much dumbfounded as worried. 'She has?'

'Yeah. She says you're some kind of computer genius. I wish I was good at that stuff, but I never paid much attention at school. Besides, I'm a bit thick, me.'

239

'I bet you're not really.' Robbie shuffled his feet bashfully. 'I could . . . I mean if you wanted me to . . . I could maybe . . . teach you some stuff. Only you probably wouldn't be interested. I guess.'

Kelly rewarded him with one of her open, artless smiles. 'Yes I would. That'd be cool.'

The two of them might have stood there admiring each other indefinitely if Carmen hadn't appeared behind Robbie's left shoulder. 'Hi, you must be Kelly. Robbie, what are you doing leaving her standing out on the doorstep? Bring her inside.'

Carmen and Lorna watched the two teenagers vanish into the house. 'I can't believe it,' said Carmen, shaking her head. 'He looks almost . . . pleased.'

Lorna laughed. 'Did you see the way he was blushing? You know what I think?'

'Yeah I do,' replied Carmen. 'You're thinking that my hard case of a son has just discovered love at first sight. Jesus, I hope you're wrong.'

Carmen delivered her verdict as Lorna drove her and Chris across the dreaded Bluebell Estate.

'She seems a nice kid. Bit daft, but then she's only fourteen, God help her.'

'And Robbie certainly likes her,' commented Lorna with a smile.

Carmen uttered a groan of embarrassment. 'Please, Lord. Spare us from besotted teenagers. Last I saw, he was showing her how to shoot aliens on his X-Box. Very romantic.'

'Does that mean yes then?' asked Chris, cutting to the chase before Lorna dared.

'I suppose so.' Carmen sighed. 'But I'm such a soft touch, you knew I could never say no. Just as long as she behaves herself and the kids get on with her, I'll give it a go.'

'Chris, give Carmen a hug,' ordered Lorna. 'I can't take my hands off the steering wheel. Thanks Carmen, you really are a star.'

'Yeah, yeah, whatever.' Carmen readjusted herself after Chris's rather amateurish attempt at a hug. 'Anyhow, all of this is academic if we can't get Kelly's mother to give the baby back.'

Lorna gritted her teeth. 'We will,' she promised. 'Whatever I have to do, we will.'

Big words were all very well, but actions proved slightly more difficult.

Chris unhooked the piece of rusty wire holding the front gate together, stepped over the disembowelled remains of a sofa and led the way to the front door of Mrs Picton's dingy semi. The houses on either side had nice clipped hedges and fresh paint; hers looked like a statement of apathy in brick.

All three of them stood looking at each other. 'What are we going to say?' asked Carmen.

'God knows,' replied Lorna. 'We'll have to wing it. Just remember to send all my body parts to the same hospital.'

'I think I should—' Chris made to knock on the door, but Lorna stepped in front of him.

'I started this,' she pointed out. 'If anybody's getting their face punched, it had better be me.'

She rapped long and hard, but nothing happened. Then waited, and tried again. Still nothing. A treacherous, cowardly part of her was secretly rather relieved. But she forced herself to give it another go. 'Best of three?'

Just as she was about to give up, the front door of the neighbouring house opened and a fifty-something man in shirt sleeves and braces looked out. 'You looking for her next door, are you?'

'Mrs Picton, yes,' nodded Carmen.

'Well you won't find her. Or that lump of lard she lives with. They've gone out.'

'And taken the baby with them?' ventured Chris.

'Yeah. By some miracle they have. This time.'

'What do you mean?' demanded Lorna. 'Do they leave the baby with somebody else when they go out?'

The man next door gave a macabre chuckle. 'What – actually pay somebody to babysit? Her?'

A cold shiver ran down Lorna's back and she stared up at the blank, cold windows, wondering what lay beyond. 'You're not saying she leaves the baby on its own in the house? Surely not?'

His expression grew evasive. 'I'm not saying nothing, me. But I've got my suspicions.'

A middle-aged woman who might have been the man's wife appeared in the doorway beside him. 'You from Social Services?' she asked. 'It's about bloody time. That one you sent last time was just a kid. I mean, we tried to tell her but no, she's all "oh, Mrs Picton's a very committed grandmother".'

'Committed,' grunted her husband. 'She should be. And the way she treated her own daughter, throwing her out on the street like that . . . What kind of woman is that to be looking after a baby?'

Chris exchanged looks with Lorna. 'Would you be willing to tell somebody about this?' he asked.

The man looked at him blankly. 'I'm telling you, aren't I?'

'The thing is,' Lorna admitted, 'we're not official.'

'Oh,' said the woman. 'What do you mean, not official?'

'We're just here as Kelly's friends,' explained Chris, 'trying to help her get her baby back. Would you be willing to tell what you've told us to the police?'

At the word 'police', the couple's expressions darkened. 'I don't know about that,' said the woman. 'We keep ourselves to ourselves.'

'Please,' urged Lorna. 'Please help us. Before it's too late.'

After she'd dropped Carmen off at her house, Lorna gave Chris a lift home.

'I still can't believe they said yes,' she said. 'It just doesn't seem real.'

'They only said maybe ... and only to a chat with Social Services,' Chris pointed out. 'Off the record. I was so sure I'd blown it when I mentioned the police and they clammed right up.'

'At least we called the police, and they promised they'd keep a close eye on the Pictons. I guess we've done all we can do for now.'

'This is only a first stage, you know,' Chris pointed out. 'Even if the police do get the baby out of there, Kelly's going to need some proper advice: somebody who can stand up and speak for her. Not just a bunch of well-meaning amateurs like us three.'

Lorna giggled. 'You make us sound like a comedy act or something. Like the Three Amigos.'

'Well, let's see ... we've got the fat one – at the moment that's Carmen – and the stupid one – that's me. And the good-looking one. Bet you can't guess who that is.'

She took her eyes off the road for a second and saw that he was looking right at her. 'Don't be silly Chris, I'm just ... just somebody's mum.'

They drove along in silence for a little while.

'I'm so sorry about Clawdius,' said Chris. 'I know how much he meant to you. And I was fond of the old chap myself, you know.'

Lorna smiled, cheered a little. Unlike other people, when Chris said he understood, he meant it. 'Remember that time he fell asleep on your arm, and you ended up taking your shirt off rather than disturb him?'

'He was worth it. Clawdius was a dude. Will you get another cat, do you think?'

'Leo's desperate for us to,' replied Lorna. 'But Clawdius was ... well ... Clawdius. I'm not sure he could ever be replaced. Oh Chris,' she said, her voice breaking at a sudden, unexpected lump in her throat, 'I miss him so much.'

'I know you do, love.'

'He was all I had left, Chris. The last link with Ed.'

To her surprise, Chris chuckled. Hurt by such unwonted insensitivity, she snapped, 'I didn't realise you found my grief so amusing.'

'I'm sorry, I didn't mean it like that. It's just that you seem to have forgotten the most important thing Ed ever gave you. Something nobody can ever take away. Think, Lorna.'

Puzzled, she met his gaze in the rear view mirror. He was smiling, the way you do when something's really obvious but the other person just doesn't get it. 'What are you on about?'

'Your children, Lorna! He gave you two great kids. If that's not a link with Ed, I don't know what is.'

'Oh God,' said Lorna. 'I'm so stupid.'

'Under pressure, maybe. Stupid, never,' retorted Chris. 'But you might like to turn right here, unless you fancy doing forty the wrong way up a one-way street.'

'Shit!' Lorna signalled belatedly and swung the car right, provoking outraged honking from the BMW behind. 'Are you sure you don't want to get out and walk the rest of the way? I'm not sure it's safe, driving around with me today.'

'That's OK, I'll take my chances.' Chris winked. 'You can't be any worse than one-armed Mick at work, and even he's never actually killed anybody.'

She stuck her tongue out at him. 'Gee thanks!'

They drove on through the traffic, occasionally exchanging the odd comment but basically saying very little. One of the really nice things about Chris, thought Lorna, is that I never have to talk to him if I don't feel like it; and he always seems to sense my mood without being told.

But today was different somehow. Today, there was a heaviness building in the air, and Lorna knew it wouldn't go away until she'd told Chris what was on her mind. Or rather, who.

'Chris,' said Lorna.

'Yes?'

There was a brief pause. 'Things aren't going right with Eoin.'

Chris's breathing halted for an almost imperceptible moment, then he replied: 'Oh,' very quietly and calmly as if she'd just mentioned that it might rain tomorrow. Just 'oh', nothing more. She was glad he didn't say anything more momentous; that would have been harder to take, somehow. Calm, impartial advice; that was what she needed right now.

Once she'd broached the subject she'd been dreading, everything came spilling out. 'You remember all that bad stuff that girl Sadie told me about him? The stuff I thought she was making up to spite me?' He nodded. Lorna swallowed down her pride. 'Well, I think it might be true.'

Chris shot bolt upright in his seat. 'What? Are you telling me he's hurt you? Because if he has—'

She cut in hastily, before Chris lost his legendary cool. 'No. No, he hasn't actually done anything. It's just a feeling . . . some things he's said. We had an argument about the kids the other evening, and he was acting like some kind of Victorian parent. And then, when I told him he was talking rubbish . . . well, just for a moment I thought he might . . . you know.'

Without her realising, her fingers had tightened so much on the steering wheel that the knuckles were showing bone-white through the flesh. 'The thing is, for all I know, I may have got it all wrong. I could be over-reacting. I just don't know what to do.'

'You mean – you're thinking of ending it between you?'

'Yes. I don't know. I mean, I almost did there and then . . . Anyway, the fact is, I'm not sure there's any future for us as a couple. And I wanted to ask you . . . what do you think, Chris? What do you think about Eoin? What do you really think? I know I can trust you to tell it like it is.'

'What do I think?' Deciding whether or not to tell the truth had never been a problem for Chris, but right now it was the hardest decision of his life. In the end he took the coward's middle path. 'I think he's . . . not Ed.'

'Yeah. I know.' Lorna wiped the merest suggestion of moisture from the corner of her eye. 'I can see that now. The funny thing is, when I first met him I liked him because he reminded me of Ed. But all that was superficial. Underneath he's a total stranger, and I'm not sure I like what I'm finding out about him. Eoin's not what I thought he was. And you're right: he's certainly not another Ed.'

Chris turned his head to look out of the window, rather than let Lorna see the tension on his face. 'Then again,' he remarked softly, 'nobody can be Ed, can they?'

'No. Never.'

He made a supreme effort and turned to her with a smile. 'So in the end, I guess all you can do is listen to your heart.'

On Friday afternoon it was business as usual on the Labour Ward, and Eoin was not at all happy about that.

'Quarter to two already,' he muttered, one eye on the ward clock. 'They're supposed to be picking me up at half-past five so we can drive down and catch the overnight ferry to France.'

'Well, you know babies,' trilled June Godwin, preparing for yet another induction. 'Little darlings always arrive at the least convenient moment.'

'Not if I've got anything to do with it,' replied Eoin. 'Haven't these women ever heard of elective caesareans?'

244

Lorna looked up from the drug chart she was checking. 'That's a joke, right?'

Eoin scowled. 'What do you think?' And he marched off towards the delivery suite with an expression like thunder.

'What's got into him?' asked Andrew, with a disdainful look at his retreating back. 'Chipped his nail varnish again?'

Kathryn tittered. Lorna tried to be professional, and not reflect on the fact that Eoin was probably in a bad mood at least partly because of last night, when she'd told him he wasn't welcome in her bed and that frankly the way things were going, he wasn't really welcome in her life either, simply because she couldn't trust him any more. That kind of rejection could seriously dent a man's ego – especially when he knew quite well that he deserved it.

'You not going away for the weekend with him then?' asked Kathryn.

'Nope. Jumping off cliffs isn't my idea of fun.'

'Pushing certain people off, on the other hand . . .' commented Andrew, rubbing his hands together. He consulted the white-board on the wall by the midwives' station, which was rapidly filling up with expected and unexpected arrivals. 'Now ladies, I can offer you raised blood pressure and twins in delivery room C, or a very large and scary-looking partner in room D. What am I bid?'

Lorna's delivery was turning out to be rather less dramatic than expected. It never failed to amuse her, how the mere sight of a hypodermic needle could reduce a six-foot-four nightclub bouncer with death's-head tattoos to a pale-faced wimp with a sudden desperate need to escape for 'a bit of fresh air'.

As for his wife, her labour pains had stopped practically the moment she entered the delivery room, which was how Lorna came to be heading for the ward kitchen to make her a second plate of buttered toast.

Eoin intercepted her in the corridor. 'Well that's one down,' he declared with obvious satisfaction. 'All I have to do is get round the other one, and I'll be on the road to La Belle France by tea-time.'

'What do you mean – one down?' asked Lorna.

'Caesarians, remember? I've already persuaded that fat girl with the spots that it's the sensible option, and—'

'Wait a minute,' interjected Lorna. 'Are you talking about that nice Mrs Potts? Because if you are, there's absolutely no reason for her to have a C-section. Her labour's textbook!'

'Yeah, textbook for a first pregnancy, which means we'll all still be stuck here at two in the morning, waiting for the damn thing to arrive! I just persuaded her we could help things along a little.'

245

Lorna's mouth fell open. 'You did what!'

He shrugged modestly. 'Hey, why not? We've got a whole theatre team downstairs, just longing for something to operate on. Anyhow, I'm off to work my amazing charm on some other gullible female—'

The scales fell from Lorna's eyes like a sheet of ice from a Swedish roof in April. How could I not see? she asked herself. How could I have been just another of your gullible females?

'Oh no you're not,' she declared. 'I've got a few things I want to say to you.' And seizing him by the elbow, she practically dragged him through the door of an empty side room.

He was so surprised, he didn't even protest.

It was Eoin's turn to look aghast. 'What did you say?'

Lorna fixed him straight in the eye and repeated the words, nice and slowly so that he didn't miss any of the meaning. 'I said, you're an arrogant, selfish, immature, misogynistic son of a bitch and the only thing you give a damn about is yourself.'

'What the hell did I do to deserve that?' he demanded, the very picture of wounded innocence.

'Do you want the full list, or just the edited highlights? And no,' she added as his mouth half-opened, 'I'm not pre-menstrual. I can't be: I haven't cut your ears off and stuffed them down your throat.'

He had the good grace to look shaken. 'Just my ears?' he enquired.

'To start with.'

Eoin sat down heavily on the unmade bed. 'I don't understand you,' he complained. 'One minute you're all sweetness and light, the next you want my balls on a plate.'

She laughed humourlessly. 'Of course you don't understand me – you don't understand women. Any women. And do you want to know something else? Maybe you're right and I am stupid, 'cause I only just managed to work this out for myself: you don't like women either.'

'That's absolute bollocks!'

She took a couple of steps towards him. 'What's more, I've got a sneaking suspicion we scare you.'

'Scare me!' He responded with an uneasy sneer. 'What are you saying, I'm gay or something?'

'If you were, maybe you'd be a bit nicer to know. No Eoin, you're just a good old-fashioned women-hater. I don't know how I didn't see it before . . . the way you patronise the patients, the way you try and order the midwives about as though they're some kind of lower form of life. You know, I must really have had it bad for you, God help me. If I hadn't, I wouldn't have had you in my house, let alone anywhere near my kids.'

246

There was a mixture of rage and incomprehension in Eoin's eyes. 'You little bitch! I can't believe I'm hearing this.'

'I can't believe I'm saying it,' admitted Lorna. 'But it's about time somebody did.'

His eyes narrowed. 'Who have you been talking to? That bloody bitch Sadie again?'

'What if I have?'Lorna replied.

'I told you, she's a—'

'A malicious liar, yes I know. Like all women, eh Eoin? Save it, I'm not listening any more. I've had it with all of this, and I've had it with you.'

'Lorna—'

''Bye Eoin. Have a nice life.'

As she emerged from the side room, her face flushed and her heart racing, she almost collided with Andrew, who was standing in the corridor outside and had obviously heard every word.

He didn't actually say anything. But as she walked past, he gave her a one-man round of applause.

Lorna was round at Carmen's when she got the phone call from Eoin.

'Don't go,' urged Carmen. 'It's some kind of trick . . . he wants to get you alone so he can get his own back on you for dumping him.' She watched as Lorna grimly put on her jacket, picked up the car keys and slung her bag on her shoulder. 'I have a really bad feeling about this, Lorna.'

'Don't worry,' Lorna reassured her with a confidence she didn't entirely feel. 'I'm meeting him in a crowded bar, not a dark alley. And I have to talk to him. I need to hear what he has to say, and besides – there's something I need to ask him . . . a favour.'

'All the same—'

'Make sure Leo does his teeth properly, and no eating biscuits under the duvet. Mum and Dad'll be back from their jive class about nine. See you later.'

As she drove across town to the bar where she and Eoin had shared so many evenings, Lorna thought back to what Carmen had said. Carmen was no fool; maybe she was right to have misgivings. Maybe when Eoin had phoned her to ask her to meet him for a chat, she ought to have refused and left it at that.

But she couldn't. It wasn't weakness on her part, at least she didn't think so. It was curiosity. And in any case, the minute he started insulting her she'd just stand up and walk away. That was the theory, anyway.

The bar was heaving, and at first she couldn't make him out. Then a hand landed on her shoulder and she almost jumped out of her skin.

'I arrived early and bagged a table in the corner over there. I got you a white wine, is that OK?'

'Er . . . yeah. Fine.' It felt very peculiar, greeting Eoin without a kiss; not because she wanted to kiss him, just because old habits die hard. In silence, she followed him through the jumble of people to the cramped corner table.

'Do you want anything to eat?' he asked.

Lorna shook her head.

'Me neither.'

'I thought you were supposed to be in France,' she said by way of conversation.

'I kind of went off the idea.'

'Any special reason?'

He grimaced. 'It's hard to have fun when your conscience is playing you up. But you're so perfect I don't suppose you've ever been in that position,' he added with just the faintest edge of malice.

'You'd be surprised.' Lorna fiddled with the stem of her wine glass, curiously unsettled by the idea of Eoin having a conscience. 'Why did you want to meet up tonight?' she asked. 'I was a bit surprised when you called me.'

'I almost didn't,' he confessed. 'I thought you might just scream abuse at me and then slam the phone down. But I'm glad you came. After what you said . . . I guess I just wanted to get a word in edgeways.'

'I meant what I said,' she warned him.

'Yeah, I know. And in many ways you're right about me. I do have faults, a lot of faults. I can be a total pig when I want to be, and sometimes when I don't. I gave my wife hell for no good reason and I don't suppose she'll ever forgive me for that.'

'And what about Sadie?' demanded Lorna, determined to get some answers now that she'd come this far.

Eoin's shoulders sagged. 'Yes, OK, maybe I did get angry and push her, and maybe she did fall and break her fingers. But it was an accident.'

'An accident. Yeah, right. Isn't it always an accident?'

'OK, so perhaps I'm public enemy number one where women are concerned. But you're wrong about one thing.'

'Oh? And what's that?'

'I do care about more than just me. I care about my son so much it hurts, all the more so since it's my own damned fault that I'll probably never see him again. And . . . and I care about you, too.'

There was a dull ache in Lorna's chest. 'Please Eoin, don't say things you don't mean.'

His hand reached out for hers and captured it before she had the wit to

248

pull away. 'I do mean it, Lorna. I swear it.' He looked into her eyes and let go of her hand, and she drew it right back under the tabletop. 'Do you really hate me that much?'

'I don't hate you,' she replied. It was true. She realised now that she didn't care about him enough to hate him.

'Then just try to believe me when I say you meant a lot to me. You still do. But I know that's all over because well, basically I cocked it up. The thing is, I was sort of hoping—'

'Hoping for what?'

'That if we can't be . . . together, we could still be . . . well . . . friends.'

Lorna met his gaze and for the first time felt she was seeing through the slick exterior to the rather lonely, unsuccessful personality beneath. She'd promised herself that no matter what he said, she wouldn't feel anything for him again. But it was hard not to feel something, some spark of warmth that still lingered after what they'd shared together.

'I . . . guess,' she said, with an effort. 'But if you really want that, will you do something for me?'

'As a friend you mean?'

'As a . . . friend. You know Kelly, the girl who's going to live with Carmen?'

Eoin's newfound enthusiasm sagged visibly. 'Oh God, not her again. What's she done now?'

'Nothing,' replied Lorna sharply. 'Nothing but try to get her life together so she can have her baby back.'

'So what does this have to do with me?'

Lorna cut to the chase. No longer afraid of him, she knew that he felt a debt towards her and had no scruples about calling that debt in. You've hurt me, Eoin, she said silently; and now's your chance to pay me back. 'You have a lot of mates. Well-connected ones. And I'm willing to bet that there's at least one lawyer among them.'

'Several actually.'

'Including one who specialises in family cases?'

Light dawned. 'You want me to—?'

'That's right. I want you to get on to this lawyer of yours and get him or her to help Kelly.'

'Let me guess – free of charge?'

'Well of course,' she replied with the thinnest of smiles. 'As a friend.'

Chapter 27

When Chris got the phone call from Lorna, he was just about to go out for a swift half with one-armed Mick from work; but straight away he made an excuse and headed out to the Yellow Parrot bar instead.

He didn't really know why he jumped whenever Lorna called. Or rather he did; he just didn't like admitting it to himself. Unrequited love wasn't exactly the coolest thing to admit to, not when you were a big, hairy bloke and it had been going on for the best part of fifteen years. Anyone else would have given up years ago and settled down with somebody else, just as pretty and funny and talented as Lorna but with a lot fewer emotional minefields to negotiate. But it was no use wanting to be anybody else: he'd tried that, and it didn't work. And he could tell from the sound of her voice that she needed him.

When he arrived, he found her slumped over her fifth glass of wine at the same corner table, her eyes pink and swollen and the scant remnants of a giant bag of crisps scattered across the scratched veneer.

'Hey, kid,' he said, bustling over with deliberate cheerfulness. 'What's up?'

She looked up at him with eyes that struggled to focus. 'I . . . think I'm a bit . . . pissed,' she announced with a drunkard's laboured precision. 'Will you drive me home?'

'Of course I will.' He slid onto the bench seat next to her. 'What do you say we have a coffee first, eh? Maybe a black one?'

She didn't object, so he ordered a small cappuccino for himself and a large Americano for Lorna, with an extra shot of espresso for good measure.

'Chris,' she said.

'What is it?'

Lorna made an effort to rake her dishevelled hair back from her forehead, but succeeded only in looking even more like Johnny Rotten. 'Do I look like shit?'

'N—' he began, then remembered that even drunk, Lorna could always tell when he was lying, and turned it into 'Sort of. A bit.'

She took a moment to absorb this information, then nodded. 'That's all right then, 'cause I feel like shit.'

Then, entirely without warning, she burst into floods of tears and Chris had to grab a handful of paper napkins to try and stem the flow. Everybody was staring at him as though it was all his fault, but he didn't give a damn about anybody but Lorna. 'Hey, c'mon,' he urged softly, 'whatever it is can't be that bad.'

'Yes it can. It can be worse. Ed's dead, and Clawdius is dead, and Eoin's a bastard, and I'm all alone and I don't think I can take any more.'

He slipped an arm round her shoulders. 'You'll never be alone,' he promised. 'You've got Leo and Hope, and your mum and dad. And . . . I know it's not much, but you've got me.' He tried to sound jocular, but there was an edge of desperation in his voice that he hoped she wouldn't notice. 'You'll have to try an awful lot harder if you want to get rid of me, you know.'

She laid her head on his shoulder, burying her face in his shirt, and he felt his heart race. He longed to draw her close and kiss her, but he knew deep down that it wouldn't be right. She was only doing this because she was drunk and maudlin, and because she trusted him . . . like a brother. Would it always be that way? Or could things change if you really, really wanted them to?

'I don't deserve a friend like you,' she mumbled into his shirt.

Plucking up courage, he stroked her hair. 'You deserve a lot better,' he replied, without a trace of false modesty. 'And you certainly deserve better than Eoin Sullivan. Did you give him his marching orders?'

She raised her head and nodded dumbly.

'For what it's worth, I think you did the right thing.'

'I know I did. So why do I feel so bad?' She buried her face again, and slid her arms around his waist, as though he were some kind of super-sized teddy bear.

'You'll feel better in the morning,' he promised. 'Too much wine never did agree with you. Do you remember that school disco when we all smuggled in Liebraumilch inside Coke cans?'

Lorna laughed through her tears. 'And Mrs Roseby sussed us out, and I got stuck trying to leg it through the window of the Boys' toilets.'

'That's nothing. I was sick on her shoes.'

Lorna went quiet. 'Ed wasn't there that night, was he? He was off somewhere playing football or something. He was good at all that stuff.'

'He was good at everything,' replied Chris a little ruefully.

They remained like that for a little while, Chris sitting with his arm round Lorna, and Lorna with her face buried in his shoulder and her arms about his waist. Chris could happily have stayed that way forever.

Now's the time, a voice inside his head told him; if you don't say it now, you never will.

'Lorna,' he began softly.

She murmured something in reply.

'There's something I've been meaning . . . wanting . . . to say to you for a long time.' He swallowed hard, his throat suddenly dry and constricted. 'It's about the way I feel.' He waited for her to say something, but as she didn't he felt emboldened to carry on. 'The thing is Lorna, I'm in love with you. I've been in love with you ever since I met you, and if I live till I'm a hundred I'll—'

He felt Lorna's head move sideways, and he glanced down, expecting her to say something profound.

But her eyes were tight shut, her mouth was wide open, and the only sound that came out was a tiny snore of contentment.

'It's all her fault, Mum,' complained Sarah as Meg made sympathetic noises on the other end of the phone.

'I know you're not finding pregnancy easy, dear, but I don't quite see how you can blame Lorna for that,' she said diplomatically. 'It does seem a little unfair on your sister.'

On the other side of the room, Lorna and George exchanged weary looks. At least I'm not the only person here who's getting fed up with Sarah and her hour-long phone calls, thought Lorna, still trying to shake off the after-effects of her hangover. Dad looks like he could happily swing for her.

Pregnancy had had a marked impact on Sarah. Before she got pregnant, she had hardly ever phoned anybody unless she wanted something or wanted to foist an unwanted possession onto some defenceless family member. This was not such a problem when the possession was a cashmere sweater or a couple of West End theatre tickets; but her fondness for dispensing 'cute' china models of fat cherubs and pigs in dungarees had had a knock-on effect on car boot sales the length and breadth of the South-West.

But ever since the hapless Gavin had impregnated her, Sarah had been on the phone non-stop, alternately complaining and demanding advice, and frequently doing both at the same time. Today, alas, was no exception.

'Of course it's her fault, Mum!' insisted Sarah, so shrilly that Lorna could hear every word from the other side of the living-room. 'She never told me about the stretch-marks, for a start off.'

253

'Tell her everybody gets stretch-marks,' said Lorna.

Meg put a hand over the receiver. 'She says you never see Liz Hurley or Kate Moss with stretch-marks. Why's that?'

'God, I don't know – maybe they're just good at hiding them. Tell her to slap a load of cream on her belly, that might help.'

'She says, double or single?'

This was all too much for Lorna. Marching across the room, she seized the telephone from her mother. 'Sarah, I hope that was a joke, I really do. Or you're going to give birth to a baby with the IQ of a peanut.'

Sarah's response to this was to turn on the waterworks. 'Why's everybody being so cruel to me?' she wailed. 'I'm in a very fragile condition, you know. The doctor says I'm very small for my dates.'

Lorna struggled not to lose her temper. 'If you ate properly, instead of trying to diet—'

'But I have to diet! I'm getting so gross! Gavin says I look just like a Morris Minor from behind!'

Give me strength, thought Lorna. 'You're supposed to be fat,' she snapped. 'You're pregnant!'

'Yes! And if I'd known what a nightmare it was going to be, I'd never have let Gavin anywhere near me. It's all your fault,' she repeated. 'You're a midwife. You had a duty to tell me the whole ghastly truth.'

Despairing of getting any sense out of her sister, Lorna handed the receiver back to her mother. 'Apparently it's still all my fault. Oh, and she's still on that stupid diet.'

Meg did her best to sound like a stern Victorian matriarch. 'Sarah, you absolutely have to start eating properly . . . What's that? I don't care if he is a qualified vegan naturopath, I'm your mother and I'm telling you to get some proper home-cooked meals down you. Besides, you can worry about your figure after the birth.'

Sarah gave a dramatic shudder. 'Please, Mother! Don't mention birth to me. The very thought of it makes my pelvic floor sag.' Her tone changed. 'Oh, by the way – have you decided what plastic surgery you're having yet?'

Meg cleared her throat awkwardly. 'Er . . . well . . . I haven't actually made up my mind whether I'm going to have any at all. Your father doesn't seem to think it's a very good idea.'

'Too right I don't,' boomed George. 'I don't hold with all this messing with nature. It's not dignified.'

Sarah tittered. 'Oh Mum, that's so old-fashioned! And you simply can't let a prize like that go to waste. Between you and me,' she confided, 'I'll be first in the queue for a tummy-tuck once I've got rid of this wretched baby. Not to mention a boob-lift, judging from all the horror-stories I've heard.'

254

'Perhaps dear, but don't you think I'm a bit past it?'

'Of course you're not! Don't you let Dad bully you, Mum. Why shouldn't you have a fabulous new figure and a face-lift? Maybe Dad's worried you'll get yourself a sexy new man!'

It wasn't until a little later in the day that Meg recalled the other thing that Sarah had said. 'You don't mind if we pop off for a few days next week do you, Lorna dear?'

Lorna looked up from sorting out the children's washing. 'Of course not. Where are you off to – anywhere nice?'

Meg looked slightly awkward. 'I . . . er . . . sort of promised your sister we'd go and see her.'

'Oh,' said Lorna. 'Right.'

'She wants to show us the new nursery now it's finished. And she's got this bee in her bonnet about converting the old stable block into some kind of super deluxe granny flat.' She gave Lorna an apologetic smile. 'You know how persuasive your sister is.'

Yes, thought Lorna, unable to suppress a pang of resentment. Too right I do. Whatever Sarah wants, Sarah inevitably gets.

So maybe I'd better not count on Mum and Dad being around here for too much longer.

It wasn't an easy task for Carmen, getting down the stairs to the basement with two mugs of tea and a packet of biscuits on a tray. Not when she couldn't see anything beyond the swell of her own stomach.

Kelly took one look at her teetering on the penultimate step and dropped her paint brush into the tin, with a spatter of magnolia emulsion. 'Mrs Jones, you shouldn't be doing that, you'll hurt yourself!' With more enthusiasm than skill, she grabbed the tray and almost pulled Carmen over with it. 'Sorry,' she said, wiping her cheek with the back of her hand and smearing it with paint. Her shoulder-length brown hair tied in high bunches, she looked for all the world like an over-eager spaniel. 'I was trying to help.'

Carmen cleared herself a space on top of an upturned crate, tested it for strength and then lowered herself onto it. 'It's about time I had a serious word with you, young lady,' she said.

Kelly's bunches wilted. 'Oh God I'm sorry, what've I done now? Was it the wallpaper in the baby's room? Only I thought you was supposed to put the paste on the wall. I've never done wallpapering before.'

'Calm down, it's not the wallpapering.' Carmen pointed to the other empty crate. 'Sit down before you fall over.'

'But—'

'Sit.'

Like the obedient spaniel she was, Kelly sat.

'First off,' said Carmen, 'you can stop calling me "Mrs Jones". I'm not a Mrs – never have been – and nobody calls me anything but Carmen unless I've just clamped their car, and then it's usually something with four letters. So Carmen will do, OK?'

Kelly nodded meekly. 'OK.'

'And the other thing is, you can stop trying so hard.' Kelly opened her mouth to speak, but Carmen stopped her. 'Yes, I know you're worried I'll throw you out, but it's driving me mad, you being on your best behaviour all the time. I'm not saying you can play me up, but please can you just be yourself for a bit?'

'Er . . . yeah. OK,' replied Kelly, somewhat bemused. 'If you want. But I thought you'd want something better than that.'

Carmen frowned. 'Why?'

'Well, being me didn't do much good with me mum, did it?'

'I'm not your mum. Now, how are you getting on with painting that wall?'

They stood side by side and contemplated Kelly's handiwork.

'It's a bit . . . wiggly looking,' said Kelly.

'That's because it needs another coat. And it helps if you paint in nice long strokes, straight up and down.'

'Oh. I never thought of that.' Kelly looked at Carmen. 'I'm a bit crap at this, aren't I?'

'So was I at your age. But I've been on my own a long time, and it's amazing how much you learn when you have to. Anyway, a couple more days and you'll have this room looking great, you just wait and see.'

'I could finish it tomorrow if I stayed home,' ventured Kelly hopefully.

Carmen laughed. 'Maybe, but you're not going to. Tomorrow morning you're going back to school. It's not a bad place, Robbie will show you the way round.'

'Aw Carmen . . . do I have to? I've had a baby now, I'm a mum.'

'Yes, you've had a baby. But if you're going to get her back you'll have to show that you mean to do the best for her. And that means getting an education, so that later on you can get a job and bring her up properly. You do want her back, don't you?'

'Of course I do!' Kelly's eyes flashed real hope. 'Do you think . . . will they let me?'

'I don't know, love. But if you do your best and I do mine, who knows what we can manage?'

Footsteps on the stairs behind Carmen made her turn round. Robbie was standing there, in his oldest T-shirt and a pair of jeans he hadn't worn since his auntie Grace told him he looked 'sweet' in them.

256

'Hiya Kelly,' he said.

'Hiya Robbie.'

Carmen looked at him curiously. 'Is this some kind of campaign to persuade me you've got no decent clothes to wear? 'Cause if it is—'

Robbie shuffled his feet and minutely inspected the toes of his trainers. 'I heard you working down here,' he said sheepishly. 'And I was wondering . . . can I help too?'

Chapter 28

When Eoin mentioned at work the next day that his 'lawyer friend' would be calling on Lorna that evening, she half expected a visit from someone middle-aged, in classic pinstripes, or from some slightly louche young man with a fast brain and an even faster car.

She certainly wasn't expecting Caroline.

The petite blonde in the designer casuals looked more like a surfer babe than a solicitor. But the card she handed Lorna read: 'Caroline McWhirter, LLB: junior partner, Ryhope & Swales.'

'Hi, I'm Caroline. You must be Lorna. Eoin's told me all about you.'

'Really?' Lorna wondered just how much. 'You've come to talk about Kelly Picton?'

'I wanted to get the basic details from you before I go round and talk to the girl herself. You don't mind if I come in?'

'Not at all.' Lorna stood back to let her in. 'First door on the left, make yourself comfortable and I'll put the kettle on.'

'Thanks. Make mine milk, no sugar please.'

As Lorna filled the kettle and arranged biscuits on a plate, two thoughts ran through her mind. First: could this young girl of Eoin's really help Kelly? And second: was she yet another of his endless exes?

The following morning, Carmen's postman arrived early. After last night's visitation from Caroline McWhirter, she was half expecting something from the solicitor's office or Social Services, but there were only two envelopes, both with London postmarks. Bending down to pick them up required a considerable amount of Mind Over Bump, after which Carmen could think of only one thing: tea.

'I can do the kids' breakfasts if you want,' volunteered Kelly, who was already in the kitchen putting the kettle on, and who had the look of someone who'd been up since dawn looking for things to do. 'And I've made a start on the packed lunches and sorted the washing and stuff.'

Carmen gave her a reproving look. 'What did I say about trying too hard?'

'I'm not!' protested Kelly. 'It's just all this business with Lee-Anne. I've never spoken to a solicitor before, 'cept when Linda first got done for possession. I need something to take me mind off it. And yes, I have done me homework,' she added, pre-empting Carmen's next question. 'Robbie helped me.'

Carmen wasn't sure whether to be highly delighted or vaguely concerned. 'I'm really glad you and Robbie are getting on so well,' she said slowly, 'but you will be . . . careful, won't you?'

This was met by the blankest look Carmen had seen since she'd tried to explain to Lorna how a carburettor worked. Then Kelly's eyes widened and she let out a gale of laughter. 'You don't think . . . me an' him? Me an' Robbie?'

'What's wrong with Robbie?' demanded Carmen, somewhat taken aback.

Kelly wiped a tear from her eye. 'Nothing's wrong with him! But he's fourteen!'

'So are you,' pointed out Carmen.

'Exactly. And how many fourteen-year-old lads did you fancy when you were fourteen?'

'Oh. Yes. I see what you mean. They did seem a bit . . . immature,' admitted Carmen.

'Hey, Carmen. You're not really worried, are you?' The hilarity faded from Kelly's eyes and she came over to where Carmen was sitting. 'You don't think I'd go and get myself in the same mess twice over? I mean, I'm stupid but I'm not that stupid. Robbie's just a mate, Carmen, honest he is.'

'Well I hope he knows that,' replied Carmen, ''cause whenever I see him he's following you round like a lost poodle.' She let out a long, slow breath, forcing herself to relax. 'I'm sorry love,' she said. 'I just don't want you ending up like . . . well, like me.'

'I reckon there's a lot worse things I could be,' retorted Kelly. 'But I won't let you down, I promise.'

'Just don't let yourself down. That's all I care about.'

'OK. It's a deal.' Kelly sprang back to life. 'Now, are you going to let me do those sandwiches or what?'

'Oh go on then.' Carmen capitulated without much of a struggle. When your back ached, your ankles were swollen and you'd been up all night with Becca's tonsils, it was hard to refuse a helping hand. 'Just make sure you're not late for school, OK?'

'Yeah, yeah, I know. If I don't go to school it'll make me look bad.'

Kelly crossed to the bread bin and took out a large sliced wholemeal loaf. 'How long is this going to go on for?' she asked, standing there with the loaf dangling in its plastic bag. 'How long before they let me have my baby back?'

'I don't know,' Carmen confessed. 'But Caroline said she'd do her best to get things moving.'

'Will she really help me?'

'Well she said she will.'

'Why? Why would she want to help me?'

It didn't seem like the time to explain about sexual dynamics. In any case, Carmen wasn't sure she'd ever quite understood the relationship between Lorna and Eoin herself. So she decided to go with: 'As a favour to one of Lorna's friends, I think.'

'Not that doctor with the fart under his nose?'

'Er . . . possibly.'

Kelly plonked the loaf down on the worktop in a gesture of resignation. 'I'm stuffed then, aren't I? Stuck-up git hates me.'

Carmen sighed. 'No he doesn't. Besides, that's got nothing to do with it. Lorna asked him to get his friend to help, and she will. Now – are you going to get on and make those sandwiches, or shall we just sit here and wait for the hard-boiled eggs to hatch out?'

While Kelly got on with making big, messy sandwiches that dripped mayonnaise from every corner, Carmen turned her attentions to the post. As she turned the first envelope over to slit it open, she saw the return address on the back: 'Grant & Neill Publishers Ltd, London NW1,' and her heart skipped a beat.

She hardly dared breathe as she unfolded the single sheet of crisp, white paper and scanned the contents. 'Dear Ms Jones . . . *Adventures of Fat Penguin* . . . we are very sorry but . . .'

Oh dear, yet another rejection letter. Maybe she'd been wrong about Mr Scholes's stories, and yet all the kids she'd tried them out on had loved them to bits, even the ones who couldn't normally sit still for more than thirty seconds at a time. She was about to scrunch up the letter and throw it away, when she noticed the final paragraph. 'Although they are not suitable for our list, because we concentrate on publishing fiction for teenage readers, I think they might be of interest to our sister company, Blue Elephant Books; and I have therefore passed on the manuscript to one of my colleagues there, for her opinion.'

Well. Maybe it wasn't all bad news after all. Maybe there was still hope for Fat Penguin. Never give up Carmen, she reminded herself; that's always been your mantra, and there's no reason to change it now.

She slit open the second envelope almost without thinking, her mind still on the publisher's letter. When she did focus on what the envelope contained, it gave her such a shock that for a moment, nothing in the world existed except herself and the sheet of paper.

Kelly's voice cut through her trance. 'Anything interesting?'

Carmen forced herself back to the world of here and now. Kelly was looking at her over her shoulder, a knife in one hand and the jar of mayonnaise in the other. 'What?' asked Carmen.

'Is there anything interesting?' repeated Kelly. 'In the post?'

'Oh.' Carmen swallowed. 'No, not really. Just routine paperwork, you know.'

She folded the letter and put it back into the envelope, its heading imprinted on her brain: 'Re: Mr Maurice Randolph Cissay.'

It was from the missing persons' agency Victor had put her in touch with. Would she please fill in the enclosed form, giving as much information as possible about Maurice? They sounded very helpful, and quite optimistic of being able to track him down.

But was that what she wanted? A little shiver ran down her spine as she touched the letter in her lap.

No, she thought; it's not what I want – but it's what Robbie wants, and that's what matters. And that's why I'm going to fill in this form.

Some time that evening, a call came through to the Social Services emergency line from the local police station.

'A young child, you say?' The on-call social worker keyed the details into her computer. 'On the Bluebell Estate?'

'A baby apparently,' replied the young constable. 'Little girl, no more than a few months old, according to our informants. We've been watching the house for some time, following information received.'

'And the parents have definitely left her alone?'

'Two adults were seen leaving the flat around six-thirty, all dressed up as if they were going out for the evening. Since then, the people in the house next door say they've heard the baby crying pretty much non-stop. I don't know how people can do this sort of thing, I really don't.'

'Have you set the wheels in motion?'

'Of course.'

'I'll be with you in fifteen minutes.'

Lorna was in the bath when the phone rang, and left a trail of foamy footprints as she ran across the landing to the bedroom extension. Whatever it was, it had to be important: nobody phoned anybody at half-past six in the morning unless it was a matter of life or death.

'Lorna, is that you? It's Carmen.'

Lorna dripped onto the carpet, dabbing ineffectually at herself with a towel that was several sizes too small. 'Have you any idea what time it is?'

'It's about Lee-Anne,' said Carmen breathlessly. 'Social Services have taken her into care.'

'When?'

'Last night, apparently. I only just heard from Caroline. You remember that couple who live next door to the Pictons? Well, they finally came up trumps and grassed on them. That bitch left the poor little kid all alone in the flat while she went out partying with her bloke.'

Lorna sat down on the end of the bed, completely oblivious to the wet, bottom-shaped mark she was leaving on the pale pink satin bedspread. 'Hang on . . . let me get my head round this. Lee-Anne's been taken into care?'

'Yes.'

'Because they neglected her?'

'Yes!'

'Well that's good, isn't it? I mean, they're hardly going to give Lee-Anne back to her grandmother after this.'

'No,' agreed Carmen. 'But that doesn't necessarily mean they'll give her back to Kelly either. From what I can gather, there's going to be a big case-conference, with everybody there – lawyers, social workers, police, the lot – and they'll decide what's going to happen to Lee-Anne. Poor Kelly's terrified. She's convinced they'll take one look at her and believe all the lies her mother told the social worker about her.'

'Poor Kelly,' murmured Lorna, imagining how she would feel if someone had come along and tried to take one of her babies away. And how she'd have felt if she was only fourteen at the time. Even thinking about it was almost too much to bear. 'Tell her . . . tell her not to worry, because she's got a good solicitor.'

'I thought you weren't over-fond of Caroline.'

Lorna smiled. 'Only because I thought she might be another of Eoin's exes. Yeah I know, pathetic isn't it? Now I've talked to her, I reckon she's far too smart anyway. So tell Kelly to do whatever Caroline advises, and she'll be all right.'

'You've forgotten the most important thing of all,' said Carmen.

'What's that?'

'She's got us.'

Over the coming days and weeks, Lorna was so taken up with work, the children, getting over Eoin, accommodating her sister Sarah's diva-like behaviour and monitoring the battle for baby Lee-Anne that she barely noticed that Chris wasn't around.

263

And when it did enter her mind to call him, or ask him to come out with her and the kids, it never seemed like a number one priority. Chris was sure to be there, just like he always had been. No matter how long she left it before she called him, whenever she did he'd be on the other end of the phone: the one element of her life that had never changed, and never would.

But in spite of all the diversions, Chris was the first person she rang when she heard the news about Lee-Anne. Whatever her joys and her sorrows, she'd always shared them with him.

'Chris?' she bubbled. 'It's me, Lorna. Sorry I haven't been in touch for a while, I've been really busy. Are you OK?'

'Fine.'

'Guess what, I've just had some great news: Kelly's being sent on a parentcraft course, and if that works out Social Services say she can have Lee-Anne back, as long as she stays with Carmen.'

'That's good.'

'Of course the Health Visitor will be keeping a close eye on them too, and I said I'd get involved as well, and—' Lorna paused. 'Are you sure you're OK?'

'Yes, fine. I told you. Why?'

'You just sound a bit ... distant. Anyhow, I was wondering if you'd like to come round next Thursday evening – Carmen and I are having a little celebratory get-together for Kelly. What do you reckon?'

'Sorry. I can't. I have to be somewhere else.'

Certain he was only teasing, Lorna parried with: 'There'll be home-made chocolate brownies.'

There was a short silence that seemed interminable, then Chris replied. 'I can't come on Thursday, because I'm off to Annecy on Monday.'

This was surprising in the extreme. Give or take the odd annual holiday in Spain, Chris never went anywhere. 'But that's in France, isn't it? What on earth are you going there for?'

'To work. There's a new twinning scheme between the local council and theirs – they send us a couple of council workers, and we send them a couple in return. They were a carpenter short, so I volunteered.'

'B-but ... you don't even speak French!' stammered Lorna.

'I expect I'll get along.'

Lorna's head was spinning. She felt as if she were inside a snow-dome that someone had suddenly shaken and turned upside down, and all the things she had thought solid and fixed were breaking free and floating past her ears. 'How long is it for? When will you be back?'

'Well, it's supposed to be for a couple of months, but some people stay longer. One or two have got themselves permanent jobs – they do say it's

264

nice over there, and the money's good. I guess I'll take it as it comes.'

'Why did you leave it to the last moment to tell me? You weren't just going to skip the country and not even tell me at all? You weren't, were you?'

'Of course not,' he replied; but she wasn't sure she believed him. 'Anyhow, I'd better go – got a lot of stuff to sort out before I go.'

'Send me a postcard.'

'Count on it.'

'And . . . come back.'

He didn't answer. But if she'd been able to see across town and into his living room, Lorna would have understood why. It was taking every ounce of his energy not to cry.

Chapter 29

Time passed, and summer stretched on towards autumn. Hope learned six new words, had her first proper toddler tantrum, and joined the Little Pixies Nursery School with her friend Ziza from down the road.

In every garden across Gloucestershire late-summer flower buds swelled and went pop; and like them, Carmen got rounder and rounder until she was sure she was on the point of exploding. While it might have seemed at first that Carmen was the one doing all the giving and Kelly all the receiving, things had swiftly turned themselves upside down.

'You'd really miss her now, wouldn't you?' said Lorna as they sat in Carmen's garden, listening to Kelly belting out 'The Wheels on the Bus' to her baby daughter through the basement window.

'All except the singing,' Carmen admitted, flinching as Kelly aimed for a top note and landed several tones short. 'Still, Lee-Anne seems to love it, so who am I to complain? To be honest, I'm not sure I could manage without Kelly, the size I am now. She does so much in the house I feel a bit guilty sometimes.'

'You shouldn't feel guilty; you've done an awful lot for her too.'

'Yeah, I know. But all the same, she's still just a kid. I'd like her to have some time for enjoying herself.'

'You're really good to her, you know.'

Carmen shrugged. 'Maybe I'm just making up for the fact that nobody had much time for me when I was her age – and look what happened to me.'

Lorna closed her eyes, focused on the crystal-clear trilling of a black-bird in the upper branches of the holly tree, and tried to transport herself far away, into a more tranquil dimension. 'You know, it's funny,' she observed.

Carmen lay back in her ancient deckchair, eating Maltesers from a box perched on the apex of her bump. 'What is?'

'The way you get so used to people that you almost forget they're there, and you can't help taking them for granted. And then they go away and you suddenly realise they're not there any more.'

Carmen opened one eye and turned it on Lorna. 'I have a feeling we're not talking about Kelly any more. Am I right?'

Lorna gave up on her half-hearted attempts to achieve spiritual tranquillity, and sank limply into her chair, which creaked at the extra strain. 'I don't half miss him,' she confessed. 'I never thought I would – not so much. But I do.'

'Would this be about Chris?'

'Well I'm not talking about Eoin! In fact, I sometimes wish *he*'d go away so I had a chance to miss him. Not that I would though.' Lorna helped herself to a fistful of Maltesers from Carmen's box. 'I still can't quite believe Chris went away just like that – I'm sure he wasn't even going to tell me he was going.'

'Maybe he thought you wouldn't care one way or another,' ventured Carmen.

'But of course I would!' protested Lorna. 'How could I not care? We've been friends since . . . since forever.'

'Since you met Ed, in fact.'

'Well . . . yes.' She turned to look at Carmen. 'Why would he think I wouldn't care?'

Hmm, thought Carmen. Time to choose my words carefully. 'Between you and me,' she said, 'I think Chris cares an awful lot about you—'

'He's got a funny way of showing it.'

'– but he maybe thinks you only want to stay close to him because he was Ed's best friend, and he reminds you of him.'

'That's not true!' exclaimed Lorna.

'Sure?'

'Yes.' She stopped to think. 'All right, maybe it was a bit like that, to start off with. Having Chris around, to share memories with, made me feel that Ed wasn't so far away. But it's more than that. I like Chris because he's . . . Chris. And that's why I miss him.'

'Perhaps he more than likes you,' suggested Carmen. 'Perhaps he wants to be more than friends, but he senses that you don't.'

That stunned Lorna more than it ought to have done. 'No. Chris wouldn't feel like that about me. Would he?'

Carmen didn't answer.

'No, I'm sure you've got it wrong. He's never said a word to me about anything like that. I've never even considered it . . .'

'Honestly?'

Lorna felt an uncomfortable fluttering sensation in the pit of her stomach that felt a bit like pigeons coming home to roost. 'Of course not! It wouldn't be right, would it? Or at least . . . it wouldn't *feel* right. He's always been like a brother to me.'

'Ah but he's not a brother, is he?' Carmen pointed out. 'And you don't have to miss him any more if you don't want. You told me yourself he got back from France a fortnight ago. What's stopping you phoning him and meeting up for a drink or something?'

She's right, thought Lorna. Absolutely nothing is stopping me. Absolutely nothing except this silly, paralysing fear of stepping into something I'm totally unprepared for.

'Oh, I couldn't,' she replied, burying her face in her book. 'If Chris wanted to see me, I'm sure he'd have phoned me by now.'

Meg was an expert at multi-tasking. Which was just as well, since she was trying to dead-head the fuchsias in Lorna's conservatory at the same time as fielding yet another of Sarah's marathon telephone calls.

'Yes dear, no dear . . . now don't be silly. Of course you won't need surgery on your belly-button, it's perfectly normal. Now, are you taking those iron pills like the doctor told you to?'

She snipped deftly at withered flower-heads while Sarah wittered on about nausea, constipation, funny brown blotches and hair sprouting in unexpected places. 'It's a global conspiracy, Mum, that's what it is,' she declared.

'What is, dear?'

'The way society lures women into getting pregnant, with all those cute TV adverts about baby-milk and disposable nappies. They never tell you what it's *really* like, do they?'

'If they did that, dear, nobody would ever have children.'

'Exactly! I just can't believe I fell for it.'

'Never mind dear,' soothed her mother, counting the drops of Baby Bio as she filled her miniature watering can, 'it'll soon be over and you'll have a lovely little baby to make up for it all.'

'Mum.'

'Yes dear?'

'I'm not even sure I like babies. I mean, I went over to see Diana's last week and it was all smelly and it puked up on her shoulder. And it screamed when we were trying to have a sensible conversation about shoes. They're not all like that, are they?' she enquired fearfully.

Meg toyed with the idea of telling her the truth, but swiftly discarded it. Sarah was the kind of girl who might go and do something silly, like bludgeoning Gavin's brains out, if she realised what the next few months were really going to be like. Meg had often wondered how she and George had managed to produce such a diverse bunch of children.

'Oh, all babies are different, just like grown-ups,' she said, neatly side-stepping the question. 'And all mums think their babies are perfect, so I wouldn't worry. Anyway, your father and I will be coming up to see you next weekend, so chin up and—'

She was cut off in mid-sentence by an ominous creak overhead, and instinctively looked up. 'What the -?

'Mum?' Sarah did not take kindly to losing her audience in the middle of a conversation. 'Mum, are you listening to me?'

The only answer she received was a splintering noise, followed by a thunderous crash.

Lorna put the phone down, counted to ten and returned to where her mother was sitting on the despised green sofa, a cup of hot, sweet tea within arm's reach.

'Sarah reckons I'm practically a murderer,' she announced. 'She says you could probably sue me for post-traumatic stress disorder.'

'Oh, take no notice of your sister,' advised Meg. 'She always did have an over-developed sense of the dramatic. Now, if you'll let me get up I must go and sweep up that mess in the conservatory.'

'Oh no you don't!' Lorna and George responded in unison; and Meg found herself pushed firmly back among the scatter-cushions.

'You need to rest,' said George.

'Dad's right, you've had a shock. And in a way, Sarah's right,' Lorna added, though the admission nearly choked her. 'After all, it's my conservatory roof that fell in and nearly squashed you.'

'That's like saying your father's responsible for the bump on your brother's nose, seeing as it was George's bicycle he fell off when he was fourteen,' snorted Meg. 'And that's just nonsense. How were you supposed to know it was going to collapse like that?'

It was a fair point, but it didn't do much to halt Lorna's guilt-trip. I should have known, she told herself. And the little demon on her shoulder grinned, and whispered in her ear: 'Chris would have known.'

George rubbed his hands together in the time-honoured way that meant 'let's get down to business'. 'I'm just popping out to the shed to fetch a ladder,' he announced. 'Better get that hole covered up before it rains.'

'No you're not, Dad,' said Lorna. 'I'm not having you up a ladder, messing about on the roof.'

'Quite right George,' agreed Meg. 'We don't want you having one of your dizzy turns.'

'But somebody's got to do something!' he protested, straining at the leash like an under-worked collie.

270

It's no good trying to wriggle out of it, said the grinning demon. You know you're going to have to do it, whether you like it or not.

'I'll sort it out,' said Lorna. All eyes converged on her.

'Do you want the *Yellow Pages*, dear?' asked her mother. 'If you're going to be phoning a builder—'

'No, it's OK,' replied Lorna. 'I'm . . . er . . . going to phone Chris.'

On her own in the master bedroom, Lorna stared at the telephone receiver for ages before finally keying in Chris's number. It wasn't that she couldn't remember it – after all these years it came to her as automatically as her own. It was something much less tangible, something almost akin to fear, which kept her from simply dialling him without thinking.

And yet she'd always felt more comfortable in his presence than with anybody; in some ways, even more comfortable than she had felt with Ed. It was pretty obvious that something had changed. Why, and what did it all mean? That was the question. She still wasn't quite sure if she really wanted an answer.

The phone rang at Chris's end for a long time. Just when Lorna thought she might be off the hook, and have to call a builder instead, he picked up.

'Hello?' He sounded tired and sleepy.

'It's . . . um . . . me. Lorna.'

After a painfully obvious pause, he repeated 'Lorna?', as though he couldn't think of anything else to say.

'It's been a long time,' she remarked.

'Yes . . . wow . . . what is it? A couple of months?'

'Thereabouts.' She could have told him the exact length of time since they last spoke, in months, weeks and days, but that wasn't something she was about to admit.

'How've you been doing?' The awkwardness in his voice was like the excruciating politeness that reigns between strangers who sense that they have little in common and probably won't meet again. Coming from Chris, it sounded all wrong. Coming from him, it hurt.

'Fine,' she lied. 'You?'

'Fine. Great.'

'Did you enjoy France?'

'Yeah, it was really . . . amazing. Fantastic experience.'

'But you still came home again,' she pointed out. 'The last postcard you sent, you were talking about getting permanent work out there. Does that mean you prefer living here after all?'

'Oh well, you know,' he replied jokily, 'All that perfect weather, gourmet food and top-dollar wages – who wouldn't prefer rainy summers and undercooked burgers in Cheltenham? I'm glad you rang,' he said suddenly.

271

Lorna swallowed hard. 'I thought you might not want me to. Otherwise you'd have phoned me.'

'Oh. You mean you were waiting for me?'

'Yeah. I guess.'

There was a pause, and then they both started talking at once. A moment's embarrassed laughter didn't actually break the ice, but at least it cracked the surface. Lorna realised that her chest was aching from the effort of not breathing properly. This was all very silly, very juvenile.

'You first,' said Chris.

'No, you,' Lorna insisted.

'Would you maybe like to meet up sometime?' he ventured.

'Yes, I'd like that.'

'Where – here, the pub, your place? Some time next week?'

'Er ... my place might be best,' Lorna confessed. 'And you couldn't possibly make it sometime today?'

'Today? Why today?' A glimmer of realisation pierced Chris's consciousness. 'Hang on – has something happened?'

'Sort of,' she admitted, hating herself for the sordid truth. 'The conservatory roof fell in this morning, and nearly brained my mum.'

'Ah,' said Chris. 'So that was the only reason you phoned me then?'

'Not the *only* reason,' protested Lorna.

Chris sighed. And when he spoke again, the edge of eagerness had been replaced by a fatalistic monotone. 'Just give me time to put my jacket on and pick up my tools,' he said, 'and I'll be round to sort it out.'

Seeing Lorna again after several weeks' enforced exile wasn't quite the way Chris had imagined it. He'd expected it to hurt a lot more, and he really hadn't been prepared for the warm glow that insinuated its way into his bones the moment she opened the front door to him and smiled.

Come on Chris man, he told himself; don't go wobbly on me again. You said you were over her now. Yeah, he answered himself; and I said I'd stay away, and look what became of that.

It was even harder to be cool and dispassionate when Leo and Hope hurled themselves at him and demanded to know where Uncle Chris had been for so long, and whether he had any sweets in his pockets. Of course he did; he always did.

Lorna, Meg and George shooed the kids out of the conservatory and stood round the bottom of the ladder as Chris shinned up for a close look.

'Is it bad?' asked Lorna.

He looked down at her from the top of the ladder. 'Well it's not good. But at least it's only wet rot, not dry. All this timber will need replacing though.' He came down a few rungs. 'Good job it was safety glass, or you'd have been cut to ribbons, Mrs S.'

He jumped down onto the floor. 'Right. Well if you hang on here I'll go and fetch some tarpaulins from the van. There's a storm forecast for tomorrow, and we don't want the rain getting in, do we?'

'I'll give you a hand if you've got another ladder,' volunteered George.

Chris patted him on the shoulder. 'The offer's much appreciated, Mr Scholes. But there's not really room for two of us up there. Maybe you could pass me up my tools and suchlike? That'd be a real help.'

Bless you, thought Lorna. Bless you for not telling him he's too old and a liability.

Afterwards, while her mother and father were picking the last splinters and stray nails out of the fuchsias, Lorna and Chris went into the kitchen for a glass of Meg's home-made lemonade.

'Wow,' said Chris, downing half a glass in one gulp. 'This stuff really hits the spot. I'd forgotten how great your mum's lemonade is.'

'My mum's just great, full stop,' replied Lorna. 'I don't know how I'd have managed without her and Dad, this last year.' She looked up at him. 'And I don't know how I'd manage without you, either. Ever.'

He shrugged. 'Oh, I'm just your average carpentry superhero – have moulding-plane, will travel.'

'I'm not just talking about DIY. I'm talking about ... you.' Embarrassment got the better of her. 'Fancy another?'

'Sorry?'

'Another lemonade.'

'Oh. Yes, please.' While she poured it out, he watched her, aware of each familiar gesture; the way she flicked her hair behind her ear before she picked up the jug; the way she rested the spout on the rim of the glass. He had never imagined that he could know someone so well and yet in some ways be so distant from her. 'Lorna ...'

'Hmm?'

'You remember I told you I was thinking of reviving the Long Stands?'

'The group? Yes, but I assumed you'd given up the idea when you went off to France.'

'Actually, we've had a couple of practices since I got back, and I've ... er ... written a couple of songs.'

Lorna didn't conceal her surprise. 'You've *written* them? Yourself? But I thought the Long Stands only played covers.'

'We did, mostly. But the lads and I thought maybe it was time to move on a bit – aim for new horizons.'

'Wow,' said Lorna, genuinely impressed. 'I never knew you were a poet.'

273

'I wouldn't put it quite like that! I don't suppose they're very good songs. Charlie the bass player takes the mickey out of them non-stop.'

'Do I get a chance to find out?'

'That's what I was going to phone you about. Or at least, I was until I chickened out. Me and the guys have got a gig at the Old Spot on the nineteenth, and I sort of wondered if . . . you know . . . you'd like to come along.'

'I don't know,' said Lorna, her mind suddenly filled with images of the last gig she'd attended: Ed's last gig. The one he'd performed at the week before he died. 'I'd really like to, but . . . I'm not sure.'

A kind of shutter came down behind Chris's eyes. 'That's OK,' he said briskly, downing the rest of his lemonade. 'I didn't expect you'd be that interested. I'll be in touch about the conservatory, OK?'

And he left her with a peck on the cheek and a sudden feeling of emptiness.

'I've really waited far too long,' said Lorna, eyeing the small carved wooden box on her living room mantelpiece. 'I should have done it ages ago.'

'What about the back garden?' suggested Carmen. 'He spent a lot of time there.'

'Yes, but what he really loved doing was squeezing through the hedge at the bottom and going into the park over the road. He used to spend hours lurking in the rhododendrons, pretending he was a mighty jungle predator, or ambushing little kids for their ice creams.'

Carmen laughed. 'How do you know all that? Can you read cats' minds or something?'

'Only Clawdius's,' replied Lorna. 'He was special. And that's why I have to scatter his ashes where he would have wanted them to go.'

She sat Hope on her knee and explained to her and Leo that they were going to do something very special for Clawdius. 'We're going to take him back to his favourite place, so his spirit can run about in the sunshine for ever and ever.'

'Will we be able to see him, Mummy?' asked Leo.

'No,' she admitted. 'But whenever we go there we'll know he's never very far away.'

'Like Daddy?'

She smiled. 'Like Daddy. Now, let's get your shoes on and pop Hope in her buggy. We're off to the park.'

The small procession entered the gates of Dunsford Park to the accompaniment of the fountain plashing into its round concrete basin, and flurries of children squealing as they chased each other in and out of the floral displays. In the distance, an ice cream van was doing a roaring trade in 99s; the queue stretched halfway down the path to the park gates.

A grey squirrel watched with interest from the fork of a tree as Lorna, Carmen and the children headed for the edge of the lawned area beside the fence that Clawdius had so often squeezed himself through. If she half-closed her eyes, Lorna could still see him popping back through the garden hedge, with twigs and leaves and bits of chewing gum stuck in his fur and half a choc-ice clamped in his jaws.

'Here?' asked Carmen, leaning her bulk against a waste-bin to take the strain off her ankles.

'Here,' nodded Lorna, taking the wooden box out of her handbag and reverentially lifting its hinged lid.

Perhaps it was pure coincidence, or maybe it really was the playful spirit of Clawdius the cat that caused a freak gust of wind to blow across the park at that exact moment. Who could tell?

But the two little girls were more than taken aback when the wind belted right past their ice cream cornets, leaving something very peculiar in its wake.

'Mummy!' cried one. 'Mummy, there's funny grey powdery stuff all over my ice cream!'

Lorna didn't dare laugh. But in her heart she knew that Clawdius was home at last.

Chapter 30

'The thing is,' Carmen explained, 'I look at Kelly and I think, what kind of future is she going to have?'

Victor doodled on his notepad. 'What kind of future would you like her to have?' he asked.

This seemed like a rather stupid question to Carmen. 'I don't know . . . a good one. One that's nothing like mine!'

'Don't you think you're being rather hard on yourself?' he asked. 'I know your life hasn't perhaps followed the path you would have chosen, but how many people do you know whose lives have?'

Carmen grunted. 'And how many do you know who've got four illegitimate kids, another on the way, a rubbish job, and have never had a successful relationship with a man in their lives?'

'More than you'd imagine,' he replied. 'And most of them would be jealous as hell of you.'

She blinked. 'Jealous of me? What are they – mentally defective or something?'

He laughed. 'I like you, Carmen. You're a breath of fresh air.'

'Oh,' said Carmen, not sure how to take this. 'Well, as long as somebody finds me amusing.'

Victor shook his head. 'I'm not laughing at you, Carmen. I'm laughing at myself. Here I am, the epitome of middle-aged stuffiness, sitting here trying to advise you on how to sort out your life, and as far as I can see you've sorted it out already, without any help from me.'

'That's rubbish!' objected Carmen. 'My life's a mess.'

He looked straight at her, and she felt unaccountably uncomfortable. 'Is it? Is it really? When's the last time you couldn't pay the bills?'

'Well – I am careful with money. And the bit of Child Support I get does help too . . .'

'Or feed your kids?'

'I—'

'Or make them feel loved?' He didn't give her a chance to answer that one. 'Your life's not easy, I'll grant you that, and it's certainly not paradise, but when your kids grow up I bet all they'll remember is the happiness you gave them. And speaking as someone whose mother was an alcoholic with bipolar disorder, I know how much that means.'

'Your mother?' She frowned. 'But you're so—'

'Middle class?' he suggested. 'Well-educated? Yes, I suppose I am. But believe me Carmen, misery doesn't give a damn what your background is, or how much money you've got.'

'OK, but that doesn't stop somebody like me wanting to be able to stop counting every penny,' retorted Carmen. 'And when the new baby comes, I can't just leave it with that kid Sharon from down the road. She wouldn't know which end was which. So what do I do? Take it out clamping with me?'

He laughed, but kindly. 'I know you. If you had to, you would.'

'Well I'd rather not, if it's all the same to you.'

'You're a talented woman, Carmen,' Victor replied. 'At don't look so surprised – you know you're smart. What we have to do is find ways for you to make the most of it.'

'Best of British luck,' muttered Carmen. But the weird thing was that when he talked to her like that, she really began to believe that she was worth something. And that was a whole new experience for Carmen Jones.

'What's up with you, Lorna?' asked Andrew, plonking his lunch tray next to hers in the staff canteen. 'I've hardly heard a peep out of you all morning.'

'Oh, nothing really,' replied Lorna, pushing half a sausage round her plate with a slightly bent fork.

'It's not Dr Arse-Face Sullivan, is it? 'Cause if it is, I wouldn't worry. I heard he's off on a fortnight's holiday next week. Jumping off cliffs in Brazil or some such bollocks.'

'Yes, so I heard.'

'With a bit of luck he'll get eaten by a crocodile or something.'

Lorna looked up. 'They don't have crocodiles in Brazil.'

'Well what do they have then?'

'I dunno – piranha fish I think.'

'OK then, with a bit of luck he'll get eaten by some piranha fish.' He bent round, stuck his face right in front of hers and did his impression of a piranha, but he couldn't raise a smile. 'Oh dear, you have got it bad haven't you?'

'I'm all right, I'm just feeling a bit ... redundant. My little girl – you know, Hope? – she gets so excited every morning when I'm getting her

278

ready for nursery. I know she enjoys it much more than being at home with boring old Mummy.'

Andrew smiled. 'She's only tiny, love – you know what they're like at that age. Everything's better than being at home with Mummy. Until they fall over and hurt themselves, and suddenly Mummy's the only thing they want in the whole world.'

Lorna knew he was right. She'd felt the same way the time Hope had called Meg 'Mummy', and that had all blown over. But she couldn't shake off the feeling that her baby wasn't a baby any more, and that before she knew it, Leo and Hope would be piercing their navels and she'd be a lonely middle-aged widow with an empty nest.

She yawned. 'It wouldn't be so bad if my bloody sister wasn't acting like she's the only woman ever to get pregnant. She's got Mum and Dad rushing all over the countryside doing errands for her, and if she gets her way they'll be moving in with her so she doesn't have to soil her manicured hands changing nappies.'

'You don't like your sister much, do you?' he observed.

'Let's just say she was always the one who got her own way, even when we were little. And ever since she married money, it's like the rest of us don't matter except when we can do something useful for her.'

'Still,' Andrew pointed out, pulling a stringy bit of pork out from between his teeth, 'your mum and dad did move in with you to help with the kids, so you can see where she's coming from.'

Lorna could have decked him for being so reasonable. She wasn't feeling at all reasonable herself, and right now she needed somebody to feed her strawberry meringues and tell her it was perfectly OK to be unreasonable. Instead of which, she had Andrew.

'Yes, all right, I know,' she muttered. 'But Sarah's got en-suite bedrooms as far as the eye can see, a paddock and a rich husband. I was on my own with two kids and no job.'

Andrew chuckled to himself as an idea popped into his head. 'Tell you what,' he said, 'you and your kids should move in with your sister – after all, you're the childcare professional in the family!'

The sheer awfulness of this idea took some digesting. 'Andrew,' she said, slowly and deliberately, 'please don't say things like that, not even in jest. Put me and my sister in a house together, and believe me, sooner or later somebody is going to die. Oh, and it won't be me,' she added with a waspish smile.

It wasn't just Sarah who was striving for Meg and George's attentions. Around lunchtime, the doorbell went and when George returned he was carrying a large, flat parcel.

279

Meg hardly dared look. 'Not another one from David?'

''Fraid so.'

'He really is terribly persistent, isn't he?'

'Well, you know David. He wouldn't have got where he is today if he hadn't been a bloody-minded pain in the backside.'

'George!' exclaimed Meg, stifling a giggle.

'Call a spade a spade, that's what I say.' George ripped off the paper and revealed an enormous illustrated gift-book, lavishly embossed with gold and entitled: *Virtuoso Garden Design: Lessons from the Masters*.

'Another gardening book, how lovely,' said Meg flatly. 'How many is that now?'

'Five. Do you suppose he thinks we're terribly slow on the uptake?'

'No,' sighed Meg. 'I think it's called saturation bombing. He's not going to give up until we agree to move in with him and design his garden for him.'

'Not to mention all that babysitting he wants us to do,' George reminded her. 'He seems to imagine that because we don't actually own a house of our own at the moment, we'll be desperate for him to put a roof over our heads.'

'I suppose he might just be trying to be charitable to his old mum and dad?' suggested Meg hopefully, then she saw the look on George's face. 'No, you're right,' she sighed. 'This is after all the boy who sold off all his sister's toys while she was at Brownie camp. You know something, George?'

'What, love?'

She got up and poured herself a very large measure of gin. 'I know you don't approve, dear, but believe me, that cosmetic surgery safari is starting to look very tempting indeed.'

Carmen was not having the easiest of days at work. Chappie had gone off sick with – of all the ludicrous things – a snake bite on his bottom, having rolled onto a sleeping adder while engaged in al fresco rumpy-pumpy in the Forest of Dean. And when Chappie went off sick, it meant even more work for Carmen.

Thank God for maternity leave, she told herself as she drove into the railway station car park. A warm glow of contentment spread through her at the thought, putting a silly smile on her face. One more week of this and I'll be slumped in front of *Richard and Judy* with a family bucket of KFC. No more scratchy green uniform for ages and ages. No more abuse from people too mean to shell out two quid for a parking space.

But for now, alas, it was business as usual.

All the same, Carmen had to admit that she was definitely feeling better than she'd done for several weeks – livelier somehow, more up for getting stuff done. The previous day, she'd even had the energy to clean the kitchen and get herself a smart new haircut. Maybe all that fruit and veg she'd been dutifully stuffing down herself had finally started to take effect. It was about time: thus far, the only effect she'd registered was terrible wind.

She walked along the lines of parked cars, checking for the regulation stick-on tickets. Yes, yes, yes ... aha, no. There was always one. In this case it was an elderly red Fiesta with saggy seats and giant stick-on flowers all over it. She didn't need to ask herself who it belonged to: it positively screamed 'student'.

Normally she wouldn't have hesitated. Student or not, this idiot had parked without paying, in spite of all the warning notices, and if she had to clamp people like that it was their own silly fault. But today, Carmen was feeling unaccountably sentimental. What if the car belonged to some lovelorn teenager who had only dodged the parking charge so he could afford a bunch of flowers for his girlfriend when he met her off the train? What if the Fiesta's owner depended on it to get her to the five horrible part-time jobs she was forced to do to pay her college tuition fees? What if the seventy-five-quid fee for unclamping her car meant that she couldn't eat for a week and her pet kitten died of malnutrition? What if—?

Good God woman, you're going soft in the head, she told herself. What on earth is wrong with you today? But she still couldn't quite bring herself to slam on the wheel clamp – at least, not without giving the miscreant one last chance.

She waddled down the ramp leading to a side entrance that opened directly onto Platform 1. Sure enough, there was a gaggle of teenagers with bare midriffs and A4 binders hanging around the vending machine.

'Excuse me – any of you own a red Fiesta?'

'No.'

'Why?'

'Nah, mine's the yellow Lamborghini.'

Laughter all round.

'You're quite sure about that?' demanded Carmen. 'Because I'm about to wheel-clamp it if it's not out of that car park within the next two minutes.'

This met with shrugs of indifference, and Carmen had to conclude that – for once – her hunch had been wide of the mark. Ah well, one last attempt and then she'd clamp the bloody thing and that was that.

As she pushed open the door of the station buffet, the feeling she'd taken to be a warm glow of contentment headed abruptly south, and metamorphosed into something more like a pang of indigestion. Bloody wind;

281

it was stuck right under her ribs. Folic acid or not, that was the last portion of sprouts she planned on eating for a very long time.

The pain came again, stronger this time, and momentarily took her breath away. This was not funny. She shook the dizziness out of her head and rapped on the nearest tabletop to get people's attention. 'Anybody in here own a red Fiesta with flowers stuck all over it?'

'Yes ... well not exactly ... I borrowed it from my grand-daughter,' replied a grey-haired lady in a 'Save The Whales' T-shirt. 'Oh dear, I do hope nothing's happened to it.'

'It will do if you don't move it, madam. I'm afraid it's illegally parked, and – owwww!'

Carmen suddenly doubled up as pain butted her in the stomach like a runaway rhinoceros.

'Are you all right, dear?' asked the old lady, peering concernedly over the top of her bifocals.

'Do. I. Look. All right?' gasped Carmen.

And before she had a chance to say, 'I think the baby's coming,' it already had.

Chapter 31

By the time Lorna got to Crocus ward, Carmen had already been checked over and was getting dressed ready to go home. Lorna found her full of energy: hopping around her bed on one leg, trying to pull on her trousers with one hand and holding the ward's cordless phone in the other.

'Now listen Kelly, don't take any nonsense from Becca, she's perfectly fine with baked beans – and tell Rosie if she plays you up there'll be big trouble when I get home. What's that – Charmain's dental appointment? Oh hell, I'd forgotten about that. Look, they're discharging us soon; leave it till I get home and I'll sort it out.'

She switched off the phone, threw it onto the bed and finally spotted Lorna. 'Hiya kid. What do you reckon to my sense of timing?'

'Oh, definitely star quality,' declared Lorna, tiptoeing across to the cot at the end of the bed where Baby Jones was dozing. 'Well, well, who's a special little girl then? It's not everybody who's born in a railway station buffet.'

'Don't remind me!' Carmen hid her face in not entirely feigned embarrassment. 'And of course the manageress just had to have one of those mobiles with a camera. I'll never dare set foot in there again!' But Carmen's smile couldn't help breaking through the embarrassment. 'Isn't she gorgeous?'

'Stunning. Just like her mum. Have you got a name for her yet?'

'You know, I was so sure she was going to be a boy, I didn't really have any girls' names worked out. But then that nice girl Honey came up with "Eva". What do you think?'

'It's nice. Delicate. Why "Eva" though?'

Carmen chuckled. 'Apparently there was this Sixties' singer called Little Eva who sang "The Locomotion".'

'Oh – right! A train joke. Trust Honey to think of something like that. It is a nice name though.'

'Right then, we're agreed.' Carmen stroked the soft, dark fluff on the baby's head, and she opened her tiny blue eyes and gave an enormous, toothless yawn. 'Eva it is. You know,' she went on, 'I never ever thought I'd be glad to have another baby, but I am. I can't stop grinning!' She lowered her voice. 'I'm sure that Finnegan woman thinks I'm a bit funny in the head.'

Lorna waved away her friend's concern. 'Oh I wouldn't worry, she's like that with everybody. Anyway, she's just jealous. May I?' she asked, motioning to pick up the baby.

'Of course! You might have missed Eva's big entrance, but I still want you to be her godmother. You will, won't you?'

'You bet.' Lorna grinned broadly. 'As long as you don't mind me being a shockingly bad influence on her.'

'Oh, I'm counting on it.'

In recent weeks, Kelly had been obliged to revise her opinion of Social Services and 'do-gooders' in general. And since the arrival of Eva they really couldn't have done more to help keep Carmen and her household afloat.

From Kelly's point of view it was almost a disappointment. What with the social worker, the home help, the maternity nurse and the health visitor, not to mention occasional visits from a home tutor, she was completely out of excuses to sneak a bit of illicit time off school and help out in the house.

Not that Carmen would have let her get away with it. She'd even arranged for Kelly to transfer to a school with a mother-and-baby unit for the new school year, so that there wouldn't be any problems with childcare. It was the first time anybody had cared very much what Kelly did, even when she was a little kid, and it took a bit of getting used to. Consequently there'd been some lively arguments and slamming of doors before it finally dawned on Kelly that she was starting to like being somebody else's responsibility, the way Lee-Anne was hers.

While Carmen was feeding Eva upstairs and Lee-Anne was having a nap, Kelly got on with her chores. She might not be much good at cooking or ironing, but she was a whiz when it came to vacuuming the house. Spiders, bits of fluff, small children . . . nothing was safe from her avenging vacuum hose.

It was while she was going over the hall carpet for ferret hairs that she noticed something creamy-coloured had got itself trapped down the side of Carmen's old pine dresser. She tried Hoovering it out, but it was too big, so she got down on the floor and squeezed her arm between the dresser and the wall.

It was a posh-looking envelope, a bit crumpled round the edges, postmarked a week ago and addressed to Carmen. Must give it to her when I've finished, thought Kelly, shoving the envelope into her jeans pocket and promptly forgetting all about it.

While George and Meg were at Sarah's for the weekend, Lorna got back into the way of being a single mum again. It was hard work, just as she remembered, and yet it did have its good points too. For example, there was a lot to be said for not having arguments about whether or not children ought to wear vests, the merits or otherwise of organic carrots, and whether the under-sevens should be allowed to watch *Doctor Who*.

With her mum and dad away, the kids were hers again; just hers and nobody else's. She felt a little guilty for admitting it, but sometimes she couldn't help envying the closeness that had developed between the children and their grandparents, simply through spending so much time together.

On Sunday afternoon, after games in the park and pizza for lunch, Lorna dropped Leo and Hope off at Lennie's for a couple of hours. Caspian and Jacintha weren't exactly Lorna's favourite children, but she couldn't help feeling sorry for them – and their mother, who had been virtually ostracised by all the other local mums since her husband got six months for aiding illegal immigration. Lorna knew what it was like, trying to cope without a man around, and she did what she could to help. Making sure the kids all stayed friends was one small way of making her feel less isolated. Still, at least Lennie's husband would be coming back.

Back home, she tidied up the children's toys and decided to treat herself to a nice relaxing bath. She was just sliding under a thick layer of rose-scented bubbles when she heard a car draw up outside and a key turn in the front door. Mum and Dad must have decided to come back a bit early. Hardly surprising really; a whole weekend of Sarah was enough to try the patience of a saint.

'Hi there,' she called out, not expecting an answer. 'I'm in the bath.'

She closed her eyes, wriggled her toes and lay back on the bath-pillow, pretending she was floating in some tropical lagoon; and she might well have drifted off into dreams of tropical hunks if she hadn't been rudely interrupted by the bathroom door suddenly opening.

Her eyes shot open and her morale plummeted. Sarah was standing in the doorway. Sarah with several pillows shoved up her jumper, perhaps, but yes, it was definitely Sarah.

'Hello little sis,' said Sarah as though she'd just popped back from a trip to the corner shop. 'I need a wee.'

'Excuse me!' exclaimed Lorna, shooting up in the bath and belatedly covering her breasts with sponges. 'I'm having a bath!'

'Yes I noticed,' replied Sarah, heading for the toilet and – to Lorna's horror – dropping her vast mum-to-be knickers around her ankles. 'And I'm pregnant. Which is why I need a wee.' She sat down on the loo. 'If you won't get en-suites installed, what do you expect?'

She's only been here thirty seconds, though Lorna, and I'm already grinding my teeth. 'What are you doing here?' she demanded, attempting to ignore the backing track of rushing waters.

Sarah looked at her smugly. 'Dearie me, little sis,' she commented, 'anybody might think you weren't pleased to see me.' She stood up, flushed, wriggled back into her knickers and plonked herself down on the toilet seat. 'Mum and Dad invited me back,' she said. 'Wasn't that nice of them?'

Before Lorna could remind her whose house Mum and Dad had invited her back to, Meg walked in through the door.

'Hello Lorna dear, I see you and Sarah are already having a chat. I knew you wouldn't mind if we brought her back with us. Not now that Gavin's office has sent him out to Tanzania. We couldn't leave her all alone in that big house, could we?'

Sarah smiled like a cat with a cream overdose, while Lorna glared and tried to sink lower into the bubbles. 'I'm trying to have a—'

'Bath? Yes dear, so I see. Where are the children?'

'At Lennie's. I'm picking them up at four.'

'That's nice, dear. They'll really enjoy seeing their Auntie Sarah'.

'And they'll be good mothering practice for you, won't they Sarah?' Lorna at least had the satisfaction of seeing Sarah's smile slip several notches.

'If you'd told me pregnancy was going to be like this,' Sarah declared bitterly, 'I'd have had myself sewn up and become a lesbian.'

'Yes dear, of course you would,' smiled Meg. 'I'll just get your father to bring up your bags and put up the Z-bed in Hope's room. George?'

There was a sound of puffing, panting and luggage being dragged up stairs, then George's head appeared round the door. 'Oh. Hello Lorna, are you having a bath?'

'Actually I'm trying to drown myself,' she replied.

But nobody seemed to notice.

That evening, after Sarah had been forced into reading the children a bedtime story and Hope had cried because she wanted Fat Penguin, Lorna attempted to slink away; but it was not to be. Her mother caught her tiptoeing down the hallway with her car keys and the next thing she knew, all four of them were trapped in George and Meg's sitting room, having a 'nice family chat' and being subjected to the *Wonders of Childbirth* video Meg had been hanging on to ever since Lorna gave birth to Leo.

The only small consolation, as far as Lorna was concerned, was observing the changing colours of her sister's face as the cheery voiceover talked them through the whole gory process.

'This is disgusting,' said Sarah faintly.

'It's perfectly natural, dear,' Meg assured her.

'Not for me it isn't.'

'Look,' said Lorna, 'if I can manage it you can too.'

Sarah looked at her sniffily. 'You've got childbearing hips; I've got the delicate, thoroughbred build. And my obstetrician says I'm emotionally fragile,' she added, as though it were the equivalent of winning a medal. 'I mustn't be traumatised.'

'I take it you're seeing him privately?' enquired Lorna.

'Well yes, of course! Why?'

'They don't use phrases like "emotionally fragile" in the NHS. They give you a stick to bite on and tell you to get on with it.'

'Lorna!' scolded Meg. 'Stop frightening your sister. Sarah, she's only joking. Did you tell Lorna you've decided to have the baby here in Cheltenham?'

'Here?' Now it was Lorna's turn to change colour.

'Not in *your* hospital, heaven forbid!' exclaimed Sarah. 'No, I'm signing up for an elective Caesarian at the Regency Clinic.'

Meg gave her a reproving look. 'Sarah dear, you didn't say anything about Caesarians! Don't be a silly girl. You know Mother Nature knows best.'

Sarah glanced queasily at the TV screen. 'Mother Nature is a sadist.'

At that moment, the front door bell rang and Lorna escaped to answer it. Carmen was standing on the doorstep, baby Eva in her arms.

'Carmen! Is everything all right? There's nothing wrong with Eva, is there?'

'No, no, nothing like that. I just need to speak to George. It's quite important.'

Lorna's nose wrinkled. 'Dad? Why Dad?'

Carmen produced the cream-coloured envelope from her pocket. 'I've got some news for him. And I think he'd better be sitting down when he gets it.'

George just kept staring at the letter, his hands shaking and his eyes failing to take in what they saw. 'Tell me again,' he said faintly. 'Tell it to me . . . slowly.'

Carmen knelt down by the arm of his chair and laid a hand on his arm. 'I sent off your Fat Penguin stories to some publishers. I know I should have asked you first, but I thought you might say no. And I didn't want you to be disappointed if nothing came of it.'

287

'But something has,' said Lorna. 'Something really good.'

'Yes. This is a letter from a publisher, offering to pay you that amount of money,' Carmen pointed to the page, 'for *The Adventures of Fat Penguin*, and that much there for another two volumes. Isn't that great?'

George passed a hand across his brow. 'I can't believe this,' he said. 'I just can't take it in. They're just silly kids' stories out of my head! I'm not a proper writer.'

'You're a wonderful storyteller, Dad,' Lorna assured him. And she gave him an enormous hug. 'Well done, you're a star.'

Sarah seized the sheet of paper from her father's hands and scanned it. 'He's going to need an agent,' she said. 'Somebody who can make a fuss and get more money out of them. They're obviously mad about the stories. I bet he could squeeze thousands more out of them if he tried.'

'Well . . . maybe,' acknowledged Carmen. 'I mean, professional advice is good: you wouldn't want to sign anything unless you knew it was OK.'

'What matters is that he screws them for every penny he can get. These publishing firms are loaded. Maybe we can play one off against another. This could be bigger than Harry Potter!' Sarah's eyes were filled with an eagerness Lorna hadn't seen since she'd found out that Gavin earned a six-figure salary and immediately fell head over heels in love with him. 'Dad, I'll get on to Gavin's accountant and make him give me some top names. Before you know it, we'll be talking big money!'

Lorna and her mother exchanged looks. 'Hey, this isn't just about money,' said Lorna. 'It's about Dad fulfilling a dream.'

'Yes, yes, I know,' snapped Sarah, 'but what's more important, dreams or cash in the bank? Dad's got a chance to get back all that money he lost – and more! He can provide for the future.'

'For your future, you mean?' Meg looked at her daughter sadly. 'Sometimes I think that's all you care about, money,' she said. 'I'd like to think I was wrong, but even when you were a little girl you only wanted to play with the rich children.'

Sarah fixed her mother with a look of wounded indignation. 'What is this – national "get-at-Sarah" day? Here I am, trying to sort out your and Dad's finances—'

George looked up. He seemed to have shaken off the initial shock. 'I'm quite capable of sorting out our finances, thank you Sarah,' he said. 'I may have had some bad luck lately, but I'm not completely senile.'

'Dad,' protested Sarah in exasperation, 'Gavin knows all the big movers and shakers. He can get you top representation, and that means top money! Isn't that what you want?'

He looked at her and sighed. 'Not if it means thinking like you do,' he replied.

With an angry exhalation of breath, Sarah flung the letter back and him and stalked out of the room – as fast as her girth would allow. 'I'm going downstairs for a glass of wine. No, make that three.'

'You can't have wine,' Lorna reminded her, 'you're pregnant.'

Sarah just gave her a furious look. 'I shall have what I bloody well want! When you come to your senses, you can come and apologise to me.'

Lorna followed her out. 'Come on Sarah, calm down. There's no need to get all worked up.'

Nobody was quite sure what happened next – whether she stumbled at the top of the staircase that led down to the basement kitchen, or whether she caught the heel of her mule in a bit of loose carpet.

But the next moment she let out a little cry of surprise and fright, and fell headlong down the stairs, arms flailing desperately to save herself.

'Sarah!' shrieked her mother.

By the time Lorna reached her sister's side, she was sprawled, motionless, across the bottom few steps. One leg was twisted under her body at an unnatural angle. And at first sight, it didn't look as if she was breathing.

When Sarah regained consciousness, at first the only thing she was aware of was the pain: a dull ache in her left leg, and something much sharper in her lower belly that pulled and stabbed when she tried to move.

And then she realised that there was something else, and a horrible, cold emptiness washed over her like a dark sea. 'W-where—?'

'She's coming round.' She recognised that voice: it belonged to her mother.

A flurry of images filled her head, and she remembered being angry and then falling, and then . . . nothing else.

And then she heard her sister say, 'It's OK Sarah, lie still. You had an emergency C-section, but you're going to be fine.'

Gingerly she opened her eyes, blinking in the glare of the overhead lights. Four faces were looking down at her: they belonged to Mum, Dad, Lorna and some bloke in a nurse's tunic. Her lips and throat were dry, but she managed to croak, 'Where's my baby?'

Somebody took her hand. It was Lorna. Somehow Sarah knew instinctively what she was going to say. She was going to tell her that her baby was dead; that she'd killed it when she fell down the stairs, and that it was all her fault. She had never imagined she could care so much about anything. Tears spilled from her eyes and poured down her cheeks. 'My baby. Where's my baby?'

'Your baby's fine,' smiled Lorna. 'You've got a lovely big boy with his daddy's blue eyes. He was a wee bit cold so they've taken him to an incubator to warm him up. But he's absolutely fine.'

Sarah looked up into her sister's face, searching for lies, hoping for truth. 'Promise?'

'Promise. Have a little sleep and the nurses will take you to see him when you wake up.'

'I-I'm sorry,' whispered Sarah.

'There's nothing to be sorry for,' replied Lorna. And to her surprise, she meant it.

Chapter 32

The next time Lorna saw Carmen was when she went round to pass on some more of Hope's hand-me-downs for Eva and Lee-Anne.

'Tell me if they're no good,' she urged. 'Only I thought they might have a bit more life left in them and some of them do look quite nice on.'

Kelly rummaged through the bag and held up a little pair of pink dungarees trimmed with yellow ric-rac braid. 'Look Carmen, aren't these cute? And they're Baby Gap! And isn't that babygro the sweetest thing you've ever seen? Oh thanks, Lorna. These are great.'

'Yes thanks, I really appreciate it,' echoed Carmen. 'It's six years since I had a baby in the house, and you forget how incredibly fast they grow out of everything.'

'I know what you mean,' agreed Lorna. 'You put them down for their afternoon nap, and when you come back an hour later they've gone up two sizes. Anyhow, I'm really glad – this stuff will come in useful.'

'Didn't you want to hang onto it for when you have another baby?' asked Kelly, for whom the phrase 'none of your business' had no meaning. 'What?' she demanded as Carmen looked at her in despair.

Lorna laughed. 'I don't think I'll be having any more babies, Kelly.' A brief pang of sadness accompanied the thought, but she was used to shrugging it off. 'I've got enough on, coping with the two I've got.'

Kelly wasn't quite so easily fobbed off. 'But what if you meet someone and he wants kids?' she persisted.

Carmen intervened. 'What if you stop asking personal questions? It's not very polite.'

Kelly looked wounded. 'I was only asking.'

'It's OK, I don't mind,' Lorna assured her. 'But I've not had much luck with dating, and George Clooney never returns my phone calls. So I reckon it's going to be just me and the kids.'

'And your mum and dad,' Carmen reminded her, folding the clothes into neat piles on the kitchen table.

'I'm not so sure about that,' replied Lorna. 'They might want a place of their own again, now Dad's earning money from his stories. Of course if Sarah gets her way, they'll be moving in with her – but only if David doesn't get his bid in first. I'm not surprised Mum's still threatening to go off on that safari thing.'

'God, families,' said Kelly, perching on the edge of the table with her legs swinging. 'Why do they always end up hating each other?'

'They don't, not always,' Carmen corrected her. 'But sometimes they forget they're a family and start competing with each other or just stop caring what the others feel, and that's always bad news.'

'Speaking of families,' she added, 'how is Sarah? Back to her usual self?'

'Not quite, thank goodness,' answered Lorna. 'She's still basking in the glow of motherhood. And Ethan's doing really well, considering he was several weeks premature. But she's started ordering everybody around again, so I'm sure it won't be long before I feel like strangling her again.'

'Is she still holding court in your guest room?'

'Yeah. Luckily Gavin's firm are letting him come home early on compassionate grounds, so we shouldn't have to put up with her for too much longer. It's probably just as well. Leo asked her yesterday why she didn't have a smiley face like Grandma and Mummy.'

'And what did she say?'

'She just glared at him and slammed the bedroom door in his face.'

'So she's definitely the maternal type then?' said Carmen, tongue firmly in cheek.

'Oh, definitely. If she was a rabbit, she'd probably have eaten the poor baby by now.' Lorna crossed the kitchen to fill the kettle. 'Anybody else fancy a cuppa?'

Kelly bounced off the table. 'I can do that, I'm good at tea.' And she promptly took over, polishing the mugs on the seat of her jeans before arranging them in a neat line on a tray.

'Kelly's got something to ask you, haven't you Kelly?' prompted Carmen.

'Carmen!' protested Kelly, visibly squirming with embarrassment.

'Well you have. Go on, ask her then!'

Kelly cleared her throat. 'Lorna,' she said slowly, 'I'm not having Lee-Anne christened, 'cause I don't believe in any of that stuff, but Carmen said if I wanted I could have a naming ceremony in the back garden. And I was wondering ... will you be one of her sponsors? It's like a god-mother without the god bit,' she added by way of explanation.

Lorna was genuinely delighted. Just to have been able to do something

292

for Kelly had been sufficient reward; to be thanked in this way touched her more deeply than she could say. 'I'd *love* to!' she exclaimed.

Kelly looked quite surprised. 'Really?'

'Really. Just tell me when and where, and what you want me to do. It'll be an honour.'

'Not to mention an excellent excuse to get out of the house and away from your beloved sister,' pointed out Carmen. 'Speaking of which ... haven't you got a date coming up this week?'

At first Lorna didn't know what she was on about, then she realised and felt her cheeks redden. 'No I haven't!' she retorted. 'I'm just going to the Long Stands' gig, that's all. And I'm only going because I sort of mentioned to Chris that I might,' she added.

Kelly and Carmen looked at each other meaningfully.

'Yeah,' said Kelly, 'but you wouldn't have done if you didn't like him a lot, would you?'

'There's a big difference between liking someone a lot and ... and anything else!' insisted Lorna. But if they'd asked her what that difference was, she'd have been hard pressed to come up with an answer that made any sense.

'You can't go out,' protested Sarah as Lorna buckled up the belt on her jeans and emptied her pockets of bits of Lego and half-chewed fruit gums. 'You said you'd have a look at my operation scar.'

'I had a look at it yesterday,' Lorna reminded her with strained patience, 'and it's healing perfectly well. There's nothing at all to worry about.'

Sarah pursued her across the bedroom to the wardrobe. 'But it's all red, and my stomach's flopping over it like ... like an apron or something! I can't stay like that, it's not normal!'

'Of course it's normal,' Lorna told her, trying not to clench her teeth. Sarah was costing her a fortune in cracked fillings. 'You've had a cut in your tummy and the muscles will take time to knit together and get strong again. It would help if you did those exercises the physio showed you,' she added.

'But they hurt,' whined Sarah. 'And they're boring. Can't I just have a tummy-tuck or something?'

'Please yourself,' replied Lorna with a shrug, 'but I can't imagine any reputable surgeon wanting to put you through another major operation so soon after having a baby. Besides, what about Ethan? You're breastfeeding, and if you had an operation the anaesthetic would affect your milk.'

Sarah shuffled her feet and looked awkward. 'I've sort of decided I'm not cut out for breastfeeding,' she mumbled.

'What?'

'It hurts and I'm sure it's making my boobs droopy!'

'And that's more important than your baby's health, is it?'

Sarah pouted. 'God, you can be a real pain sometimes, Lorna. A real schoolmarm. It's a wonder you ever got married, let alone had kids.'

Lorna narrowed her eyes, and even Sarah had the wit to see that she'd overstepped the mark. 'All right, I'm sorry, I didn't mean to upset you about Ed and all that stuff. It's just, you're getting at me and it's not fair.'

'I really have to go out now,' Lorna announced, picking up her handbag, 'or I'll be late for the gig.'

'Can't I come too? I'm sure Mum and Dad would look after the baby as well as your two.'

Lorna's heart sank. 'Don't you think you ought to stay home with Ethan? It's his mum he wants right now, not his gran.'

This suggestion met with a sniff. 'It's all right, I know when I'm not wanted. That Chris told you not to bring me, didn't he? He never did like me.'

It was perfectly true that Chris would have run a mile if he'd thought Sarah was coming to hear the band play, but Lorna wasn't about to upset her sister any more than she had to. 'Don't be silly, of course he likes you. I'll take you along next time.'

'Huh!' scoffed Sarah. 'If they're as bad as they were last time I heard them, there won't be a next time.'

It was great to get out of the house, and even better to get away from Sarah for a couple of hours. But as she got closer to the venue, Lorna couldn't help having flashbacks to the days when Ed had played there with his band.

The Old Spot pub was within walking distance of St Jude's, in a small alley behind St Mary's churchyard. Every aspiring Cheltenham band aimed to play there, and gigs were pretty hard to come by, so obviously somebody there must have thought the Long Stands were still worth listening to.

She tried to pay on the door, but a guy with a broken nose, whom she knew from years ago, waved her through with a grin. 'Good to see you again.'

'You too.' She struggled to recall his name but failed. All of this seemed such a long time ago, as though it belonged to a completely different life.

Seating was on a first-come, first-served basis, and she squeezed onto the end of a row about halfway back from the stage, between a bloke she vaguely recognised as the music critic of the *Cheltenham Courant* and a couple of Goths who looked like they'd got the wrong night.

When the band walked out onto the stage, to the accompaniment of cheers, whistles and clinking beer glasses, Lorna could hardly bear to look. She half closed her eyes, and imagined Ed standing out there in front, grinning and blowing kisses to the crowd. But the image wouldn't come. Try as she might, the space where he used to stand remained blank, even in her mind's eye, until at last Chris walked out into the lights.

He looked as nervous as a skydiver who'd inadvertently left his parachute at home. 'Hello Cheltenham,' he murmured into the microphone. The audience responded with a few half-hearted grunts.

Come on Chris, you can do better than that, Lorna willed him.

She saw him take a deep breath. 'I said, hello Cheltenham!'

This time, everyone relaxed, shouting and stamping their feet. And as the band thundered into their first song, a cover of 'Johnny B Goode', Lorna saw Chris's features begin to relax. He might not be a showman like Ed had been, but he was a damned fine musician. All those years when he'd played rhythm guitar in Ed's shadow, he'd been hiding a stylish technique and a distinctive baritone voice, quite pure but with just an edge of rough charm.

Within minutes, Lorna's fears of old ghosts had been dispelled, and she was rocking along with the rest of the audience as the band pounded its way through all the old covers and one or two new songs – all with lyrics by Chris. She found herself surprised at how good they were: witty in places, poignant in others, or sometimes just crazy. The Chris she was looking at on stage was someone she hadn't met before; someone who wasn't afraid to shine.

She felt sorry as the gig drew to an end. It had been a good night, and she'd make a point of hanging back and telling Chris so. The Long Stands might never be top-forty material, but he'd done a fine job of resurrecting them and dusting them off for the twenty-first century.

Just when she thought it was time to go, Chris stepped forward to the microphone. 'Ladies and gentlemen, just one more song before we say goodnight.' His tongue flicked nervously over his lips. 'It's called "Be My Baby", and I wrote it especially for a lady in the audience. I hope she'll know who she is.'

He was looking straight at Lorna. But surely that was just a coincidence. Wasn't it?

The song began quietly, with just Chris's voice and the acoustic guitar:

'At fifteen you were pretty, like a perfect summer's day,
At sixteen you were beautiful, you stole my heart away.
I couldn't help but love you, and my love could only grow,
But you belonged to my best friend, so you could never know.'

No, it can't be true, she told herself. I'm imagining it. He's singing this for someone else, some other woman, not me. Nobody could feel this way about me. Most of the audience were happily swaying along as the rest of the band joined in, but Lorna was sitting ramrod-stiff, frozen to her chair by the sound of Chris's voice and the look in his eyes as he sang the song.

Her song.

As the final chorus rose to a crescendo, the first tears began to well up in her eyes. She tried to blink them back, but they just wouldn't be denied.

'I dream we'll be together, though I don't know where or how,
But I know my heart would be set free if you'd be my baby now.'

The last, plaintive note lingered on the air for a few seconds before the audience burst into appreciative applause. But Lorna wasn't going to stay around to hear it. She couldn't. Already she was fighting her way out of her seat, through the ranks of chairs and bodies, stepping on toes, provoking curses, stumbling towards the doors through a blinding curtain of tears.

'Are you all right, love?' asked the man with the broken nose on the door.

She didn't answer; just ran out through the alleyway and into the churchyard, where she finally stopped, panting for breath and sobbing as if her heart would break; sobbing like she hadn't done since the day Ed died.

If someone had asked her why she was crying, she couldn't have come up with a single coherent answer. She was crying for Ed, for Clawdius, for herself, for everything that she had lost . . . and perhaps also for something that she had found.

But had she found it too late?

Chris left the stage in a panic, throwing down his beloved guitar and pushing aside a group of students who wanted to ask him something about his amps.

'Hey, man—'

'Later.'

What have I done? he agonised as he ran out through the back doors of the pub and into the warm, late-summer night. Oh God, what have I done?

'Lorna? Lorna, are you there?'

She didn't answer, and his mind started racing. It wasn't safe for a woman to be wandering around here at night on her own. Nasty things had happened to people in this dark alley, not to mention the churchyard . . .

He found her huddled up on one of the benches amid the yew-trees in the churchyard, knees drawn up and her shoulders heaving as she sobbed into her jeans.

'Oh God Lorna, Lorna I'm so sorry,' he said, trying to comfort her but not knowing how to begin. 'Please forgive me, I didn't mean to hurt you, that was the last thing I wanted to do.'

She raised her head and looked at him with tear-filled eyes. 'Please Chris . . . don't apologise.'

'B-but look what I've done to you. I've been so selfish. If I'd just kept my big mouth shut—'

Their eyes met. 'If you'd kept your mouth shut I'd never have known,' she replied between sobs, 'would I?'

Her words flashed through him like a lightning bolt. 'You mean—?'

'I don't mean anything,' she replied, pushing back the wet hair that had plastered itself to her face. 'I don't *know* anything any more. The only thing I'm sure about is, I need time to think.'

'Will you let me take you home?'

He held out his hand. She hesitated for a moment, and then took it.

'Don't leave me,' she whispered. 'I'm afraid.'

Chapter 33

When Carmen received the letter about Maurice, it came as a huge shock. In the weeks since she'd contacted the missing persons' bureau, she'd imagined many scenarios, each more gruesome than the last, but this one had never even crossed her mind.

She thought about taking the letter to the community centre, to ask for Victor's advice, but she knew she mustn't expect him to solve every problem that arose in her life. Besides, wasn't it Victor himself who had told her to start believing in herself and relying on her own judgement?

Of course that was fine in theory, but when you were dealing with an over-sensitive teenage boy the practice wasn't quite so easy. Should she tell Robbie outright what the letter said, or throw it away and pretend that it had never arrived? It wasn't a real question though, because she already knew the answer. She'd promised Robbie that she'd be honest with him, so that's what she had to do, even if the truth might hurt him more than a whole bucketful of little white lies.

'You in there, Robbie?' She knocked on his bedroom door and waited for the usual noncommittal grunt before going in.

He was sitting cross-legged in the middle of the floor, surrounded by cardboard, glue, acrylic paints and what looked like the mangled remains of several wire coat hangers. 'Don't step on anything, Mum,' he ordered her. 'It's not dry yet.'

Carmen did her best to make out what it was. 'It's very ... colourful. What is it?'

Robbie concentrated hard as he threaded string through a hole in a blue teddy bear's head. 'It's a mobile for Kelly's baby. She said she couldn't afford one, so I thought I'd make her one as a surprise. I printed the teddy bears and stuff off a kids' site on the Internet. Do you think she'll like it?'

'Of course she will.' Carmen cleared a space for herself and sat down carefully on the end of Robbie's bed. 'You don't think you're getting a bit too close to her though, do you? She's quite ... advanced for her age.'

Robbie gave her a long-suffering look. 'Relax Mum, she's my *friend*, that's all! A mate. Ryan's the only other proper one I've ever hand, and sometimes I get fed up talking about football and prison all the time.' He turned his attentions back to the mobile. 'That's not the only thing you came to talk to me about, is it?'

'Actually no,' Carmen admitted. 'I've had some news about your dad.' She produced the letter and offered it to Robbie, but he just stared at it.

'He's dead, isn't he?'

Carmen shook her head.

'In prison then?'

'No, he's not in prison. Here, read for yourself.'

Robbie flinched from the letter. 'No, I can't. I want you to tell me.'

'OK.' Carmen took a deep breath. 'Your father's married with three kids, and he's living less than forty miles from here.'

'Oh,' said Robbie.

'He's quite well off too. Apparently the last time he was arrested he fell out of the van and got injured, and the police had to pay him a lot of compensation.' She had to force herself to say the rest of it. 'If you like, we can get in touch with him and see if he wants to meet up.'

Robbie looked down at the cardboard teddy bear in his hands. It smiled back up at him, empty-headed and trusting, the way he must have looked up at his dad in the days before he went away.

'Does he know we've been looking for him?'

'No. And I don't have an address for him. But the agency will pass on a letter if you want to write to him.'

There was a lengthy silence, punctuated by the sound of Robbie clicking one length of wire against another.

'I don't want to,' he said at last. 'I don't want anything to do with him.'

'But you've been desperate to see him for months!' Carmen watched as Robbie fought to find the right words to express himself. 'What's changed your mind?'

'I thought he was in prison,' said Robbie. 'Or really sick. Or hiding out somewhere where he couldn't get in touch with me, so it wasn't his fault that I never got to see him. But it *is* his fault, isn't it? All of it. He only lives up the road, and he's got these three other kids, and he couldn't even be bothered to find out if we were alive or dead.' He looked his mum straight in the eye. 'Why would I want to see him, Mum? He's not my dad any more.'

Carmen gently stroked his hair, and for once he didn't make the typical teenage gesture of shrugging off her touch. 'I'm sorry, son. I really am.'

'It's OK, you don't need to be,' he replied. 'I don't need a dad; I've got you. But Mum—'

'But what, love?'

'There's just one thing I'm scared of. What if I take after my dad? What if I turn out bad like him?'

Carmen wrapped her arms around her son and hugged him so hard he could scarcely breathe. 'Robbie love,' she declared with all her heart, 'you couldn't turn out like him if you tried. Never in a million years.'

Lorna had hardly seen Chris during the days since the gig at the Old Spot. She knew he was keeping the promise he'd made her: to give her the time and space she needed to think. But Meg was convinced that the two of them had had some kind of row, and that this was why the conservatory roof remained half-finished.

She was still harping on this theme as Lorna was getting ready to leave for a night shift at the hospital.

'Lorna dear, you really should try to stay on good terms with Christopher,' Meg advised her as she darted around the living room looking for hairgrips, car keys, Polo mints and a host of other last-minute essentials. 'He's such a lovely boy.'

'Mum, I *am* on good terms with him!' insisted Lorna, praying that her mother would drop the subject. 'I expect he's just been extra-busy this week, and that's why he's not been round much.'

Meg looked unconvinced. 'It'll be autumn soon,' she pointed out, 'and you can hardly face winter with only half a roof on your conservatory, can you? Whatever you two have been having this silly row about, I strongly suggest you sort it out. All it takes is one little apology.'

Lorna looked up from rooting under the sofa cushions for small change. 'Mum, I haven't got anything to apologise for!'

'It doesn't matter whose fault it is, dear, just say you're sorry and put an end to it. Men love women who apologise; it makes them feel all masterful. Besides, Lorna, a woman on her own can't have too many friends – especially big strong male ones with useful household skills!'

'Yes Mum, I'm sure you're right, but—'

'And you do realise that your father and I may not be around forever to help you?'

'Oh,' said Lorna. 'Does that mean you're definitely moving in with Sarah and Gavin?'

Meg looked as if she'd swallowed a hedgehog. Sideways. 'Lorna dear, we may be getting on but we're not completely senile. And now Sarah and Gavin are back home with the baby, I'm sure they'll manage perfectly well on their own.'

'So it's David you're going to then?'

301

'All in good time dear, all in good time. For the moment we're not going anywhere. And we certainly won't be moving on until you've sorted out some suitable working hours. All these nights are totally unsuitable for a single mother with a young family.'

'I know Mum, but once I've finished these last few I'll be free to negotiate my own hours with the hospital.'

'Good.' Meg glanced at the clock on the mantelpiece. 'Well I suppose you'd better make a move, or you'll be late.'

'See you in the morning, Mum.' Lorna dotted a kiss on her mother's cheek. 'And thanks for everything.'

'That's all right dear,' Meg replied with a wink. 'You can pay it all back when your father and I are ancient and obnoxious. Between you and me, I think George has always rather fancied himself as an old git.'

Being on nights on the labour ward wasn't so bad in itself – except for the fact that it was always busy, since most babies seemed to insist on being born at three o'clock in the morning. The worst bit was being on call in case one of the home birth patients went into labour in the wee small hours.

On this particular night it was Lorna's turn, and her hopes of an easy ride were dashed when the phone rang just after midnight with news of an impending birth.

Somebody slapped a scrawled note into her hand. 'Ruby Craven, thirty-five, it's her third and there were no complications with the first two. Address is on the paper. Have fun!'

Grabbing her bag and her coat, Lorna legged it down to the car park. Ten minutes later she was still there, swearing loudly and aiming kicks at her car. At the end of her tether, she grabbed her mobile and dialled home.

'Mum? Yes I know it's really late, and I'm sorry, but it's a bit of an emergency. I have to go out on a delivery and my car won't start. You couldn't get Dad to drive over and pick me up, could you? I wouldn't really feel safe in a taxi. Thanks Mum, you're a star.'

She might not have thought quite so highly of her mother if she'd realised that the moment she rang off, Meg flicked through Lorna's phone book, found the number she was looking for, and dialled Chris.

'Oh God, I'm so sorry,' babbled Lorna as Chris drove her through the darkened and deserted centre of Cheltenham. 'My mum should never have phoned you, only she's got this weird idea that we've fallen out or something because you haven't been round at the house for a while.'

Chris's eyes met hers in the rear view mirror. 'Have we?' he asked.

302

'What?'

'Fallen out.'

'Of course we haven't!'

'You see, I wasn't sure whether I ought to call you or not,' admitted Chris. 'I mean, I really wanted to, but I'd sort of promised I wouldn't crowd you. And then I thought, if I don't call, maybe she'll think I didn't mean what I said, and then the song and everything will have been completely pointless. Basically,' he confessed as the car headed through the grim maze of streets behind the industrial estate, 'I'm just no good at this emotional stuff.'

'Yes you are,' protested Lorna. 'That song you wrote was beautiful.'

'Really?'

'Really. I would never lie to you.'

'Well I'm glad it was OK. But I'd still have been a lot happier making you a chest of drawers. I think God probably intended me to go and live on top of a mountain with just a goat for company.'

Despite her awkwardness, Lorna laughed. 'You do talk some rubbish, Chris! You're one of the sweetest, most sensitive guys I've ever met.'

'Ah, but is that good or bad?'

Tentatively, she reached out and touched his hand. 'Good,' she said softly, feeling her heart flutter in her chest. This was crazy, like being sixteen again. Her emotions were all over the place. 'You know something, Chris? You ...' She looked down at her knees in embarrassment. 'You sort of make my heart smile. Does that make any sense?'

'It does to me.' The car turned into Ondurman Street and slowed right down. 'What number did you say?'

'Thirty-five. This must be it, here.'

They drew up outside a row of old workmen's cottages. The houses themselves were well-kept, and the owners of number thirty-five had done their best to cheer it up with hanging baskets and a concrete rabbit; but there was no denying the fact that this was not the pleasantest of areas. Somewhere in the distance, a dog howled and rattled its chain. It sounded more like a wolf on the Russian steppes.

Chris looked at the house dubiously. 'What do those people think they're doing, sending you out here on your own in the middle of the night?'

'Oh, we usually have a chaperone,' said Lorna, 'but there's a staff shortage at the moment.'

'Are you sure you're OK, going in there on your own?'

She smiled. 'Of course I am. And I've got my mobile, so I can phone for a taxi when it's all over. I'll be quite safe, really.'

'I could wait for you.'

303

'I could be in there for hours! No, you go home and get some sleep. Thanks so much for bringing me here, though.' Her hand lingered in his and he gave it a little squeeze.

'The pleasure's all mine.'

As births went, it was straightforward and really rather swift. In fact it was one of those occasions when Lorna felt more like a spectator than a midwife. By half-past six in the morning, Mrs Craven was sitting up in bed eating toast and nursing her baby son as though giving birth was something she did every day of the week.

With the family's thanks still ringing in her ears, Lorna yawned and stepped out into the cool of early morning. The streetlamps were dimming, and birds were starting to twitter in their roosts along the ridge tiles of the houses opposite.

It was then that Lorna spotted the car – Chris's car – still parked outside the house where she'd left it. Surely he hadn't waited there for her all this time?

She walked down the path and across the cracked pavement to the car, bent down and looked inside. Chris was fast asleep, his head resting on the steering wheel, his tousled hair straggling over his face and his lips very slightly parted.

With a soft click, she opened the passenger door and slid inside. She'd meant to shake him awake and tell him off for being so silly; but as she looked at him sleeping peacefully there, a huge wave of love washed over her. And she knew, in that instant, that this was much more than just the love of one friend for another.

She smiled. 'Sleeping Beauty.'

And as dawn came up over the sausage factory, she awakened him with a kiss.

Sasha Temple-Marsh was not a happy bunny.

It was her last day working at Avocado Productions, and whose fault was that? Not mine, that's for sure, she told herself as she sat alone in the video screening room, balefully watching a re-run of the pilot for *Rather Your Job*.

If it hadn't been for that bloody doctor, throwing his weight around and getting all the juiciest footage cut from the programme, it might actually have been a ratings winner, instead of the turkey it had turned out to be. If it hadn't been for him, the pilot would have turned into a series and she would still have a future in television.

Dark and snake-like, the idea wriggled into her brain. There was a pile of blank videotapes over there. It wouldn't take more than a few minutes to copy all that unused, incriminating footage onto one or two, and send them – anonymously of course – to people who might be very interested to see how professional an obstetrician Dr Eoin Sullivan really was.

Perhaps today wasn't turning out to be quite such a terrible day after all.

Chapter 34

Eoin was on top form as he swaggered through the swing-doors onto the Labour Ward.

'Nice tan,' commented June Godwin, and the new Nursing Assistant went all gooey-eyed and giggly at the sight of so much prime-quality bronzed manliness. 'Do we take it you had a good time?'

'Bloody marvellous, more like,' he replied, leaning against the midwives' station with studied casualness, and fixing Lorna with an especially dazzling smile as if to make sure she knew what she'd missed. 'I'm telling you, you haven't lived until you've hurled yourself off an eight hundred-foot cliff, with nothing but split-second judgement between you and a horrible death.'

'I'll take your word for it, thanks,' said Lorna.

Eoin shook his head sadly. 'Poor Lorna, it's such a pity you couldn't conquer your fear. You really don't know what you're missing.'

'Actually I know exactly what I'm missing,' she replied curtly. 'That's why I was so keen to miss it.'

'Never mind, I met this local girl called Consuela and we had a great time. Very understanding girl, Consuela; very ... open-minded. Give anything a go.' He rubbed his hands together. 'OK, what've you got lined up for me today? Don't tell me – a load of twenty-stone forty-year-olds carrying triplets. Wheel 'em on, the way I'm feeling I can take anything.'

'That's good,' remarked Andrew Rennie, emerging from the office, 'because the Chief Executive's PA's just been on the phone, and he wants to see you at eleven-fifteen in his office.'

If Andrew had hoped this news might put the wind up Eoin, he was in for a disappointment. The doctor's chest swelled visibly. 'I knew it,' he declared. 'I knew they couldn't pass me over for promotion, not after that last set of exam results. Mark my words: this is about that new registrar's post they're creating over at Gloucester Royal.

307

'At his rate, this time next year I'll be a Consultant Obstetrician; just you wait and see. You should have stuck with me, Lorna; I'm really going places.'

At about the same time that Lorna was glaring at Eoin's retreating back, Carmen was taking a seat in Victor's consulting room.

'This is Eva,' she announced, holding out the bright-eyed bundle for him to see. 'You know so much about me that it didn't seem right, you not having met her. Eva, this is Victor. He's been a very special friend to your mummy.'

Victor's eyes crinkled when he smiled, and he looked years younger. 'Pleased to meet you, Eva,' he declared, taking one of her tiny hands in his and gently shaking it. The baby looked up at him wonderingly, and let out a loud burp. 'Oh I quite agree,' he added solemnly. 'This is a very horrible tie; I should've thrown it out years ago, but I never was much for fashion.'

'We don't think it's horrible, do we Eva? We think it's ... different. Different is good,' Carmen added firmly.

'It can be,' conceded Victor.

'Well that's what you taught me; you can't go back on it now!'

Victor laughed and sat back in his chair. 'You do realise you don't really need me any more?'

Carmen's mood turned instantly from ebullient to glum. 'Yes I do! I'm useless on my own.'

'On the contrary, I think you're a marvel. You're smart, you're independent, and you've started believing in yourself. No more destructive relationships; no more sacrificing yourself for people who do nothing but hurt you. And we're well on the way to finding you a job you really like. What more can I help you with?'

She swallowed hard. 'You can't abandon me!'

'I'm not. I'd never do that. All I'm saying is, maybe you only think you still need me.'

'No,' she answered softly, putting all her heart into the words, 'I really do.'

They looked at each other for a little while; both thinking, both silent. In the end it was Carmen who broke the silence.

'Kelly's having a naming ceremony for Lee-Anne in my back garden next Sunday afternoon. Will you come?'

He looked surprised. 'You really want me to?'

'Yes, really.'

'OK then, I will.'

'It won't be posh or anything.'

'Great. I'm not big on posh.'

Carmen relaxed a little and her smile returned. 'You know what you were saying, about destructive relationships and all that? Well, I've definitely promised myself I'm never going through that again. You were right: it's not fair on the kids and it's not fair on me either.'

'Good for you.'

'So – no more men for me then. Consider them history.'

Victor raised a hand. 'Hey – I didn't say that! When did I say no men again, ever?'

She felt puzzled. 'I thought—'

'Then you thought wrong; and it's my fault for giving you the wrong impression.' He slid his hand across the desktop and just for a fleeting moment, their fingertips touched. 'There's just one thing I want you to promise, Carmen.'

Their eyes met. 'What's that?'

'I want you to promise you'll never say "never" again.'

Meg was so appalled, you could have knocked her backwards onto Sarah's cast-off settee with a flick of a feather duster.

'Suspended? Eoin's been *suspended*? But what on earth for?'

Not without a trace of satisfaction, Lorna explained about the anonymous videotape that had landed on the Chief Executive's desk, bearing the missing footage from the pilot of *Rather Your Job*.

'Oh dear,' said George. 'You mean the bit where he went off and left that poor girl in the bath and she took ill?'

'Exactly.'

'Ah,' said Meg. 'Well I suppose in the circumstances he did behave rather unprofessionally . . .'

'Debs could've died, Mum! Eoin was so busy trying to impress the presenter, he completely neglected his patient.'

'Dear me. And he had such nice manners too. What do you suppose will happen to him?'

'I don't know,' Lorna replied; and in her heart of hearts she didn't actually care that much, either – particularly since she'd found out that Eoin's first reaction, on being confronted with the tape, was to accuse everybody from Andrew Rennie to the patient's husband. If I'd been there, she mused, he'd have accused me too without a second thought. 'I expect there'll be some sort of investigation. Still, Eoin knows all sorts of influential people. Knowing him, he'll just get himself transferred somewhere else and do it all over again.'

'Goodness. It has been an upsetting day for you.' Meg sat down on the green sofa and patted the seat next to her. 'Sit down, Lorna. Your father

309

and I have something to tell you. I do hope it's not going to upset you even more.'

Lorna sat down slowly. She looked from one parent to the other. 'Is this about you moving out?' she asked. There didn't seem much point in beating about the bush. It wasn't as if she hadn't had plenty of time to get used to the idea. In a way, it was a relief that the issue had finally risen to the surface.

George looked faintly surprised. 'Oh,' he said. 'Well, yes, actually. How did you guess?'

'Dad, you and Mum have been making noises about it for months – ever since Sarah got pregnant and started trying to get you to move in with her!'

'Have we?' Meg was aghast. 'And there I was, thinking we'd been so discreet about it. The last thing we wanted to do was give you any cause for concern.'

'And we'd never even have considered moving on until Hope was at nursery school and you'd sorted out your work, love,' added George. 'We've been very happy here, love, and you've been very good to your old mum and dad.'

Lorna eyed the pair of them expectantly. 'So, who's won the battle then: Sarah or David?'

Meg and George looked at each other and burst out laughing.

Meg wiped away a tear of mirth. 'Lorna sweetheart, we love them both dearly, but do you really think we could face living with either of them?'

'Oh.' Lorna was completely flummoxed. 'But if you're not moving in with Sarah or David, where are you going?'

Meg took her daughter's hand. There was an excited twinkle in her eye. 'What with your father's stories, and our bit of money from selling the old house, and those few prizes I sold on the Internet, we've enough money to buy a nice little place of our own.'

Lorna's jaw dropped. 'A house?'

'Well no, dear,' her mother admitted. 'A static caravan. But it's on a lovely site in Wales, not far from Ed's parents, so we'll still be able to come and see you and the children.'

'When we're around, love,' her husband reminded her with a nudge.

'Ah yes, that's the other thing,' Meg went on. 'We've got ourselves a new career, as house-sitters. All we have to do is go and live in people's homes while they're away, take care of their gardens and their pets, that sort of thing, and we get paid for it!'

'And do you know, there's such a demand for older people with good references,' George added, 'that we've already been booked for our first assignment over Christmas.'

'Yes,' enthused Meg. 'And guess what – it's in Spain! But we'll only go if you're sure you can manage without us,' she added. 'We want to be absolutely sure that you and the children will be all right.'

Lorna gave her mum a hug. 'We'll be fine,' she said.

'Promise?'

'Promise. But we're going to miss you terribly.'

'Nonsense. You'll be glad to see the back of us – interfering with things and always getting in the way, and generally driving you round the bend—'

'No, Mum!' Lorna felt a lump come to her throat and she squeezed her mum's hand hard. 'All I'll remember is how you two helped me get my life back when I was barely managing to hold things together.'

They chatted for a while about Meg and George's plans. 'Oh, I forgot to mention,' Meg added casually, 'I've decided to go on that cosmetic surgery safari after all.'

If you'd dropped a bomb down George's underpants he couldn't have looked more horrified. 'B-but Meg!' he protested. 'I thought we'd sorted all this out! I love you just the way you are!'

'Wow,' said Lorna, not sure whether to be appalled or impressed, or both. 'That's an awfully big decision, Mum.'

Meg looked at their two faces. 'I wish you two could see your expressions,' she commented. 'You look as if the Martians have invaded Stroud. And you don't listen, you know,' she went on. 'I said I was going on the safari – I didn't say I was having the cosmetic surgery done, did I?'

'Oh!' Lorna blinked. 'Can you do that?'

'Why ever not? I've always wanted to visit South Africa. This just means that I can thoroughly enjoy the safari bit, while all the others are in agony and wrapped up like Tutankhamun's mother-in-law. Imagine – having a facelift and then being bounced around the veldt in a Land-Rover. Not what I'd call a holiday at all.'

A little colour returned to George's pallid features. 'All these years, and your mother still keeps me guessing,' he commented.

'It's a pity your father can't come too,' mused Meg.

'Oh no it isn't,' replied George. 'I come out in prickly heat when the temperature goes over seventy, remember. And I'm allergic to mosquito bites.'

'Speaking of guessing,' cut in Meg, 'I've a feeling Lorna's got something she'd like to tell us, haven't you dear?'

'Have I?' Lorna tried to look innocent, but her ears were burning.

'Some rather good news about you and that nice boy Christopher?' hinted Meg with a smile.

It was pointless trying to hide anything from her mum, so Lorna spilled it all out: her hopes, her fears, her guilt, her joy. And as she did, the last barriers to her love began to melt away like April snow.

It was the most perfect day imaginable.

Everybody who mattered was at the naming ceremony for baby Lee-Anne. Everyone from the social worker and the police constable who had rescued her from her grandmother's house, to Debs and Honey from Crocus ward, George and Meg, Lennie, and even Chappie, who had honoured the occasion by having a Number One and a new tattoo. What seemed like hundreds of children were scampering about all over Carmen's back garden in the late-afternoon sunshine, pursued by Chappie's two over-excited terriers, one with a Stars and Stripes bandana round its neck, and the other wearing a small straw hat with holes cut for its ears.

The ceremony was conducted by a friend of Carmen's who knew a bit about Wicca and had put together some nice, simple verses welcoming baby Lee-Anne into the world and into the arms of the Goddess. Everybody cried and laughed a lot, including the baby, and as she solemnly promised to be Lee-Anne's sponsor and to guide and help her through life, Lorna felt a real glow of pride and responsibility. This might not be sophisticated, but it was sincere. Just like Lee-Anne's mum.

'Victor,' said Carmen, walking across the lumpy old lawn to where the counsellor was standing, a little apart from the others. 'Thank you for coming. Are you OK, all on your own over here?'

He shrugged and gave an awkward smile. 'Oh, I'm fine. I just haven't had much experience of the big family thing, I'm afraid. Never quite sure whether I belong in these gatherings.'

'Of course you do. You're my friend and my guest, and as far as I'm concerned that makes you part of my family.' Carmen held out a hand and, to his own surprise, he took it. 'Come on, I want to introduce you to some people.'

The people she had in mind were Lorna and Chris, who were having a conversation with Chappie about wheel clamps.

'Of course, your British ones are better quality,' he opined through a mouthful of barbecued sausage, 'but your American ones go on faster, and of course they're cheaper.'

'Of course,' echoed Lorna, trying not to catch Chris's eye for fear of corpsing.

'So what about ones from other countries?' enquired Chris.

Chappie sucked in breath through his cheesy teeth. 'Ooh, you don't want to get involved with them cut-price clamps. Fall apart as soon as look at 'em. Mind you, your actual Denver Boot from Denver—'

Carmen arrived like the Seventh Cavalry, with a middle-aged guy in tow. He had a bad haircut, terrible taste in jumpers, and the kindest face Lorna had ever seen.

'You must be Victor,' she said, sticking out a hand and hoping she was right.

'How did you know?' he asked, taken aback.

'Oh, Carmen's told me ever such a lot about you.'

Chappie regarded the newcomer through narrowed eyes, like the baddie in a spaghetti western. 'So, you're the one who's stealing my best operative off me, then?'

'I'm your only operative, dimwit,' Carmen reminded him.

'Yeah, well, but that's not the point is it?' Chappie complained lamely. 'What's an area manager without his area?'

'Sorry mate,' said Victor, 'but it's your own fault for training her so well.'

'It is?'

'Oh definitely. You've made her really attractive to the job market, you see.'

'Oh. Well if you put it like that.'

'So you're definitely taking the job with the Teenage Pregnancy Initiative?' enquired Chris.

Carmen nodded. 'Hope I'm up to it. Still, they'll train me. And nobody knows more about teenage pregnancy than me.'

'Except me,' interjected Kelly, popping up at her elbow. 'Hi Lorna, hi Chris. Come on Carmen, I want to show you this really cool rattle Robbie's made for Lee-Anne.'

Victor hung back, but Carmen grabbed him by the elbow. 'You don't get away that easily.'

When everybody had wandered off to the barbecue, Lorna and Chris strolled down to the bottom of the garden, where a couple of upturned plastic milk crates served as a makeshift bench.

'Ed would have loved this,' murmured Chris as they sat side by side, watching the children and the dogs weaving in between the adults' legs as music played in the background.

'In a funny way, I think he's here,' replied Lorna. 'I don't mean actually watching or anything weird like that, I just mean . . . like a sort of feeling. A presence in the air. It's as if wherever people are happy, Ed's there too.'

'I never knew anyone who was happier or loved life like he did. Maybe he *is* here.' Chris moistened dry lips. 'Do you think he understands? About us?'

'I've never been sure about many things,' Lorna replied, 'but I'm sure about this. Ed would understand completely . . . but this isn't about Ed

313

any more, Chris, it's about us. It's about being brave and loving each other and living for the future.'

As the sun began to set behind the rooftops of Cheltenham, Lorna slipped her hand into Chris's, and together they set out on the magical mystery tour of love.

Epilogue

Nine months later . . .

The register office was filled to capacity, and there were tears in Lorna's eyes as the recording of the 'Wedding March' came to an end. She turned to look at Chris and felt the warmth of the love in his gaze.

'I never thought I'd see this day,' Chris whispered.

Before the registrar stood Carmen and Victor, the bride and groom, with Carmen's children in descending order forming an honour guard of pageboys and flower girls, and Kelly as a sort of unmarried matron of honour. Victor looked as if he might explode with pride. Carmen was so overcome that it took her three tries to get through her vows. Her sister Grace sobbed so loudly that hardly anybody could hear anyway.

'I can't believe she's wearing a *dress*!'' hissed Meg from the seat behind.

George came back with: 'Well I can't believe she's not pregnant.'

'Maybe sometime,' Carmen told people coyly at the reception afterwards, when they asked her and Victor about starting a family of their own.

'But for now we just want to enjoy being together,' said Victor. 'It hasn't sunk in yet that this beautiful lady has actually agreed to marry me.'

While the guests attacked the buffet lunch in the function room upstairs at the Old Spot, and George regaled listeners with 'Scandalous things I have discovered in other people's houses', Leo marched up to Chris and tugged at his sleeve.

'Uncle Chris.'

He looked down. 'Yes?'

'Were you in my mummy's bedroom last night?'

Chris and Lorna froze. It had to happen sooner or later, thought Lorna. Let's just hope he doesn't take it too badly.

Chris cleared his throat. 'Er . . . yes.'

315

Leo grinned happily. 'Oh good, because Mummy gets lonely on her own, and sometimes at night when it was very dark I used to hear her crying. She doesn't cry any more. Uncle Chris.'

'Yes?'

'Thank you for our new kitten. We're going to call him Fang because he bit Caspian and it was really funny.'

He skipped off happily to join his sister, uncle and his two sets of grandparents, who were enduring Sarah's histrionic account of how truly dreadful it had been, discovering that she was pregnant again only three months after giving birth for the first time.

'Leo seems happy,' commented Chris, with an edge of insecurity in his voice.

'He *is* happy; he loves you.'

'I can't replace his dad though.'

'He knows that; he doesn't expect it. Nor does Hope.'

'So I'm not just second best?'

'Never in a million years!' exclaimed Lorna. 'Nobody expects you to replace anyone, Chris. We all love you for yourself.' She cuddled up close to him. 'Is there any way I can show you just how much I love you?'

'Well . . . maybe just one.' Taking all his courage in both hands, Chris proceeded to do the scariest thing he had ever attempted in his life. Dropping to one knee in the middle of the canapé-stained carpet, he asked:

'Will you marry me, Lorna?'

In the split second that it took her to answer, Chris suffered every torment that Hell could devise, and a few thousand more besides. And then Lorna's face blossomed into a beaming smile, and she fell to her knees, threw her arms around him, and said 'yes, yes, yes!' over and over again.

A long time later, when they finished kissing and came up for breath, they found that everybody was cheering.

And somewhere, hidden among the crowd, was the ghost of Ed Price. Still around, still looking out for the love of his life, but happy now; at peace. And smiling.

Split Ends
Zoë Barnes

Eight years ago, when Hannah was a struggling single mum, Nick Steadman seemed like Mr Right and Prince Charming rolled into one. Kind, strong, reliable - and the perfect step-dad to Lottie - what did it matter if his taste in trousers was more M&S than D&G?

OK, so their relationship's never been based on passion, but it has plenty of respect, friendship and trust. Trouble is, after eight years together they're beginning to realise that friendship isn't enough.

The solution? An amicable divorce. Which would be just fine if it wasn't so hard to explain to nine-year-old Lottie. And if Hannah didn't find herself a teeny bit annoyed at Nick's ability to move on so quickly.

Not that she isn't happy for him and his new lover. Of course she is. After all, they agreed they'd be mature, grown-up and rational about their separation. They may be divorced but they can still be friends.

Can't they?

Praise for Zoë Barnes:

'bloody good read' *New Woman*
'Top ten book...feel-good escapism' *Heat*

Love Bug
Zoë Barnes

Don't get bitten...

If love is a bug then Laurel Page is immune. Been there. Done that.
Got over it. All she wants now is a quiet life. And while running a
dating agency may not seem like the logical career path for a
woman who has so fervently sworn off romance, for Laurel it's perfect. There's something deliciously safe about other people's
romantic problems. Laurel's had enough drama in her relationships
to last two life times.

And then Gabriel Jouet walks into her office. Tall, dark and oozing
with Gallic charm, he's an unlikely client and almost enough to
make even Laurel contemplate abandoning her vow of singledom.
Almost... But Laurel's scars run deep: Cupid really would have to be
stupid to pick on her again...

Praise for Zoë Barnes:

'Zoë Barnes writes wonderfully escapist novels, firmly based in
reality' *Express*
'An enjoyable and moving read...funny and likeable novel' Maeve
Haran, *Daily Mail*

Just Married
Zoë Barnes

Emma and Joe Sheridan have just got married. Emma has been in love with Joe since school – marrying him was the happiest day of her life. But now the honeymoon is over and Emma's having to cope with the reality of married life. She's living in a new town, has a new job and a new husband who hasn't quite left his bachelor days behind him. Then there's Emma's interfering mother-in-law who's expecting the patter of tiny feet before Joe's even carried her over the threshold!

Still, at least she and Joe are together at last. But Joe and Emma have never lived with each other before – and apart from the odd holiday – have never spent more than two weeks in each other's company. Setting up home together for the first time might be romantic, but nobody told them that living happily ever after takes a lot of hard work...

Praise for Zoë Barnes:

'A great book for anyone who likes their romance laced with a healthy dose of real life' *Options*
'entertaining and lighthearted' *Observer*

Ex-Appeal
Zoë Barnes

Gina had fallen for Matt Hooley when they were both teenage rebels. Together, they were going to save the world - until their mothers put a stop to it, and made sure they never saw each other again.

Now, fourteen years later, Gina still regards Matt as 'The One'. No one else has ever come close to measuring up. All of her other boyfriends have eventually stumbled at some hurdle or other, cursing 'Saint Matt' as they fell.

Gina's always had a daydream that one day Matt would come back and carry her off on his obligatory white charger. But never once in her fantasies did he ever arrive complete with an ex-wife and three kids! Worse, her teenage rebel has become thoroughly respectable. Well groomed, wealthy, middle class - he could even pass for an accountant!

How can her Mr Right have gone so wrong...?

Praise for Zoë Barnes:

'lively and compulsive' *The Mirror*
'A good giggle' *Essentials*

Bouncing Back
Zoë Barnes

All she needs is a job, a man, and a life!

Everyone has one really bad day in their life. One *really* bad day. For Cally Storm it's the day she loses her job, her marriage and her home. While everyone around her seems to be settling down with Mr Right and 2.4 children, Cally is back living with her mother. Still, when you've hit rock bottom, the only way is up…

Everyone's got an opinion on what will turn her life around; a new wardrobe, a new bloke, a new career… But the only job she can get is at a local wildlife park. Still, life with her ex-husband has ably equipped her to deal with all lower forms of life! And as for romance – well, if good men are so hard to find, frankly she'd rather not bother. Only she's reckoned without the collective matchmaking efforts of her friends and a strange – almost animal – attraction to her unconventional colleague, Will. Can this wrongest of Mr Wrongs ever turn out to be Mr Right?

Hot Property
Zoë Barnes

Dream home? Dream man? *Dream on!*

When Claire inherits a house out of the blue – she thinks she's struck it rich!
But, while the word 'cottage' inspires images of romantic idylls and roses round the door, there's nothing remotely heavenly about Paradise Cottage. It's a tumble-down wreck in the middle of nowhere – more in need of a demolition expert than a decorator.

Still, Claire's not one to shirk a challenge. Much to the amusement of her hunky new neighbour, Aidan, she decides to renovate the cottage herself. After all, problem-solving, trouble-shooting – it's what Claire does best. She's used to planning events for thousands of people. She can sort out one little cottage…can't she?

Hitched
Zoë Barnes

Gemma and Rory have been best friends and happily in love since university. They're both twenty-five, living together in a nice flat in Cheltenham, solvent. So when Rory gets carried away by the atmosphere one New Year and proposes, Gemma finds herself saying yes. It's the obvious next step.

Of course, it will just be a small wedding. A quick jaunt to the registry office and off to the pub with close friends and family. And then they'll carry on as before.

That's when all hell breaks loose...

It means a lot to Gemma's parents to be "Respectable" - and with one gay daughter and another a teenage eloper, Gemma is their last hope for a white wedding with all the trimmings. And Rory's family have just "come into money" and are dying for an opportunity for ostentation on the scale of the Roman emperors. Suddenly, their plans for a quiet wedding are crushed in the stampede towards yards of frothing tulle, page boys, seating plans for the feeding of the five thousand and an all-inclusive honeymoon in the Maldives.

And slowly but surely, Gemma and Rory's relationship begins to buckle under the strain...